Also by Trevor Ferguson

High Water Chants
Onyx John
The Kinkajou
The True Life Adventures of Sparrow Drinkwater
The Fire Line
The Timekeeper

AS JOHN FARROW
City of Ice
Ice Lake
River City

DRAMA
Long, Long, Short, Long
Beach House, Burnt Sienna
Barnacle Wood
Zarathustra Said Some Things, No?

FILM
The Timekeeper

THE RIVER BURNS

BURNS

TREVOR FERGUSON

Published by Simon & Schuster Canada
New York   London   Toronto   Sydney   New Delhi

Simon & Schuster Canada
A Division of Simon & Schuster, Inc.
166 King Street East, Suite 300
Toronto, Ontario M5A 1J3

Copyright © 2014 by John Farrow Mysteries, Inc.

First Simon & Schuster Canada edition April 2014

SIMON & SCHUSTER CANADA and colophon are registered trademarks of Simon & Schuster, Inc.

For information about special discounts for bulk purchases, please contact Simon & Schuster Special Sales at 1-800-268-3216 or CustomerService@ simonandschuster.ca.

Designed by Aline C. Pace

Manufactured in the United States of America

10 9 8 7 6 5 4 3 2

ISBN 978-1-4767-5184-9
ISBN 978-1-4767-2641-0 (ebook)

For Freya and Craig,
Leah and Jamie,
good moms and dads,
and the new ones,
Inga, Erik, and Rundle.

THE RIVER BURNS

AUTHOR'S NOTE

Readers acquainted with the town of Wakefield, Quebec, will discern contradictory evidence here: the novel liberally mines the community for its history, culture, architecture, and geography while, with equal enthusiasm, reconfigures the same. Dates, for example, go unmentioned, yet details will demonstrate that the Wakefield Bridge fire does not occur at the same moment in this account as it does in history. In this imaginative rendering the facts are given due credence and respect, but I contest that they cannot be granted governance. A cause for the evident discrepancies lies in the paramount reality that persons in this narrative are fictional creations who do not depict, nor are they intended or likely to depict, anyone living or dead, and if a resemblance does occur it is unwitting and only through that rare fluke we term coincidence. Historical events inspired the novel's genesis; skeletal aspects are mirrored here; yet the gentle shifts to time and place underscore that the novel is compelled by its own intentions and design, at variance with the known record in search of a veracity of its own, and is a work of fiction.

I

TRANSGRESSION

1

Quite early on a splendid summer's morning, as sunlight shimmied across the treetops or sashayed within a mischief of breezes to brighten patches of farmers' fields and meadows below, while streams navigating the hills remained wholly shaded and residents of Wakefield stayed asleep or tottered through dawn's familiar routines, Dennis Jasper O'Farrell caught himself *having a moment*. Not that he would admit to such a thing. He considered even the expression lame, unworthy of use in any serious vein. Making sport of his wife, he might toss out the line, "You're having a moment there, sweets," but in the company of pals—loggers and truckers—a phrase of that nature never slipped off his tongue. And yet, that morning, he acknowledged the thought. Stranded at an intersection, both hands on the steering wheel of his pickup, the brake pedal jammed to the floorboards, he veered precariously close to uttering a stunned admission aloud. "Holy *sh*—! Can you believe this? I'm having a *whatchamacallit* here, a moment."

He'd awakened to the dull buzz of his crotchety alarm. Having been dreaming, the narratives soon forgotten, he flipped through a series of nonsensical suppositions as to what the sound could be when his hand reached across and, as if with sight although his eyes remained shut, tapped the button home with a soft *donk*. Many mornings he required a further nudge from Val, but today he made it up on his own to a sitting position on the edge of the bed before he succumbed to being fully upright. An initial evaluation concluded that his trucker's aches were minimal this morning. Once on his feet he received the first of the electrifying images that were to alter his inner polarity. Val's right foot, little of the ankle visible, poked out from the chaos of blankets. She was a sloppy sleeper. He told her one time that if left outside to sleep at night she'd level a forest, that he ought to invest in a catcher's mask and a jockstrap for his own protection while in bed. Oh, she pretended to be gung ho for the jockstrap. The blankets this morning were shovelled up around her in haphazard waves, but one foot, as if dismembered, tranquil in its slumber, stuck out from the fray.

The turn of her heel, the slope down to the wee toe, the perfectly rounded cut of the nail, the curl of middle toes, and the atomic twitch, like a clock's rhythmic tick, of the biggest, the faint delta of veins so fine and precise they'd be impossible to paint, struck him as being one of the truly beautiful sights he'd witnessed at six o'clock in the morning—*ever*. Floor dust embedded on the bottommost pad. He stood riveted a moment while simultaneously unaware of his own astonishment, as though he was still dreaming. The beauty of the foot—offset by a rummage of blankets and illuminated by a sunrise on the opposite side of the house, so that only a scant reflection off leaves of a glow beyond their bedroom window abetted him—signalled his receptors and snared his interest. The slight blond hairs on the big toe that he never bothered to notice before—lovely. And yet, Denny simply was not prepared nor inclined to be spellbound by such a moment, certainly not by a foot (oh, by the wily wink of a nipple, or a thigh's gleam, that would be different), and so moved on to the bathroom for the bright gush of his morning piss and the commencement to his day.

He stood still in the tub awhile, eyes closed behind the drawn curtain with its print of mauve falling petals, his face tilted upward while the shower's considerable velocity raged down upon him.

By the time Valou thumped her tiny fist upon the bathroom door he was officially awake. The occurrence was not daily but lately happened often enough to be considered a new and confounding habit. Denny deciphered that his youngest, his only daughter, waited first for one of her brothers to command the upper-floor washroom before crawling from her own bed, as if being second in line to the toilet gave her permission to enter the master bedroom unannounced to try her luck at the ensuite. She knew darn well that it would also be occupied, the difference a private calculation: bug a brother and suffer his rebuke, or bother her dad and receive in return his loving attention first thing in the morning. Obviously, Denny deduced, puttering downstairs to the other available loo did not constitute a third option. He might have to do something about this latest trick, but not this morning. Wrapped in his housecoat, which spent the night hung on a hook, he opened the door and merrily swooped her up into his arms.

Her little squeak of a cry as she landed on his shoulder helped form the next searing impression of his day.

Rather than accept that he'd been struck numb twice that morning, Denny happily planted a noisy raspberry on Valou's tummy, kissed her cheek while she giggled, and set her back down on the floor in a single motion.

"You're a gimmick," he remarked.

"You're a gimmick," Valou chimed back.

He touched the top of her head and shut the door behind her, and then, as though he possessed the ears of a hawk circling above the treetops, able to pick out the imprint of a timid mole tentative on mud (he entertained that very thought, then chose to modify it—*hawk* eyes, *dummy, not* ears), he heard the soft pad of Valou's bare feet across the tiles as she approached the toilet. He hoped the lid was left down, and if not, that she'd remember to clunk it down herself before climbing up. This early, Denny remained slow. Remembering to drop the lid hadn't been an issue for months now, perhaps more than a year, that incident when she partially fell in and had the dickens of a time getting back out, hollering blue murder, happened eons ago, and really he was the one failing to remember that she'd long grown past the issue.

While sipping coffee downstairs in the kitchen waiting for toast to pop, he was struck again by Valou's squeak of a cry, as if hearing it for the first time, as he scooped her off the floor and she landed upon the comfort of his fatherly shoulder. Heartbreaking—even as the thought was being entertained he was actively, consciously, pushing the notion aside—how love sang between them. *Sang.* Oh, joy in his sons crushed him, yet when affection for his daughter stung him, Denny caved, as though the very sting was unbearable. An unwavering emotion fixed in such a way that he need never tend to its care or broach an adjustment, yet the physical manifestation of it, that tingling nip in his gullet, felt so fleeting . . . or so he was thinking, even as he successfully shoved the thought so quickly aside that it lay keenly vanquished and he was merely sipping from his cup.

A Blue Riders cup, his hardball team, from the year they were champs.

He swung the bat well that summer.

Toast popped. He thickly buttered the slices and slathered on jam.

Red currant.

A delightful first crunch, the sound as well as the taste, and Denny ate and drank contentedly.

The slow, easygoing, wide yawn and stretch of morning.

Before departing the house, he poured coffee into a thermos he then clipped to the underside of his lunch pail's rounded lid. He snuck a peek at his lunch today (peanut butter and banana—stupendous), grabbed hold of his denim jacket, and headed out, letting the light screen door *kff-chook* behind him like a muffled cough before remembering that he was not supposed to let that happen. He hesitated on the stoop, as if to give Valérie a clear vocal shot at him, but apparently— and he remembered the silence, the *silence,* of her sleeping foot—she remained too groggy to complain. Coffee's scent, wafting up from the kitchen, would rouse her soon enough.

If not the coffee, then Valou.

Denny adjusted his jacket collar, which got itself pinned behind a shoulder, but he was promptly off the porch and crossing the yard. First stop, retrieve Valou's trike. Another gambit of hers, to leave her tricycle in the path of her dad's pickup. He gave it a little shove with his knee and the toy scooted off the drive, spinning safely onto grass. His daughter was perfectly capable of leaving it out of harm's way on the lawn. That she failed to do so might prove to be neither carelessness nor accident. She used to be an amazingly obedient wee child, nothing like his sons, and he grappled with an impression that she *wanted* him to be forced to move her trike. Just as she wanted him to climb out of his truck to move it when he returned up the driveway at the end of a day's work. The little nipper was actually competing with her devil-may-care brothers, or perhaps learning from them, plotting for attention even if it arrived in the form of mild fatherly wrath laced with an end-of-the-workday irritation.

The little nipper.

He loved trucks, but mostly he loved his own. A midnight blue F-150, a mighty truck, although he had no particular use for its power or cargo capacity, other than for the commute into the woods where his truly massive rig stood parked. More truck than he required. A good car would do, be cheaper, and save on gas. While hunting in the fall, he found the pickup useful, even if his last successful hunt was years ago and not in this particular vehicle. Still, it seemed inane to him to drive to work in, say, some teensy Toyota only to climb up a ladder into the cab of his big rig. Unsafe, went his thinking, to switch from tiny to huge, whereas the progression from a big pickup to a monster logging truck kept his skills up and the roads safe. Proposing that argument to Val when he was dickering over what to buy, he was taken aback by her scoff, then by a laughter so bewildering, so genuine and not the least forced, that he kept the thought to himself ever since. Still.

"Denny," she told him back then, "it's called peer fucking pressure."

He bought the truck anyway.

He caught the weather report on the A.M. station, the promise of another scorcher, then switched it off, preferring the sound of tires on the winding hilly curves as he swept down into Wakefield. Sunlight occasionally flickered through the foliage. The road ran alongside a stream. Few other vehicles were out that early. Stores remained closed and homes slept soundly. Rooftops slouched. Walls gently snored and chimneys rasped. He did not always mind the speed limit precisely but he made a point of it this morning, enjoying the discipline of keeping the needle bang on the mark. He loved his truck and he loved this morning drive when he could kick off the air-conditioning and slip the windows down, rest an elbow on the sill and drive. Just drive. Like that. Like gliding on a breath of summer.

In town, he came to an intersection governed by a stop sign that frequently he rolled through. The streets were free of traffic and pedestrians alike. Cops, he knew, weren't up. Any cop awake was probably his older brother anyway. So. Nonetheless, he came to a complete stop. And stayed stopped. How light shone on the glass of the restaurant to his right, the chairs within upside down and sitting on tabletops, dust motes floating in the air, how neatly the old timber buildings squatted awaiting the day, the heat, the norm, how calm the landscape beyond the street appeared to him, the trees, the broad river, the hills already drooping before the promise of another languid day and yet somehow the whole scene shot through with light, how birds flitted from tree to bush, catching time on their own amid the planted shrubs before humans and their raucous chaos descended, and Denny feeling, keenly, his beloved family at his back and the job and a day's honest labour before him, and he felt struck, now for the first time with meaningful awareness, by a certain blissful essential certainty within his marrow that sang, *sang,* along his bones. He was hugely content, and glad to be at the intersection seated in his F-150, the motor sweetly purring, and suddenly he was dismayed and thought, "Holy *sh*—! Do you believe this? I'm having a *whatchamacallit here,* a moment."

Denny hesitated, in surprise, in dismay, permitting the time to linger. He felt spooked, not sure that he appreciated being overcome by a surprising, lurking joyfulness or whatever it was, an exquisite pain similar to the random charley horse in the night he experienced on occasion, excruciating, that pain, yet at the same time mesmerizing so that he missed the agony once it passed, and he wondered also if he wasn't having some kind of a freaking stroke or maybe one was imminent and he ought to go see a doctor although he knew that he never would, tell him he was on the verge of a fatal aneurism if he didn't intervene immediately, *like right now,* and why, he'd ask him, why is this happening to me?

But he knew what was wrong with him.

He didn't need to ask or be told.

He simply chose not to admit it.

Then his reflexes took over and he slid his foot off the brake, pressed the gas, and careened away from the intersection. Away, too, from his own thoughts and mood as if fleeing the scene of a crime, or fleeing a powerful inclination to commit one.

■ ■ ■

AT A FORK IN THE road, Denny O'Farrell went right. Unbeknownst to him, going left would have taken him past his brother, out of uniform but standing by his patrol car, who was talking to a man they'd both known since childhood.

Ryan O'Farrell was leaning back against the front-side fender of his vehicle, ankles crossed, arms comfortably folded over his chest. He was wearing his policeman's baseball cap, but otherwise decked out in civvies, jeans, and a short-sleeved, teal, soft cotton polo.

"Nice of you to not bring your gun," the man said.

"So we're both underdressed for the occasion," Ryan remarked.

Save for a thin deer-hide vest better suited for an adolescent half his size, and a torn flag of denim shorts, worn loosely, slit up the sides and cut away as though every stitch of excess fabric was abhorrent to his nature, the man with the darkly bronzed skin sat in the dirt, as carefree and as confident in his minimal attire as the policeman in his off-duty garb. Ryan noticed a bicycle resting on its side down in the ditch.

"That's new," Ryan pointed out.

"It's not stolen." The man went by the name Skootch.

"Did I infer that it was?" Ryan asked. "But you inferred something about my brother. Do you want to spill the beans or go on talking in riddles?"

Although on the ground, Skootch sat on a level higher than the road or Ryan, at the top of a bank above the ditch. Behind him stood the thick forest that provided a livelihood for so many, and for him a home.

"Rumours aren't riddles," Skootch contested.

"They're lies. Not worth the time of day to listen to."

"Sometimes that's true. Sometimes truth is in the listening."

"Now we're back to your riddles."

Skootch untangled his limbs and rose up from the ground. He was tall, as skinny as a sapling. White whiskers speckled his chin.

"Why oh why, Ryan, did an acquaintance of mine get sent to the pen? Christ, Ryan, three to five?"

"Know him well, did you? Do business with the man?"

"Ryan, he was a reserve outfielder. I won't miss him that much. But apparently your putting him away inspired my third baseman to skedaddle. A middle-of-the-night type thing. He went all paranoid on me. At this point in the season, where am I going to find someone to play third? Unless, you know, you want to make a comeback."

"You didn't ask me out here to play third base."

"I wanted this meeting because stories are making the rounds. Call them rumours. But truth flies around wherever it flies. Out of the mouths of babes or out of the mouths of babbling idiots sometimes, you just never know. If it's true, it's true. If not, then no harm is done if I give you a heads-up anyway."

"Go on."

"Like I said, it's your brother. Denny's one hothead mother."

"I'm not sure that he is."

"Some loose talk gets spun. People say he might take matters into his own hands. Commit an act of veritable destruction, something of that nature."

"Skootch—"

"Why would I tell you this, Ryan, if I didn't have our own best interests at heart? Yours and mine, both? I've got nothing against Denny. You know that. I'm partly squealing on him for *his* sake. So he can be stopped. I believe he needs to be stopped. I don't like it that you put my third baseman away—"

"Your reserve outfielder, actually."

"Same difference. I need a third baseman now because of it. You know what team I'm playing this week, couldn't you have waited? Anyway, I don't like what you did but this is not about that. It's about Denny. All I'm saying is what you already know. If he shoves, there will be some push back. It might not be insignificant. You know what I'm talking about, Ryan."

That's all that the policeman needed this summer, a running battle between loggers and conservationists with his own brother at the forefront. Ryan took the other man seriously.

"So you're hearing that this is about Denny. Reliable sources?"

"At first I wasn't so keen to believe it myself. But word has a way of going around until it sounds convincing. *Various* sources. You know that I move in mysterious ways. I keep strange company."

The man skipped down the steep slope into the ditch and righted his bike. He pushed it up the embankment so that he emerged on the road just in front of the police car. He lifted a leg over and seated himself, the bike looking ridiculously small for a man with such long legs. He scratched his dribble of chin whiskers.

"How about," he asked, "if you leave my ball club alone for a while? You've done your damage. Now leave us alone until the season's over.

As a favour to me, who's just done a favour for you. Anyway, you've got worse things to think about now than my team's record."

"I don't have a clue what it is, nor do I care."

"Like I believe you. But you've got a bigger problem to think about now and I'd appreciate it if you concentrate on that, for all our sakes, and for more goddamn reasons than baseball. I'm trying to keep the peace here, Ryan. Just like you. I'll see you around, okay? Thanks for the visit. It's been a slice."

He paddled the bike with his feet awhile before he raised them onto the pedals, then he was soon zipping off down a hill and out of sight.

Ryan watched him go, then stared off into the dark woods. The sun was coming up warm. He returned to his car, started her up, did a three-point turn, and drove back to town and another day on the job, feeling uneasy.

2

So, too, was wizened old chirpy Mrs. McCracken an early riser. Townsfolk assumed her good habit had formed through forty years of getting up early to teach children the geography of their planet, and Mrs. McCracken willingly suffered that perception. Privately, went her theory, as long as people remained sufficiently gullible to believe that load of bull roar she was spared further embarrassment. Following the terribly premature death of her husband, Mrs. McCracken started waking up an hour earlier each morning than her previous custom. Schoolwork had nothing to do with that. Four decades later and within the month following her retirement, she commenced getting out of bed an hour earlier still, school not being the instigator of that routine either. Nor did Buckminster, her tabby, precipitate the new regimen, although she was fond of blaming him. "That cat!" And while she needed to be up at a reasonable hour to tend to her newest occupation, baking pies, folks weren't going to consume her wares or even make a purchase before noon. Mrs. McCracken got up early for one reason only. She was lonely. Flat-out fatigued by solitude. Being full of zip and the town's busybody ameliorated her condition, but any time spent in bed while awake was difficult to bear. Once an eye cracked open she was up and at 'em, usually three steps ahead of her alarm clock.

Her full name bloomed as Alice Beauchamp McCracken. Not a soul called her Beauchamp. Only the government, the bank, and one or two credit card agencies knew it to be her middle name. Yet no one had called her Alice in such a dreadfully long time either. Peers who might have done so were now deceased, and a few younger people whom she believed called her Alice once upon a time had since succumbed to the common weal. She was Mrs. McCracken to the world, to the point where she'd begun to refer to herself only that way. When introduced, a fairly rare occurrence, whether she was meeting a Dick, a Mary, or a Siobhan, she replied, "I'm Mrs. McCracken, how do you do?" Schoolteacher force of habit, perhaps. Upon spying a bill or an official notice that carried her given name or even the first initial, she was oddly surprised, as though the address must be a typographical error.

And yet, *Alice Beauchamp McCracken* one day would be inscribed upon her gravestone. She'd made the arrangements.

A scooter morning. Fresh berries. She'd beat the heat and arrive at the fields early, be back in time to bake a blueberry pie. Mrs. McCracken started up her Vespa GTV 250, a scooter that could truly scram.

She lived near the old covered bridge and, obedient to its rules to a fault, slowed down and came to a complete stop before traversing onto the wood surface. The same could not be said of the vehicle approaching from the opposite end. This early, she had no clue whom the interloper might be, but he was under an obligation to stop and to ascertain that he would indeed be first onto the single-lane bridge. He was not first, not by the length of her scooter, and he was not waiting for the vehicle travelling from the opposite side of the river, namely Mrs. McCracken on her Vespa, to cross the bridge ahead of him. They were on a collision course, and knowing full well that she possessed the right of way Mrs. McCracken would not back down. If it meant that her full name was to be inscribed on her gravestone sooner rather than later, so be it.

The car, an old roadster she soon established, an antique, seemed to be of similar mind, the difference being that only Mrs. McCracken on her scooter would be shunted off the bridge upon impact over the side rails and through the half-height opening into the rapids below while the old green roadster, a heavy Studebaker as it turned out, might suffer, at worst, a scratch.

Not even a dent, Mrs. McCracken calculated as she sped along.

Maybe she'd end up a very big muss on the windshield.

That might turn his stomach. He'd be sorry then.

The prospect, perhaps, caused the Studebaker to begin to slow, which allowed Mrs. McCracken to honourably do the same, and the two headlong adversaries stopped at the bridge's centre, the scooter's wee front tire a speck away from the car's bumper.

"You're in the way!" the driver, an older fellow with a shining pate and white paintbrush moustache, called out. She could not yet distinguish his florid, chubby face through the windshield but knew that she didn't know him.

"I started across the bridge first and you never stopped!" Mrs. Mc-Cracken berated him. "Obey the rules! They are put in place to be obeyed!"

"Move to the side, for crying out loud! We can both pass by!"

"This bridge is one-way-at-a-time only. Back right up right now or I'll have the police here quicker that you can say, *How did I wind up in jail today?*"

That charge got him out of his car and he slammed the door as if to confirm his position. She nearly broke out into laughter, he was so short, except that that would be unkind. "You got to be out of your freaking tree, lady!"

"*A*, freaking is not the name for any tree. Nor do I believe it serves as a legitimate adjective for any object, animate or not. And *B*, I am not out of my tree because I have never been in one. Now, return to your car as a gentleman ought to do and back this monstrosity up!"

"Monstrosity!" He failed himself then, actually looking at his vehicle to detect if there might not be some merit to her defamation. "Monstrosity?"

"Fine," Mrs. McCracken backtracked. "I'll withdraw the insult. Uncalled for. Back up your fine antique car, please, sir. I'll tell you why you must if you really want to know."

He was beginning to appear amused. "Tell me why. I'm interested."

"This is quite a small town. Not a village. But small. The police know me. They do not know you." She removed her cell phone from her berry-picking pack strapped to the rear seat and held it up to a strobe of sunlight slicing through a gap in the ancient roof. "Shall I awaken an officer at this hour?"

The visitor looked at his car, at the scooter, and at the acerbic old woman.

"What are you doing on that thing anyhow? You must be eighty."

"I am not," she told him, strident for the first time, "*eighty.*"

"Lady, I've got a car show to get to. Near the city. Something tells me, the only way I'm going to get there is to back up. So I'll tell you what."

"Do that. Tell me what," Mrs. McCracken encouraged him.

"I'm going to back up."

"Fine. That'll be just fine," she determined.

"Fine," he agreed, and got into his car, and backed up.

When he reached the other side and steered off to the oncoming lane, Mrs. McCracken scooted on by him heading uphill without a word, a flash in the sunlight, her dress a yellowy-white flag in the breeze, her blue helmet ablaze, then she was gone. This time, the driver checked who was coming—no one—before driving onto the old covered bridge.

18

3

Denny called it smoking, although he rarely lit up anymore. Smoking meant just hanging with the guys and the morning found him by the old covered bridge where he and his friends Samad and Xavier waited in line with their big rigs. The guys still smoked and he had a tendency to stand downwind so the scent would find him as the others puffed away. He might breathe in deeply but he didn't call it inhaling exactly.

Quitting was his idea. He did it of his own volition and without prodding when Val first got pregnant. He didn't want her smoking, so he didn't either. Harder for her than for him. He still missed it, though, and the other guys could tell. The easy part was driving smoke-free in his cab. The hard part was hanging out with the guys and having a few beers after a ball game. He could crumble pretty easily but he never did in any big way, even though he and Val were done with making babies, and despite allowing himself a once-in-a-blue-moon smoke with a beer. He was feeling so jumpy inside his skin today he felt like having that smoke. He knew to resist when the urge was strongest. The urge. Strange, that. As if something living inside him craved a different life.

Denny shuffled a stone around with his toe and munched an apple pinched from his lunch pail. He looked up as another logging truck, out of sight, geared down for the stop and the protracted wait.

He sneaked a deep breath of secondhand smoke.

Having shed his jacket, he was now feeling the heat of the sunlight on his bare forearms.

The driver of the last truck to arrive was another close pal, André Gervais, who came down the hill, swinging his arms high as he did whenever he walked down a slope, as though he needed the motion to keep up with the momentum of his runaway hips, pulled along by his belly's ample ballast. As he moved, the flesh on his face jiggled down into his jowls. He joined the truckers who were waiting for the bridge to clear—except that it wasn't clearing. A family stopped in the middle of the old covered bridge and the father was coaxing his kids from the car to gaze upon the rapids rushing below. The dad held up his youngest to spy the water above the half wall.

"Oh, pitch a tent, why don't you?" Denny muttered, just loudly enough for his pals to hear. Also waiting to cross from their side was a plumber's van and a pair of sedans that appeared to be travelling in tandem. The drivers were out of their cars, gabbing, but neither smoked. To Denny they looked like men who'd never smoked, but he didn't know why he thought that way or why the presumption made him feel indifferent to them. As though he'd never say hello unless they did first and probably they never would. Denny spoke so that they couldn't hear him, just his pals. "Play a round of mini-putt, for Pete's sake. Cook up a barbecue while taking food out of the mouths of my kids."

Samad Mehra commiserated with him on the thoughtlessness of tourists. He'd arrived from Delhi as a pensive child, a man now of diminutive stature who admired Denny and could be counted upon to agree with him whenever he held to an opinion. Denny did not necessarily admire that trait in Samad but he accepted it and came to expect it. Xavier Lapointe was apt to pick an argument just for the fun of being ornery, but this morning there was no disputing the annoyance they faced. Xavier couldn't believe that anyone could so freely waste people's time as that family was doing, and if the tourist dad didn't get a move on in one second flat he was going to walk down there and either make him move or remove him altogether.

"I pity his kids," Xavier said.

"How come?" Samad asked him. He was expecting a serious reply.

"It won't be pretty when I go down there and toss the dad over the side. Those poor kids, to see their dad wash away like that."

"Scar them for life," Denny noted.

"That's what I was thinking," Xavier concurred. "It's a shame."

"The sooner you get it over with . . ." Denny suggested.

Samad was chuckling to himself, but when he looked at Xavier's face he grew worried.

"X," Samad said. He knew that his friends could be rash, and feared that they might misbehave in his company some day. His wife often warned him about that very thing. She didn't trust men in groups without women.

"Don't X me," Xavier said.

"Oh, he's going," Denny foretold. "Soon as he's finished that smoke."

"Soon as," Xavier agreed, and Samad worried more.

Arriving, letting his arms flop down to his sides, André Gervais assessed the situation in a jiff and said to everyone, but pointedly to Denny, "Hear about it? The company got the government to agree on a public meeting. Finally."

He was speaking French and when he finished chewing his apple, Denny spoke French back to him. "What kind of meeting?"

"A meeting meeting. What other kind is there?"

"What'd they say about it, anything?"

"They said not to get our hopes up. Not too high anyway."

"Oh, that kind of meeting," Denny said, and Xavier and Samad laughed.

The tourist was packing his kids back in his car so Xavier stayed put. Crushed his cigarette butt under his boot. "Know what I'd like to do with a guy like that someday?" he asked, in English now. They freely switched languages with no apparent cues. "Give him a dose of his own medicine."

"Like how?" Samad wanted to know.

"One truck blocks one end, another blocks the other end, and he has to sit on the bridge until we decide to move. Except we go for lunch instead, have a beer afterwards. He has to hold his kids over the side to go wee-wee. He has to listen to them bawl because they're hungry and thirsty."

"Wee-wee?" André asked. "Wee-wee?"

Xavier said, "Shut up."

"Wee-wee?" André repeated, making Samad laugh.

Xavier got defensive. "I got kids of my own. You got to talk like that."

The tourist family left the bridge, finally, and the driver of the first truck in line, who'd been napping in his cab, got ready. The big diesels collectively rumbled in idle, but now the driver tapped his accelerator and just the sound of a diesel being summoned gave Denny a charge. He looked around as if afraid that the others might detect how absurdly ecstatic he was feeling at that moment. He didn't know what was wrong with him today.

The turn was a tight fit for a big truck and they watched as the rig went wide around the bend to get the back end through. The driver took it slowly. The way the old bridge creaked under the weight of the cab then sagged as the load of logs was shouldered by the trestles, the diesel coughing up black smoke from the stack, and under that cacophony the rush of the river as it fell through the rapids, the full scene under the heat of the sun churned in Denny as a physical sensation, as if the pistons were calibrated with the rapids and in tune together, causing him to vibrate. André nudged him out of his daydream.

"What?" said Denny.

"Go to that meeting," André urged.

"If we can't get our hopes up, what's the point?"

"You're the one who said it, Denny. It's been your argument. First, take the legal route. Then nobody can complain."

He was known to say that. *First.* The legal route was proving to be a dead end. *Then.* He said it often. *Nobody can complain.*

"Yeah. Maybe."

He didn't want to think about the legal route because he didn't want to think about the alternative. The bridge was a major pain. The worst sort of bottleneck. None of them were living the lives they imagined for themselves when they were kids together playing on the river, imitating their dads who drove logs down to the mills every spring and fall. Those big log drives were spectacular to witness and this river, the Gatineau, was the last to see them disappear. Environmental issues precipitated the change. Instead of driving log booms on the water, they were driving trucks. Only the world didn't catch up to that shift, and they were forced to cross the river on a bridge unfit for the weight of their vehicles or the new volume of traffic. The bridge needed to be replaced but had its own diehard backers, those who wanted the relic to remain forever, for the sake of tourism and for their eternal heritage and for its own exquisite beauty.

Denny held nothing against heritage or beauty but the bridge was useless.

He craned his neck. He wondered if he was not feeling so odd to himself these days because he had so much to gain and so much to lose and he was balancing right on that fulcrum, not knowing which way his life would tilt. One moment's adrenaline-induced excitement flipped into the next moment's tumble down a steep descent.

Over the hill came Mrs. McCracken on her scooter and she parked right down in front of everyone in the space vacated by the rig that was now on the bridge. Nobody minded. She'd go ahead of the next truck and no one counted her as a separate vehicle so that both truck and scooter could cross simultaneously as long as she went first. If she went second someone on the other side might not see her and turn onto the bridge after the truck passed and smash her. They had everything worked out. As a rule, no other vehicle was allowed on the bridge with a heavy truck even if they were going in the same direction, and now that a truck from their side was crossing they'd wait for the next vehicle coming from the other side before the plumber's van was allowed to cross. It's how their days went now. Mostly just waiting to cross. They told the government it was inefficient, but so far no one was listening and this was how they got to spend their working hours, hardly making a dime.

Mrs. McCracken switched her motor off, peeled off the helmet, and fluffed her white hair that she wore curled. Samad called down to her, "Blueberry pie today, Mrs.?"

"Freshly picked blueberries," Mrs. McCracken emphasized, "are the key."

"Bake trucker-sized pies," Denny advised her. "You'll make a mint."

She wasn't sure if that meant they should be bigger or smaller.

"Something we can eat on the go," he explained.

"Tarts!" she chimed in.

"Bigger," he said. "A tart's not trucker-sized. Bigger than a tart, smaller than a whole pie."

"Oh, I see," she said. She seemed to be thinking about it.

"Depends on what kind of tart you're talking about," Xavier pointed out. "I like mine small and curvy."

"X," Samad forewarned, worried.

"What?"

"It's Mrs. McCracken."

"School's out, Samad. She's not going to give you the strap."

"I might," Mrs. McCracken let it be known. "Did you hear the rumour that the school gave me a strap as a retirement gift? That one went the rounds."

"Good for a laugh but I never believed it," Xavier said.

"I never denied it," Mrs. McCracken pointed out. "But you're right. You're not in school anymore. A lot of good it did you when you were. In any case, you're allowed an occasional double entendre, even when it is in my presence."

"Double what?" Xavier asked. "Espresso?"

Samad and Denny laughed.

"You boys," Mrs. McCracken said.

"Oh God, no. Don't tell me," André said. He seemed stricken.

They looked where he was looking and his pallor and trepidation was such that even Mrs. McCracken gazed in that direction. On the other side of the bridge a bus was destined to cross next. Rather than proceed at a fitting pace, slow enough, the elderly passengers disembarked and were proceeding to walk across. A few were being pushed in wheelchairs. Among those who walked were the sprightly and the spry and a number of them kept up a good pace, yet others demonstrated a lethargy, or the carnage of difficult knees and hips, and so hobbled along while still others appeared barely ambulatory.

"What the hell is that?" Denny asked.

"I heard about it," André intimated. "Had to see it to believe it."

Denny noticed the two men who owned sedans moving closer to them to observe the activity on the bridge and he no longer felt his previous antipathy.

"Heard about what?" Denny asked.

"Fuck," Xavier said.

"Language," Mrs. McCracken chided him.

"Those inspectors? Out to check the bridge? At first we thought they were on our side."

"Government inspectors you're talking about?"

"Highway Department, whatever. So there's a new regulation now. Buses have to off-load before crossing."

"What the fuck for?"

"Ryan O'Farrell! Language!"

"Ryan's my brother, Mrs. McCracked. I'm Denny. You never could keep us straight."

"What did you call me?" she demanded to know.

"You started it."

"They have to off-load," André explained. "After the passengers cross on their own, then the bus drives over empty. So passengers won't be on board if the bus falls through the bridge."

"Fuckin' hell!"

"Mr. O'Farrell!"

"Come on, Denny," Samad whispered. "Don't piss her off."

"I know you think Ryan's your big success story," Denny rebuked his former teacher, ignoring Samad, "and I'm your big failure, Mc-Cracked. You wanted me to be more than just another logger but here I am, logging. Get over it. You have to look at the situation we're in today. This is what matters now."

She appeared nonplussed, yet could not follow his thread.

"You're partly responsible," he accused. "You're one of them who wants to keep this bridge. And it's partly because you don't like loggers. You never want to see our side. The worst thing is, you're spearheading—that's the word—you're *spearheading* the people who want to keep this bridge. Look! We can't cross and now the whole morning's shot."

"You can go around, Mr. O'Farrell."

"We don't have a choice now, do we? Is that what you want? But *think*. Try to get hold of this. The detour adds an extra nineteen kilometres per trip, one way. Never mind our time, do you know what that costs at the end of a day, just in fuel? Eleven trucks. Thirty-eight clicks round-trip. Make it four round-trips a day, five on a good day but you can forget about five now. Do the math. You taught it."

"You were good in math yourself."

"No, McCracked. That was my brother. Ryan. I'm Denny."

"Denny," she said, as though to nail that down for good.

"I've done the math. It's over sixteen hundred clicks a day. Do you know how much fuel that is, how much money, not to mention the drivers' time? And don't talk to me about the company. These are *our* trucks. We pay the mortgage on them. We pay the fuel bill. Not the company. The company pays us by the load, not the time, so they don't care how long it takes any more than you do, just so long as the logs get moved."

"I'm not going to stand here and argue with you, Mr. O'Farrell."

"Can't even remember my name."

"You disparage mine. Why should I speak yours?"

"Hey, Crackers, did you hear about the meeting coming up? You'll have to stand and argue with me then."

"That's fine. There's a proper forum for every discussion, Mr. O'Farrell."

"Just don't get your hopes up. Things can go wrong."

"Denny," André said, catching him before he said too much, and Denny relented. The problem with a secret plan was keeping it secret.

"We better get turned around," Samad said, as though he wanted the conversation to conclude as well. "It'll take forever."

"Might as well," Denny agreed. "The old folks won't cross anytime soon."

Those who were spry and sprightly were now stopped to admire the view.

"If they do," André said, "we'll just run them down."

"I heard that," Mrs. McCracken said.

"You hear everything," Denny said.

"I do," she said. "I remember everything, too. Except maybe names."

"Guess what?" he said as he started towards his truck. "So do I."

Denny didn't know why he said that or what it was supposed to mean. He was mad at himself as he knew it sounded stupid. He strode back to his rig. Now he needed to make up for lost time with speed. He'd drive angry. Probably get a ticket for his trouble when he was past the county limits where his brother's jurisdiction ended. Down the road, those tickets were whoppers.

4

Whenever Alexander Gareth O'Farrell went to his knees to rout the latest trespass of weeds to sully his garden, past glories snared him like a vice. He'd grunt. Wince. Remember a time. *Oh*, there'd been the romance of those days, driving logs downriver for milling. Being a river rat and regarded as one of the very best helped him to woo his wife, a woman he considered above his station. There was that. Yet an infatuation with the river worked more powerfully within him than in others. As a boy on the verge of manhood he opted for the life through pure attraction, not because he found himself bereft of better choices. Now that he was on the cusp of old age he doubted that he could disentangle the various sentiments involved to explain himself, but the romance, or so he believed after a night of drinking and reminiscing, guided him as securely as a well-paddled canoe throughout his working life, up and down the humps of injury and perpetual pain, hardship, sacrifice, and fear. To be out on the water on a fall day, driving rafts downstream after the hills corroded to brilliant yellows, reds, and oranges, the *ping* of winter in the crisp air, signalled that he was distinctly alive, and the romance of those times aided him to overcome an abiding weariness and bequeathed to him his legendary endurance. He'd balance on a spinning log, strut across to the next raft, and work his peavey to free a jam against a rock, an obstacle he recalled from the previous year and the year before that, and never was he imperilled on that precise spot but in other places, yes. Often in relatively benign situations. He nearly mangled a foreleg once, a finger was amputated, an ankle got turned and jammed, a knee was twisted in unholy screaming disarray, his tailbone was battered, his scalp wickedly thumped after his hard hat flew off. Other assorted agonies. At times he would arrive back ashore bloody and bent, half-drowned, spitting up the river from his thorax and lungs. Romance helped him sail through the experience and now the romance of his memories encouraged him to carry on. For Alex, now retired, going down onto his knees mimicked the prayerfulness of others as he muttered involuntarily, as if to a host deity, wincing, fretting, obliged with each expression of soreness to reclaim that brief yet ancient time.

He'd taken his lumps on the water.

Now he scratched in the dirt.

Gardening was never his thing.

After his wife's passing he foresaw a choice. Permit the care and labour that she invested in her gardens over their lifetime together to go to seed, and probably go to seed himself, or pick up a gardening spade and dig in. He dug in. He was even beginning to fathom her enjoyment in the wonders of a garden, and successfully compiled a catalogue of dos and don'ts. Begrudgingly, he admitted that despite the perpetual body aches the work bore upon him he was probably better off for it than if he just put his feet up and napped. Not that he did not nap. And hoist a few glasses. Yet he felt more comfortable taking it easy having first put in a few faithful hours on his knees.

A way to handle this pending old-age thing.

The heat was coming on. Toxins, he surmised, the crud from a life lived without regard for his eating and drinking habits, oozed from his pores.

Alexander O'Farrell lived by a mountain stream that seemed quite still unless the viewer concentrated on observing the flow, the water cast into a lull by a small dam downstream. His was the first of six homes constructed above a straight patch of bank. The opposite side of the dead-end road that served their locale fell vacant, a farmer's field fallow this year, so he was surprised when he heard a rattletrap percolate towards the cluster of homes, then stop before it reached any. Through a clump of birch he spotted an orange sedan, now parked, where a young man organized his materials. As he appeared to be on his own Alex ruled out the Jehovah's Witnesses—no such sport today—yet hoped that his luck would hold, that the visitor would prove to be a salesman. So few were left nowadays. The stranger came around a cedar clump, tall, redheaded, flush with the confusion and anticipation of youth. Alex welcomed the good fortune that now beamed upon him. Not wishing to meet any man while down on his knees, he gathered himself to his feet, grunting a little, then waited to hear the fellow's ungodly pitch.

In a suit that ill-fitted him, probably culled from a rummage sale when first he got the job, the arrival was stymied before he began. He was undecided on the etiquette of approach. Should he cross the lawn? Or carry on down the road, the long way, and use the stone path? Alex waited for him to figure that out, and gave him marks for choosing to march straight across the lawn.

"Morning," Alex noted.

"Good morning, sir!" the young man enthused. He was trying to offer his hand while shifting the weight of his awkward sales catalogue from one arm to the other. "My name is Jake Withers, and I—"

"Whatever you're selling, son, I'm not buying. Just so we understand each other."

Jake paused. Already this was not going as well as planned. He was still waiting for the handshake.

"I represent the Rathbone Company?" The statement emerged as a question, as though he doubted his own claim. Alex rescued the hand hanging in midair and took it in his own and, cruelly, compressed it. He could see Jake's eyes blanch with the pain. Then he let go.

"Is that a fact? Don't know those people. You don't sound so convinced yourself."

"Yes, sir. I work for—I represent the Rathbone Company? And I'm asking you today to imagine the one alteration that will transform your property."

"You're asking me to use my imagination. Is that a fact."

"Yes, sir. Now picture this." He turned to his left, and cast his free hand over the ground, as if to emulate Moses dividing the waters of the Red Sea. "A gleaming black driveway."

Alex looked over at his pocked gravel drive and saw a thing of beauty.

"Eh? Eh?" Jake pressed.

"Excuse me just a moment, will you, son?"

"Yes, sir!" the young man consented. He walked with the older man until Alex turned into his house and then the younger one stood still. He silently rehearsed how he was going to embellish this deal, then close it. "Sir!" he called out before Alex made it inside the house. "You got a beautiful spot here."

Alex turned, smiled. "Thank you, son."

"I'll tell you what I'm going to do."

"Excuse me for one moment, son."

"For the boost to your property value that this will give you, you should be paying me double. Really, it's like I'll be paying you. But this is what I'll do. Sign on the dotted line today, I'll give you a ten percent discount. Just like that, right out of the blue. No need to haggle. That's over and above the big boost to your property value that I'm talking to you about today."

"Am I excused or not?" Alex inquired.

"Sure, sure," Jake Withers said. "Go right ahead, sir. I'll be here."

"I'll only be a moment."

"Go right ahead, sir."

"Thanks."

Looking at the visitor from inside the house through the screen, Alex wondered if this was the lad's first attempt at a sale ever. He returned outside onto his sunlit porch carrying a shotgun cordially pointed at the ground.

The young man's pupils dilated. "Is that thing loaded, eh?"

"Not much point if it's not."

"What do you shoot out here? Ducks? Is it ducks?"

"This time of year, no."

"Then what?" He was trying to be brave and friendly but Alex could tell that his knees trembled. His whole torso quavered.

"Old people in this town, we just don't like scammers. So we're armed."

"Look, if you don't want your driveway paved, eh, that's okay."

"That's all right with you, then?"

"Yes, sir!"

"I'm glad to hear that, son."

"I was only trying to help you out with your property values."

"That's a lie. This is why we hate scammers. They lie. You don't give a shit about my property values. Do you? Admit it now, Jake Withers."

"I was just trying to help you out, sir."

"No, you weren't. You were trying to make a sale. That part I don't mind so much but you were also trying to screw me over. That's the part I mind. Why don't you just admit it and then get on with your life? Maybe do something useful with it while you're still young."

"Look, I'm going to go now."

"You're always free to go, son."

Jake Withers hurried off, but he was not heading back to his car.

"Hold on there, son."

Petrified, the young man stopped. He turned slowly.

"Don't go pestering the neighbours either."

Jake Withers hesitated. He gazed at the wild old man, perhaps for the first time he really looked at him, at his dusty, weathered face, a scratch of white morning stubble across his chin, at the receding hairline and thinning salt-and-peppery tufts, at those unflinching steely eyes. He looked like an old crabapple tree in an abandoned orchard. The old man was ornery, he could see that, probably not worth standing up to, but he did so anyway. "Sir, I got a right to earn a living, don't I? I'm just calling on people today. I'm not causing you any harm. I'm not making trouble."

For the first time, the boy sounded genuine. Alex liked that, but felt a need to explain the rules of the road to him. "When I want to shop, son, I go to the store. People here, we don't expect the store to come to us."

"I don't want any trouble, sir, but if you don't let me go door to door, like I have to do, it's my job, well then . . ."

He waited, as though the consequences were obvious.

"Well then what?" Alex asked him.

"You won't leave me a choice. I'll call the police on you. I don't want to, you understand that, I hate the police. But maybe I won't have a choice."

Alex was curious. "Why do you hate the police?"

He shrugged, explained, "I got no reason to like them."

The reply disappointed Alex, since it seemed rote, an impulse informed by hearsay, not experience. "Actually, son, I don't want trouble either. That's why I'm keeping you away from my neighbours. If you think I'm a bothersome bastard, a few doors down you'll find worse than me. Don't think it's only the men either. There's one woman— Look. What you need to know is this—nobody's gonna let you pave their driveway."

The young man stood on the lawn, undecided.

"There're better jobs than this," Alex reminded him.

Jake Withers studied the row of houses. Driving by on a scouting trip, he thought he'd struck the mother lode. He was less certain of that now. While it was true, as the man said, there were other jobs, he never seemed to land them, and anyway it was also true that there were other driveways, including those in more civilized communities. He strode back to his car, tossed his book of glossy photos of pavement samples into the backseat, and slammed the door. Going around to the other side he nearly slid down the embankment, but he found his footing and clambered up and piled himself into the car. He bolted forward, then braked, turned into Alex's gravel drive and backed up in a cloud of dust to change his direction, then roared off again, hammering the steering wheel with a fist. His eyes welled up. Before he did anything else, he was going to call the cops on that old man. He was going to mess with that old geezer and settle this score no matter what. The only way to do that was to sic the cops on him. See if he liked that so much.

To hell with him and his shotgun anyway. He was going to make that call.

On his front lawn, Alex O'Farrell ruminated that not every sport gave him the kick it once did. That's what happened when a part of him sympathized with his victim's circumstances. Wisdom was a bother, and made him less ruthless. Poor kid. The sun was hot now and Alex was perspiring and dirty from his garden work. He turned back to the house, ready for a quick shower and a morning nap. After that it would be noon, and time for lunch.

Another day. At least this one dished up a dose of entertainment.

5

She begrudged this train its old-world comforts. Especially its nostalgic joys, the cosy mystique. She resented the staged evocation of an earlier, purportedly simpler, time. The lives of young women were different then. *I should've caught a derelict bus* if buses were available to catch, *been aggravated throughout the trip,* crouched in a seat that long ago lost its cushioning while penned in by a lout with a shrill voice and a ringing desire to chat her up. *Hitchhiked, then, okay?* Picked up by a half-blind octogenarian, *half the ride veering over the white line* taking the curves in the wrong lane, dropped off by the roadside in a sweltering broil. A crazy idea, the craziest. Then get picked up again and *probably molested. Worse. Dumped in a ditch after. Crazy, crazy notion.* This train, though, *is a pretty crazy idea, too.*

A seer's advice. Drive your truck into the ground, she was told. But don't stop there. Travel to the end of the line.

She was running away.

Going where that witchy woman said.

Schoolkids ran away, didn't they? Teenagers. Husbands fled. Draft dodgers and deserters. Thieves on the lam. Lovers eloping. Cats ran away sometimes *but they came back* after crossing whole continents if you could believe the myths *and what adventures they experienced! The best*. Was that it, then? She was looking for adventure? *Deadbeat dads ran off.* Fraud artists who tripped up got the hell out of town, trying to beat it down to a Caribbean island void of extradition laws. Wives ran away from desiccated marriages. *Lambs fled wolves.* Or so she supposed. But lawyers, lawyers didn't run away. *Or did they?*

Always, they had better things to do.

And yet, *I'm a lawyer* and although others might vehemently disagree that she had nothing better to do she'd decided that her best option in life was to *Scram. Beat it. Run. So I'm running away.*

Vamoosing, she called it.

Perhaps this is what lawyers did. *They vamoosed.* In style.

I'm a storm now. The wind. That's the thing. I can't argue career choices when all I am now is a whole gale in the dark of night. Even when it's noon.

The sedate comfortable pleasure of an antiquated steam engine and passenger train wending its way along a lovely riverside on a sunny day seemed, in oblique ways, enchanted. But she would much rather arrive wherever she was bound like a thunderclap, all wind and downpour, crackling hail and tempest.

I'm pending, she supposed. *The calm before the—*

Raine Tara-Anne Cogshill, who commonly and professionally used only the first half of her middle name, knew little of the place where she was headed. She just wanted to be travelling *on the run* and got into a slight tiff when she was refused a one-way ticket. The ticket seller, an older man less tall than herself, was adamant. Only round-trip fares were sold. She was resolute about not returning, while he was equally stubborn, stating that she would either pay to come back or she would never leave, not on this train. The quandary was solved only when he commented that once she paid for the *round-trip ticket* no one could prevent her from missing the return leg.

"So, nobody will stop me from *not* getting back on the train?" she wanted verified.

"The railroad has no hounds," he told her. "We won't hunt you down."

So she bought a round-trip ticket with no intention of using the return leg.

A brochure informed her that the town at the end of the line was charming, quaint, and small enough that she could walk to everything. Perfect.

"Enjoy the trip," chirped the man at the ticket counter.

"Only the first half," she told him, and boarded.

As the train approached Wakefield it slowed, not that the relic was ever swift, but half speed became one-fifth, and as it entered the town's limits where the narrow-gauge tracks were planted hard against the main drag, with virtually no separation, men, women, and even children on foot were strolling faster than the train in its deliberate crawl. She could climb out and push and arrive at their destination sooner and assumed that this was supposed to be charming, too. A lawyer's frenetic pace still resided in her bloodstream. Perhaps she had that to subdue. In places there seemed to be no gap between the tracks and road and in other sections between the tracks and a walking path. Under the passenger car window, patrons having an early lunch on a restaurant's rear patio were so close she could count the chicken wings *four down, four to go* on their plates and study an emblem on the flatware. *I know zip about heraldry.* This was unlike any town she'd visited. Where else did cars, pedestrians, *and diners* jostle for space with steam locomotives?

Perfect.

A weekday, a goodly portion of those onboard were either retirees or railroad aficionados on a mini-holiday, and none of the latter and few of the former were in a rush to disembark as they pulled into the station. They loved sitting on the train in the station. Only slowly did they stow scant belongings into light backpacks, retrieve cameras and binoculars. Tara Cogshill carried a purse and a small backpack that contained the sum total of her earthly possessions—she'd sold her stuff and her furniture, dropping a good deal of her clothing off at a Goodwill. If she was truly leaving she wasn't going to bring her belongings with her. She'd left the bed of her little red pickup bare, guessing that sooner or later the truck would break down. When it did, she was unencumbered, a garage taking the truck for parts, and she had next to nothing to carry off it. The only item beyond bare necessities that she could not do without was her cell phone, although she'd been tempted, during the train ride, to toss it in the river. One final act of separation, but she resisted. This was a new beginning, a fresh start, and she was well satisfied to be first off the train.

Tara declined the conductor's hand to guide her onto a step. *Hands off.* A beauty, and due to her striking looks she was accustomed to the attentions of men, including those who would find any excuse to graze her skin. She hesitated on the train's lower rung and allowed her eyes to adjust to the sudden brightness. The delay was not meant to put herself on display. The opposite, she wanted to take in the moment, for this step off the train marked the conclusion of her old life, and a fresh start.

She stepped down onto the platform. Feeling famished.

Soon enough, resigned to it, tourists disembarked as a swarm, ready to commence a bee-like buzz about town. Tara looked around awhile, just observing, deciding on a direction, then adjusted her backpack—thinking that perhaps she'd brought along more than she needed—resisted the bakery across the street, and started walking.

So, town. Her lips moved with the intensity of her query. *Whatcha got?*

6

After lunch, the men waited for timbers to be loaded on their trucks. They were deep in the forest now, comfortably in the wild and their element. Amenities were primitive, yet their lives in town and even at home fell away once they entered this realm. Here, the order of their lives went unchallenged. Each man's worth was attributed and valued. Standing amid the rampant noise of machinery and the constant dust, encircled by the forest's stately presence, they felt privileged. In another era, their forebears passed whole winters in these woods before emerging to the care of families and friends. This generation entered the forest they depended upon for their livelihood daily and departed again each evening, yet here they feel at ease, and the truckers believe that it is legitimate to call themselves loggers, no matter that none of them cut down trees or load the logs onto flatbeds.

Machines perform the bulk of that labour now.

Above a scrimmage of screech and roar, the men talked. So familiar was the robust bedlam at their backs that they never noticed themselves raising their voices. If magically the cacophony could be switched off they might be shocked at how boisterously they were shouting, of how their neck muscles bulged and contracted with the strain.

They had much to bellow about, the day an affront, a partial misery.

News about the bus being off-loaded and the old folks tottering across the bridge had gone around. Versions were embellished to include more buses, more wheelchairs, more elderly over ninety, virtually all of whom were dependent on canes or walkers. Wildly exaggerated, the stories still polished an essential nugget of truth, that not only were matters with the bridge not progressing, they were deteriorating more rapidly than anyone could salvage.

"At some point, you gotta call it what it is, what this is here."

"What do you wanna call it?"

"The last frigging final fucking straw."

"You're right. Totally. Call it that."

Denny O'Farrell remained quiet. He wanted to hear fresh ideas, not another endless rant. Only ideas could save him now. He heard the complaints, repeated them himself a thousand times. What he needed was a proposal equally as abrupt and as convincing as their anger, and far less terrifying than the gambit he now embraced. He remained still, and quiet, because he was beginning to feel boxed in, surrounded, ambushed by his own notions, as foreign as they might be. He'd proposed a plan, to a few, and those within his inner circle were bound to secrecy. They would not proceed unless they had no choice, and right from the outset Denny prayed that matters would never reach that juncture, that declared point of no return.

Yet the moment appeared to be drawing near.

"A blockade!" one of the big talkers pronounced, as if the scheme hadn't already been recklessly discussed multiple times, and rejected as often. Denny supposed they'd argue it through once more for good measure. Samad was there, smoking and nodding but not saying much, and Xavier was chipping in with comments. André made suggestive gestures in response to aggressive statements, but mostly he made eye contact with Denny as though to confirm that the time to do something was coming soon. Denny wished he'd stop. The big talkers could be counted on to work themselves into a lather, but they'd think differently when things became complicated, or dangerous, or rife with consequences. They wouldn't talk so loud when matters got down to the nitty-gritty, the particulars. When the time arrived for risky action, some men would find an imaginative way or even a dumb way to be absent. Oh, but they'd still goad others to do the dirty work. They'd inflame others with talk about dumping logs across highways or planting bombs in government buildings or abducting key figures or, since the environment garnered such attention these days and the environmentalists opposed their idea of a new, fast bridge, why not create an oil spill in the river and see how people liked that, eh? Guys like Big Bill Fournier and Max Klug and Lee Stemniuk, those guys, they were talking big because they always talked big, and Denny once thought that they were the guys, the leaders when you needed to change the world. Over time he learned otherwise. Those guys never took a risk, but oh man, they loved to talk, they loved to pressure others.

Someone once mentioned firing a bullet out of the dark forest through a windshield. That way, no one could ever find out who pulled the trigger. A few guys talked about something like that because they themselves would never hold that rifle in their hands, but someone like himself, who might actually do something, kept his mouth shut. The only way, he thought.

"What do you think, Denny?" Big Bill Fournier was asking him. "You're so quiet. What's up with you?"

Thanks to that remark, quite a few of the men were looking at him now, not just André. As if they knew. Or if they didn't know, they were good at guessing. He was leaning back against Big Bill's truck, both hands in the front pockets of his jeans, sticking to the shade. A damn scorcher today. Perspiration matted the front of his shirt and every man's shirt showed dark patches under the arms. He could smell their sweat. Big Bill's diesel rumbled at idle at his back and he felt that gentle shake although, as close as it was to him, the engine was virtually inaudible, overwhelmed by the charge of the forklifts snapping up timbers like twigs then releasing those logs to drop onto the beds of the trucks, including at the moment his own. A thunderous tumble. One after another. Every truck, not only Big Bill's, rumbled with its engine on, the three being loaded and the four in a row waiting. What was he supposed to say?

"We've been down this road before," he yelled, unaware that he was yelling. "Blockades don't work if the first guy in line loses his contract."

"But if everybody goes," Big Bill was saying as if he hadn't said it before, "every last one of us, at the same time, they can't fire all our asses."

"Sure they can," Denny pointed out to him.

"They don't have to," Samad interjected, because he'd heard this debate a hundred times over himself, everyone had.

"Start at the front and work their way back. Cancel contracts on the first couple of guys and it's over," André said.

"The rest will fall," Xavier conceded. "Like bowling pins."

"Guys, we can hold tight, refuse to load up if somebody's canned."

"Then stand first in line," Denny suggested. He'd never been that cruel before. "We'll line up behind you, Big Bill, back you every inch."

Without saying so, Big Bill's body language conceded that that strategy put a different spin on things.

Denny wanted some other idea, which he knew he didn't have, and probably his unhappiness stemmed from an intuitive conviction that the only workable idea was the one that he and André would not speak aloud in the company of others. This was going to fall on him, he could feel that. Maybe that's why he'd been mean to Big Bill, called him out for being a wuss. This was going to fall on him, and Big Bill Fournier, a big talker, could never get to the bottom of what that might mean.

"It sucks," Denny said above the raucous booming down the line, and he didn't mean the bridge or how their day was going. He meant that any solution would by necessity fall on him and he hated that. André was still glancing over at him and he wanted to punch him in his left eye, close it with his fist.

Lee Stemniuk, usually a mild-mannered sort with only a pair of bar fights to his credit, said, "Maybe we can kidnap some fucker's ass."

They chuckled a little, but Denny looked up, gazed at Lee.

"Whose?" Big Bill wanted to know. He wasn't taking the idea seriously either but he wanted to play along, have a lark.

"Some CEO fuck," Lee said, and shrugged. "Some politician shit maybe."

Denny wasn't laughing and despite the heat he crossed his arms over his chest and buried his hands beneath his biceps. He didn't like the rancour embedded in the false humour. He knew that some of the men discussed these things in whispers, and considered it all, and went on flirting with it all. *Kidnap some fucker's ass. Get attention that way. They'll find out how serious we are then. A new bridge in the blink of an eye after that.* Lee was a mild-mannered man who could get rowdy when pushed, he'd seen him in one of his two fights, but the day was doing this. The heat, the blocked bridge, the long drives that limited the number of loads they'd carry, the forfeit of a measure of their pay, the rising cost of fuel, the buildup of frustration, the erosion of hope—

these things caused Lee to make a joke, but under that joke lurked a venom, and a potential that Denny judged to be dangerous.

"Fucking assassination, that's the way to go," Big Bill added on.

Unimaginable deeds felt plausible when they could laugh about them.

"Pop off the old people," Xavier put in, and he took aim and fired an invisible rifle, "when they walk across the bridge instead of taking the bus. That'd get a reaction."

"You think?"

They were laughing and having a good time now, their humour virulent, but Denny knew they were building themselves up to justify an action, some kind of an action, any action. Denny didn't crack a smile. He wasn't going to build himself up that way. When it came time to take that action, he'd probably do it. Otherwise it might not get done, or worse, the wrong sort of thing would happen instead, something that could damage their prosperity, even wreck their lives. So the matter fell to him. He not only had the vision to know what to do and how, he was willing to see it through. And he was not some hothead, although he knew people liked to think so. He made it a personal point of honour. Everything needed to be carefully considered, with attention to detail, and just. He could never speak of his solution to anyone beyond his trusted group, not ever, for that would be tantamount to a public plea of guilty before the commission of the crime. The wrong remark now could land him in jail later. So he detested the heated words spitting around him, as no one seriously contemplating an action would dare speak of it aloud. Something was brewing, so deep, so dark, that not only could he never speak of it, but neither could he bring himself to laugh along with these other imaginary escapades. His silence, he assumed, could never convict him.

Yet André, one of his trusted confidants who should know better, was looking right at Denny at the same time that he was laughing at Xavier, and Denny could punch him out, swing both fists to pummel the bastard. Why, he lamented, couldn't someone else take charge?

"Fuck off!" he whispered to André, words the man could not hear but could see on Denny's lips.

"What's up with you?" Big Bill asked.

Denny chose to retreat.

"I'm loaded," he yelled. "I'm bugging out."

He and Samad and Xavier walked back to their rigs. The others mounted theirs as well, preparing to move up the line.

Denny climbed into his truck and settled behind the wheel, and that's when he felt it again, only this time he admitted that he knew why. He knew why Val's foot appeared radiant to him that morning, why Valou on his shoulder seared his soul, why dust motes floating in the sunlight stunned him. What was perfect in his life, golden, both the apparent and the subtle treasures, lay in jeopardy, at risk. He so wanted to be delivered from a gambit that would put him and those he loved in harm's way. He alone would deliver himself into the heart of that trouble, so he alone could spare himself the grief. While he considered his choices, what he loved in life shone upon him with foreboding luminescence, as if talking back to him, shining in his eyes, as though to counter his folly, his zeal. As though to say *Hey! You. Denny. Stop.*

7

A late lunch. Beans bubbled in a pot. A visit was in the offing. Alex O'Farrell smiled when he spotted the squad car pull into his drive. He withdrew a second beer from the fridge, uncapped it, and at the sound of the knock turned the heat down and took the bottle out front with him. Opening the door, he proffered the beer.

"Beans on the stovetop. I'll bring out a plate."

"I can eat," the officer said, and accepted the beer. Collapsed down onto the porch bench, he exhaled in appreciation of this refuge from the sun. Under the line of his cap he mopped his damp brow, then tossed the cap on the bench and relaxed his gun belt, letting it slip lower on his hips. His crotch felt damp and he sat with his knees wide apart. Alex returned with two plates of brown beans and chunks of bread twisted off the loaf.

"Hot one."

"Say that again."

"Hot food on a hot day, your momma used to say."

"She was wrong then, she'd be wrong today."

Alex grinned, sat down, and began to eat. "So," he sighed, after his first mouthful.

"It's like this, Dad," Ryan Alexander O'Farrell commenced.

"Oh, don't tell me," Alex advised him.

"You can't answer your door to salesmen with a shotgun in your hands."

"What if he'd been a thief? Or one of those goddamn psychopaths who drive across the countryside on killing sprees? The reckless ones."

"Don't play the old-woman act on me," Ryan O'Farrell dismissed him. "Not a psychopath on earth is dumb enough to take you on."

"Ryan, I was taking what you call . . . preventative measures. If he'd gone down the road . . . what if he rang Old Gal Sally's bell? She might've used her slingshot on his eyes. You'd be up here for a different reason then. That boy, that Jake Withers, he'd be a blind man, stumbling around holding his arms up, singing 'Show Me the Way to Go Home.'" He took a swig from his beer. "Anyway."

Ryan waited, then said, "Anyway what?"

"It's good to see you, too. How've you been?"

"Not bad. You?"

"Hanging in."

"The garden looks good."

"Don't mock me, son."

"Wouldn't dare."

They both ate their beans and swigged beer. Ryan hoped he'd not need to interview anyone later, especially if they happened to be in close quarters.

"Don't you eat cold food ever?" he asked his dad.

"Like ice cream?"

"Like vichyssoise or gazpacho. I'm sweating bullets here."

"Don't blame the food. It's that uniform you're wearing."

"Salads, for instance."

"I cook. Don't worry about me."

"You cook. Out of a can."

"Keep it up. I'll fetch my gun again."

They finished and stacked their plates and Alex knew that Ryan would never accept a second beer but asked him anyway. Ryan shook his head. He wasn't in any hurry to leave, though, and leaned back against the wood bench that his father built years ago when his mother was alive. She'd wanted a porch with a smooching bench and saw to it that her husband built both for her. She was a woman easily satisfied in life. Ryan never thought about it before but it occurred to him that he was more his mother's son, in many ways, than his father's. His brother Denny, on the other hand, was so noticeably his father's son. Wild, in his way, untamed, impetuous.

"So who're you dating?" Alex asked him.

Ryan was being poked. So he poked back. "An hour ago, give or take, a pretty girl stepped off the train." He whistled.

"That good-looking?" Alex was interested, as he hadn't actually heard his son say boo about a girl in years.

"Take your breath away. Mine anyway. Good thing it wasn't you seeing her. She'd take your life away. You'd have a heart attack."

"So what're you doing here? Off that train, she's in town for about four hours, no?" Ryan made a gesture, and his father detected his regret, which he understood. "The uniform," Alex figured.

"Doesn't help," Ryan agreed. "But if you don't see me again, you'll know why. That one, a man could follow to the ends of the earth."

Alex was flabbergasted. "For God's sake, Ryan, take the day off. I haven't seen you this smitten since high school."

Ryan sighed heavily, released a slow gush of air. Alex interpreted that response as well.

"Don't sell yourself short."

"I won't. I don't. But, whoa. Another level. Know what I mean?"

Instinctively, Alex wanted to buck him up, counter his perspective. Yet he murmured, "Mmm." He knew what Ryan was talking about. Some women did seem to exist on another plane. And Ryan was a cop, which in his experience meant that the women who were attracted to him specifically because he was a cop were women he didn't particularly want around. While others were repelled, or possessed wiser instincts. As well, Ryan had endured misfortune in love. Only natural for him to hesitate.

"What about you?" Ryan asked. Time had passed since his last visit.

"What about me?" Alex was genuinely clueless, until he saw his son's slight grin. "Get off it."

"What? You're a man. You always liked women. Even Mom knew that."

"What do you mean even Mom knew that?" Alex picked up the plates to help him escape this situation, but as he stood his son retrieved his gun belt and followed him back into the house where he snapped the belt back on.

"Everything's about petunias and jackmanii vines now?"

"For God's sake."

"What?"

"I'm not older than Moses but I look it."

Ryan grinned. "Deception. That's your ploy. Always has been."

Alex put the plates down in the sink. "Whatever you think you know, I don't want to know you know. So bite your tongue."

"Done. But seriously. Are you going out? Staying in? What?"

"Go. Chat up your beauty queen off the train. If you want to double date, give me a holler."

Ryan took a glance around the house. His father wasn't old yet, although he knew that simple tasks were physically demanding for him, that stoically he suffered his aches and pains. So he was pleased to note the state of the rooms. Tidy. The man was tidier now than when he had a wife who cleaned up after him, that was for sure. Ryan's job took him into other people's homes at the worst of times—compared to his peers in similar circumstances his dad was doing well. Hanging in there. Keeping it together. He should see him more regularly, do more things with him, yet somehow that simple notion was fraught with difficulty. As if spending time with his dad underscored that he himself remained alone in the world, not only as a bachelor but dateless, in a dry spell following a losing streak on the heels of what he referred to as a bad breakup, if he made any reference to that time at all. With most people he avoided the memory, and people knew it was his way of blunting pain. He'd been left numb by the experience, disoriented, defeated. Spending time with his dad reinforced the notion that he might inherit his circumstances, become old and awash and alone. In the main, he spent substantial time with his dad only during hunting season, and he supposed that that was not going to change.

His father came up behind him.

"So. Dad," Ryan said. He turned. "Help me out on this. Why pull a shotgun on that poor kid?"

"He's almost as old as you are."

"Not nearly. I'm thinking you had an ulterior motive."

"I wanted to save his skin. Spare him from the wrath of my neighbours. I don't suppose you're going to arrest me."

The two men faced each other just inside the dining room, the heat of the day slipping in through open windows, fluttering the curtains a touch.

"Your brother," Alex said, "can't get over that you're a cop. I understand it, though. What else would you do with a mind like that?"

"Suspicious?"

"That's not the word. Inquisitive. Also . . . I might blush here because this makes me so proud . . . brilliant."

Ryan knew that his father was not about to blush. He also knew that he was right in that something was on his dad's mind. He'd been lured here.

"So what's up?"

"How about a Coke? I got diet. The other stuff pisses right out of me. You can still be on the job and have a Coke, no?"

Quietly, Ryan said, "Sure." He sat in a hardwood chair by the table. Cooler than the sofa. Whatever was stuck in his dad's craw sounded serious. He automatically hoped it wasn't health-related.

In the kitchen, Alex uncapped a beer for himself and poured the Diet Coke. He returned to the dining room. "I put it in a glass," he said. "With ice. We can pretend we're like civilized people."

To Alex, his son seemed to take his remark to heart, perhaps invest more in his words than he intended to say. "Out with it," his son nudged him.

"It's all just talk, Ry." He raised his right hand and made it vibrate. "The wild man of the river. You know my reputation."

"Is it? With a basis in truth, no? Anyway, it's more than reputation, Dad. You're a freaking legend. Your name carries weight. I know what I'm talking about. Denny and me, we grew up with it. We were expected to score the pretty girls, the girls expected it of us. Well, that part wasn't so bad."

"I wouldn't think so." Alex laughed from his belly a moment, then took a swig of his beer. He wanted to say more, but it seemed that something was also on Ryan's mind.

"We fought the toughest fights. Drank more than anybody else, took the biggest risks, on and off the river." Ryan responded to a need to run this down, as they rarely got into such territory. What they knew about each other was usually kept under wraps. "You were the river rat everybody else followed and looked up to. People took their cue from you. You got the logs downstream, but you also led the strikes when that needed to be done. You straightened people out sometimes, made them wise up. But you also settled them down when that was necessary, and then, Dad, when it was time to get them off their butts again, you riled them up. Call it mythology, okay, but I heard tales about you from enough sources, including from Mom, that they're bound to contain more than a grain of truth."

The reminiscences did not seem to hearten Alex. "Old times," he commented. "I have a hard time swatting a fly now. Life on the river makes you older than you are. Weathers you. Pulls a tear in every muscle you own. Mangles your bones. Are you still on me for working over that driveway salesman?"

"You know I'm not," Ryan said.

"This is about Denny," Alex confirmed, with a note of sadness.

They sipped their cool drinks, and Ryan caused the ice to rattle around in his glass.

Then they both went still.

Ryan broke the silence. "Big shoes, Dad. That's what you left us to fill. I get to act as the tough guy off and on when it's my job. But with Denny, some people think of him as the heir to your spirit, your legend. He's working as the modern-day equivalent of a river rat, a logging trucker. I think it's almost automatic that guys look up to him because of his surname. You know it. Is this why I'm here?"

"Denny's done a good job, for the most part. People respect him."

"I think so, too. He gets people to do what's right, most of the time."

"What happens if people believe that the time has come to dream up something that's more drastic? That might not be right?"

This was why he'd been lured here. "Like what?"

"There's a ton of shit in the air, Ry. You haven't heard?"

"I got my ears to the ground."

"Denny's mixed in?"

Ryan put his glass down. He didn't want to squeal on his only sibling to a parent, but this was no trifling matter. "You know him, Dad. Do you think he'd walk away just because things get tough to handle?"

Alex contemplated the question, staring off into space awhile.

"Let me put it another way," Ryan proposed. "If it was you, and you were a young buck again, would you be mixed in?"

Alex nodded. He understood.

"I'd be mixed in," he agreed. "The sad thing is—me, not being a river rat anymore—if you asked me to take sides today, it wouldn't be for the loggers. Not automatically. It would be for the river. I love the river and I'm sorry it took me so long but I realize that we damn nearly killed it. I love the trees. Even though I'm willing to cut them down, I want them to grow again. I also love good clean air, now more than ever. Maybe you two think you had a hard time living with my reputation. Trust me, it's been no easier for me."

"Meaning what?"

"Meaning if I talk to people about clean air, let's say, for some of them it's like I reached down inside their gizzards and pulled out their spleens."

Alex continued to nod when Ryan said, "I'm worried, too, Dad."

He acknowledged his son's serious tone with a nod. "Maybe I

shouldn't interfere. You're all grown men. But sometimes I can feel my blame in this. That it's my fault in a way. The legend thing is bunk but I agree with you, it's out there. I feel my part in this because I led the logging drives that nearly killed the river. Some would say they did kill it. That the river's as dead as a doornail."

Ryan could not comfort his father with idle remarks. Pain was evident behind his eyes.

"Talk to Denny," Ryan urged.

"That's what I think you should do." He added with a tight, sly grin, "Isn't that why I asked you here?"

Ryan pursed his lips, and thought about it. He concluded, "In this case, Dad, better you than me."

Alex swirled the beer around in its bottle, creating a bit of foam. "Okay," he said. "We'll see. Maybe you're right."

8

She cased the joint. Her term for browsing, a little joke to herself in the midst of an uneasy mood. Tara was drawn inside by a sign in the window advertising employment. *Bet I look like a shoplifter to you, don't I? Ha!* His eyes, she determined, didn't merely fall upon her the instant she stepped through the door, rather his gaze slithered across the floor, then snaked around her legs. She felt bound by a constrictor. Long ago Tara made peace with a constant in her life—men were free to gaze, she didn't mind that so much, as long as they didn't give her the creeps. This one? *Borderline. Look, I'm not out to steal your precious merchandise, okay? Is that what you're hoping for? So you can pat me down? Demand to see what I've stuffed down my bra? Ah, wouldn't you like to know.* She circled the crowded aisles, a deliberate prowl. On the hunt, but for what? *A lure.* A hope. A path. *Some kind of a sign.* A sixth sense foretold that it might be lying around here somewhere. *Don't get your hopes up, Mr. Snaky Eyes. A lot of your stuff comes in between second-rate and doesn't rate. My shoplifting standards run higher than this.* She sniffed potpourris and cast an eye into amazing kaleidoscopes of ascending sizes and grazed her fingertips along the felt finish of a chessboard. Within the congestion of souvenirs and artefacts and the wares of artisans a few items were at least mildly interesting. Several she counted as tempting. *But it's only your wallet I'm after, Snaky. Yeah, come on over here. Bring cash. Oodles.*

When the shopkeeper did commence to drift her way, she moved off, slithering a little herself.

Yeah, smile, buddy. While I pick your pocket blind.

She didn't know why she was entertaining this fantasy today. Being out on her own with no fixed address made her feel like an outlaw for a change, rather than an officer of the court. Tara could no more pick a wallet than she could rob a bank or shoplift penny candy. She knew she should *get real in a hurry*, she had a life to remake. *This time.* This place. Here. *Now. I know. So get on it.* At university, a fellow student once called her a ballbuster. Upset, she wondered how widespread the sentiment travelled before understanding that the guy was not merely being a dork, he was being a jealous *competitor*, someone who wanted her marks, *my scholarships*, her awards, her class standing, *probably even my looks. But what's mine is mine, buddy.* He had no legitimate claim on any of it or on her. She'd long since lost track of him but assumed that he was doing well, *creeping up the corporate ladder, whack job?* He'd be cheered by her current circumstances, and Tara hoped that he never found out about her sudden, lapsed interest in their profession. Her demise.

He'd be unbearable.

She was not poor, but she was out of work and, essentially, home-less.

What have I done?

Thinking of him motivated her. Whatever she did next wasn't the point, *not so much.* The main thing was not to fail. Maybe that was her old lawyer training and natural competitiveness muscling aside fresh desires, but she couldn't kick the habit. She'd cut herself loose. Given up everything. She fled. Yet she was no saint and *I'm no latter-day hippie-dippie. Gawd.* She needed to succeed at something, only it had to be *something else.*

An anteroom allowed her to slip away from the shopkeeper's scrutiny, but few treasures there sustained her interest. Until a notion, undefined, ephemeral, provoked her. *The possibility of a maybe. Hey. This is a thought.*

More than a common consideration perhaps, an intuitive flash.

On closer inspection, the little room presented itself as a quaint disaster. A confusion of tastes, a litter of bad ideas, a place where items impossible to sell were ostensibly displayed when really they were being shunted aside in the faint hope that somebody might steal them or accidentally break them, or that their creators would return to remove them to a loving home under a rock somewhere. *Way deep.* Plaster owls and plastic bouquets and commemorative plaques and plates honouring old inaugurations or civic anniversaries or jamborees. A hodgepodge of kitsch. Unwanted, untended, each surface dulled by dust. Too late to vacuum and now the shopkeeper was edging her way. *You're not so borderline creepy anymore. Just more creepy. Do you, like, practise? Is it an art form with you?* As he entered the room and moved closer she marked down his appreciative gaze to being an ill-concealed leer. *There, that's it, that's the look I despise.* The man's left hand plucked a figurine from a shelf as if the scantily clad buxom Indian princess and her brightly beaded elephant really did deserve and command the whole of his attention.

She turned to him and, before she could rethink or censure herself, put forward, "About your sign in the window."

That changed his expression entirely.

He needed to collect himself, to reconfigure his approach. He put down the Indian princess. "You have experience in retail?"

"For this job?" She should not have said that, her tone an insult, but the words slipped out lickety-split. Tara recovered with a smile and cheerily declared, "Plenty." Then quickly rambled on. "I'm not asking for a job. Here's the thing. I'd like to present you with a business proposition."

She was thinking on her feet *lightning speed*.

At least he seemed as startled on the outside as she was internally.

She quavered, grateful for the opportunity to say next, "Ah, there's a lady at the cash, sir. You may want to attend to her first."

He nodded, bowed slightly, and backed out of the room. *Dude, you back out of a room bowing, who does that?* He beamed broadly upon his paying client, yet his glance repeatedly returned to the small antechamber and the mysterious visitor there.

Tara contained her desire to bolt. If she fled now she'd be *running away from running away*. Instead, she wandered out to the main section of the store. Someone entered—a little old lady balancing a pie on each palm—and she turned at the sound of the door's jingling bell. The old lady grinned *beamed!* and shyly she returned a faint flicker of a smile. This seemed a friendly sort of town.

The scent of berry pies reminded her that she was starving.

The bell began to jingle repeatedly, a crescendo to any retailer's ears as passengers off the train kept wandering in. If nothing else, they found a reprieve from the heat. Tara stepped up to the side of the cash while the proprietor rang up a sale and the elderly visitor waited patiently, balancing her two pies. The woman beamed brightly once more and said, "Another hot one. *Whoo!*"

Tara felt a need to match her friendliness. "You aren't going to— Well, you look like you're going to—"

The old lady gazed first at one pie, then the other, then fell into a fit of the giggles. *She gets me*. Just like that, *This old lady gets me*.

"Oh no, dear," she laughed. "I'm not going to throw these in anyone's face. Although *you* could. They're for sale. You can buy one in a moment."

"A little difficult to carry in a backpack."

"You're off the train?"

"I am."

"On your own?" Rather than curiosity, the question expressed dismay.

"Another reason I can't buy a whole pie just yet."

"People are after me to bake smaller ones. I'm considering it."

The first customer in line moved off with her bag of trinkets, allowing the elderly woman to put her pies down on the counter. Each was protected by a cellophane wrap punched with small steam holes. The proprietor was marking up the sheet that maintained a record of their transactions while she removed the wrap.

"They smell great," Tara marvelled. "You must sell a lot of pies."

"I started as a cottage industry. Now I'm a major conglomerate."

Tara laughed. "Because of you I need lunch. Suddenly I'm famished."

The proprietor's look mingled surprise and intrinsic regret.

"You're swamped, sir. I'll be back," she said, which appeared to mollify him. "We'll try again after lunch."

Without waiting for a response, Tara used only a facial expression to say good-bye to the old lady as she departed the counter and the store. The wee bell tinkled overhead. On the street she was surprised, and waited a moment to verify the image. The pie lady emerged to find Tara admiring her scooter, which carried two more blueberry creations cradled in a basket.

"This is yours?" Tara asked her.

"Are you worried I'll run over your toes? You should be. I might!"

"On purpose?"

"No, silly. But accidents happen. Especially when I'm driving."

The woman started up the scooter and pulled on her helmet. Slow-moving traffic obliged her to delay a moment. Tara felt transfixed by this geriatric on a colourful, gleaming motorized bike sporting a bright blue blaze of a helmet. She was finding this town charming in unexpected ways.

"I'm Mrs. McCracken," the old lady told her in response to her scrutiny, her voice muffled by the helmet and its visor.

"I'm Tara."

"Of course you are, dear," Mrs. McCracken declared, almost as though she did not believe her, then swung her scooter out into traffic.

■ ■ ■

AS SHE ARRIVED HOME, MRS. McCracken felt perspiration leak down the back of her neck. A change of dress might be in order, although she reconsidered as she entered the relative coolness of her home. Fans fluttered the curtains and the house itself stood in the lee of a tall sugar maple and a great eastern pine. The cooling effect may have been more psychological than what could be demonstrated on a thermometer, but certainly the shelter of the house was welcome after the blazing sun.

"I could bake a pie on the sidewalk," she told Buckminster, her tabby, who, languid on a patch of cool bare floor, could not care less.

She needed to tidy up the kitchen after her baking and deliveries and was concluding the chores when the doorbell sounded. Her old one broke and a new remote bell that allowed her a choice of chimes was installed by her neighbour's gaunt son. A mystery, that boy. Just when you were guessing that he was good for nothing he turned out to be good for any chore that contractors charged a fortune to accomplish. He accepted payment but without concern for the amount and only seemed happy when he was tinkering. He came over sometimes to see if she'd baked more pies than she was able to distribute, but unfortunately, he wasn't the one at the door today.

She spoke through the screen to a red-haired lad, a stranger.

"Hello?"

"Good afternoon, ma'am!" he fairly bellowed. "My name is Jake Withers and I represent the Rathbone Company?"

She didn't know what was wrong with a whole generation that couldn't make a simple statement without it sounding like a question.

"Is that a good thing?" she asked.

"Pardon me?" Jake Withers was having difficulty making out the woman's form on the other side of the screen, although she seemed slight, old, and, from the sound of her voice, easy pickings.

"I've never heard of the Rathbone Company."

"We're very well established. I can show you references."

"I've never met a Rathbone. Are they from around here?"

"Well, we're a company, you know. A company. We're from everywhere, like. We're old."

"Old is good."

"If you were to come outside, I'll show you how I can accelerate your property value."

Mrs. McCracken opened the screen to have a peek at him. He seemed like a nice enough young man. He was backing away from her, which she appreciated. He was not acting as though he planned to storm the premises and tie her up to a kitchen chair. These sorts of things never happened *here*, of course, but one never knew when *somewhere else* suddenly became your very own doorstep. She stepped outside into the glaring light.

"Property values don't interest me one whit," she explained to him.

"I'll die before I sell. So improving property values can do nothing more for me than raise my taxes. But feel free, talk away."

Jake Withers, she saw, was staring at the patch of yard where her scooter stood parked. Old ruts from another era remained perceptible along the rising lawn to the garage behind the house where her husband used to park his car. Lawn tools were stowed back there now, and her scooter over the winter. "Just imagine," the young man brayed, "a gleaming black driveway. Ma'am, for the addition to your property value you should really pay me double, but I'll tell you what I'll do. I won't charge you double. In fact, because you're a senior and I respect seniors, I'll give you a discount right off the bat. Ten percent, no questions asked. I'll also cut the deposit in half. Ma'am, it's too hot a day to bicker or barter, so I'll just give you the best deal possible and lay it on the table. Or on the lawn, *ha-ha*. First, I want you to imagine that gleaming black driveway up from the road to your garage. A beautiful thing, no? A beautiful thing, indeed. Imagine it!"

"Would you excuse me a moment?" she asked him quietly, and went back inside.

Jake Withers had heard that phrase earlier in the day, or one like it, and this time his antennae were alert.

"You don't own a shotgun, do you?" He chuckled nervously.

"Certainly not," she assured him, and carried on inside. She emerged shortly carrying a croquet mallet.

"What's that?" Jake Withers asked her.

"What does it look like?"

"I'm not sure. It's colourful enough."

"A croquet mallet."

"What's it for?" To err on the side of caution, he took a farther step down.

"Given that you want to destroy my croquet lawn with your ridiculous driveway, I thought that it might be perfectly fitting for me to bop you one over the head. It won't hurt that much. I am old, not so strong, so there shouldn't be too much blood. Don't you think that's fitting?"

"Oh, come on!" Jake Withers did a complete spin. "What is wrong with you people in this town! I'm here to pave your driveways and increase your property values and you treat me like *I'm* the criminal! *You're* the criminals! With your shotguns and your weapons! I'm just trying to earn my living here!"

"Not at the expense of my lawn, you won't."

She didn't have to run him off, he was already leaving on his own accord. He threw his driveway samples into his backseat and flung his hands in the air as he berated the wind. Whatever he was muttering to himself, the flurry came upon Mrs. McCracken as unintelligible.

She watched him drive off, then returned with her mallet to the cool sanctuary of her home where Buckminster yawned in apparent approval. "I'd be better off with a dog," she told him. "A yappy mutt." The cat had heard the threat before, and so stretched out, nonplussed, to help cool his furry self.

■ ■ ■

UP FROM THE RIVERBANK, IN from the pubs and cafés, out from the curiosity shops, and down from the trails through the woodlands, excursion train passengers flowed back towards the town's centre and the train station. Tara Cogshill found herself carried along by that current, but as she passed the store she visited earlier she stepped inside. The man with the combed-over haircut and slender nose was hoping for her return. She confessed that his eyes were not so beady, that they were probably his finest feature, soft with a greyness, but believed that they ought to be beady given his subtly creepy demeanour. *Icky.*

"You mentioned a business proposition." He wrung his hands together as he spoke. "I confess that I am quite stumped as to what that might entail. How it relates to the sign in the window—I confess to being baffled."

Tara smiled. He wasn't that bad a guy, not really. She'd met worse. "You asked if I have retail experience. Isn't every business, ultimately, about selling? Commerce revolves around buyers and sellers. Intrigue is one lure. If you are willing to concede that I garnered your interest, then you kinda have to concede that I've proven something here."

"Ah, excuse me? Proven what?"

"That I have enough experience to sell. In this case, I'm selling, in a manner of speaking, don't take this the wrong way now, myself."

Good speech. Major pat on the—

"So," the shopkeeper supposed. Tara demonstrated that she was giving him her fullest attention, even as he grew hesitant, still baffled. "So you do want the job."

"Hardly," Tara let slip.

He nodded, as though to confirm his own assessment. "I didn't think a job in retail was part of your—how shall I put this?—persona."

Sounding creepier, dude.

Taking a breath, she pressed on. "A business proposition, sir, that's what interests me. My name is Tara Cogshill." She stuck out her hand. "You are?"

"Willis Howard. I'm pleased to meet you, Miss Cogshill."

"Tara," she corrected him. She wondered if she should not correct him twice, for did he not give his names in reverse order? "I'm pleased to meet you . . . Mr. Howard?" He didn't contradict her, so his first name must really be Willis. "Despite the fact that your anteroom over here is a disaster."

"Ah." Willis Howard stepped back, peered over his shoulder. "I do have my secret plans. It's a question of time and, of course, resources."

"Precisely. That's where I come in. At the moment I have time. In a modest way, resources, too."

"Ah. You want to redesign my store?"

"Not a chance. Not your store."

"The anteroom?"

"Own it, actually."

"Excuse me?"

"The products inside, at least. I'm proposing a store within your store. Which saves me the headache of setting up a business in a town where I've only just arrived. I don't even know my way around yet. This spares us becoming direct competitors, as well. My start-up costs will be minimal. Maybe I can get off the ground without high risk."

"And," he said, speaking slowly, smiling as though he found the idiocy of her proposition as amusing as it was irritating, "I'm selling you part of my store because—" He let his voice trail off, waiting for her to finish the sentence. Rather than do that, Tara strolled over to the room in question and gave it another look.

She faced him.

"Dull, useless, wasted space that produces negligible revenue. You can't put items of value in here because you can't keep your eye on them. You can't put big-ticket items in here, such as those grandfather clocks, because if you spent time in this room with a customer your clientele on the other side might rob you blind. You cannot afford—it's illogical—to hire someone merely to keep an eye on this tiny room. So you've made it a junk room that just doesn't pay. No, the only solution that makes sense is to allow me to take over the space, run my own business, one that's complementary to yours, and pay a percentage of sales in lieu of rent. A win-win-win proposition."

Her proposal flew out with such alacrity, the bows tied and the buttons done up, that Willis Howard was unable to mount a quick defence. He realized that that was exactly what he was attempting to do—defend himself, and his shop, against her onslaught.

"I'm—sorry. I don't think so, Miss, ah—Tara."

The moment he spoke her name she knew she'd won.

"So I should get on the train, then?"

"Excuse me?" Once more caught off-balance.

She showed him her return ticket. "The train? I get on it?"

In his hesitation Willis Howard was truly lost.

"Departure time is in nine minutes," she reminded him.

Tara started to back away, holding up her ticket. Facing him. Stepping towards the exit, bopping in a slightly exaggerated fashion, as if she, the fish with a hook in her mouth, was pulling the fisherman into the drink.

"There's a number of complications. Issues. Agreements. I can't have you in direct competition with me."

"Everything can be worked out down the line. Do I go or stay?"

Abruptly, Willis Howard put aside the negotiation. He simply regarded the young woman before him. She was what he would call, in his own personal vernacular, a straightforward, shining beauty. The vulgarities which sometimes attracted him on the Internet did not come attached to this young woman. Tall, willowy, elegant, even wearing a backpack she exhibited a suave and sophisticated bearing. He assumed that she came from money, perhaps power, good family—something about her pores. Breeding. In any case, he'd not spoken to a woman so pretty at such length over the course of his lifetime, not even as a shopkeeper to a prospective patron. Whatever the ramifications for his business might be, they were now being superseded by a baleful and pathetic internal desire not to let her out of his sight.

But he just couldn't commit to this flimflam arrangement.

Tara pushed him over the edge. "Did I mention that, when my room is bereft of clientele, I can help out on your side of the store, at the cash or wherever? Of course, you'll have to agree to look after my wee alcove whenever I need time away, and when things are quiet."

"It's so complicated."

"Simple, actually. Time's on our side. We'll work it out."

She was nearly out the door. Out. Gone. That light.

"I accept," he agreed. Just like that. "We'll try it. I just need to know—"

Tara interrupted him by ceremoniously depositing the ticket back in her pocket, then holding up her hand. "The details come later. There's something I must see to before the train departs, Willis. I'll drop in tomorrow, okay?"

He nodded, sensing as he did so that this would not be his first such acquiescence. And knowing that, oddly for him, he didn't mind. Not so much. Not yet.

■ ■ ■

SHE WANTED TO SEE THIS done. A trick for the tourists. A nostalgic gesture. She wasn't able to wholly imagine how it was possible so needed to see it for herself. She was like that. At the end of the railway line, the old steam engine that dragged them to Wakefield required that it be turned in a half circle, in order to pull the passenger cars back home while facing elegantly forward. The engine was detached from the train and slowly it eked onto a set of rails laid upon a circular wood platform. Passengers took hold of braces that served the purpose and walked the engine and the round table around until it faced the opposing direction. Tara wanted to see this done, but before the engine was a quarter of the way through she joined in, amazed by how little effort it took. She laughed with the others as the little engine was spun, then shyly stepped away. Travellers were happily embarking, going home. She was not. She was on her own, staying put.

It's official.

I'm here now.

Tara walked away without turning back. As the locomotive pulled out from the station, she was still ambling along slowly, yet faster than the train. Farther along, she could sense it catching up. By then it was time to turn off the road and stroll to an inn she'd first spotted in a pamphlet. She was excited. Feeling exhausted and alone. Everything so far in her new life, from birdsong to the shining water tumbling down the mountain creek to the town itself to her soft steps in the roadside dirt to the way her body slipped and sang along her bones, as if she was dancing on a speckle of light, thrilled her. This was the first big surprise. She expected to feel nothing but sadness for a good long while, to be weepy and forlorn, consumed by defeat, a rejection to herself, as though she intended to be in mourning for her old life and a once-promising career. Instead, she rejoiced.

9

That evening, in the moist, heat-induced tanginess of humid air, Denny O'Farrell tended to the backyard barbecue. His domain. The property bordered a forest. During the summer, the foliage dense with luxuriant growth, he could seldom distinguish his neighbours' homes on either side. Only an occasional, excited, disembodied voice might rise up from other yards to announce a child's presence or a parent's reprimand. His own yard perpetually struggled between its domestic purpose and the wild surrounds. Denny never replaced his old dog when he passed away two years previously, but remnants of Coot's manic diggings remained, the grass scraped bare in patches, the excavations of shallow bone holes never backfilled. In their fervour the kids did their worst as well, running and scrapping and tumbling in the dirt. Tougher weeds abounded, springing from the selvage on the forest's perimeter, taking hold and laying siege. He'd given up on grass, although it grew high around the twin car engines which dominated the backyard. At one time he intended to restore them, or create one functioning engine from the two, but that wasn't going to happen. He'd finally admitted as much to himself, if not to Valérie, and the motors now sat rusting as inexplicable sculptures. Old tires and still-good winter ones fell about in haphazard array, tunnels through a mountain range one afternoon, mini-trampolines the next. At the back of the yard stood a homemade swing set that each child used briefly around the age of three, only to reject in favour of portable toys. His children seemed to share the same adage, that if a toy could not be dragged through the woods where it was undoubtedly clobbered and humiliated for hours on end, then it wasn't worth the playtime. Some toys, of course, never returned from the deeper woods.

Val left her imprint on the backyard as well, it wasn't only Denny's and the kids' doings. She constructed the picnic table herself after giving up on her husband getting around to it, and under where they sat their feet gouged small dirt valleys in the earth, puddles when it rained. She purchased new lawn chairs while allowing old ones to descend into ruin along the perimeter. The decrepit wheelbarrow twisted onto its side spilling a cascade of flowers was also her idea, one that worked, and save for the tomato plants remained pretty much her only attempt at a garden. Following that success she tried something similar with an old wagon discarded by the boys, but no sooner did she plant annuals in it than the boys reclaimed their property, doing so without permission. She made them replant the flowers in the front yard that year but Valérie learned her lesson. Leave their stuff alone, no matter how old or dysfunctional.

An idea to plant cylinder heads with chrysanthemums was scratched.

The backyard adopted its own style. The old and neglected found a home, and consequently the space was much used, typically cheerful and loud.

Boy-Dan, who nicknamed himself when he first learned to talk, a tag that stuck, shouted out the explanation of a point, "It's called a baker's dozen, Dumbelina."

Denny turned over the chicken breasts on his grill, only vaguely attentive to his kids' incessant chatter.

"That just proves bakers can't count," Davy astutely parried.

"All right! Geez. We take twelve horsemen each. Okay?"

This division of the spoils held one point of interest for Valou. "How many cannons for me?"

"You got tanks," Davy reminded her.

"I want cannons, I said! I told you six times already!"

"But I'm the fort!"

"I'm the navy," Boy-Dan decided on a whim. Until that moment, no one was aware of an ocean. "The ships are mine."

"Then how come you get the horsemen?" Boy-Dan was the oldest but Davy didn't let him get away with a thing.

"Fine. Split up your stupid horsemen. I get the ships."

"Davy! Davy!" Valou cried, her voice a veritable shriek that her father considered silencing.

"What?"

"I'll trade you. One cannon for a tank. Even steven."

Davy was perhaps willing to make that deal, although first he wanted to consider his options, see if a superior trade might be doable. Their negotiation was interrupted just then by their grandfather coming around the side of the house, which caused Valou to drop the whole matter.

"Grandpa!" she cried out.

"Va-looooou!" hooted Alexander O'Farrell, opening his arms wide to snag her.

She ran up to him with her good news. "We're building a fort!"

"Make sure you don't get stuck in the tower."

"It's only a play fort!"

Alex gathered her up into his powerful arms and hoisted her to his shoulder.

"Play forts have the scariest towers," he warned her.

As he lowered the lid on the barbecue Denny was engulfed by smoke, and waved a forearm to clear it. "Hey, Dad, how goes the battle?" he asked.

"Good. You?" He sought confirmation from his granddaughter on his shoulder. "It's not so bad, eh, Valou? How goes the world with you?"

"Help yourself to a beer," Denny invited.

"Don't mind if I do. Thanks." He went up the steps to the broad wood porch on his achy joints, lifted the cooler's top with his foot, then sat and swung Valou onto a knee in one motion. He executed the move with practised perfection, but this time he winced. His left hand dropped into the cooler and he uncapped a bottle and took a swig and only then did Valou slide from his lap and dash back to join her brothers before they won the war without her.

Val poked her head out the screen door.

"Bonjour, Alex. Stay for dinner?"

Alex offered his typically shy shrug. "Valérie. I don't know."

"You should. We have enough."

Where the war waged among ships and forts, tanks and cannons, the voice of the innocent pointed out to her grandfather, "You always do."

Alex laughed a little at that. So did Val. Whenever he came over at this hour, he stayed for dinner. A foregone conclusion. Stripped of artifice, he consented to the invitation. "That would be nice. If you've got enough."

"We've got enough," she assured him, and let the door bang shut.

Warm from the walk over, Alex took another long swig then bent forward, resting his elbows on his knees as he observed his grandkids in their play. His gaze eventually settled upon his son and somehow Denny had expected that, although he didn't know why. He looked up, inquisitive.

"What's going on?" Denny asked, and grinned, trying to be casual, holding his own beer in one hand, tongs in the other.

"Funny," Alex said. "That's more or less what I came here to ask you."

Denny furrowed his brow and gave him another questioning glance, then opened the lid again and was concealed behind a billow of smoke. He squinted and angled his head away. Being the cook bought him some time.

In the kitchen, Val checked the vegetables. She'd made enough. She didn't know why Alex couldn't call first, or come over sooner, but this was his way. So be it. A few of her friends complained about their in-laws but she never did. An extra chicken breast was intended for Denny's sandwich tomorrow, but now she'd snap open a can of tuna for that, no big deal. Nor was cost an issue. They had mouths to feed and Alex never brought food or beer, but a few times a year he'd take home the electricity bill, or ask, "What's this about?" as he picked up her credit card statement off the small desk in the hall where it awaited payment.

As if he didn't know. She'd say, "Alex."

He'd say, "Never tell your accountant what he hasn't already guessed." The bill would vanish into his jacket pocket, to be paid by Monday.

What accountant? What did that phrase even mean? He repeated it when, once a year, he mentioned that he was taking care of the mortgage that month.

"Alex, we have money."

"You pay your own way. I know that. You also have three kids, and your kids have a grandpa mooching off your table half the time, drinking your beer and whisky."

He brooked no argument, she found out, and so it went. If she was mildly embarrassed earlier on, she no longer felt the need. He wasn't only helping them along, the arrangement made him more comfortable about dropping by for dinner whenever he pleased. He walked a mile to their place, through woods, across a field, then down their road, uphill on the trek back home. The stroll was part of the attraction. Getting his exercise as well as being fed.

On the flip side of the coin she could call him at any time. He stood guard over the kids while she borrowed his car to run an errand, so it worked out. To be on the safe side, though, she put an extra potato in the microwave. She could have that while the others ate the ones that made the kitchen feel like a sauna, boiling away.

Denny came up onto the porch and stood leaning against a support beam, beer in hand and held against his chest. "Same old with me, Dad. Nothing much is up. Batting average has slipped a touch, but there's been a few indications that my good stroke is coming back."

"In my day—"

"Logger sports, Dad. Maybe you had no time for baseball, I know that, but you had time for logger sports."

"Logger wars more like it."

"Yeah. I'm sure that's true. Baseball can be like that sometimes."

"You mean the tree huggers."

"Mostly them, yeah."

"The thing is, Denny, I didn't come over to talk about your batting average."

They sustained a moment's eye contact and Denny grew uncomfortable. "Shit," he said.

"What?" Alex asked.

"Is it those rumours? I heard a few whoppers myself. About me, about different people. Seriously, Dad, don't pay them any mind."

"Denny," Alex shushed him under his breath. "Ssshhh. Look."

Denny's glance went first to his children, and they were fine, then to the edge of the woods. Alex left his beer on the bench and stood slowly, trying to rise and yet be motionless at the same time. He edged back towards the screen door.

Val's heart constricted as Alex slipped into the kitchen, making doubly sure not to let the door slam or make a sound as it closed behind him, then crept on the balls of his feet to the den.

"Oh no," Valérie whispered.

He put a finger to his lips.

"The kids."

"They're safe," he whispered back and carried on to the gun rack.

She looked out the window. She couldn't see the children. Denny was standing with his back to her, staring out at the forest. "Denny!" she warned under her breath. Yet she meant for him to hear her.

She saw Alex in the den loading a rifle.

"Shit!" Still, she knew only to whisper her alarm.

Valérie went to the door and saw the boys on the back porch, safe, sound, and accounted for. But where, where was Valou?

"Denny!" She tried to get his attention yet still remain virtually silent. "Valou?"

Alex O'Farrell tapped his daughter-in-law's shoulder and she moved aside just enough to let him pass with the rifle, then she followed him out the door. Valou remained in the yard, but she was coming their way, a valiant effort to make no sound as she sneaked up on her tippy-toes to the porch steps. Alex passed the rifle to Denny, who took aim.

Deer grazed at the edge of woods and yard.

Risky. This was not hunting season.

He was waiting for a doe to step onto his property.

"Denny!" she whispered hotly, her anxiety apparent while hushed. "Valou!"

Her daughter was not safe, still not out of harm's way.

Just then, a deer glanced up, startled as Valou tripped on a miniature cannon she missed seeing, stumbled, and Valérie jumped to catch her, although that was impossible, and she lightly jostled Denny as he fired. Quick as gusts, the deer vanished amid the trees.

The shot boomed in their ears and echoed off the trees.

"You missed," Alex remarked.

"The doe spooked."

Valérie erupted.

"Denny, you shithead! What the fuck's the matter with you!"

"Mommy, you said a bad word."

"Block your ears, Valou. Put your hands over your ears right now."

The urgency in her voice compelled her daughter to obey. The little girl cupped her palms over her ears, though with negligible effect on her hearing.

"Boys! Same thing!" She pointed a forefinger at each of them. "Right now."

They cupped their ears also, although long ago they learned to make it look good yet fully admit sound.

Denny ejected the spent shell.

"You stupid dumb ugly—" Valérie mouthed her expletive, so that the children were excluded from hearing her talk that way but Denny still got the message. She was seriously pissed. He wanted to defend himself but thought better of it.

"You shot right over her head! Right over her head! You freaking imbecile! You idiot!" Storming inside, she punctuated her rage by slamming the door.

The children uncupped their ears and awaited their dad's reaction. He'd provide their cue as to what to think. When he shrugged, Davy and Boy-Dan looked set to bust a gasket.

"It's an old family tradition," Denny told them, but he kept his voice low. "Shooting deer off our back porch. Moms never like it. But when we have venison to eat, they change their minds."

Valérie shouted from the kitchen. "Take your little sermon and stick it!"

Speaking below a whisper, Denny added, "But very slowly."

"You missed the doe by a foot and a half," Alex said. "I don't know why you bothered if you were going to shoot that far off the mark."

"But I missed Valou by five feet. Not like when you shot deer over my head."

"I never came that close to you," Alex protested.

"One time, the bullet whizzed past my right ear. *Wheeeet!* Inches."

"You exaggerate," Alex said.

"Mom was going to kill you. You don't remember?"

"A vague recollection maybe."

They both knew they were talking for the sake of the kids, teaching them the ways of moms and dads. A racket inside the house interrupted their conversation. Pots were tumbling inside a cabinet. A clatter of cutlery. Dishes were not being broken, though, which Denny deduced was a good thing. Val was venting her upset yet exercising reasonable control.

After the last pot rattled itself into stillness, Alex whispered, "Maybe I should go." He thought he was speaking only to Denny.

"Stay right where you are, Alex," Valérie commanded from inside. "Go now and I just might kill that evil son of yours." The door flew wide open. "Kids. Inside. Wash up. Don't you dare argue or delay."

They did not intend to defy her mood and jumped to the task.

She addressed the men. "Nitwit and Bigger Nitwit, don't think this is over. Alex, put the rifle away this instant and make sure you lock that door or you will not leave here alive. Fuckhead, set the damn table."

She let the door slam.

The two men stood still in the deadfall of silence.

"Fuckhead," Alex said. "I guess that would be you?"

He and Denny shared a glance, acknowledging that in the greater scheme of things they were getting off lightly, then moved on to their assigned tasks. Denny gathered up the cutlery. His shot missed. Everyone concluded it happened because Valou tripped. But he didn't think that way. He had the deer lined up. An easy shot. Somehow he missed. By as much as his dad said. Denny didn't want to let on that he was perplexed by that, that he couldn't figure it out. Still, he'd eluded that private talk his dad wanted, and for now and through the evening could keep him at bay, without being caught alone in his company. So all, at least, was not lost.

10

Night's fall is sudden upon a river town nestled amid rolling hills. Alexander Gareth O'Farrell detected a breeze through his bedroom curtains as he adjusted the blind half down, wanting to thwart the awakening glare of morning without impeding any possible circulation of air overnight. Across the stream below his window, a stillness remained palpable. Creepers burst out, a cacophonous blast, the racket easing as suddenly. A buzzy moth tested the screen, lingering awhile after the blessed light is shut, as if hopeful yet, ever expectant.

For Alex, sleep has not been a simple chore these summer nights, given the old injuries. His body resists being prone and struggles to find positions that ache less. The heat is welcome to succour these wounds, yet remains a distraction as he tosses and turns under a thin sheet. When that proves too warm he kicks out a leg, though he still desires his chest covered. Enough breeze will touch his skin to indicate that he will doze, eventually, in comfort. Yet soon his eyes blink open. He's caught wondering what that light might be. A waning quarter moon rising. The angle at the other window never so perfect as now to admit the shine. Alex inhales at length. Then breathes in calm rhythm. He feels, before he shuts his eyelids once more, the whole ache of the night upon him like these aged Gatineau Hills, ponderous, immense. Feels, as though at his feet, the scud of pond scum where the stream pools below his yard.

■　■　■

FOR RAINE TARA-ANNE COGSHILL THE night exposes her as restless. The steady purr of an overhead fan a push and pull, the shimmy of air across her skin, alternately warm, light then heavy, cool, the humidity distressing.

She rises and gets dressed, and wanders outside.

By the backyard swimming pool and hot tub, lovers irritate her. To come upon them entwined is a catalyst for her own loneliness that, for the moment, feels unbearable. A trail follows the surge of water down through the woods and she surrenders to that route. The inn an old mill transformed. Here, water rushes over the dam, loud, hypnotic, and, oddly, triumphantly soothing. The terrace has been abandoned by diners, yet a few patrons committed to their drinks linger on above the tempest of the falls. The path down through the trees takes Tara lower and a boardwalk guides her to a place to sit by the stream, to catch water in her fingers over smooth broad stones. She adjusts her weight on a boulder and crouches there in the moonlight, the water dripping from her fingertips, a longing which to her feels vaguely soulful apparent in her gaze. Staggered by the confluence of events that have carried her here, she's a twig, she feels, on the tumbling stream.

She considers something outside her norm. Solitary in this darkness she could undress, wade out upon the smooth flat stones, succumb to the embrace of the river where the stream idly circulates, turns, and gyrates awhile before travelling on. She could swim, dog-paddle in circles at least, in the deep black pool under the leer of wanton moonlight winking through the trees.

■ ■ ■

KITTY-CORNER ACROSS TOWN, MRS. ALICE Beauchamp McCracken has enjoyed her evening. Never did she mind the heat at night and for a change the shows on television amused her. If given her druthers, she is content with cops and robbers, or their near equivalent, cops and killers. Vile big-city goings-on. She is confident that she has prepared herself well as she crawls into bed—doors locked, pills taken, water on the bedside table, Buckminster safely ensconced, alarm set—and yet, she is no sooner under the sheet and comfortably upon her side than she struggles back up again. She's forgotten the light. Switching it off, she's astonished by the moon's bright glow bearing down upon her. The interruption changes her plan, and she informs Buckminster, who has at that moment landed on the opposite side of the bed with a bound, "I think we need the symphony tonight, dear."

Having missed the introduction, she does not know which otherworldly philharmonic comes through on the radio, nor is she adept at attributing music to composers. Mrs. McCracken enjoys the dulcet tones of the announcer and so regrets having missed them. Some nights, his words alone lull her to sleep.

His talk, tonight, proved unnecessary. An interval of at least forty minutes passed, the station programmed to play that long, when Mrs. McCracken awakens to a thump, one she cannot trace to a percussion section as the radio has automatically switched itself off. The night, as she listens for further sound, bears the silence of its warmth, when not enough breeze passes by to a rustle a leaf.

She hears the tinkling of glass.

Her hair stands on end.

Swiftly wide awake, intent, petrified, without knowingly commanding herself to do so, Mrs. McCracken sits erect.

All ears. All fear.

Buckminster, too, cranes his head up, listening.

Mrs. McCracken cannot properly interpret what it is she hears next. While her imagination conjures the covert entry of thieves she also tries to dismiss the threat as an old lady's batty nerves. She knows from long experience with false alarms that there is no earthly reason why she should guess at a sound's significance when she can as easily, and probably more quickly while saving herself considerable fret, go investigate.

Bravely putting her feet down on the floor, she works them into her slippers. Her lightweight housecoat, a flimsy thing, awaits on the bedside chair and she throws it on. She hurries—then thinks that she has detected something. What was that? Someone . . . whistling? *Impossible!* Mrs. McCracken pulls out the drawer of her bedside table and reaches in to where her husband's antique duelling pistols sleep. She withdraws the case and places it on the bed, opens it, and takes out both pistols, one in each hand.

They are both fully loaded.

They always are.

With blanks, but what thief knows that? Her secret.

Mrs. McCracken sucks in a sharp breath. With a wag of her chin she commands Buckminster to be still, although he shows no interest in moving, *no gumption whatsoever*, then she steps through the bedroom doorway.

Silence.

She moves to the landing at the crest of the stairs.

Her hearing seems electric, superhuman.

A frog by the shore of the Gatineau, a long way's off, croaks.

A board creaks and she flinches. She almost leaps.

Then, in defiance of her trepidation, she heads down the stairs.

A whistling!

One step at a time, slowly, slowly, until two-thirds of her descent is complete.

Mrs. McCracken sees a thief move before she hears his next whistle. She spots his nasty dark form scurry rat-like through the living room in haste. Then she detects more such phantom shapes. The temerity not to at least be quiet! As bold as you please! A whole gang of intruders, or ghosts, or wraiths at this hour of her death but in any case she's having none of it and Mrs. McCracken raises her right pistol in defiance of them. Then raises the left. She stands there waiting for the next spooky shape and when one crosses her line of sight she fires.

The roar of the blast nearly knocks her over, the sound of it alone, and she's aware then that the apparitions are on the run, and that she's hearing things, shouts and words and multiple voices and crazy running, and she's aware that she's still firing, point-blank, both guns, as if the weapons have seized control of her hands and blast away indiscriminately as she sits where she's tumbled on the stairs, wildly shooting thieves.

Later she guesses that only their laughter made her stop. Their laughter and their coarse invective. Not that she wanted to stop or considered it prudent, but she ceased the noise of her pistols to ascertain if her ears really heard what she thought she was hearing. And they did. The intruders were *guffawing, that's the word for it. They're guffawing!* Yelling, also, and swearing vilely, although probably not in fright as first she suspected. They sounded more like fans at a hockey game whose team just scored. *They're hooting!* She wanted to keep on shooting them but felt too perplexed. Why were they laughing at her in her own house while she was trying to shoot them dead?

At least, she summed up then, *at least,* they were leaving.

One said to another, "Come on. Let's piss off."

She didn't know how many they were. Three? Four?

She tried to shoot once more, but the hammer clicked, her ammunition spent.

Oh dear.

The roaring of the gunshots in her ears, her nerves assailing her so that she could neither think nor breathe nor cry out, Mrs. McCracken fell back lower on the stairwell, convinced that the end was near. She'd done it now. *You old galoot.* She was in for it. She'd given herself a heart attack and could only wait for the ambulance, preferably, or perhaps she'd have to wait for that dreadful morgue's pathetically morbid van, *black, if you can believe.*

Oh, you've gone and done it now, you silly old ninny. Foolish girl!

■ ■ ■

GOOSE-BUMPY COLD, THE WATER, BUT she didn't mind. She held on to a rock on a shallow ledge, allowing her legs to float up in the current above a deep cavity, gently kicking her feet to keep her more or less stationary. Tara looked a sight, she knew, her bum up above the water's flow, the twin orbs, she guessed, shining in moonlight. No one seemed to be peering at her, though, and anyway, what of it? She had the lone woods to herself and if an intruder impinged on her sport she'd throw stones, plenty were handy, and shout, scream if it came to that. The inn was nearby. Yet it seemed that she was free to commune with the stream under an overhanging arbour of branches in perfect solitude, as if the forest conspired with her to conceal her frolic. Imagine, being this free, to cavort, like some mystical nymph from antiquity, a captive maiden on the lam, a nun popped over the wall. Sheer bliss. *I love it.*

Yet she emerged. Her body adapted to the water temperature, the coolness a delight after the day's swelter, but soon she shivered. Easy does it on the slippery stones. She wished now that she planned this and brought down a towel, at least. Tara dabbed her skin with her summer dress, then drew it on over her head and along her wet torso. She pulled back her hair, wet in places, and retied a band to hold an impromptu ponytail. She sat by the stream, needing to dry at least a little before the trek through the lobby to the elevator and up to her room.

Out of the water, the sensation of being buoyed by it remained. She felt suspended, and consciously breathed deeply awhile.

Through the trees, flickering moonlight teased her.

She felt it, like a bump, and could have stopped everything right there but chose not to do so, allowing herself to nudge a certain eroticism distilled by the muggy air. The woods could hold her now, be her lover here. She resisted any imprudent behaviour in the stream but the forest's intentions remained indecent. She could walk a path that appeared to have been cleared by moonlight. She saw a fence. Annoying. Limitations. Lines drawn. She was not the first to be down here, not the first to have done this, although perhaps the first to have done this on her own. Maybe. Insect rattle and squeak. The tumbling stream. Leaves shimmering. Her movement was not involuntary, fully premeditated, for she cast a long glance over both shoulders first and back up towards the mill to check that she stood there alone and unobserved. She commanded her senses to be sure, to make absolutely certain that she could not be seen, a ghost in this realm, before she reached up under her left breast and held that slight weight and raised the breast higher before she tweaked the nipple already stiffened by the water's chilly wash.

Her hand eased back to the middle of her chest where she felt her heart thump.

Then she stopped.

Looked around once more.

If she carried through on fantasy now these woods would indeed be her lover. These trees. This very breeze. The stirring caress of the water.

Tara fell still, feeling somewhat mournful.

She was thinking of this: she missed no one. She remembered no one.

Did anyone, anywhere, she pondered, miss her?

■　■　■

A STRANGER MIGHT THINK SHE'D shot the devil through his evil eye. Such hubbub!

That dodo police officer *Oh, I know he's had his troubles but he's parked on my lawn!* never turned off the rotating red light clamped to the roof of his car. *What was he thinking? To draw more attention from the neighbours like that.* The moment he arrived, hurrying across the grass to see to her welfare, he managed only to utter her name, "Mrs. McCracken," before she felt compelled to interrupt.

"How do you keep that thing up there?" she asked.

Momentarily at a loss, he swallowed his next question and looked back at the unmarked car. Despite the paucity of clues, he extrapolated her meaning. "With a strong magnet. Mrs. McCracken, are you okay?"

"Makes sense," she considered, and held the door open for him to enter. She was wearing her light green housecoat with the floral print. Slightly warm but sufficiently modest for male guests. "Come in. Don't mind your shoes."

And now, two more cop cars were on her lawn, one with its high beams practically blinding her if she looked out, the other darkened, save for the light from an interior computer screen. Neighbours on every side mocked her by keeping their houselights on. They were probably serving tea and biscuits. Tomorrow, there'd be stories to re-count, for sure.

Her gunfire awakened a pocket of the town.

The first officer to arrive was one of the O'Farrell boys, she never could keep their names straight. This one must be Ryan, the smart one, but she didn't want to risk asking him to confirm that again as she'd already asked him once and forgotten the reply. Probably more than once. For the time being, she'd call him *officer*, and let it go at that. He sat with her while other policemen roamed her well-lit home—every light in the house was on for who knows what reason.

"If you think my robbers are hiding under the sofa you'll be dis-appointed."

One man sidled past the O'Farrell boy—oh, he was probably more than thirty but any man under fifty seemed a mere lad to her now, or was it that memories of them as eight-year-olds in her classes and later as teenagers held the greater sway?—he sidled past and broached some *indication* through his facial expression. She looked over at the O'Far-rell boy to see if he understood.

Evidently, he did. "Nothing's been taken," he surmised.

"I told you. I interrupted their plans."

"Or they couldn't find anything worth stealing."

Was she being insulted? She gave him a stern, quizzical look.

"In the dark, I mean," he qualified.

"They were not ghosts."

"I suspect juvenile delinquents."

"What's your name, dear?" she asked him.

"I'm Ryan. Denny's my brother."

"I get you two mixed up."

He laughed. "I know. Maybe if you say what you think is the wrong name, you'll get it right."

"Oh, I've tried that. It becomes a ping-pong ball. Right. Wrong. Denny. Ryan. I should just call you *officer*."

"You've mentioned that."

What was he insinuating now?

"Will you be posting a guard?" Mrs. McCracken inquired.

He smiled. Somehow, she knew that he was going to do that, smile. Did she already ask that question? Did he smile like that previously?

"There's another possibility, Mrs. McCracken. A stronger possibility, maybe. They might not have come here to rob you."

"Then why? Surely not to do me harm!"

"A prank maybe. Kids. Summer vacation. A few are looking for adventure, shall we say. A prank, which might've begun as a dare."

"Officer—there, I said it—Officer, you're being silly," Mrs. Mc-Cracken scolded him. "What was their purpose, to break into my house and run back and forth across my living room rug? Only to be shot at in cold blood?"

"And laugh while the pistols were being fired."

Another silent communication passed between the O'Farrell boy and a third officer. Policemen were departing her house, leaving every interior light on as if she was made of money.

The O'Farrell boy faced her. "We've cleaned up the glass, so you won't cut yourself, and taped plastic in the window to keep the bugs out."

"Thank you. But tape and plastic won't keep the thieves out."

"They've done their mischief."

"And what mischief is that, Officer? Scaring an old lady half to death?"

"Partly. Also, they got you to fire your guns, Mrs. McCracken. Everybody knows that you only shoot blanks with those things."

"Who knows?" she stormed.

"It's common knowledge."

"How does anybo—" she objected, but stopped herself.

He gave a little knowing nod that irritated her no end.

"I may have mentioned it in passing," she added.

"Word gets around. But that tells me that local boys did this. I doubt if they'll be able to keep the story to themselves. We'll keep our ears to the pavement and hear what we can hear."

"Then there's a chance," she perked up, "that we might get a break in the case? I may yet receive justice?"

"We'll see. I'll hang around outside for a while. As a rule, these types of dares are attempted only once. No repeats. I'm sure you'll be safe now."

"With tape and plastic on my window, I lack your confidence."

"As I said, I'll hang out for a bit. Give you a chance to sleep."

"Sleep? It'll take me half the night to turn off these lights."

"I'll do that for you. Downstairs, in any case."

She stood up with him.

"You know," she said, "I've only mentioned it to a few people."

He tapped her shoulder gently. She liked that. "A few too many perhaps. Personally, I've known about it since . . . oh, high school."

"That was a while ago."

"I think you even mentioned it in class."

"You were boys and girls! What's the harm?"

"The point is, everybody knows. Some kids had a little sport with you."

"Hooligans, I call them. They don't deserve to be referred to as kids. You were a good student. I remember that. Brighter than your brother."

"Denny's bright, Mrs. McCracken. Maybe more rambunctious than the rest of us. School just wasn't for him."

She adjusted the collar of her housecoat when really she'd rather remove it, feeling the heat. "You have a point, I suppose, about the blanks. Perhaps I did mention that fact one too many times."

"You practise firing them on your front lawn."

"Only on holidays! What are you insinuating? That this is my fault? Those boys could've given me a heart attack! Then you'd have a murder on your hands. Have you thought about that?"

"Let's be grateful that never transpired."

"Oh, I am, Officer. I truly am."

"Ryan," he said. Then smiled, briefly.

As Officer *Ryan* went through the downstairs rooms switching off lights, Mrs. McCracken eked her way back up the stairs, wondering if there was anything she was forgetting to do. "Come along, Buckminster," she said, although she knew that his comings and goings were only on his own accord and to his own schedule, that he acquiesced to none of her requests even when he might prefer to do so, all on account of some innate feline stubbornness that was simply incomprehensible.

11

Willis Howard never noticed himself being scrutinized. Across the street and a few doors down, Tara-Anne Cogshill was seated upon a community bench. She took note of his arrival as the somewhat dowdy shopkeeper unlocked the front door to his shop, right on time. He wiped his feet before he took two steps back to cast a glance over the entire storefront, as though to confirm that the exterior trappings of his premises didn't corrode overnight. He then stepped forward and wiped his feet a second time on the welcome mat—and wasn't it nice to live in a town, she considered, where a store's mat could be left outside on the main street and not be stolen, the thief's question being not *Do I want it?* but rather *Why not steal what's not nailed down?* The door unlocked now and his feet well wiped, he continued to take time to evaluate the display window. Following this thorough deliberation, the shopkeeper seemed satisfied and the newcomer to town, half hidden behind a telephone pole, checked her smile. The fellow amused her, she allowed. She doubted that the presentation changed during a season, yet he still made a daily inspection as if labouring under the suspicion that a few delinquent trinkets or curios might, in his absence, have spent the night carousing. When next he returned to the front door he wiped his feet yet a third time, removed the bundle of keys hanging from the lock, and entered.

Tara felt an affection for the man's addiction to routine. As much as her amusement, that's what initiated her smile. She herself didn't suffer that gene.

Inside, he flipped the sign from CLOSED/FERMÉ to OPEN/OUVERT.

Willis Howard was ready for business.

Tara crossed the street and went in.

The wee bell above the door tinkled.

"Ah," he greeted her, "my partner so mysterious." He was behind the cash, adjusting items on the countertop. She guessed that he meant to sound more sarcastic than he did and less intrigued, but he failed to pull that off and, consequently, gave himself away. "I give you marks for punctuality."

"Sir, what's your middle name? May I ask? I'm curious."

Despite a promise—indeed, a full-blown commitment—to not allow himself to be stumped in her company again, he was. "What?" he asked. "Why?"

"No particular reason. Consider it a hobby of mine, middle names."

"Ephraim," he acquiesced. "What's yours?"

"I use my middle name."

If he wanted to ask what her first name might be, he didn't.

"I see," he demurred. Then recovered to say, "Good morning."

"Good morning, Mr. Howard. How are you?"

"Ready and able, I guess. Another scorcher in the works, huh? Ah, if I'm to call you Tara, Tara, as you've suggested, then you must call me Willis."

"I shall. And I won't call you Willis Willis either, Willis." She noted his consternation. "Forget it. Bad joke. I guess we need to get things rolling."

He clasped his left wrist in his right hand and held both arms over his stomach. "I've been wracking my brains to assess how this might work, Tara. I confess that I find myself at a significant loss. You know what they say, the devil is in the details. The problem is, I can't think of a single detail to help us make this arrangement work."

Guessing again, she suspected that the speech was prepared in advance, probably rehearsed at some length before a mirror.

"Ephraim," she mused, "is not in widespread use, at least not anymore."

Again, he was caught off guard. "Willis neither," he mentioned. "I suppose my parents expected more of me." He smiled, but she could tell that the moment he spoke the words he wanted to snatch them back.

"Your peers thought less of you, I bet. That's a difficult handle for a kid."

Not for the first time in this conversation, he seemed flummoxed, waiting.

"So," Tara decided. "The details. Shall we root out the devil then?"

"It's a small room," he reaffirmed. "I don't know what commerce anyone can conduct in that space sufficient to earn a livelihood. This store does pretty well, but I would not want to depend on any one segment to make ends meet."

"Changes are in order, obviously. For instance, how many grandfather clocks do you sell in a year?"

Magisterial, four governed the wall at Willis Howard's back—sentinels, an honour guard in full plumage. With the store empty and the background music not yet switched on, a combative ticking resonated across the wide-planked floor. They seemed, in their way, to suspend time within this room, with its nod to a bygone era that perhaps never actually existed, at least not in the way so many perceived.

"I'm uncertain of the exact number."

"A big-ticket item like that? Your biggest, probably. You must have an idea."

"One, from time to time," he confessed. "Two in a good year."

She indulged in a moment of minor facial theatrics. If he was going to deliver prepared speeches, then fudge the information he did provide, then she needed to disrupt his line of communication. Even his way of thinking.

"I'll bring the clocks into my section, Willis. We'll segregate them in their own quarters, rather than see them elbow for attention amid doilies and—what is this anyway? Some sort of faux native embroidery. Made in Thailand. Figures. People going home on a train won't think to buy a grandfather clock—"

"We deliver."

"—but people interested in a grandfather clock might enjoy taking the train up from the city to view one."

"That would mean—" He stopped himself. He didn't want to be caught saying the word, as though to introduce the idea would already be a concession.

"Advertising? Yep. That, too. But we need to think big. And small. You realize, of course, that you are perfectly located. By the time passengers off the train stroll up from the station they're dying to get out of the sun. This is a nice cool room, temperature-wise, with loads to look at. That's ideal. It's why you're successful. Then they hike to the inn, have a drink and a sandwich up there, and on their way back to the train they already know that they'll be stopping in here, if only to cool down. On some days, I bet, they pop in to escape the rain."

"True." The tapestry she painted was one that assured his ongoing prosperity. "In the spring and fall, people drop in to warm up."

"Exactly. Too many use the store as a way station, with no intention of shopping. We can't do much about them. Except to serve lemonade."

"Lemonade? I'm not a lemonade stand."

"You are now. And cookies. Hot chocolate in the cooler months. You'll be surprised, Willis, shocked, in fact, by what a difference a few extra dollars multiplied by quite a few of those five hundred passengers a day will make to your bottom line. *Our* bottom line."

He appeared to be doing the math in his head.

"Does it have to be lemonade?" he asked. "If they spill—"

"We'll have a good laugh and mop up the mess. Anyone who is particularly guilt-ridden about a spill will find something else to buy, but those just breezing through will feel . . ." She searched for words to convey her vision for the store. ". . . more welcome. They'll spend more time. The atmosphere changes because the place will feel busier—in fact, it'll be more crowded. The longer folks linger the more likely they'll find something to their liking." She paused, smiled at him, and brushed a finger across the dust on a grandfather clock. "Now, Willis, some things will have to change."

"For instance?" The trepidation in his voice verged on fear.

Tara held up her dusty fingertip.

"That's one more reason I advertised for help," he defended. "My previous lady moved on to another position."

"She still needs to be replaced."

"I thought that's where you came in."

She shook the same finger at him. "I'm not your employee. We've been over this. And I'm certainly not your cleaning lady."

Willis Howard retreated. "I'm given to understand as much. I gather that you are, in fact, taking over my business. Bloody hell, Tara."

She chose to interpret his petulance as a form of gumption, which she appreciated.

"*Affecting* your business. Not nearly the same thing as taking it over. It's not even my intention to transform the store, merely *affect* it in a positive fashion. We'll need to put our heads together and see what we can sell to men, for instance. This is a very feminine store, Willis."

"My shoppers—

"—are women. Of course they are. That's why you put husband benches outside. Keep them. We'll sell lemonade to the guys outside, but more will be coming through and spending time inside in the weeks ahead."

"Why's that?"

Tara chose not to reply. She moved through the wares of the store, familiarizing herself with items for sale, checking a few price tags. He followed her with his eyes. He was about to repeat the question when she turned and faced him, and then he understood.

"You're blushing," she chirped.

"Please." Willis sounded doleful.

"Don't worry about it," Tara advised. "We may have to punch a hole in the wall to serve lemonade both inside and out. But I'll leave that up to you. The grandfather clocks should come into my section, though, where I can segregate the interested clients and give them the quality time they deserve."

"When you're not serving lemonade, at least."

"You'll operate the taps at those times. Or the extra help will."

He exhaled with some high degree of consternation.

"Here's the thing," she carried on. "This is an artsy town. At least, it has that reputation. Other stores carry local artists and artisans, but you don't, at least not with any emphasis. We'll change that."

"You don't understand."

"What don't I understand?"

"That crowd. Those artists. The painters and sculptors and, you know, the trinket makers." A note of derision tinged his voice.

"Yes?" She waited. Clearly, the subject irritated him.

"They're a different breed."

"You don't get along with them."

"Not particularly."

"Willis, you see, this is where I come in. This is where I can help. I'll get along with them. You don't have to. Once we develop these relationships, the store will be known to be more hip, more people will seek you out. You have candles, but let's go further than that. Incense, incense holders, a pipe or two, stones and beads, nothing ridiculous, you understand, just a nuance to suggest that the place also caters to the younger set, which will help encourage the artists to show here, and once they do, that'll affect our crowd as well. I'll take care of that end. We'll add genuine original arts and crafts—higher-end work—then we'll be laughing."

"Along with grandfather clocks," Willis muttered.

"We're nothing if not eclectic. Not only people on foot, off the train, but the tourists who arrive in their own cars and, more importantly, the locals who live in the area, and particularly among that group the cottagers up for the weekend. We're expanding our clientele. Willis, the store must become a destination. We have the summer to see to it. Now, your name."

"My name? Potpourri—"

"Potpourri is fine." She shook her head. "A tad typical, but it's established and works in both languages. I don't suggest changing it. I mean *your* name. You see, we're going to modernize the store a little, yet we must not lose its charm. If anything, we want to evoke an old-world ambiance."

Willis Howard vigorously nodded to endorse this point. Finally, she said something he could agree on. Then a worry crossed his visage. "I'm not changing my name."

She laughed. "Of course not, silly. I'm proposing that your name, Willis Ephraim Howard, Esquire—the esquire part abbreviated, of course, and in smaller type—"

"Type?" he asked, but he was really thinking that she'd called him silly. He *loved* that.

"—carved in wood. On a large sign. Over the cash. That'll do a lot to improve the ambiance. Give it the feel we want. I'll bet women will ask to have their pictures taken with you under that sign, Willis. I'm talking about a large sign, you understand, hung on chains from the ceiling. It'll differentiate your business from mine. I'll put my name above the door to the side room. A smaller sign, that. But it'll create a sense of moving from one shopping experience to another."

"I see."

"Do you? This is a new vision for you. I've given you a whole whack of stuff to take in at once, so you may need some time."

"I may need . . ." he started to say, then paused to consider what exactly that might be, ". . . some time," Willis Howard concluded. Then finally he chose to seize the initiative, which was his intention that morning. He simply failed to do so for as long as a second. "Have I told you," he asked, knowing full well that he hadn't, "about the loft?"

■ ■ ■

TRUCKERS GATHERED ON THE WATER'S side of the road in the shade of their vehicles, waiting there to cross the bridge. When she rode on past the big rigs and parked her scooter in her customary spot, Mrs. Mc-Cracken also stepped around to that side, perhaps to join the guys in conversation but certainly to get out of the sun. Her hairline dripped. Her dress was damp where it touched her skin. At midday, the heat was suffocating, the sun's blaze intense.

Covertly glancing at one another, the men shared secret smiles. Today of all days, they were delighted to have her in their midst.

"One hundred and three degrees," she said to no one in particular. "It might get hotter. Don't ask me what that is in Celsius. My brain can't handle the strain."

"You shouldn't pick berries this late in the day, Mrs. McCracken," Samad noted. Unlike the others, he wasn't struggling to keep a straight face and didn't share in their whimsy. He seemed genuinely concerned for her well-being. "Not in this heat."

"You could catch sunstroke," Xavier butted in.

"I agree with both of you," Mrs. McCracken stated as she wiped her brow with a handkerchief. "I already picked berries early this morning, Samad. Baked my pies and made my deliveries. Now I'm after the last blueberries of the season. Which I'll freeze."

The men shuffled their feet around, and glanced at one another, and occasionally a grin caught at their lips before fading again into the obscurity of their silence. Mrs. McCracken was surprised, for usually they were a talkative lot. The heat, perhaps, subdued them.

Xavier, his expression placid, intruded on the quiet. "So, Mrs. McC, if you don't mind my asking, did you blow anybody's brains out last night? Or just scare the bejesus out of them damn thieves?"

So they knew. If she'd known that, she might not have joined them to pass the time. She dabbed her brow, guessing that she was in for it now.

"Did you miss on purpose?" Max Klug tacked on. "Or did you aim to kill? It can be tricky in the dark. Maybe you were nervous, firing so many rounds."

"You fellows," Mrs. McCracken remarked. "I suppose you need to have your fun, even if it is at an old lady's expense."

"Did you warn them first?" Xavier inquired. "Or just start shooting?"

"How's she going to warn them?" André objected. "Stop, thief! Or I'll fire blanks in your face!"

For the first time, the men burst out laughing.

"You fellows," she said. "I scared them off, didn't I? They ran for the hills."

"Hell, you used to scare us off," Xavier recalled. "You didn't need to say nothing more than 'Good morning, children.'"

They laughed even harder then. The memory of her stark greeting, which always sounded like an accusation, tickled their funny bones.

"What we should do is hire you," Xavier suggested. "You could stand guard at the other end of the bridge, Mrs. McC, and blast away at anyone who wants to cross. At least until we reach the other side."

"Or, she could just say 'good morning,' that would do it," Klug said.

"Sounds like a plan," André agreed. He looked at Denny O'Farrell, who was quiet and seated on the ground leaning against a tire. Denny was observing Mrs. McCracken and sucking on a long blade of grass that he played with in his fingers as well, although he looked up at André when that man spoke. Then he looked away again.

Denny stood up. He dusted off the seat of his jeans. The delivery vehicle they'd been waiting to cross to this side was almost over and now was the time for everyone to move up one. Mrs. McCracken walked back to her scooter, relieved to be released from their teasing but at the same time regretting that it was time to go. She was tucking her hair in under her helmet when the O'Farrell boy, instead of returning to his truck, stood before her, his knees on either side of her scooter's front tire.

She looked at him, expecting something, but she didn't know what.

"You must've been scared," he said.

She certainly didn't expect this. *Kindness.* Or was he planning to trap her into uttering some admission he could then use to betray her? To make fun? Even so, the inherent sympathy in his voice required her to respond.

"It nearly gave me a heart attack, if you want to know the truth."

"I bet," he said. "I'm sorry you went through that."

"It seems to bring no end of amusement to your pals."

"You know how it goes. It's our way of saying we're relieved you're okay."

More kindness. She was finding this nearly as unbearable as the sun.

"Mrs. McCracken, you know we got that town meeting coming up. Thursday night. About the bridge."

"It was supposed to be tonight. They postponed."

"Yeah. Well. We got a ball game tonight, some of us."

"I see."

"We're on different sides of this issue, you and me."

"That seems the case." If only she could remember his name. His brother, last night, was also kind to her.

"You're a tenacious fighter. I remember what you did for Maria Sentis. Remember her? And I know who you were helping there. I'll never forget that."

"When I take on a cause, I give it my best. Whether it's the unfortunate woman of whom you speak or a defenceless old bridge. Look now. We have to go. We're holding up traffic."

"Actually, it's the bridge that's holding up traffic, Mrs. McCracken. In more ways than one. Just remember, something's got to give. If we don't get a new bridge—"

"This old one cannot come down!" she said sharply.

"Fine. But I think it will, unless you agree with me. We can't wait five or ten years for a new one. We need a new bridge. Will you think about it some more? It's important."

Mrs. McCracken started up her scooter. "I appreciate, Mr. O'Farrell—"

"It's Denny."

"Denny. Thank you for your civil tone. We'll see what can be done at the meeting."

He stepped aside, and Mrs. McCracken scooted on her way, followed by Big Bill Fournier and his rig. Denny walked back under the blazing sun, beads of perspiration in his eyes, to move his truck up. No one was waiting to cross from the other side, and with any luck everyone might get their loads over, one after the other without a further long pause.

■ ■ ■

JAKE WITHERS STARTED LATE IN the day, due to a bleak outlook and diminished morale, and considered not bothering to get out of bed. He hated his clothes but put them on, which only deepened his ennui. Breakfast was tasteless. He complained to himself about the heat as he clambered into his car and driving around town he found excuses not to intrude upon the lives of elderly men and women toiling in their gardens under their wide-brimmed white hats or lounging on their porches with lemonade and fans. "Bastards might even shoot me," he moaned aloud. "Fucking hellhole." Clearly, quite a few people needed new driveways but he'd lost his zeal to rectify their plight or to improve their property values. "Too damned ignorant to know what's good for them."

Jackson Eugene Withers of the Rathbone Paving Company ("When you introduce yourself, son, for heaven's sake don't mention the word *paving*, not at first, nobody wants to hear that word before they know what it is you have to say for yourself") had lost his direction. If yesterday, his first on the job, was not a banner day, then today, his second and possibly his last on the job, was surely destined to be much worse.

He was feeling so sorry for himself he could spit. He could even weep.

Still, he was formulating a plan. A partial plan. The more he dwelled on it, the more positive his outlook grew. He liked this kernel of an idea if for no other reason than it excused him from knocking on people's doors. As well, the strategy took him away from a town he was quickly learning to hate. Previously, back when he still idly calculated his monstrous commissions, for he intended to break all existing sales records for paving driveways, he came across a long, winding road in dire need of asphalt. A drive crying out to be paved, the gravel was rutted and pocked. He wasn't able to see far down the slope but noticed that, on the curves, the side walls were giving way. What stood at the bottom of the drive went unobserved, the view blocked by woods, but in his experience long drives led to big mansions and he knew that this one sale could give him enough of a boost to keep him going. Perhaps, he might generate a big enough commission to pack up his scant belongings and go off somewhere else and make his fortune.

He could take a vacation if he made this sale.

Dreaming about a big score mollified his conscience. He possessed a lengthy list of houses to visit, a list now ignored. People were too testy in the heat. He couldn't sell to them. He was perspiring too much and needed to cool down. How could he sell during the middle of the day? The thought of equipment heating asphalt in their front drives was too daunting for most people, he'd be squandering his opportunities if he approached them now—better off leaving everybody in town until later.

So he drove out of town.

He legitimately missed the long switchback drive when he first passed by, and circled around. This time he drove by on purpose, to collect himself and rehearse his pitch. At a slower speed, he motored by a third time to see what he could glean from down the slope. He was right that nothing could be seen. He then remembered a roadside stand about a mile back and guessed that he should really have a pop to cool down and maybe a dog to buoy him up before he made this cold call. Later, refreshed and fed, he passed the driveway yet another time. The world looked cooler down there, and when he approached the drive on his fifth pass he decided that the time was at hand and willed himself to make the turn and start down the driveway under the shelter of the trees.

The road was even rougher than predicted. Rougher than he'd hoped. He might call it a donkey path when addressing the owner. A smart-ass line like that just might seal the deal.

Jake Withers was increasingly excited the farther the road continued. The drift was decidedly lower, but there were inclines, dips, and twists and it was much longer than he assumed. He wondered why anyone would design so many twists. Due to the road's length, he would offer a 20 percent discount. "Right off the bat," he practised aloud in his car, "although I shouldn't." He sounded convincing to himself. "On account of the road's poor condition I should charge you top rate per foot, especially with these twists and bad spots. We'll have to build the roadbed up as well and none too soon, let me tell you." That he was in no position to give anyone a discount was not relevant. He'd first inflate the price before marking it down, no big deal, no harm done, and that way everybody would feel good about the transaction.

If he pulled down this contract he might request a bonus.

By the time the road was bottoming out and a clearing was visible through the trees, Jake Withers was certain of his success both in this job and in life. The car shook upon uneven rock and he swerved to avoid a jutting thick branch that might have taken out his windshield, then he came down onto a muddy plateau and skidded. He braked gently, but felt his tires sliding off the edge of the roadway. He gunned the engine then, which only made the wheels spin more and sideslip. He braked hard, then gunned it, but he was spinning his tires now and going nowhere.

He tried, but he could not get going, and managed only to sink his right rear wheel and its axle deeper. Jake turned off the engine. He needed to collect himself. He gathered his profanities and lined them up on the dash to be screamed aloud, one by one.

But instead, Jake Withers hung his head on the steering wheel and remained silent. He wondered if life would ever be worth living, and would he live to see the day? Only the suffocating heat inside the motionless car roused him from his trance. He wanted to breathe. He looked around, and pulled himself out of the orange Dodge. He examined his straits. At least, he thought, he'd proved the need for a new road surface here, no one could argue against that.

A man was lumbering towards him, a tall, thin man, smoking, moving through the dappled light of the shade trees that were less dense now. Beyond this stand of trees, a clearing showed a clutch of cabins and sheds and, beyond them, a swath of the river. No mansion anywhere. A few fires were burning, which struck Jake as odd in this weather, for although he'd thought that this place looked cooler, it plainly was as hot down here as anywhere else without so much as a whiff of breeze.

The lumbering man stopped to gaze at him across a ditch. He stood quite still, obviously taking in Jake Withers and his stuck car with as much interest as Jake Withers was investing in him. Then he walked closer and started talking before he was near and before Jake Withers took the opportunity to commence his own spiel, or plea for mercy.

"My God, look at what you're wearing," the stranger railed at him, but Jake Withers was plainly more interested in what the other man was wearing, and also, not wearing. His appearance terrified him. Over his bare chest he sported a narrow vest, which Jake guessed to be deer hide, maybe moose, and multiple long strings of beads. Feathers of some sort, perhaps from nothing more exotic than chickens, fluffed out from the vest's chest pocket like a banker might display a decorative handkerchief. He also wore beads in his hair, which was long and braided in places and coiled in a bun at the back of his neck and here and there knotted in a haphazard way. He didn't have pants on, or nothing that Jake could call pants. He didn't want to use the word *thong* but the skimpy little flag of attire reminded him of just that and as he got closer Jake Withers noticed the dance of mosquitoes around the man's hairy legs. He realized then that he was under attack himself and thrashed away, to beat them off his face. "You'll die of heat prostration. You'll just die."

"What?" Jake asked. "What?"

"That jacket. That coat. You must be swimming in sweat."

Jake finally looked down at himself, to see what he was talking about. The jacket, never intended for summer use, was indeed uncomfortable. Under it, his shirt was soaked through. Even his tie looked damp.

"What are you dressed up like that for to come down here?"

No ready explanation came to mind. "This is a business call," he said. "But a friendly one just the same. My name is Jake Withers, and I represent the Rathbone Company?"

"The Rathbone Company! My God. The Rathbone Company!"

Jake Withers first thought the man was barefoot but noticed now that he wore sandals with soles no thicker than skin. He'd seen sandals like those for sale—buffalo hide, as he recalled. He didn't know why that stuck with him. He supposed that they were better to have on than just going barefoot.

He guessed that the man was about ten years older than him, mid-thirties or so. His face was weathered, gaunt, the eyes proportionally large even when he appeared to be squinting half the time. He was smoking still and now Jake noticed the peculiar scent.

"Do you know," Jake asked, both surprised and encouraged, "the Rathbone Company?"

"Sounds like you sell fertilizer. Do you?"

"No."

"Because the Rathbone Company sure sounds like shit to me."

Jake Withers found himself with nothing to say.

"Seriously, friend. What did you come down here to sell me?"

The young man knew that he no longer wanted to say. If he could simply get back in his car, turn around, and drive away, he would. Given that his car wasn't going anywhere, he assumed that he wasn't as well.

"Maybe I could think about a discount," Jake said.

"Save yourself the trouble. I appreciate an honest bargain as much as the next guy, but I'm not one to haggle. Can't stand it. One time, I picked up this box, see, it was just an empty box, in a flea market. I didn't even want to buy it, it was an old box, a crate really, nothing more than a battered worn-out milk crate, except that it was old, but I was looking at it and when I saw the price I couldn't believe it. 'Twenty bucks!' I hollered. I didn't mean to attract attention to myself, I was just so surprised. I mean, it was just an old crate. The seller says, 'Okay, fifteen.' What? I was so embarrassed to be haggling for something I didn't even want, I gave him the twenty. Then I went down the line and sold it to another dealer for ten. Cost me ten bucks for my dismay. So, no, I don't haggle much."

Jake Withers stared back at this man of the forest with the gnarly face in his skimpy garments and mosquito-infested skin and crazy story and found out that he still couldn't manage anything to say that would make sense. The man was holding out the smoke to him. Jake waved it off.

The man inhaled and squinted, held the smoke in his lungs, and studied him with his squinty yet oversized eyes. Streaks in his eyebrows and a crust of grey whiskers under his chin belied evidence that he didn't look old enough to be turning white.

The man finally exhaled, and asked, "So what do you want to sell me?"

Jake looked up at the track he'd just come down. "Well," he said.

The man waited.

"Maybe I could— Maybe you'd like to have your driveway paved."

Time seemed to drift away, like the smoke from the fires in the camp. Jake Withers felt pinned by the gaze of the stranger before him, unable even to adjust his posture, let alone move. Behind the man, smoke from those strange fires curled skyward, unimpeded by any breeze, and amid the cabins and fires women and men saw to tasks or basked in conversation or watched over children who played. Jake Withers was thinking that the children were quiet kids and that the women, who weren't wearing much in the heat either, were suntanned. He entertained the notion that they were *sun-kissed* and he didn't know what prompted such a weird idea and hoped he wasn't blushing. Then he was finally released from the moment by the broadening smile on the face of the man before him, a spell broken, and he was set free.

"That's pretty funny, Jake," the man said, although he wasn't laughing himself. "My name is Gordon. A few friends call me Gordo but more often I get called Skootch, on account of my last name is Skotcher. They call me other names that I don't want you to repeat out loud in polite company so I'll let those go. So," he concluded.

Jake waited. Then he said, "So?"

"You're stuck."

Jake agreed. Then he thought to say something clever, and came up with, "That's because you need a new paved driveway."

This time Skootch reared back and enjoyed a good laugh. He clutched his stomach, which Jake noticed was muscled and taut and suntanned, unlike his own which was none of those things. He used to be athletic but that time was only a memory now. "That's a good one," Skootch said, coming closer. Then closer still, until he touched Jake's shoulder and turned him, pointing back up the hill.

"See, that stream trickles down through here and I suppose, I suppose, we could put in a culvert and let the road go over the water instead of the other way around, but—and you can do this in the dark once you know how—when you feel the hard stone that jangles the car, then you know to veer left, that lets you pick up the harder mixed gravel and keeps you out of the mud. So, no, we don't need our driveway paved. Not today. Not this week."

Both men, as if responding to a cue, took a long look at the predicament in which the right rear wheel of Jake's car found itself.

"That'll take some pushing," Jake said.

"One unholy mess," Skootch concurred. "A lot of spinning mud. We won't even discuss the inconvenience of pushing you out in this heat. Holy."

Jake considered the news. He didn't know where he was. If he phoned for help he wouldn't be able to direct how help could find him.

But he doubted there was a phone around. This excursion was going to cost him dearly.

"I guess," Gordon Skotcher ascertained, "if you came down here trying to sell snow to Eskimos, which, frankly, makes more sense than trying to pave my road, then you're a desperate man. In your heart. Desperate, and in the wrong business. Is this the final frontier for you, Jake? Is it? Or are you starting out in life? Answer me honestly now, because I could use a man like you."

"What do you mean?"

"What do I mean about what? Honesty?"

"No. That you could use a man like me."

Him staring at Jake's sunken tire caused Jake to do the same.

"I don't judge you," Skootch said. "The Rathbone Company, I might judge them someday. But I don't judge you. Everything in life is sales. We're buying or selling, it's got to be one or the other. Say you don't disagree with me."

"I don't."

"One of my clan has moved on, Jake. I need someone in sales. I can find you a good territory. Easy work. You can keep your jacket on. Keep your car. That's what makes you valuable to me, in a sense. Your car. Even your jacket. In any case, your look. This is the day that changes your life, did you know that?"

"What do you want me to do exactly?"

"Exactly? Sales, Jake. That's it. Not even. Deliveries, really. But deliveries is sales. Are you trustworthy? That's what I need to confirm here."

"What do I deliver?"

"What do you want to ask me a question like that for, Jake? Seriously, now. What did the Rathbone Company say that you'd be selling for them when they set you up to pave the world? To take beautiful green grass and bury it under that ugly black asphalt gunk?"

"I know what you want me to deliver," Jake Withers told him. And then he said, "I'm not naïve."

"Jake. Look. Over there. What do you see?"

He saw the smoke and cabins and people in their daily lives.

"Woods. Cabins. The river."

"No, Jake. Seriously. Seriously now. What do you really see?"

He took another look, wondering what it was he was supposed to see but obviously did not. He began to concentrate more keenly on what he'd seen before, but was noticing more acutely now, and thought that he might be on the right track. At least, he knew what he was seeing now. Could this be what Skootch meant? Could he dare say it?

"What do you really see, Jake?" Skootch was whispering now. "Tell me what you really see."

He coughed, and thought it through. "Women," he admitted. "Girls."

"Women," Skootch repeated. "Girls." He let that settle. "Many are spoken for. Some are not. A few are in transition, or they will be someday. Women. I would say, if you're not too superficial about these things, that this statement is entirely true—they are beautiful women. Now, I've only got one more question for you, Jake, and it's neither here nor there. I'm just hoping, I guess, that you can help me out in more ways than one. Do you or do you not play baseball?"

Jake shrugged.

"What does that mean?" Skootch inquired.

"I haven't for a while. I used to be pretty good."

"Jake. Are you yanking my chain here? What position?"

"Third."

Gordon Skotcher spun in a circle three times. Then he shouted out for those in the clearing to hear. "He plays third!"

"You need a third baseman?"

"Yes! Jake! I mean, we need a ninth player, but if you also play third, that makes you heaven sent. Quit your job, Jake. For God's sake, come and work for me! Say yes. I'll pay you way more than the Rathbone Company ever promised and they probably lied. Keep the car, keep your silly suit. The girls will forgive you once they get to know you and find out that you play third. Can you hit? Don't tell me. Let it be a surprise. We'll find out tonight. *You play fucking third? Holy shit!*" He did another spin. "Listen. Quit Rathbone, but keep whatever they gave you. Company ID. A catalogue. Samples? Is there such a thing as sample asphalt? Whatever. Just in case you get stopped someday, that's who you are, their representative. Do you realize how perfect you are, Jakey-boy? Do you have any idea?"

"How much," he wondered, "will I make with you?"

"Name your price, Jake! I bet I can double it. *Everybody! Hey! He plays third!*"

In the clearing, mainly men but a few women as well raised their arms in quiet, and largely disinterested, celebration of this pronouncement.

"Come on, Jake," Skootch said. "We'll get you shoved out of here. Then you can meet the ladies. I'll look after the introductions myself. We'll have a beer or three. Do you have your own cleats?"

How different his life would be, Jake Withers was thinking, if he never drove down this road. How unjust.

■ ■ ■

"YOU THINK IT'S JUNK," WILLIS said as they surveyed her alcove.

"I don't think it. I know it. It's junk," Tara reiterated. She spoke softly, not wanting to overly antagonize him.

Willis Ephraim Howard was nobody's fool, although at times she

116

was lulled into the mistaken sense that he could pass for one. He was correct to point out that the likelihood of her earning a living from one insignificant section of the store was remote. That reality needed to be addressed, and she was keen to move quickly to make her wee sector viable.

"Junk is not without value," he maintained. "Some people buy this stuff."

"Granted. I'm not throwing it out. But you do see our problem here." Careful to include him, she did not want the solutions to fall only upon herself. "By concentrating the worst of the kitsch in one room, the space becomes an object of amusement for your customers. Amusement and derision. For some, even if they want to buy something in here, they won't, due to that stigma. How can someone buy something off these shelves if their friends are smirking at them just for looking?"

Willis conceded as much.

"Let's do this," she pressed on. "Take the junk—our specialty items, we'll call them that—and make them disappear. Reposition them around the store. Spread out, they won't be an eyesore. Their impact will be diluted. People can still turn up their noses at this or that but without a stigma being attached to the entire inventory. Everything becomes part of the eclectic charm of the place."

Tara found that when she explained things, Willis Howard was flexible.

Train travellers were arriving in waves, interrupting them. She smiled at the difference a day made. Yesterday she'd been a tourist. Today she was part of the scenery, and contested for market share.

Whenever she took a break from the store she ventured upstairs to the loft. Although small, the attic admitted ample light with a view of the river above the treetops. A kitchen nook was in place long before Willis Howard purchased the building, and while it was problematic for him to rent the space to just anyone, as the only entrance was through the store proper, in years past he leased the premises to students up for the summer as employees. Consequently, the room was not too shabby, brightly painted, and could easily be cleaned of its cobwebs and aired of a mild mustiness. The captain's bed was constructed in situ, with drawers beneath it, as getting any large piece of furniture up the steep and narrow stairs would prove too daunting. She planned to toss the single mattress, start fresh with bedding, but the other sticks of furniture—a wooden loveseat and a beanbag chair, a folding table and three hardback dining chairs—*why three?*—could remain for now. Standing by the window, watching the river flow, she couldn't believe her swift good fortune, nor the breadth of the tasks that lay ahead. Her new life, then—her grand adventure—had truly begun.

Other adventures could wait. Walking down the street for lunch turned out to be a case in point. Truckers honked as their big rigs crept through town. Yeah, big men in their big trucks with their big horns. They were probably married and those who weren't probably didn't have a word to say once their beefy palms were off their bellowing horns. So there was that. Then there was another guy, a cop, who stopped his car and looked once, twice, as if sizing her up for a prison cell, before he drove on. *No. Not a prison cell.* Normally she wouldn't glance over but a police car tricked her into thinking that something official might be up. But no, just another guy giving her the eye, so she walked on. That kind of stuff could wait, but in any case, she knew policemen from her days in court and none of them particularly appealed. *Firemen, though. Ah. Maybe.* He was cute, though. Really cute. *Probably married, the creep.* She smiled through lunch, wondering about the breeze her grin sailed in on.

After lunch she surveyed the competition. Potpourri was unquestionably the largest, the most long-standing, and the most successful of the town's gift shops, and so benefitted in particular from the broadest inventory. Other stores showcased artisans who were either local or relatively local, and Tara committed a few names of the better crafts-people to memory. Lemonade might give her a modest daily income, but she needed quality merchandise to bankroll the broader enterprise.

Back at the store she ordered her mattress and bedding from a chain in the city. Before coming here from the coast, she threw out a relatively new queen-sized bed that never would have made the trek in the back of her pickup, or alongside her on the steam train, but even had it survived—and wouldn't *that* have made for an entrance into town!—it never would've come up the narrow stairs to her new premises. This proved, in a way that she found gratifying, the wisdom of leaving all her old stuff from her old life behind in its entirety to start anew. Less satisfying, she acknowledged, was that she'd now have to shell out cash to have something to sleep on.

She'd stay on at the inn while awaiting delivery.

12

From this plateau, the Gatineau Hills concealed the horizon in all directions. No one could gauge a change in the weather with acuity, although those who were preparing to play or settling into the stands to watch the game detected an electrical charge in the air. A languidness affected the motion of women whose slow, deep strides in the heat bore them along the dusty tire tracks up the hill to the plateau's mown field, and affected the men as their arms arced through soft tosses, their gloves lazily sweeping the air for an easy catch. No player exerted himself for a ball slightly out of reach, no one drilled it, no one hustled, the air too humid, the day's heat pervasive still. Breath felt difficult. Soon the sky would be ransacked by a cooling storm, although players and fans alike assumed that prior to matters becoming nasty they'd hear the approaching rumbles of thunder, spy a telltale black anvil cloud forming beyond the hills and so have time to pack up and leave. With any luck the teams might sneak in five innings, enough to make the game count, and the boys would be back in the pub for a few cold ones before rain pelted down and violent wind and lightning chased them off.

No minute could be spared. The teams were ready on the dot of seven.

The first pitch a strike. A few fans clapped.

"Swing the damn bat," griped the catcher to the hitter, his voice growly. "We don't got all night."

"Keep your jockstrap on," the batter, a trucker, answered back. The Blue Riders, Denny's team, worked in the forestry industry in some capacity. They had enough players that they could play against themselves if their opposition failed to show. Customarily, they wore uniforms, shirts at least, although tonight a portion of the men chose shorts and a few opted for mere T-shirts. The team boasted of relief pitchers should their starter falter, and pinch hitters, and spares who were better fielders than some in the lineup and would play if the team built a decent lead, and one of their guys, a skimmer by day, did nothing more than steal bases for them, coming into a game as a pinch runner when the situation warranted. He got into games often, as the Riders were slow.

The second pitch was outside, the bat steady on the hitter's shoulder.

"Take it the other way."

"Skootch," the batter advised him, a man known as Slim for good reason, although the catcher he was talking to was skinnier still, "don't start with me. If you start with me the next ball I hit is maybe your head."

The umpire, a short, chubby druggist by day, formerly a catcher himself until a torn rotator cuff wrecked his arm, in any case now in his sixties, waddled out to the front of the plate, faced his bottom to centre field, and bent over to sweep the plate clean. The batter and catcher waited, although the plate was already spotless and the action unnecessary. The ump took his mask off then put it back on and while he was doing that he said, "Both of you, shut the fuck up. Skootch, you don't have an extra man. Not one. If you think that'll stop me from tossing you out of the game if you give me cause, think twice. I'm not putting up with this shit tonight, it's too damn hot. Do you get me?"

Gordon Skotcher hunkered down into his crouch and ran through the signals with his pitcher. When the umpire leaned in behind him for the pitch, he said, "You're a hard-ass, ump."

The umpire called out, "Steeeee!" loudly, right in his ear as the ball zipped in, catching a corner of the plate. Unhittable.

The batter smiled. After throwing the ball back, the catcher made a point of sticking a finger in his ear as though the drum was now in need of repair and a few fans chuckled. The next ball the batter dribbled down the first base line and thinking that it was arcing foul he didn't run it out. The ball took a bounce off a stone and shifted fair and the batter was left looking lazy and dumb as the first baseman snagged it, and fans, even those who rooted for the Blue Riders, booed his utter lack of hustle.

In disgrace he walked back to the team's bench, as the evening was too warm to jog.

Fans seemed into the game tonight, which was not always the case. A few spouses were on hand with their youngest kids and often they just talked among themselves at the games and asked, when it was over and they were piling their husband's gear into the back of a pickup, "Who won?" This evening they were into the game because the Blue Riders were playing a team that called themselves the Wildcats but they were referred to as Tree Huggers for being on the opposite side of every political, economic, and environmental issue from anyone who happened to work for a living cutting down trees. On occasion, fielding a full complement of players was a problem for them when one or more of their number slipped in a little jail time over the course of a summer, or another went missing and a rumour spread that he was in California, as if that could not be helped, or in Prague, as if that made any sense to anyone. A couple of their players were quite good, which only partially made up for the two who were daft, while others fell between okay and not so bad. Their main pitcher, his name was Benoit, who actually worked in a visible job as a car mechanic, snapped off a fastball that ate loggers and truckers alive. On a few rare nights his velocity fell off a notch and only then did the Blue Riders scratch a few hits off him. Most nights they couldn't touch his heater and they needed luck to eke out a run and if they expected to win they needed to pitch well themselves. They always had a chance of winning because the Wildcats were prone to making errors, especially in the outfield where some of their guys went to sleep. Their minds just drifted off to la-la land. In the main, the Blue Riders played the game for fun except when they played the Tree Huggers. That group wanted to hamper their right to earn a living, and what happened off the baseball diamond inevitably found its way onto it. They wanted to win those games too much to have any fun unless they actually did win. Each team's record against the other was about fifty-fifty.

The Riders' second batter struck out on three pitches without swinging at any of them. Skootch looked at the umpire and smirked.

"Just keep your yap shut and play ball," the umpire warned. "I don't want to hear any mockery out of you."

"Ump, I mock. That's my game."

"Not tonight it isn't." He was worried that in the heat tempers could easily flare between two rivals who despised each other, off the field and on.

The third batter up was Dennis Jasper O'Farrell.

"Hey, Denny," Skootch said.

"Skootch," Denny said.

"He's firing tonight."

"Early days," Denny reminded him.

"The storm will get here before he wears out," countered Skootch.

Agreeing that that was probably true, Denny O'Farrell felt demoralized. Especially when the first pitch blew right by him.

"Told you. He's got his pop. Hey, you going to that meeting tomorrow?"

"This is ridiculous," Denny said. He stepped out of the box to look at the signals from his third base coach who was an older gentleman in sales at his company. He was making his signals unnecessarily complicated for the situation. Two out. Nobody on. An oh-and-one count—no need for signals.

"Christ, Denny," Skootch said. "He wants you to bunt."

"How come he wants me to bunt?"

"Beats me. Unless he thinks you can't hit my guy tonight."

Denny called time and strolled down the third base line, using his bat as a cane. Dimitri the salesman, overeager, loped down to meet him more than halfway. In the outfield, players bent at the waist and tore out a few strands of grass to pass the time, and the guy in left wore his glove on his head, slouching. In the infield, the players moved dirt around with their toes and the shortstop spit a few times then dusted over the spots, creating small clumps. The Wildcats didn't wear uniforms and quite a few wore shorts. They had on different coloured T-shirts except for the centrefielder who was bare-chested.

"What the fuck?" Denny asked his coach.

"We need to manufacture a run, Denny. Put some pressure on him."

"Skootch reads our signals, Dee."

"Oh."

"Yeah. Oh."

Denny shot a glance at the third baseman, who was someone he'd never seen before, then he walked back to the batter's box. Then he stepped out to confirm the signals. He knew he was sweating but he blamed the heat. He wiped his eyes on his shirtsleeve but even the sleeve was soaked.

"Yeah, I guess I'm going to that meeting," he said. He squinted.

"He still wants you to bunt," Skootch informed him. While Denny was gone Skootch lit up a roach and now he pulled on a long drag while bringing the infield in. He offered it to the umpire as he always did but the umpire, as he always did, declined. He held it up to Denny but when Denny didn't look at him he got the message. Skootch got into his crouch and balanced the roach on the trailing edge of home plate and Denny took a couple of halfhearted half swings then stepped into the box. The pitcher wasted no time. Denny couldn't believe how well he saw the ball coming in, as if he could count the laces, and he was surprised by how slow it seemed and by the amount of time given him to make up his mind, as if the ball was a balloon and in that millisecond which computed velocity and trajectory and spin he determined that it was not slow, only that his brain was fast, and he couldn't believe how the ball just *ticked* off the bat as if the bat barely touched it, nor could he believe that he was rounding the bases at a jog, having finally gotten this guy when he was having a good night only no one would believe that now, people would think the pitcher botched the throw before believing that Denny hit the best pitch he'd ever hit in his life, taking it over the low right field fence although, admittedly, on a muggy night the ball was prone to jump, high humidity was great for home runs, and as he rounded second Denny checked out the third baseman who'd been in for the bunt, and wondered why he didn't know him, and why his hair was cut short like a regular Joe's haircut and not like some warmed-over hippie's from another era or off another planet like the rest of his teammates, and he noticed the guy's spanking-new cleats as well as he trotted past him and that made him consider at that very instant and for no reason that he could fathom his wife's right foot poking out from the sheet the other morning and as he stepped onto home plate just a second before Skootch removed the roach he felt weak, particularly in his knees and in his stomach, and Denny decided that he must have taken the bases too quickly on such a hot day, or maybe that wasn't it, and he heard Skootch say, "Nice bunt," as he was being welcomed into the hoots and applause of the audience and into the embrace of his teammates while feeling as odd in his own skin as he'd ever felt, as if he was not standing in his own flesh.

Then Denny did something he'd never done before. He looked back at the catcher, Skootch, a tree hugger Ryan's age, thirty-five, and probably the oldest guy on the field, and he saw that Skootch was looking back at him probably for the first time ever in that situation as well, and he noticed something else that amazed him. Skootch knew. Skootch knew that he just hit the best pitch he'd ever hit and Skootch could no more believe it than he could. That hit. A freak of nature. An anomaly. His rival's look was saying to him that he should enjoy it because *You'll never hit a pitch that good again*, but Denny was thinking exactly that on his own. He couldn't help himself. He shrugged at Skootch, and the ragamuffin eccentric catcher shrugged back, put his mask back on, and everyone then settled in for the next at bat.

Denny sat on the bench.

Feeling weird.

He hit his share of home runs over a summer, but none were ever so sweet or so perplexing, the way it just ticked *ticked* off the bat like that. Like snapping his fingers and it was gone, as if he wasn't the one swinging the bat, as if he wasn't himself.

Two innings later, Denny was in the field and taking an interest in the next hitter for the Tree Huggers. His counterpart at third base. He looked down the line and moved his toe through the dirt as he always did when there was no one on base, then he leaned into his stance and punched the pocket of his glove twice. Then he put both hands on his knees. Outside the batter's box, the newcomer took a few practise swings that seemed smooth to Denny, fluid.

The batter stepped into the box.

Denny thought later that it was just as it was with his swing, the way the ball clicked off the bat, and that it was just like Val's foot, the way it left an impression on him, as though its life suddenly transcended its function, as though it shone with its own light or something equally perplexing. This was just like that and so he didn't think about anything. He called time.

The ump swung his arm up.

Denny called it intuition. He had an urge to call it something.

He walked to the pitcher's mound. The catcher was going to join them but Denny held up a hand to stop him and the catcher was grateful to be spared the hike. He waited with his face mask pushed up over the top of his head and tapped his glove.

"Fuck it's hot," the pitcher said to him.

That's when they first heard it, and although the rolling thunder was long anticipated, its sound and vibration and how it echoed through the hills and seemingly grew louder and reverberated did surprise them and frighten a few. Mothers started gathering up their kids, and when Denny and the pitcher looked towards the direction of the sound they saw the first evidence of storm cloud above a nearby hilltop, black and roiling with menace.

"Look at that," the pitcher said. His name was Pierre Alfred Turcotte and he was having a brilliant night for their side. Maybe his best ever.

"Walk him," Denny said. Everyone spoke English on the diamond.

"What? Denny, I got a no-hitter going. It's a fucking perfect game."

"You're not supposed to say that out loud."

"Oh fuck. You're right. You're right."

"Walk him."

"Why?"

Denny stepped around him so that his back was to home plate, maybe to conceal what he was saying from the hitter, but he didn't want his catcher to know his ruse either until he first convinced the pitcher.

"Look at the guy. Take a good look at him."

Pierre Turcotte did so. "Yeah? He doesn't look tough."

"You ever seen a tree hugger with a haircut before? He's got shiny shoes."

"So?"

"He's not one of them."

The pitcher took another glance at the batter. "So?" he asked.

"So he's a ringer. Walk him. That storm's coming fast. Don't let him hit one out of here and tie this game. The ball's popping out tonight if a guy makes contact. I know. Did you see my hit? It's the humidity. Let's keep the lead."

"But Denny, it's a perfect game."

"It won't matter, Pierre. Check out that cloud. We won't finish the game."

That final point won the argument, but Denny was surprised that the pitcher agreed with him. Pierre was a competitive guy and this strategy required letting that go, not to mention letting his perfect game go. Denny went back to his base and the pitcher signalled the catcher to stand out of the box and then he lobbed him the ball. The catcher was confused, looking first at Pierre and then at Denny. He walked out to the mound pounding his glove.

"He's a ringer," the pitcher said.

The catcher looked at Denny, then ambled back behind the plate, and they walked the batter quickly. Following them to the plate was the Wildcats' own catcher, Gordon Skotcher, who popped up the first pitch to second base and when he ran back to his bench along the third base line, he took the long route around past Denny.

"Fucker," Skootch said.

So he was right, Denny thought, the guy was a ringer.

The next thunder roll was terrific, and both benches began packing their extra equipment and the umpire made a turning motion with his arm to speed them up and after that Pierre pitched quickly. The next batter grounded out to short on his second pitch, and the third out of the inning occurred on a fly ball to left that was as well hit as any ball that night by a Tree Hugger. Denny held his breath but the arc of the ball was too high for the ball to leave the park and the catch was made in the outfield and on his easy jaunt back to the bench the wind whipped up and dust flew in his face and they could see the lightning now snapping into the hills and one blast of thunder bore closely on the next.

The ump took a long look. The Wildcats hadn't gone out to the field yet. They were checking the sky. They were scared to go out there. They knew they could get killed. The ump held up his arm as the first batter approached the plate even though no pitcher was on the mound to face him.

Then the ump called the game off. The Blue Riders feigned being pissed off because the Wildcats were spared a defeat but within the minute the game was forgotten in the race to get off the diamond and into their vehicles parked down the road out of the reach of foul balls. Women shooed their children on. The players pulled duffel bags up over their shoulders and beat it out of there. They knew that the storm was coming too fast, that they were going to be soaked.

■ ■ ■

RAINE TARA-ANNE COGSHILL HAD NOTICED a poster for the baseball
game, and traced a path where others strolled, skirting a field of parked
trucks and vans on up through a woodlot to a higher plateau where the
diamond shone in the evening light. Hot out, still. Close. Stifling. Perspiration dappled her nose. She was drawn to the crowd by her loneliness, but didn't take the impulse to be anything serious. She considered
her mood to be exaggerated because it felt unfamiliar, as she was now
bereft of a constant whirlwind agenda. In time, she might grow into
her current circumstances, feel less vulnerable. She might manage to
enjoy herself. For the moment, Tara desired the crowd.

Located behind first and third, the stands were low, just six rows
to the top with no backrests. She chose to situate herself behind the
third base line, not noticing initially that the section was reserved for
the visiting team's supporters. Both sides were filling equally. Tara was
surprised that she didn't feel conspicuous, and supposed that the competing factions didn't know one another well enough that a stranger
stood out. By the way that the crowd was arranging itself—older folks
greeting one another and young mothers doing the same—she presumed that at least a portion was merely along for the ride, more interested in socializing out of doors on a hot night than in baseball. Many
fans, and players as well, fit her age bracket, so it was easy to feel part
of the crowd, and Tara sensed how, in time, this could become her
community. She lacked only the proper introductions.

Requiring protection from the sun, she wore a ball cap purchased
in town, her first addition to a new wardrobe. She wore a short sum-
mery taupe skirt, a collarless and sleeveless white blouse, and sandals,
the coolest outfit she could put together to beat the heat.

Tara drew subtle pleasure from the sounds of the game, the voices, how players barked encouragement to teammates and paid homage to the rituals of their sport. The soft thud of a ball into a mitt. She liked how everyone leaned one way or the other when a pop foul risked coming down on their heads. Preteen girls giggled. She appreciated the babble of small fry in and under the stands who frequently abandoned the game altogether to romp behind the tall fence of the backstop, their mothers edging over to keep an eye out. Tara noticed that a few beautiful men decorated the field, husbands probably, and when she slapped at a mosquito she detected in that action, in that quick response, the moisture on her own neck and forearms and in a twinkling the moisture on theirs. She liked the power that derived from anonymity. She was just a blur in the stands, free to notice a good set of pectorals, a six-pack, a cute tush.

Then the thunder and lightning came up and that excited her differently.

Like the others she fled the storm, walking quickly, although she was bereft of a car or truck to shield her and this sport could only have one conclusion: she'd get drenched. As the few cars that were behind her drove by, rocking in the ruts, she caught whistles from ballplayers, but no one stopped. Those cars were full. Then the rains hit and she jumped under a tree. Lightning slashed the sky and the thunder was not merely loud, it shook the ground and shot through her feet and she felt the tree tremble and its fright made her shake, too. She loved it. Branches whipped to and fro. She knew better than to seek cover under a tree in a storm, but out there, in the open, surely lightning would find her just as easily as did the fierce rain.

She wasn't there long, maybe twenty seconds, when a pickup stopped and honked. The driver seemed to be looking for her, but she couldn't be sure, as the windows were opaque with water. He flashed his lights and honked and when the truck went forward it was only by a few feet. So she took a chance and ran out and since she could not make eye contact she banged on the door's window. The window lowered a crack.

She was already soaked.

"Jump in!"

She did. How dangerous could a baseball player be? She recognized this guy and told him, "Nice hit."

"Thanks. Too bad we didn't get enough innings—it won't count. No car?"

"No car."

"I saw you duck away. Figured you might need a lift."

He was glancing over at her as his hands wrestled with the steering wheel until the truck reached a smoother section of road. He was checking her out but he was one of the cute ones she'd already checked out herself, and anyway photographs of three kids and a wife were pinned up under the windshield visor and across the dash above the glove box. A good-looking family. She felt safe enough.

"Thanks," she said. "It's really coming down." She tried to adjust her wet bangs, then folded her arms over her chest in case she was showing through her soaked blouse. She knew she probably was, a little, but didn't want to make that visual check. "I can't believe how fast it came on! Just over the hill and *whoosh*!"

"Yeah. For sure." He was able to speed up a little. The red taillights of a small car in front of him helped keep him on the road.

Rain galloped across the roof.

"Are you a tree hugger?" he asked. "You don't look like a tree hugger."

The question amused her. "What does a tree hugger look like?"

His was a lovely smile. "You know," he said, although she didn't. "Weird."

She continued to look at him quizzically.

"That's who we were playing. The other team. They're tree huggers."

"So, someone else might call a tree hugger . . . an environmentalist?"

"Some would. Other people might call them ecoterrorists. Depends on who you're talking to. I guess I'm just asking if you live here. Are you visiting? I don't think we've met."

He could have tacked on something snide, such as, "I'd remember you," but he didn't, and she appreciated that.

"Just arrived. For now I'm at the Old Mill Inn."

"I'll take you up there."

"That's out of your way."

"Nothing in this town is out of anyone's way. What, do you think I'd just drop you off in a puddle?"

She smiled. "Thanks," she said. He was right. She didn't have far to go.

"So you're visiting? Sorry about the weather."

"I'm moving here. I'll be staying upstairs at the Potpourri. Do you know it? I've joined that business."

He was looking at her with a different sort of curiosity now.

"What?" she asked.

"Joined? You mean you're working for Willis Howard?"

"Nor *for* him exactly. With him."

She could tell that he didn't believe her.

"He's surprised, too," she told him. "But I'll have a little section of the store for myself and I'll help him out with other things. Come see us! A few changes are in the offing."

He turned onto hard pavement and she had trouble locating where they were through the driving rain. The wipers no sooner cleaned the windshield than it was instantly inundated, as if they were underwater.

"Changes, huh? Does Willis know about these changes? He's like an old stick-in-the-mud, except that he's not that old. About the only thing he changes is his clothes. Yeah. Sure. I'll come by. See what you're up to."

"You don't look like a shopper to me."

He laughed lightly. "Changes down at Willis Howard's store? News like that? In this town? You might as well say you've built a skyscraper smack dab in the middle of Main Street."

She laughed. She liked him. "Good. Spread the rumour. We want people to come by, just give us a little time. Send your wife, too, of course."

He looked over at her.

"If she's the shopper in your family. Man, I feel like I'm in a sub-marine."

"Yeah. It's coming down."

"What work do you do?"

"Logging truck."

"Ah. An anti–tree hugger. A tree chopper. I'm getting the picture."

"You thought that was a baseball game? That was no game. That was war. Whose side were you on?" She was glad that he was grinning.

"I clapped for your home run, does that count?"

"Sure does."

"Good. Then I rooted for the tree choppers."

They both smiled and he drove on slowly, as visibility went down to nothing and the world went dark.

"What just happened?"

"Power failure. Typical in a storm like this."

"I love storms," she said.

He didn't answer right away, but momentarily uttered a quiet grunt.

"You don't?" Tara asked.

"I do. Actually. But it's been dry. With lightning, I worry about fires."

"Ah. Competition for decimating forests."

He glanced over at her to see how serious she might be. As quickly, his focus returned to the road. Driving required concentration.

"Do you know what I call that?" she asked him. "A common denominator. A point where you and the tree huggers can agree. You both don't like forest fires, I bet."

He was having trouble admitting to the shared ground, but conceded with a shrug and a nod, and they laughed together.

"So, who do you know in town? Or are you from here originally?"

"Never been here before in my life. I just got off that sightseeing train and never got back on. I've met Willis. Oh, and a sweet older lady who sells pies."

"Mrs. McCracken. One of my former schoolteachers."

"Really? She's a darling."

"She cracked the whip, I'll tell you that. She wasn't such a darling back then. So you just came here, and just like that, you're part of a business with Willis Howard?"

She mouthed the word *yep*.

Tara knew where she was now, heading up the steeper part of the road to the inn. She tried to see out but that was nearly impossible until he stopped right by the inn's front door. Only emergency lighting was on.

"Thanks. Really. This is very sweet of you."

He laughed, and then he said, "Whoops."

"What?"

"I caught myself. I just about said, Get out of those clothes. Didn't mean it that way. I meant, Dry off."

Her hand rested on the door latch. She wasn't sure if he was flirting now. That wouldn't be a sin but she gave him the benefit of the doubt anyway. "I'm Tara," she said. She took her hand off the latch and extended it to him.

"Denny," he said. They shook briefly, both their hands still wet.

"Thanks, Denny," she said, and stepped out into the downpour and slammed the door behind her. Two steps and she was safely under a canopy.

Denny needed to take care turning around, his visibility minimal. He was pretty sure he had room but he couldn't see what cars were parked around him so he inched forward a couple of feet then crept back, turning each time he did it, and saw that she was watching him when his headlights caught her and when they did she finally turned to enter the inn. Denny was thinking that she wasn't at her best, looking like a drowned cat with those big eyes and her hair plastered against the side of her scalp under a ball cap that was soaked through, but her makeup hadn't run and that was a realization, for he suddenly understood why, because it meant that she was not wearing any. And yet, without makeup, the worst possible hair day, clothes soaked, she was probably as striking a woman as he'd ever met. A real look to her. High cheekbones. Those huge eyes. From what he could tell her skin was flawless. Plus, a big plus, she seemed nice. He stopped outside the inn's door, pointed downhill now, and gave two big blasts on his horn.

He waited.

Two more big honks.

First, she poked her head out. Then she came out under the canopy. He rolled his window down and over the loud rain hollered, "Are you single?"

"You're not," she shouted back.

"But I have friends," he said. And then he said, "I also have a brother."

She looked at him. She made a faint motion with her chin, a slight squint under the peak of her cap, which he could not appraise.

"Actually, I have a really great brother."

This time her lips cracked. Just. "Thanks for the lift, Denny."

"You're welcome," he said, smiled back at her, and drove down the hill into town to join the guys for a beer.

13

Perpetually on the verge of calamity, the kids were up to their madcap ruckus, although for the moment the eldest appeared to be pouting for no discernible reason. No child, thankfully, was underfoot as the barbecue smoked in the breezy air, chicken breasts tweaking perfection. Valérie set the picnic table and put the salad out, covering the bowl with a clear wrap to ward off bees. She returned indoors for the wineglasses, having already opened the bottle. A Merlot. A signal.

Denny's day was decent, his time at home pleasant, and while he did feel trepidatious regarding the evening's public meeting, where he planned to speak on behalf of the loggers, he was also reminding himself that how things evolved fell out of his control.

Nothing remained to be done but to go to that damn meeting.

If blame or fault flowed from the discussion, if consequences ensued, that responsibility did not rest solely upon him. Not in the slightest.

What will be, will be, like in the old song—

Surely, if the powers that be failed to see the merit in a new, necessary, fast bridge, then did it not follow that the responsibility for whatever came along in the wake of that failure fell upon *them*, specifically? If someone, such as himself, took an action in response to their lack of action, if a crime was committed, who was really to blame? The people who did the deed, or the people who made the deed necessary? If he did something wrong because the authorities did nothing right, could he really be blamed for that?

Lifting the cover, he nudged a few chicken pieces, although they were fine if left untouched, browning nicely. He enjoyed the swift release of smoke as he closed the cover. Val came out and passed him a glass accompanied by a coy expression when, just as she returned to the picnic table to fetch the bottle, Denny's dad and brother Ryan came around the corner of the house into the backyard. Husband and wife nicked each other with a quick glance. Both knew why she selected a wine. A romantic addition to the meal was meant to preface an after-the-meeting, end-of-the-day, overdue carnal rendezvous. That was not in jeopardy, but Val conveyed her disappointment that their flirtation now lay in ruins.

"Grandpa! Uncle Ryan!" Valou squealed. Extricating herself from her trike, she ran to them.

"We have enough," Val whispered, anticipating her husband's concern.

The boys enjoyed having Uncle Ryan around, even if he wasn't in uniform. He played their games with enthusiasm. While their dad was passionate about baseball, they were more likely to get into a game of pitch and catch with their uncle, and preferred playing with him anyway because their dad was always testing out a curveball or a knuckleball and throwing it in the dirt half the time or else he wanted them to really fire it in there and when they did with all their might he never seemed satisfied.

Valérie was making the best of the intrusion and gave the men a choice of wine colour, but both requested beer. She went inside and Denny noticed the light sashay of her hips and knew that her mood was going to take them deep into the night. First, the meeting. Then the aftermath. Finally, he'd be up half the night with Val. He only wished that her intensity might have arrived on a night when there was no town meeting, but suspected that she thought this through—by the time he got home the kids would be asleep.

"What brings you here?" he asked his brother. "Been a while."

"That's why. It's been a while. How's it going?"

"Same old," Denny attested. "You?"

"Pretty much," Ryan said.

"Nothing exciting? Bank robberies? Jaywalking? Old ladies firing blanks?"

Alex O'Farrell peeled away to soak up his granddaughter's reports on her daily life, yet Denny still felt that his dad and brother were in cahoots. A vibe in the air. Somehow they were ganging up on him.

"Nothing serious," Ryan said. Denny continued to nurse a grievance about his brother being a cop. Loggers of old possessed an air about them, as if they were their own authority, not to be intruded upon by a "civilian" population. They dispensed their own justice when they considered it necessary, and in the old days a logger pretty much had to kill somebody before police investigated. While he didn't feel the need for an ethic that primitive, Denny clung to a value system in which the police represented outsiders—people naturally disinterested in them, at best, and usually inclined against them. He did not understand how his brother could think any differently. "Speeding tickets to truckers, mostly. So far you've eluded me."

"It's not because I slow down."

"That I know. Someday I'll nab you."

Val emerged with her guests' beer. "Chicken tonight. Don't argue. We have plenty."

"Thanks, Val," Ryan said. "I'm not going to turn down a home-cooked meal even if my brother is the one burning the chicken."

Denny ignored the volley. "I was thinking about you today, Ry," he said. "Bumped into this girl last night. A real looker."

"You bumped into a real looker?" Val parried. "Define 'bumped into.'"

"Define 'real looker,'" Alex called out.

"Thought of you," Denny reiterated to his brother.

"Never mind him," their father chipped in, louder still. "He's in love."

Val's interest took a seismic shift. "You've met someone? Ryan!"

Glaring at his dad, Ryan said, "No. I have not."

"He hasn't met her yet," Alex explained. "He's only set his sights on her."

"Who?" Val asked.

Denny didn't know why or how, although he was inclined to call it intuition, but he guessed who'd caught Ryan's eye.

"A new girl in town," Ryan let Val know. "Nothing's going on. Dad's just bugging me about it."

"Does she work at Potpourri?" Denny asked.

"I've seen her around there, yeah."

"How do you know who works at Potpourri?" Val wondered.

"He's smitten and doesn't even know the lady's name," Alex teased.

"It's Tara," Denny revealed.

"*You* know her name?" The third degree. "How come?"

"Val, come on," Denny said. He couldn't avoid this conversation so the best tactic was to gain the upper hand. "Just because I make a point to talk to every gorgeous chick who walks into town doesn't mean you have to get your dander up."

Wee Valou was listening and her mother chose to bring her into the conversation. "Valou, honey, say good-bye to your daddy because he's about to die young."

"Why?"

"Because I'm going to kill him."

"He's not so young," Valou pointed out.

"Tara," Ryan said. "Tara?" As though to himself.

"Willis Howard's new partner, apparently."

"Really. What? Really?"

Denny checked out his brother, who seemed adrift. He agreed with his dad that Ryan was smitten. This was welcome news. "Chicken's done!" he proclaimed. "Kids, line up according to height. Shortest first. Grown-ups in the rear."

Only after the meal did Ryan manage to catch his brother alone for a talk, and it wasn't about the new girl in town. Alex went back to spending time with the kids as if to remove them from the picture, which confirmed to Denny that he was in on this family conspiracy, whatever the conspiracy turned out to be.

"You're going to that meeting tonight," Ryan stated.

So that was it. Those bloody rumours that swim around town, like silverfish sliding up drainpipes. Denny's back was up because, while his brother was not in uniform, he still owned a uniform. From the kitchen came sounds of Val dealing with the dishes and even though he did the cooking he felt guilty for not helping out with the washing up. Especially given that they were feeling amorous. "I hate meetings, but if that's what you've got to do, then I'll go to a meeting. I promised some people I would. Sometimes you have to make a sacrifice."

"Don't get me wrong, Denny, I'm glad you're going. You should go. The loggers need to make their position known. You're the one to do it. You guys deserve a proper bridge. Let's hope something gets worked out."

"Yeah, let's hope," Denny concurred.

"You don't sound too hopeful," Ryan noted.

Denny raised one shoulder only, then let it drop. "History," he said. "We've hit our heads against the government wall before."

"I just wouldn't want things to get out of hand," Ryan put forward.

"Me neither. I mean, if McCracked pulls out her duelling pistols and starts blasting away, she could start a stampede. We could have a public riot. Blood on the streets even."

Ryan returned a tight smile, which struck his brother as nervous.

"What's wrong?" Denny asked him.

"You might think it's funny what she did, but people broke into her house. She was scared half to death."

"Yeah, I know. I don't feel good about that. I told her so. Kids, I suppose."

"I suppose. Or loggers wanting to intimidate her."

Denny was surprised. He hadn't made the connection but took it to be a possibility. He also knew that Ryan had personal reasons to come to her defence.

"I didn't hear anything like that, Ry. Not a word."

The older brother nodded to show that he believed him. "Loggers'll be on hand tonight," Ryan pointed out.

"Like me, they don't exactly race off to meetings. But yeah. A bunch of guys will show up. That's allowed."

"So will the tree huggers."

"It's only a meeting, Ry."

"Denny."

"A meeting. Define meeting—boring. Nothing's going to happen."

"You know you can't say that, Denny."

"Sure I can. I just did."

"It's unpredictable. It's a volatile situation. Twice after meetings, I broke up brawls."

"Brawls? Fistfights, Ryan. Some say you started one of them."

"I hope you stuck up for me. Pointed out how ridiculous that is."

"Yeah, I did, actually," Denny conceded. "But sometimes I think if a couple of boys want to go at it, you should just let them go at it. Nobody says it's going to solve anything, but some guys might get it out of their system."

"Thanks for the advice," Ryan said in a flat and challenging tone. "That's exactly what I came here for."

Denny backed down another step. "Okay, look," he tried to convince him, "as far as I know everybody who's going to that meeting is going there to talk. Nobody has anything in mind. Not that I hear absolutely everything but I don't miss much."

Ryan took the final swig of his beer. "Okay. But what about after that? If things don't go so well at the meeting, then what?"

Noticing his father watching him, Denny made eye contact, holding his gaze for a prolonged moment. "I don't plan that far ahead," he said. "Anyway, I think I'm expected back at the ranch. Right here. That's what I'm counting on. But listen."

"Yeah? What?"

"That new girl."

"Tara."

"I thought of you. Swear to God. I even told her I have a brother."

"Oh shit."

"What? I'm an embarrassment to you now?"

"I can meet girls on my own, Denny."

"Since when? Ryan, you're a cop. You told me before, it gets in the way. You've had shit luck."

"Quit it."

"I'm just helping you out here."

They exchanged a glance, which confirmed that Ryan was not really all that miffed.

■ ■ ■

RYAN O'FARRELL WAS OF TWO minds coming away from the house. Wanting to be off on his own, he arranged for Denny to drive their father to the meeting. He'd pick Alex up later to get him home, given that Denny wanted time for a beer with his buddies afterwards. "No, we won't be beating the crap out of tree huggers." His brother came across as calm. Ryan had no reason to believe that anything untoward sailed on the wind, contrary to the sentiment his father brought to his attention and Skootch as well. Maybe Skootch was just being a shit disturber again, keeping everybody jumpy while protecting his ball team from losing more players. As well, that girl, the one he saw walking, the one Denny called a looker but whom he considered mind-bogglingly gorgeous, the one who just wrecked him, not only was she still in town, but her name was Tara and he loved that name although he didn't think that he'd ever met a Tara before, and apparently her intention was to stay. That news stirred him up. Such good news. But a trifle scary, too. He tried to be as calm as Denny seemed to be about the meeting, and maybe he was pulling that off, but the report on her continuing presence created a roaring tumult inside him. Which is why he remained of two minds. He wondered if his brother possessed the same ability, to conceal what fomented inside him, to make it seem as though nothing was going on when really all hell was breaking loose.

■ ■ ■

DOUBTS CONCERNING HER NEW TOWN surfaced when the biggest event of the season appeared to be a meeting. People even put up flyers, *for a meeting,* tacked onto telephone poles. Her new business partner never mentioned attending, and possibly assumed she'd have no interest in attending herself, or that she was too busy making her new digs liveable. Yet Tara felt a strong pull to be among people, and so showed up at what the older women gabbing on the streets were calling "the kafuffle." If nothing else, she'd find out what could possibly be controversial about a broken-down old bridge.

The gathering was infinitely more popular than she anticipated. People were flooding in, everybody and their second cousins twice removed from up north or down south, and included in the multitude was none other than Willis Howard. She intuited that he was going to be a problem. Immediately upon sharing a quick greeting, he was revelling in her company, basking in being seen at her side in full and drastic public view.

Wearing her like a bracelet.

Willis was in the process of steering Tara to where he believed they should be sitting—if he succeeded she'd chalk up the night as ruined. She didn't have any particular concerns about how people might perceive her, but neither did she want to be judged as Willis Howard's trollop date. Nor did she want to be obliged to endure his commentary throughout the evening.

His claim on her just felt so irritating.

She preferred the rainstorm she'd been caught in the previous evening.

Tara tried to break free once, as if by accident, only to be chided by Willis for entering the inner sanctum of the tree huggers. A second move away would have put her among loggers, no better a choice in his rigid hierarchy.

"Are these like reserved seats?" she complained.

He laughed at what he perceived to be a feisty spirit. "Nothing like that." Indeed, the turnout was exceptional. More chairs were being unfolded and put out. "You don't want to sit among the loggers or the environmentalists."

"I don't, huh? Why not?"

"Each group needs to make itself look as strong as possible. We'll be with the tourism industry—the merchants and innkeepers. That way we can show that our point of view is well represented."

"Who are those people, over there?"

Willis leaned in front of her to look across the room. "Strangers," he noted. "You know what that means."

They didn't look like strangers to her. Well-groomed men in suits and ties, and women in spiffy pants suits, were reminiscent of her former enclave. She could only speculate on their purpose here. "Actually"—annoyance crept into her voice—"I don't."

"Bureaucrats. Provincial, federal, municipal, the works. Lawyers."

She cast a glance their way. That's where she should properly be seated, but she didn't want any part of that group. Tara supposed that she should just go home. She was on the verge of feigning a headache, or of declaring that it was too nice outside to be indoors and really she never intended to be in such a big crowd. But to leave would countermand her own curiosity. What could sufficiently interest this spectrum of diverse people to not only turn out in numbers but to seem so animated, so energized?

A bridge?

"Who're the other suits?" she inquired. Another gaggle sat forward of the loggers on the same side of the room.

"Logging company officials. Their lawyers."

More lawyers. More of her own kind, yet she felt so estranged from them now. Behind them arrived the minions, a broad public panoply eager for an evening's entertainment that promised to outdistance the summer fare on TV.

As Willis was seating himself she finally found a way to elegantly slip loose from his company. "There's Mrs. McCracken now. I promised to sit with her." Her first business partner lie.

Willis Howard came up with no retort. Although his disappointment showed, he politely let her go, and Tara settled in four rows behind him and a few seats over—still within the bounds of the tourism industry—beside the elderly firecracker.

"You don't know what you just saved me from," Tara whispered.

"Oh, Willis can be a bore," Mrs. McCracken chimed in. Somehow, she just got her, this woman. They smiled.

"I hear you've been firing blanks at burglars."

"Oh, shut up." Despite the words of protest, Mrs. McCracken smiled as she spoke and did not seem to mind her comment.

"Spill the beans," Tara continued. "Explain to me why so many people are here. I've heard about community involvement but this is ridiculous. Something about a bridge?"

"Oh no, not a bridge, dear," Mrs. McCracken corrected her. "Although two are involved. Our beautiful old covered one and a new monstrosity that's not even built yet and hopefully never shall be. No, dear, this is about our heritage, for starters, and it's also about our hopes for the future."

"Nothing trivial, then. Whose side are we on?"

"In tossing your fate to the wind, my dear, you have landed with the tourism industry. We are supported by the ecologically aware young people in our midst, and by different levels of government. Keep in mind that the latter can never be trusted. But we enjoy the support of the good, the pure, and the enlightened people on our planet."

She loved this gal's wit. "Such good news. And our enemies are?"

"Loggers."

"Thought so. They don't favour our heritage and future?"

"They do not. They're in it for the money."

"Whereas the tourism industry . . ."

"Oh, shut up." This time, she may have meant it.

"So what's the difference?"

"The loggers are dunces."

"Undoubtedly so. But what's their case, their point of view?"

"My dear, listen to me when I'm talking to you. They're dunces. Nothing more needs to be said."

Tara shot a glance at the enemy trenches. Men turned out in good numbers and looked ready for bear. She did not have a handle on the issues, but she couldn't simply endorse Mrs. McCracken's position without further articulation. Her elite training as a lawyer taught that adversaries could be creeps and malcontents, pathological liars and brutes, rapacious villains or wretchedly needy imps, but they were never dunces, unless you planned on losing the case, which made you the dunce.

"Mmm," she said.

"I know what that means," Mrs. McCracken opined.

"No, you do not."

"Now you be nice, dear, or I'll send you back to sit with your Mr. Howard."

Tara shot her a glance. "You wouldn't."

Mrs. McCracken clicked her fingers. "In a trice," she said. "Like that."

Laughing lightly, Tara touched the old lady's bare forearm. "I'll be good," she promised. "Boy, you people around here play rough!"

■ ■ ■

ALEXANDER O'FARRELL WAS NOT ALONE in noticing the new young woman in town. Every person in attendance at the meeting succumbed to some awareness of her presence. Her newness as well as her beauty were magnets, and while many found excuses to glance in her direction, a few numbskulls blatantly stared. Not only men were the culprits. Women glared as if mentally preparing for a catfight if she dared come into contact with their husbands. Government agents, who had no clue that she was a newcomer in town, craned their necks as if scanning the audience to assess its size, but specifically to bolster their initial impression that a rare creature resided in their midst. The evening might not be a total waste. Alex, observing her, did feel concern for his eldest son. Ryan had come to grief in his life, and this woman struck him as being a walking heartache.

He wished that Ryan thought to join him at the meeting, though. He might have found a chance to introduce himself to her. What was so important that he was avoiding this?

Alex appreciated how the young woman was relating to old Mrs. McCracken. The two interacted like schoolgirls, giggling together. He liked her, an impression not wholly tied to her fine looks. She received the attention of the room, she was fully aware of it, yet she didn't play to that attention, or exhibit any sign that it was either justified or necessary. Nor was she intimidated by the interest of the room in evaluating her, for none of her gestures appeared remotely self-conscious, and she didn't perform for the wide-angle lens of that camera's eye.

Something odd occurred that quietly strengthened Alex O'Farrell's positive view. The woman turned to look right at him. So many were gazing at her and yet she returned the scrutiny of just one man, the one who, in his estimation, was sympathetic to her plight. That perception bowled him over. Yet he did not react as he might with any other, did not turn away or pretend that his gaze was accidental. He'd been found out, observed, and so confirmed his study of her by meeting her eyes for the few seconds that she returned his look, before her attention reverted to her companion. Mrs. McCracken soon shot a glance over her shoulder. So the young woman was asking about him, and now Mrs. McCracken conveyed a report.

A walking heartache for sure, Alex concluded, unless she happened to take to his son, in which case—and he was surprised by how convinced he became of an opinion he could only call rash—they'd be well suited for each other. For he knew Ryan as no one else did, better, perhaps, than the young man knew himself, and not merely as a father might know his son, although that aspect was involved. In Alex's mind, Ryan possessed a quality that transcended the familiar, setting him apart, a native intelligence he hadn't fully tapped into yet and, depending on life's circumstances, might never fully experience. He possessed a generosity of spirit—his wife, Ryan's mother, alerted Alex to this—as rare as it was precious, in her words, and as vital as it was undefined. The boy didn't know about any of that, Alex considered, pulling his gaze away from the woman out of courtesy while thinking also about his long-deceased wife. But a woman such as this one, if his instincts regarding both young people held true, could aid him with that discovery.

As the meeting was about to begin, Alex sensed that he was the one hot to trot here, vicariously, on behalf of his elder son, and even, strangely enough, on behalf of this new woman in town. He consciously reverted his attention to the meeting to see how the younger of his two sons might fare.

The retired mayor called the meeting to order and Alexander O'Farrell sensed the partisan tensions rise, one side of the room pitted against the other, as if they were all a pack of brawling in-laws at a shotgun wedding. "This could get interesting," he whispered to those seated just ahead of him.

To bring people to order required more than the formality of pounding a gavel, although the former mayor of Wakefield, Anton St. Aubin, gave it a try. He was selected to be chairman due to his experience with similar gatherings, as the organizers prevailed upon the presiding mayor to step away from the task. No one wanted the discussion to seem controlled or even sponsored by any level of government. The meeting was meant to allow opposing factions into the same room to see what could be jarred loose from their mutual antagonism, to learn who could be placated and what could be done, if anything, to calm the waters.

Even, although this idea was deemed a pipe dream, to find solutions.

As anxious as the populace felt attending the meeting, many were not above treating it as a social outing. To get people to quiet down proved difficult. The old mayor finally resorted to virtual profanity. He roared into the microphone set before him on his table, "Everybody, will you just shut the"—he lingered for a breath to give people time to fill in the blank for themselves with the appropriate expletive, then titter, before he finished—"up."

He'd won their attention.

The old mayor, a youthful seventy-five, albeit with a widower's characteristic malaise—spills on his tie, a crumpled shirt, for he'd sloughed off his jacket as the room warmed up, and he was in need of a haircut despite a shiny, liver-spotted pate—spoke with a smile.

"How's everybody doing tonight?"

Most everyone concurred that they were doing just fine.

He announced that dignitaries and professionals were to be introduced, and as he did so they joined him at the head table facing the congested room. Only outside officials sat at the table, provincial bureaucrats at one end, federal at the other. In the middle, closest to the former mayor and on either side of him, experts on bridges, on roads, on forestry, and on the economy converged, and while no one explained who employed them—"We're consultants," the junior bridge expert attested—those in attendance could detect in the strangers' manner the long arm of government agencies.

Each man and woman at the head table was invited to speak, and each had the decency to keep their opening remarks brief and noncommittal. An operative phrase for the meeting, "We are here to listen," underscored that they were neutral observers, and those in attendance abided their statements with patience. Not that anyone believed them to be as neutral as they claimed.

The audience sat waiting for the fireworks to commence. Without the advantage of that expectation, accustomed to meetings so dull and monstrously detailed that they bordered on the carcinogenic, Tara Cogshill settled in for an evening of tedium. She took comfort in the advantage of this introduction to her new community. Loggers and shopkeepers, innkeepers and artisans, the old and a few young, misfits and the genteel commingled. She gathered, with help from Mrs. Mc-Cracken, who whispered pertinent, if blatantly biased, notes, that an old covered bridge impeded traffic, and that the forestry industry felt imperilled. "In days of yore," as one man began a poetic effusion, logs were driven south on the Gatineau River. Those great floating masses of timbers worked well for more than a century but over time threatened to choke the life of the river, and eventually were deemed an ecological hazard. So now logs were trucked out of the woods to mills.

"Those men of old," Mrs. McCracken started to whisper.

"In days of yore," Tara stipulated.

"Exactly. Back then, they drove the logs on the river with patience and expertise. They relied on their wits."

"Therefore?" She loved this old gal, loved goading her on, just a touch.

154

"Young men today are too impatient! Everything's rush, rush, rush. They can go around. They can wait their turn. They can *relax*, for heaven's sake. Given what's at stake that doesn't seem too much to ask, if you ask me."

"Isn't that the point of the meeting, Mrs. McCracken? To ask you. And everyone else while we're at it."

■ ■ ■

"WORK TO DO," HAD BEEN Ryan's excuse for bowing out of the meeting. Perhaps to justify his fib, he cruised through town, the streets starkly empty with so many at the meeting. The supermarket shut early, everyone off to do their civic duty, which at twilight contributed to a spooky, ghostly atmosphere. Ryan's tour took him past Mrs. McCracken's house, and he considered this to be correct police procedure as well. He told her one thing, yet also gave credence to a second theory regarding the rampage through her home. Blaming kids was credible, but loggers might have committed the trespass. Among their numbers were those with the temerity. And within that tribe were those with motive, for she was a formidable political opponent in the current dispute over the bridge. They might want to unsettle her, get her off her game. Should that guess prove right, they could conceivably return when her house was empty to wreck further havoc. Fortunately, her home as he drove by seemed quiet. Lovely, in a still, sedate way in the gloominess of dusk. From there Ryan drove to the old covered bridge, in part to guard against anyone taking advantage of the exceptional quiet to scrawl slogans or commit some reckless, malevolent act.

As he arrived, he came across a group of young people, each taking turns jumping off the upper rail into the water below. A serene scene of summer, which held in its moments—the girl crying out as she leapt feetfirst into the stream, the young boy fearful on the rail prior to his first jump ever, the older boy swimming across the current to a boulder near shore, still hooting with the thrill of his leap—a nostalgia for summers past, for simple joys and special memories. If he were an artist, Ryan thought, cheesy or not he'd capture this scene. Strictly speaking, the sport was not legal, although Ryan was never the sort of police officer who enforced infractions for the sake of proving his power, and he'd made the leap into the river himself countless times as a kid. Dangers lurked—only a patch of the water's surface was free of rocks and rapids—and yet generation by generation young people managed to negotiate the dangers and teach one another to be safe even as they revelled in the risks. In Ryan's estimation, no one could be protected and shielded from himself or herself at every moment. Taking reasonable risk, as a youthful folly, was probably beneficial over the long term. Let folks or their kids speed or drink in cars, though, and he was on their tail in the blink of an eye, and merciless.

As well, the river was not swimmable, due to the proliferation of deadheads, the old logs still floating around or stuck in the river bottom or lassoed by grasses or lodged in the side banks, often just out of sight where a child might slam into one if plunging below the surface. Forget about boating, as a rudder or prop might easily be ripped off. Only the rapids cleared them out from the area below the bridge each spring, so only here, beneath the bridge, could children enjoy the water.

Walking out onto the old covered bridge he was ignored by the kids at first. He was not in uniform and stayed at one end, away from the deepest diving spot. Recognizing him, the teenagers conferred with one another, which resulted in an emissary being sent to approach him. Before the dripping boy got within twenty feet, Ryan issued an edict. "Kid, don't get me wrong. I'm not giving you permission. But I'm not on duty. I'm not on duty and I'm not in the mood for a chat." The boy retreated to the company of his friends. In essence, Ryan was giving them his tacit approval, yet somehow he spoiled their fun. He never meant to do so. After a few minutes, following one more leap, the teenagers gathered up their clothes and towels and walked off the bridge in the direction opposite Ryan.

His weight against the railing, his arms crossed over it, he stared down at the rapidly flowing river.

The first girl he ever kissed was on this bridge.

The first breast touched.

He broke up a fight on the bridge once, standing between two youths wailing on each other and getting them to stop. Seventeen at the time, about two years younger than the combatants, he came away from the experience shaking. He'd put himself in danger, but to his surprise, inexplicably, he gained the approval of a number of his peers, guys and girls both, and from that moment forward he considered that an idea floating in his head was viable. He might actually carry through on an inkling. Ryan accepted that he was destined to become a cop.

Standing on the bridge as he did now, except that it was wintertime then with ice below and a chilling wind at his back, he contemplated, and absorbed, the agonizing death of his mother. And he returned on an autumn's evening to wallow in emotional wreckage when bad news regarding his girlfriend ripped him asunder. The bridge and the river below exerted this kind of pull on him. Others talked about heritage and history and tradition, but for Ryan the bridge counted in ways he was unwilling to speak about to anyone. Certainly not down at the town meeting. The bridge was his personal holy ground. A private place for an intimate correspondence with himself.

He understood that he was not at the meeting because he could never say there what he felt so deeply here, and to listen to lesser or silly testimonials might agitate him. There was that, and one thing more.

The new woman in town. Whoa. She wrecked him. He hoped her voice was a high-pitched squeak, or that she only spoke in expletives, or was as dumb as a dump truck, or as sharply stony as the boulder divers avoided when leaping into the stream below. Anything, in fact, that would rescue him when eventually they met.

He wanted to talk to her soon. That much he knew. His brother was an inadvertent spokesman on his behalf and he couldn't let that continue under any circumstance, and the way his dad was teasing and sounding him out earlier, he better not let him be his next spokesman either.

Cowboy up, he chided himself. *Talk to the girl.*

Gazing downstream, he knew why he was such a mess. Or knew several factors. He hadn't responded to anyone since his last relationship, its end an acrimonious affair. After that he felt demoralized, inordinately self-protective, alert, absurdly discriminating. He devalued his own judgement but primarily he was afraid to fall in love again. Whenever he was sent out on an emergency call he hoped that the victim was male, for if not, he became automatically critical, as if he must analyze the woman and detail her idiosyncrasies and frailties, map the dents in her character and discern the ridges and smudges on her personality before any meaningful conversation could take place. As if he was in training for his next emotional encounter, whenever and with whomever that might be. The fear of being hurt by itself did not stymie him, but the fear of falling so profoundly under a lunar sway that he could neither think straight nor act in any competent manner or distinguish what was up or down petrified him. Because he knew what could come of it when the relationship went bad. He was less afraid of women, he understood that much about himself, than he was rattled by the depth of his capacity to tumble helplessly, irredeemably, into love, and then feel stuck, even when he wanted out of it, with only himself to blame.

In going to the bridge, he needed to make sure that on this critical night it stood safe from vandals or malevolent folks with their strong opinions, but he also wanted this, to commune with the old structure and the old river amid the old hills where he communed with his mother upon her death, and where, through several critical periods in his life, he communed with the stars above, seeking his way through life just as the river steadily bore a channel through these ancient hills.

Ryan took a deep breath.

His boyhood dream was to work on the Gatineau. Drive logs downstream. Dangerous work. Good work. A labour that was no longer available. As the river flowed, so did that history, and his own—all of it churning together, and while he could not recover the old days Ryan wondered if he could permit romance to seep through his bloodstream again. He knew he was getting way, way, way ahead of himself, but he couldn't help it. The river and the first stars were answering back, and he was able to comprehend a simple but difficult thing, that sooner or later it would not be possible to avoid falling rampantly for someone. That part was inevitable. He was prone. If nothing else, this woman called Tara already showed him that the door was now open. He'd be unable to close it. Whether with her, and his senses hoped it would be so, or with another, the door was as wide open as the sky. He was a goner. He knew that now. The view from the bridge indicated that this was so.

■ ■ ■

SAGE WISDOM ARRIVED FROM SUNDRY directions, unexpectedly at times, Tara noted. But then, right after someone spoke wisely, another debater's idiotic remarks inevitably fell into step. So many who spoke seemed unable to differentiate between diehard opinion and thoughtfulness. In turn, idiocy bequeathed honourable yet mediocre thinkers with both the courage and the incentive to enter the fray, a group soon emboldened by its strength in numbers. The mediocre and then the merely garrulous spoke one after the other, until finally another sage voice piped up and altered the course of the proceedings. Then nutcases stormed the ramparts, and the cycle was faithfully reborn.

"If I wanted to be objective," she prefaced to Mrs. McCracken.

"Now, dear, you don't want to do any such thing."

"You have no clue what I'm about to say."

"Just choose a side, dear. Mine."

"You haven't spoken yet."

"I pick my spots."

In the way that the old lady held her head, chin up, eyes alert and calm, and in the way that she maintained an authoritative disposition, back straight, one wrist comfortably, delicately placed on top of the other in her lap, Tara presumed that her new pal was probably right.

They heard from those who either elegantly or falteringly spoke with an unerring passion about the environment. The gist being that trucks and logs ultimately were bad, therefore highways and bridges were bad, therefore the status quo was fine, and so the old bridge ought to be maintained as the only point of crossing in the immediate area. They summoned air pollution, noise pollution, and the dangers of high-speed traffic to convincingly support their positions, and suggested that the money saved might be better served to acquire parkland. "The faster they can move trees, the more they'll cut, and before you know it they'll clear-cut the entire forest." Members of the concerned ad hoc committee at the head table nodded and jotted discreet notes.

Those on the side of the conservationists cringed, while loggers chuckled, when a cute girl with short legs out of proportion to her frame, who wore cut flowers in her hair and across her wardrobe, screeched, "I can't stand it when I see a logging truck on the road! Someday I promise you"—her right hand struck like a cleaver through the air—"one of those loads will land on a Volkswagen! Then what? With babies inside!"

"Why is it always a Volkswagen?" a logger inquired from the back.

"Child killer!" she bellowed back at him. "You wait and see!"

"Don't worry, lady," came another's retort, "we keep our loads tied tighter than you are."

She misinterpreted his meaning. "I'm not drunk!" That didn't occur to anyone until that moment, but now no one was sure.

Those who supported tourism read prepared statements that were quietly rational and compelling. The industry was thriving. Inns, restaurants, and shops were doing a banner business, the steam locomotive came up to Wakefield for a reason and the old covered bridge, "photographed a thousand times a day during the summer and quite a lot in the winter," was a big part of creating their overall prosperity.

When called upon, logging executives ran down the numbers to impress the committee, and copious notes were taken.

Tara had no difficulty singling out those known as tree huggers, for many were at the game the night before and their haberdashery was proudly flamboyant. They supported every spokesperson for tourism and the academic ecologists, while adding wry notes of their own. "Our choices should follow the will of nature," declared a man identified as Gordon Skotcher. He wore proper trousers and a suit jacket, minus a shirt. "Our choices ought to favour people over machines, a living, breathing forest over clear-cut timber."

The tree huggers not only applauded, they cheered.

"What about jobs?" a provincial bureaucrat asked from the head table.

The speaker stared at him awhile, shifting his weight from one foot to the other before the standing microphone he gripped to steady himself. The question seemed to confound him. Finally, he answered,

"You're asking me? I haven't worked in fourteen years!" Which earned the ribald hoots of the populace, loggers and tree huggers alike.

"The panel recognizes Mr. Willis Howard," the old mayor announced, and Willis stood and moistened his lips before moving over to the microphone. He considered himself the lynchpin in the shop-keepers' drive for recognition of their economic contribution to this community. More so than any other, he resented the loggers' claim to fiscal prominence.

Yet a voice boomed out before he uttered a word. "Hang on there, chief. My hand was up long before his."

"I'm sorry if that's the case, Denny," the old mayor said, "but I have recognized—"

"Sure you recognize him, Anton. Who doesn't? I've known him my whole life. He has a shop on Main Street so he's in favour of the bridge. What else did you expect? If a tourist takes a snapshot, he finds a way to make a dime."

Tara found it curious that the only two men she'd met in town were now jostling in an argument, although Willis was hanging back, apparently confident that the mayor would uphold his status as the next speaker.

"Denny, you'll be permitted to have your say, but I didn't spot your hand in time."

"You're listening to everyone who wants to keep the bridge." Denny did not require the use of the microphone, content to loudly press his position while standing at his seat in the midst of the other loggers. He didn't mention that his side deliberately chose to sit on their hands this deep into the proceedings, and knew that his accusation wasn't fair. Years ago, Mrs. McCracken taught him to pick his spot in any public debate, and so he did. Her edict, *When you speak is equally as important as what you say,* was one lesson well learned from her. "But the loggers need to have their say, Mayor, straight from the horse's arse."

"We're getting to everyone in due course—"

"That's okay, Anton," Willis Howard conceded, too intimidated to speak over Denny's objections. He'd let him talk his mouth off and be more comfortable speaking afterwards. "Denny can say whatever's on his mind."

His tone suggested that he didn't expect much.

"As you wish, Willis. Thank you for your gracious concession. The committee recognizes Mr. Denny O'Farrell."

The loggers gave him a round of applause, as though this constituted a victory in itself. Because he'd agitated to be heard, the room was paying him particular mind now, and Tara wondered if he planned it that way. Supplanting Willis Howard might grant him a more sympathetic reception.

Brilliant, if that was true.

In any case, expectations were raised, including her own.

"This will be interesting," Mrs. McCracken proffered, confirming her own intuitive sense.

Denny edged his way past the knees of his fellow workers, choosing at this point to command the microphone. Determination affected his stride, and when he stood before the gathering he put his hands on his hips and paused to scan the meeting. The room went stone quiet— even Tara Cogshill felt a tickle in her throat, as if a cough now might be an unwarranted, unacceptable intrusion. She was impressed by his immediate command of the room.

"You've heard from my bosses, the company executives, from their accountants and their lawyers, and even though I sincerely believe that I agree with them, I'm not sure I understood a frigging word they said."

The room erupted in laughter, and Tara was intrigued now. This man could be a successful politician, the way he brought an entire gathering into his sway with just a few words. She leaned into Mrs. McCracken and whispered, "Some logger."

The older woman whispered back, "My nemesis."

Tara raised an inquiring eyebrow.

"Sitting over here," Denny went on, "I see the big shots at the table agreeing with the tree huggers and the innkeepers, with the shopkeepers and the folks who mean well but don't know diddly, you're bobbing your heads—"

"We consider everyone's standpoint fairly, Denny," former mayor St. Aubin avowed.

"Maybe that's so, Anton, maybe it's not. You don't make the decisions anymore, so how do we know?" A point was contested that he won for his side. Tara judged that if this logger was her opposing counsel in court, she'd be alert. "You're listening to the tourism industry's viewpoint, to tree hugger experts, to townspeople, some of whom only want to hear the sound of their own voices through an amplifier, it gives them a thrill."

A minor clamour of objection arose, countered by the murmur of those who agreed with him.

"I don't mean to insult anybody. Well, tree huggers, maybe, I don't mind insulting them." Even that group enjoyed his mirth. "But seriously, people. Come on! We used to drive logs down the river. My dad, who's here tonight, did it his whole life. The conservation experts warned us to stop because the river was dying. Fine, they made their point. Nobody wants a dead river. Not even the orneriest son-of-a-bitch logger you can find. We don't want that. So instead we truck the logs out now because we just happen to believe they won't fly out of the woods on their own. But trucks—need—roads! When a road comes to a river, it needs a proper bridge. That pretty bridge that we have now was not intended for big rigs or tons of traffic. Not when it was young and not now that it's an antique. I know why you're so gung ho to agree with the people who have spoken here tonight."

The face on the old mayor was reddening. "This is a fact-finding mission, Denny. I'll have to insist on that. Nobody up here, and I know that I can speak for everyone, nobody has made up his or her mind yet. It's not about agreeing or disagreeing."

"You can't say that, Anton, because you don't know for sure."

Tara glanced around the room, noticing how people were responding to the back and forth, their nods at one another. *Denny, you're winning points,* she deduced.

"Some people never want anything to change," he trumpeted. "Is the government any different? We know the answer to that one. A bridge costs money and you don't want to spend it even when it's our own money. You've got other priorities. Other ways for elected officials—whose skinny asses aren't here tonight, you'll notice—to win votes and keep their precious jobs awhile. But I'm telling you, the modern world is on our side. On the loggers' side. Maybe not the fairy-tale world of the tree huggers, peace and love and shit like that."

"Fuck you, too, Denny!" Skootch shouted out.

"Oh, go smoke a joint!" Denny called back, which, Tara noted again, won the approbation of a major portion of the assembly. "I believe in that stuff myself. Sure I do. Peace, love, nothing wrong with that. But the point is, we loggers pay the bills around here, with our sweat and our trucks and with the trees we cut down and transport. We support this town, not the guys making a mint at the inns—who take their cash south in the winter—and not the tree huggers, that's for damn sure. Nobody is saying tear down the old bridge. But build a new one. Get off your ass, stick your hand in your deep government pockets, you'll find some cash down there if you feel around and stop playing with yourself, then build us that new bridge."

The truckers were rowdy in their praise as Denny seated himself. Applause from many townspeople, who filled the back rows and lined the rear and side walls, who brandished no particular axe to grind and perhaps were open to being persuaded, went beyond token politeness.

Clapping, Tara chipped in as well, only to be scolded by Mrs. McCracken to keep it short.

"That'll be enough of that," the old lady commanded.

"I'm done, I'm done. But he did well, you must admit."

"I haven't spoken yet."

"I know. You pick your spots."

Mrs. McCracken leaned into her. "This is the spot I pick."

She stood up. Willis Howard was making his way back to the microphone to be formally introduced by the meeting's chairman, but that proved no impediment to Mrs. McCracken. Willis, a nervous Nelly when it came to public speaking, took a breath, smiled, cleared his throat unnecessarily, and double-checked his notes, a delay that cost him the opportunity to say a word. An emphatic finger poked his shoulder. He turned.

"I'll take it from here, dear," Mrs. McCracken informed him, in effect giving him the boot. Willis, who decided that he wasn't so thrilled to be speaking in the wake of the popular Denny O'Farrell after all, slinked back to his seat, somewhat relieved.

"Check that," the old mayor announced. "The committee recognizes instead the lovely Mrs. McCracken."

Her mouth a little too close and loud in the microphone so that it boomed around the room, she retorted, "Don't you dare flirt with me, you old fart."

And just like that, Tara saw that her friend now held sway across the room. Loggers were grim, Denny O'Farrell in particular, while the rest of the room was raucous with laughter and enthralled.

"I want to thank the previous speaker," Mrs. McCracken stipulated. "It's good to hear another person's perspective. I'm glad that you made a reference to our history, Mr. O'Farrell. It's our principle concern here, although I don't recall that you did particularly well in the subject."

Tara guessed that it was an inside joke, as the line went over so well that Anton St. Aubin needed to resort to his gavel.

"Our covered bridge is an important part of our heritage," she carried on.

"Whoop-de-doo!" At the sound of the trucker's voice, Tara turned to look at him. He was two seats farther down from Denny, and like Denny his voice carried well. "Whose salary does our heritage pay?"

The spry sapling of an old lady ignored him. "The bridge goes to the very soul of this town."

The panel was nodding to these comments, something that Denny mentioned but Tara was noticing for the first time herself, and it was Denny who chose to comment.

"It's a bridge, McCracked, it's not a religion."

Laughter at the name he'd chosen percolated around the room. Tara was impressed that her new friend appeared not to care. Undoubtedly, she'd heard the name before, and probably from children no taller than her thighs.

A panellist, antagonistic after being called out by a logger for bias, chose to interrupt with a query. "Ma'am, what do you say to the complaints from the forestry industry? The time delays, for instance. Are they not legitimate?"

"Oh, my dear," she chided him, "you're old enough now, don't be taken in. The truckers can be patient. These little delays won't kill them. I endure them myself picking my berries. So what? Really, ask yourself, what is the big rush? Anyway, they can go around. It's a quick hop up the road."

Denny was on his feet this time, roaring. "Thirty-eight extra clicks per freaking load. Don't bang your gavel down on me, St. Aubin," he commanded the moderator, although he'd only raised it without bringing it down yet, "this is serious business."

"You can make the little side trip if you want to," Mrs. McCracken protested. "It doesn't take that long. You do it now when you're in the mood."

"Only when the lineup's too long! Only because we have to!"

The gavel came down this time. "I must require both of you to address the panel. For now, Denny, Mrs. McCracken has the floor."

Tara was keeping her own internal tally. Mrs. McCracken's counterarguments came across as weak, and the room sensed that. The loggers scored a point.

"Given what's at stake," Mrs. McCracken contended, her sure, pure voice enunciating every syllable as if sharpening a blade, "our heritage, our history, it's a minor detour."

The committee's heads kept wagging.

"Hey, you!" Denny cried out. "Tree huggers! Get in on this! She wants us to burn more fuel. Stick up for the planet here! They want more pollution, more noise. Are you just going to sit there and let that happen?"

Opposing sides were both on their feet, and Tara, observing these people in action, noted a few telling details. Having instigated the sudden splurge of insults and rhetoric, Denny O'Farrell was not swept up by the furore himself. He was keeping tabs on the room instead, letting the verbiage fly around without responding or being emotionally distraught. That made Tara think, and she watched him closely. She was unsure how much credit she should give this man, for she recognized her own prejudice here. He was a logger, not a jurist. And yet . . . if he was Mrs. McCracken's nemesis as she maintained, then he'd found the perfect way to censor her voice. In the bedlam, she was stuck at the microphone but unable to get a word in edgewise. The perfect ploy.

Tara glanced at an older logger with whom she'd made eye contact at the onset of the meeting, a man whom Mrs. McCracken described as "the head of the clan." Alex O'Farrell was quietly observing his son, as though he also wondered if Denny was not choreographing the entire event.

At the front table, the old mayor banged the uproar to silence with his gavel. Mrs. McCracken seated herself, receiving a few pats on her back, and the old mayor decided that if he was going to get them out of there in one piece, he'd reserve the final comments of the evening for himself.

"We appreciate that the congestion on the old covered bridge is an issue. Your city council, I'm told, has put forward remedies to alleviate the problem."

"Like what," Denny called out, unhappy with this return to civility, "a new paint job?"

"They will buttress the bridge," the old mayor pressed on, "to make it safer for heavy vehicles. That way, bus passengers won't need to walk across, the trucks can go a little faster."

"We still have to wait for that bus!" another voice pointed out.

"The town will build a better turning circle, saving time," St. Aubin stated.

"Seconds, every hour," Denny qualified.

"And as I understand it, and this helps people in many quarters, an aesthetic issue, well, we'll repaint the bridge."

Denny jumped to his feet. "I knew it! Paint it white, Anton, to symbolize the whitewash that's going on here tonight!"

The old mayor resorted to his gavel to bring the room back to his remarks. Slowly, with a few errant shouts ricocheting around the room, people quieted, and he scrunched his brow.

"I believe," St. Aubin finished up, "that that sums up the town's position. Now the agencies here tonight, and the governments, they'll get together, I assure you, and I sincerely believe that they will see what else can be done. Maybe a new bridge is the answer. Maybe not. Down the road, a new one may be inevitable. It's a matter of resources, of course. Of priorities. On that, we'll have to take a wait-and-see attitude."

He thanked the individuals at the head table and the citizens for their participation. His gavel, and a halfhearted smattering of applause, declared the meeting closed.

Out in the cooler night air, Tara walked Mrs. McCracken to her scooter. "So?" she asked. "Did you win the debate tonight, do you think?"

Mrs. McCracken adjusted her helmet.

"I didn't have to win the debate tonight. I just wanted to make sure that my side didn't lose it. I'll bet you a blueberry pie that come morning, come next week next month next year," Mrs. McCracken prophesied, "the bridge will still be standing. Most likely, as the only one."

"Why the only one?" Tara asked her. "What's wrong with two?"

"Because we're too small for two, dear. We're much more than a hamlet but not in the government's mind. To them, we're nothing but a whistle-stop. A name on a map. A detour during election time. Not a soul in government is going to care enough about us to build a second bridge when we already have one which, as far as they are concerned, true or not, is adequate. I mean, who do we think we are? The rich? The powerful?"

Tara took her meaning, but still tried to speak for the other side. "The men have a different point of view. They represent commerce, big industry. Well, maybe it's only modest-sized industry. But they made several good points."

Mrs. McCracken was having none of it. "Understand me, I don't *care* if they get a second bridge as long as they don't tear mine down to build it. That's the risk I'm not willing to take. I don't believe there will be a new bridge. Like I say, we're too pint-sized a community. There aren't enough votes here and anyway, those votes are split down the middle. All I want is to make sure the authorities have it in their craw that if—a big if—*if* they build a new bridge, then they must make certain that the old one stays where it is and will be properly maintained *or there will be hell to pay*. I want them to fear our side and I believe they do. I know very well that if the old bridge becomes a secondary crossing, voices will say that it's outlived its usefulness, it won't be maintained, eventually it becomes a danger and gets torn down. So! Do you want to take that bet or not?"

"I win a blueberry pie. What do you get if I lose?"

Mrs. McCracken mulled it over, then broke into a wide grin. "Your pride, Tara. Your youth. Your beauty. I'll snap all that up for myself and you get to hobble around as an old codger."

"You witch!"

"Only for a day, let's say. So is it a bet?" The old lady's eyes were dancing.

Tara let her know that she could never risk all that.

"Yet you do, dear. You've already risked everything by coming here. Over time, you might keep your pride, I pray that you do, but someday everything else will be gone."

"Unless I give it away to you, hunh?"

"Oh, if only you could, dear. If only life was like that. But in any case, only for a day. So, no bet?"

Tara laughed happily. "No bet," she said.

14

When harvesting a field, truckers required coordinated radio communication. Much of the roadway—flat, hard-packed gravel, dusty these days—was single lane, so trucks awaited cues before arriving or departing. Upon receiving an all-clear, they barrelled down the road in packs of four or five, straight and fast, confident of no oncoming traffic.

Passing lanes existed at two locations along the logging road, for the sake of potential breakdowns but principally to allow rigs to enter and travel partway along when trucks from the opposite direction were not yet on their way. As many as four trucks could wait on each siding while the oncoming vehicles passed by. Denny O'Farrell was given clearance to carry on to the loading field, but he pulled over onto the siding anyway, drove his rig up to the farthest end, and cut the engine. Momentarily, three companion trucks motored behind in his dust. The drivers shut their engines as well, something they rarely did, a silence that felt suddenly uproarious. Denny stepped down from his tractor, tapped his tires as he walked to the rear, and joined Xavier, Samad, and André. Two men fished out their cigarettes, and Samad shined an apple on his shirt before biting into it. Denny took a long pull on his water bottle.

Foliage shaded them, the day mild and breezy, cloudy with a threat of rain. They'd not spoken in private since the town meeting the night before.

"Not even the courtesy to wait," André said, assuming that the others would catch his reference. "They didn't even pretend to show us any respect. Just flat out, no bridge."

"It wasn't flat out, but faking a response, that's no courtesy," Denny concurred.

André emphatically shook his head. "This way, see, they don't just turn us down, they don't just tell us to take a hike. This way they make sure we know that the meeting was a blow job."

"Then how come I didn't enjoy it?" Samad asked. The others were not in the mood for his joke and didn't respond.

"This way, they can tell everybody they listened. They made themselves look good. To us they're saying, forget this shit, we only listen to people on their knees."

"We can eat moose shit for breakfast, that's what they think," Xavier added, a thought that made Samad feel glum. He tossed his apple core away.

The men were quiet awhile, and Xavier did a tire check down the length of his rig and returned up the other side. When he came back, he was watching Denny, and Samad checked him out as well, repeatedly glancing his way. They knew, instinctively, that what mattered now was Denny's reaction. If anyone could find a way out of this, he was the man. But he chose not to get embroiled, neither in André's emotions nor in his own pent-up fury nor even with his frustration at being put in this position. He never asked for this, but he long presumed that the

decision would fall upon him anyway. Most people could not understand what it meant to be a leader of a pack of men, and not just these
three. He kept a lid on things, but he kept a lid on things by implying
that the lid could be removed one day, and when that day came he'd
take it upon himself to remove it. That day, it seemed, fast approached,
or was already here. Whatever the logistics of the process, the former
mayor's comments to close the meeting unofficially confirmed that no
new bridge would be built in the immediate future. Probably the government didn't want him to repeat all that he overheard, yet he may
have picked up insider knowledge which he then let slip, softening the
blow a notch by adding, "not at this time." Possibly, Denny considered,
the old mayor deliberately overplayed the government hand as a way
to tip the loggers off, to let them know the lay of the land. Always they
were advised to give it five or ten more years, to place their faith in
the god of patience, that sooner or later a new highway and with it a
new bridge would be constructed, but never, it seemed, did that loose
timeframe get reduced, not even after years went by. Not that the loggers wanted to wait that long anyway. The mayor's remarks convinced
everyone concerned that the government had made its decision before
the meeting was called, that the whole point was to mollify those who
held to a different opinion, so they'd feel included and wait out another
five or ten in peace, and now Denny was on the spot.

"We know what we agreed to do," he said.

"We know, Denny," Xavier confirmed.

Samad studied his boots. He hated this. He knew that they needed
him for a very specific reason and wished that that was not true. He
felt an ache rise through the bones of his chest, as if cracking across his
breastplate to prepare him for a surgical procedure, which was unnecessary perhaps with the end result in doubt. He wanted to run, yet hated
being such a coward. He was afraid, too, of what his wife might think.

"If anybody wants out, then now's the time."

"This is no time to back down," André objected.

Denny reeled him in quickly. "That's not your decision," he admonished him. "Every man makes that choice for himself. You don't get to make it for me or for Samad or for Xavier. Every man is on his own in this. But now's the time. After this, that's it. Whoever is in is in. Whoever is out is out."

"You can't be out," André fumed.

"Anybody," Denny reminded him, and his anger showed, "can be out."

"Well, I'm in," André told them.

Neither Xavier nor Samad shared his enthusiasm, but if this was the time to back down, then neither possessed the wherewithal to do that. They didn't know how. Samad was the least committed, the worrywart, the one among them prone to imagining the worst. But he was not a man who made decisions on his own. Even when Denny gave him an opening as wide as his truck was long he could not bring himself to step through it. Denny knew that, but he also knew that if Xavier decided to call it quits, then Samad might find the courage to join him. He and André couldn't go it alone, just the two of them. So in a way their gambit was entirely up to Xavier. Only Xavier didn't know that.

The large man was taking his time to decide. André wasn't worried but Denny knew why, because André believed he could bully anybody into anything. Denny wasn't going to allow him to do that. Xavier needed to make up his own mind and he would be free to do so without being intimidated or else he'd call this whole thing off himself.

"I've thought about it a lot," Xavier said.

"What the fuck is there to think about?" André demanded to know.

"Hold it," Denny said. "There's a ton to think about here."

"Like what?"

"Like jail time, André. Like fucking prison." Then he shrugged, as if confounded by a thought that ominous popping out of his mouth. "It's a possibility." He couldn't imagine being caught. Accused, possibly, but not tried, let alone convicted. He'd read statistics in a newspaper article that arson was the most successful major crime, and the least prosecuted, in part because the evidence normally burned away. He was determined to improve on those stats, although there were no guarantees.

His cautionary words not only silenced André Gervais but gave Xavier's deliberations more traction. Unlike Samad, he had the internal fortitude to join in with them or to stand up against them, but he did not have the acuity to strike the right course of action. Denny knew that about his friend. He told him one time that his Achilles' heel was his brain but Xavier didn't feel insulted because he didn't know what Denny meant. "Do you think we should do this, Denny?" he asked. He wanted support.

Denny refused to make up another man's mind for him. Not for something this risky.

"Somebody has to do something," Denny told him. "To be honest, I wish it didn't have to be me or you. But you have a choice. I've got a choice, too."

Xavier seemed upset. He wanted this to be simple, yet it was more complicated than he could handle. He strolled away from them, his back to his friends and to the sun, and they thought he was going to check his tires one more time when he turned around and although nothing changed and nothing could be predicted, he said, "Look. I'm in. That's that."

Samad wished he'd said nothing, Denny could tell, but the small man nodded, and put his hands in the hip pockets of his jeans and spit. These men were his friends. He said, "I'm in, too."

"Don't sound so goddamned enthusiastic," André admonished them both.

"They don't have to be," Denny censored him.

André accepted that, and then he said, "You didn't actually say yourself, Denny."

He blew out a gust of air. He really wished that someone else could do this, take the risk, be responsible for executing their plan. This is what he'd never be able to explain, thinking at that moment of his brother and father. And of his wife. They'd be disappointed in him. This wouldn't be done to hurt them, or spite them, or to prove himself in their company. He hoped they'd never find out. This was not about being the younger brother becoming his own man. He accomplished that on a daily basis, didn't he, at home and on the job, being the breadwinner and the best damn dad he could be? This was about leading these guys, whom he loved and cared for, too. They counted on him, every day, and because they counted on him he led them. Angry men who felt humiliated were capable of surrendering to their baser instincts, their bad impulses. As far as Denny was concerned, he was doing what was wrong to prevent something far worse from taking place.

"I'm in charge. That's the deal. If you don't like it, bug out now. If you accept it, then I'll decide exactly when we go. You'll do what I say. Period. Samad, you ready yet?"

Samad gave him a thumbs-up. "Already done," he let him know. Which was good. Denny forewarned him to be prepared well in advance so as to diminish any connection back to their group.

"You won't get much notice. Just be ready to go," Denny advised them, and held out his fist. Each man tapped it, then he and the others returned to their rigs and restarted the big diesels. They looked calm. They moved slowly. But each man's heart was thumping. Then they drove down the dusty road.

∎ ∎ ∎

"Hop on."

To climb aboard a flimsy, zippy scooter with an elderly driver wearing an outrageously brazen helmet felt a trifle daunting.

"Where to?" Tara asked. She squinted under a shaft of bright sunlight. She was outside without sunglasses as scudding clouds cast a pall.

"The graveyard."

"Oh! Sounds lovely."

"Sarcasm does not become you, young lady."

"If it makes me any less a *lady*, I'm all for it. But if you prefer, a trip to the graveyard sounds creepy."

Mrs. McCracken had obviously planned the afternoon outing, given that a spare helmet sat tidily strapped to the passenger seat. Tara put it on, snapped the clasp, then swung a leg up and over and made herself comfortable on the scooter's small rear seat. Reaching behind her back she grabbed the chrome bars.

"Not too fast, okay?" she pleaded.

"Oh hush."

They were off.

Stores, including Potpourri, were closed on Mondays as the train didn't run. She should probably be sprucing up her new home now that she was moved in, and she was making progress on that front. Yet Tara felt undermined, her familiar focus wreaked by a restlessness of spirit and a new and unrequited longing. Justifications came readily to hand: she'd not run away from job and home merely to lock herself into a similar manic routine. So she strolled along in search of whatever might buoy her spirits on a cloudy day, and realized soon enough that her feet were propelling her towards the old covered bridge. She thought it a worthy destination after the prior evening's debate. The bridge stood proud and was strikingly attractive—she'd not given it sufficient attention since her arrival, she supposed, especially considering how fixated others were on its stature. She was about to turn off the sidewalk onto the dirt path that was the riverside walk when the indomitable Mrs. McCracken intercepted her foray. She gathered that the old gal intended to snatch her from her apartment if she wasn't claimed off the street.

Mrs. McCracken wasn't joking about their destination. The ride to the cemetery was no quick jaunt and gave Tara sporadic cause to be terrified. Winding roads, potholed pavement, steep hills to climb. The scooter whined loudly, objecting to the day's extra weight. The pair made it to the top without the engine stalling, although Mrs. McCracken acknowledged the battle. "Thank goodness you're only a wisp of a thing."

"You're wispier."

"Thank goodness for that, too."

"Now what?"

"The graveyard, dear. It's worth a visit."

From the small parking lot they climbed farther on foot. A breezy day, with showers in the forecast, and each woman put a hand to her hair from time to time. Fighting a gust, Tara turned to face the wind a moment, allowing it to blow her hair back over her head, and in doing so saw for the first time above the canopy of trees the astonishing view from this altitude. She stood still before the rolling hills and snatches of speckled farmland. Mrs. McCracken, a few strides ahead, returned to take in the vista herself. While intimately familiar to her, she never grew tired of the pastoral scene.

"A fine place, don't you think, to spend eternity?" she asked after a few moments.

"What's your middle name?" Tara replied.

The older woman gazed at the younger. "You don't even know my first."

"Sure I do. Alice."

Seemingly without any cue, like birds turning in tandem, they both resumed their walk up the grassy hill to the rows of tombstones and markers.

"I don't tell people it," Mrs. McCracken said. "Not the middle one."

"Why not?"

"What's yours?"

"Tara. Tara-Anne, actually. Hyphenated."

"It's not much of a mystery then, for you."

"Yours is?"

"Why do you want to know?"

"It's a hobby of mine. Learning middle names. I find them"—a gang of goldfinch darted between trees and her eyes jumped with the dash of bright yellow—"not revealing exactly . . . but I think differently about people when I know their second name. Take somebody who's a Tom. There're so many Toms. Then you find out that plain Tom's middle name is Augustine, or Percival, or merely Michael, and you realize that he's not just another Tom. The parents who named Tom also held to a further idea or impression for their lad. Sometimes a grand notion. Sometimes a qualifier in some strategic way. So he's Tom, but with an added distinction, or at least a different note. We might detect that our ordinary Tom has a secret, that he derives from surprising expectations." She smiled, and added shyly, "As an example."

"Are you planning on babies, dear?" Ascending with slow, deliberate, thoughtful strides, Mrs. McCracken tucked a hand into the crook of Tara's elbow, and climbed on.

"Not in the near future, if that's what you're asking. Is it what you think? That I have babies on the brain? Naming them? A few things need to fall into place before that goes down."

"Something in what you're saying seems right to me. Initially, just about everybody is somebody's romantic notion. Sometimes, often enough, somebody's *unexpected* romantic notion."

"That's it. Anyway, I like to find that stuff out. Now, tell me yours."

"Better than that. I'll show you."

She had a gravestone in mind.

Plain and weathered, the marker stood as an upright slab no more than eighteen inches high. The birth date went back over a century.

"Grandmother?" Tara asked.

"*Great*-grandma. I never knew her." Winifred Alice Beauchamp.

"Your middle name is Winifred? Oh, poor you."

"Guess again."

"You use your middle name, like me?"

"Nope." She seemed quite proud of this contest.

Tara's mouth dropped open an instant. "Beauchamp? Your middle name is Beauchamp?"

"If you tell anyone, I'll know it was you. Do you like it?"

"Oh yes. Very impressive." She gave her a knowing look. "Figures."

Mrs. McCracken took the remark as a compliment. "It's of no particular use in my daily life. But it's going on my gravestone, absolutely. Up here, among these strangers and old relations, I'll wear it proudly. In terms of connecting the dots, if someone wants to do a who's who of Wakefield ghosts, it'll be helpful."

"You're a character."

"Am I?" the older woman asked. "And you, young lady."

"What about me?"

"You have some explaining to do."

"Ah . . . and because you feel that I have some explaining to do, you invited me to a graveyard. This makes sense how?"

To turn her, Mrs. McCracken grasped her quite forcibly by an arm. The cemetery stood as a clearing on a hilltop, a swath amid the trees that was not flat, and undulated softly. Several rows of graves ascended gradually, markers on the surface of the ground standing out like steps. "First," she answered with a deliberate aura of mystery, "let me show you in what august company I shall spend my eternity."

"You're morbid today."

"Not true. I'm feeling my oats."

Farther along, she paused before the modest gravesite of a famous man, who'd won a Nobel Peace Prize and been prime minister.

"Did you know, he's not from around here?"

"So why's he here now?"

"For the view."

"Seriously?"

"Oh, the official PM's summer residence is relatively close by. That's how he happened to find this place. So he stipulated that he wanted to be buried on this hill. He found the view enchanting."

"It is that."

"You could be buried here, too. Then you'd have the PM as a neighbour."

"And you as a neighbour, too, I suppose."

"Not to mention my cats. Come look."

In a corner of the clearing, well apart from the graves for humans, a pet cemetery was segregated off for the remains of cats and dogs, turtles and hamsters, Billy the parakeet and Marco the wandering python who got run over by a logging truck. "The poor driver nearly ran off the road trying to avoid him, but in the end he couldn't. The snake was a pet that escaped a summer cottage. He wore a knitted orange vest. I'm serious. I attended the funeral, actually. The owner was a student of mine as a lad. He was heartbroken."

Amid the flowers and stones and carved wood plaques were the

names of Horatio, Gilmore, and Frances, three cats from Mrs. Mc-
Cracken's earlier life, "before Buckminster. Another two went missing,
silly things. Grease spots on a highway, no doubt."

"Gross!"

"Life has sad realities, my dear."

"So," Tara deduced, "this is why you come here. To visit your cats."

"Do I look like a dingbat to you?" she protested. "No, don't you
dare answer that. It's true, I tend to the cats' graves, but principally I
come here to care for my husband's."

Tara felt a shiver unrelated to the premises. "Sorry. I assumed . . ."

"Do I come across as an old spinster?"

"I wouldn't say so. But you've made your own way in life, it seems.
I think I knew that but I'd forgotten."

"I was widowed young. I call myself *Mrs.* in good faith, dear. Yes,
it's so sad. If I seem like an old biddy who's been on her own throughout her lifetime—"

"You don't!"

"—it's because it's true. My poor Robby was only twenty-seven."

Tara linked the length of her arm with hers. "An accident?"

"I wish." Mrs. McCracken spoke more quietly, in deference to
their closeness and to the solemnity of the memory. "Might have been
less . . . *enraging* that way. A brain aneurism, dear. Something in his
head misfired and burst and he was dead and gone, as quick as a wink.
No prior warning. No final word. Just *poof*! Alive one second, dead the
next. A doctor said it might have happened at any time, but that it was
bound to happen, sooner if not later. My Robby was a walking time
bomb. Too bad I didn't know it earlier on. I might have been a better
wife. Or maybe I'd have set my sights on becoming a mother instead of
putting it off." She waved her free hand before her face as if to ward off
flies. "Perfect nonsense, of course. If I'd known his brain was going to

explode one day, I might never have married the poor fellow, practical gal that I am. Now isn't that a sad commentary?"

"Now you *are* being morbid. I know you're teasing me so don't bother."

"Smarty-pants. Let me show you where he rests."

For the first time that day, Tara did not particularly want to go with her, but acquiesced, and standing over the grave felt less uneasy. Mrs. McCracken bent to support pink and reddish annuals by retrieving earth that washed away, and brushed off dirt that splashed onto the tombstone in a downpour.

"There you are, my dear," Mrs. McCracken said, and it took a few seconds for Tara to realize that she was not talking to her. On her knees, the attentive widow looked up at her new young friend.

"So what's your first name, dear, since you get by with your middle?"

"Raine."

"Like the weather?"

"With an *e* on the end. But otherwise, yes. I'm a gloomy day on two legs."

The women laughed. Tara never made that reference before and didn't know why she did it now, although the day was gloomy enough and they were standing in a graveyard. Mrs. McCracken was willing to accept a hand up and struggled back to her feet.

"Well then, Rain-*e*—Rainy I should call you."

"The *e* is silent, but stick with Tara. If you don't, I'll call you Beauchamp."

"Oh, bother. But now let me show you something, Raine Tara. After that we'll talk. You are going to tell me why you're on the run."

"Who said I'm on the run?"

"Do you want to be called Rainy?"

Tara's initial defence was to cross her arms. While her posture was now self-protective, she tried to mount an argument. "A woman on the run might not want to say why. If I was on the run, as you put it, I might not even know why. Or know how to explain it."

"I agree. Then that's what we'll talk about."

Mrs. McCracken guided Tara a few stones down from her husband's final resting place. "See her?"

"Is this what you'll do to me if I don't talk?" Tara teased.

"You jest. But if she's resting peacefully now, she can thank me for that. You might hear this story if you haven't already."

Tara read the name and the inscription. She and the deceased were born less than two years apart.

"Poor child," Mrs. McCracken said solemnly.

"Who, me?" Tara asked.

"No. Her. A car crash victim. Sadly, we have too many in this cemetery. A small town's all-too-common anguish, I'm afraid. She was off to a city. Toronto, or, no, Hamilton, I think."

"That's so hard on the family."

"It was, but it also got worse."

"Worse? Than death? Really?"

"Oh, it was a bother. Something came up, to do with the other car and liability, and the insurance company wanted to know her exact injuries to figure out if she was wearing a seat belt because that information wasn't include in the original report. The point is, her corpse was exhumed and examined. When she was returned to the ground after that rude awakening, the forensic scientist in charge forgot, or so she claimed later on, she forgot to include her head."

"Oh lovely." Tara herself didn't believe that the ill-treatment of bodies mattered a whole hill of beans. The dead were dead. Respect ought to be accorded the living, though, and it would be mortifying to foresee that a dreadful end to one's life would not constitute the final humiliation. This woman once lived, and so deserved basic, civilized respect. If she was in court on the matter, that's what she would argue. "How did that come out?"

"The scientist happened to mention it. She was guiding a TV crew through her lab one day and somebody said something, and she said, 'Oh, that's Maria Sentis.' I saw it on TV. I knew where her grave was located, just down from my Robby's, so why was her cranium not in it? The thought made me ill. So I put up a major stink."

"I bet you did."

"I did. Her poor family came apart at the seams and moved away after her passing. They offered me some moral support. Do you know, that scientist, who has more skulls to play with than she can count, is an avid collector? She did not want to give Miss Sentis her head back. She claimed that it was hers now, and when that made people mad she argued that it belonged to science. Then she tried to say that I was an old ninny with silly superstitions and that Miss Sentis did not miss her head one whit, but in any case her skull was staying put, in her lab. The woman's public relations skills weren't the best, I'm afraid. She tried to make me out to be a nincompoop who wanted to put mummies back in the pyramids, which I told the press when they came calling wasn't such a bad idea, but in any case the cranium of a young woman who lost her life prematurely belonged with the rest of her, that we, as a society, with our fast cars and dangerous drivers, owed her that."

Tara was on Mrs. McCracken's side in this. "What did the scientist say?"

"No."

"She said no? Just no? What did you do?"

Mrs. McCracken's grin seemed impish, a break from the gravity of their discussion. "Tara, by the time I was done with her, that scientist wished that she was the headless one. I vilified the poor woman. She summered in a cottage up here but it's sold. She accused me of running her out of town but I never did. I swear."

Tara enjoyed the tale. "So you got the skull back."

"You bet I did. Not only that, I made her put a name to every skull in her lab, in case anybody else wanted a friend's or a relative's head back. She rued the day she came up against me, that's for sure."

Tickled, Tara let the last of her laughter subside. "You're a wonder," she said. "But the part about not going up against you—am I to worry?"

Tara moderated her remarks with a broad smile and a sparkle in her eye, yet Mrs. McCracken took the charge seriously. She bobbed her chin and squinted at her. "You, Rainy Day Tara-Anne Cogshill, have some explaining to do. Don't think that you can escape me. I'm going to know where you came from and why even if it kills me."

The younger woman took a deep breath. "How far will this go?"

Mrs. McCracken pulled an imaginary zipper closed over her lips. "Seriously?" she asked.

"Tara," Mrs. McCracken vowed, and crooked their elbows together to commence their walk and talk together, "I'll take it to the grave."

■　■　■

RYAN SCRUNCHED FARTHER DOWN IN his car seat. He knew how this could look but didn't care. He put in extra hours, paid and unpaid, and his employers and the citizens of Wakefield were aware of that. A very occasional nap by the side of the road then was not a mortal offence.

Not that he napped. Nor was it the idea. His eyes stayed open despite his desire to crash for a bit, and he adjusted the mirror to see who might come up behind him. While he remained in danger of falling asleep, and on any other day he might easily have done so, too much agitated his synapses for that to happen this afternoon. Really he looked more like a policeman trying to conceal his presence for surveillance purposes, albeit in a marked car, than a cop goofing off on the job. As further evidence of that, more than his cop radio was turned on. A CB brought in sporadic communication from deep woods loggers.

He knew where his brother was working today so chose this road to monitor, listening in to the crackling radio even while nodding off. When Denny emerged he'd drive this route and Ryan evaluated the pros and cons of stopping him, something he'd done only once, back then to give him the news that their mother had passed away. Over the years, his brother edged above the limit on his radar gun a few times, but nothing extreme, and if he stopped him today it wouldn't be to fine him. They just needed to talk. Denny would protest that he was hauling logs, that downtime and conversation cost him cold hard cash. Mentally, Ryan rehearsed a response. "I could talk to you here and now, or later at home in front of your wife and kids. You choose."

Not that he wanted to have the conversation in either location. Yet theirs should be a secret talk with no one from the public noticing, and he presumed that Denny wouldn't want his wife within earshot either.

A few cars passed by, but the first vehicle of interest that came down the road was neither one of these nor a logging truck, but Mrs. McCracken on her Vespa GTV 250 speeding along at a good clip. She looked out of control. Secretly, Ryan wished he could have a ride on that thing himself, to see how it ran. Not a motorcycle by any means, but it seemed nimble. He calculated that coming from that direction she'd been up to the cemetery, a fairly frequent trip. Ryan kept his head down as she went by, but raised it up again as the vehicle's passenger, hanging on by gripping the chrome backrest, glanced behind her at his car.

Stunned by her beauty.

Her hair flew out from under a helmet, as if waving. Waving.

Ryan hesitated, but nowhere near long enough to think this through. He started the squad car, pulled out onto the highway, and went after them. Along the way, he turned on his revolving lights, although he decided that the siren would be overkill.

Mrs. McCracken pulled over.

Ryan parked on the shoulder of the road behind the scooter.

He thought about running the licence plate, but that was a reflex, a silly one in this circumstance. He took a deep breath and stepped out of the car instead, putting on his cap as he emerged.

Mrs. McCracken watched him walk up in the rearview mirror that hung off her left handlebar. She lifted the visor of her helmet and whispered to Tara, "I was not speeding."

"Not by too much," the young woman countered. "He's being picky."

"It's the extra weight!" Mrs. McCracken defended. "It's hard to go slow down a hill."

"Now you tell me. I could have walked."

"Hello, Mrs. McCracken. How are you today?" Ryan asked brightly.

"I'm fine, Officer O'Farrell. Nice of you to stop me for a chat. Have you caught the criminals who invaded my home?"

He smiled, and shot a quick glance at Tara, who was removing her helmet and did not return the eye contact.

"Not yet, ma'am. They're still on the loose, I'm afraid."

"I have every confidence that you'll leave no stone unturned."

Tara combed her hair, knotted by the wind, with her fingers.

"You can count on it, but that's not why I stopped you."

"I do hope that you are not about to insinuate that I was speeding.

As you can see, I have a witness. She will vouch for me. And yes, I will make a federal case out of this. I don't care what your radar gun says, it's faulty."

Tara leaned forward to whisper privately in her ear. "Remember what I do for a living. Or used to do. I'm an officer of the court. I won't lie for you."

Ryan could not hear the whisper, although he wished that he could. He waited patiently for their secret chat to conclude.

"I'm not out here on speed control. My radar gun wasn't turned on."

"Oh," Mrs. McCracken said, assessing the news then recalibrating her defence, which now seemed unnecessary. "Oh."

Tara was the first to recover. "Then why were you out here?"

He was glad that she posed the question, as it gave him a chance to look directly at her. Proximity only enhanced the woman's beauty and he loved her eyes and felt a knee nearly buckle.

"Things to think about. I needed the quiet time."

"Then why did you stop us?" Her question was pointed, cutting.

"Because," Ryan started, boldly at first, but he quickly felt the air in his balloon deflate. He looked away to recover, then back at her. "Because I wanted to meet you."

Tara snapped a look at him then, her curiosity heightened, but she also felt a familiar defensive mechanism take charge. She paused before speaking, to let both sentiments subside, and relaxed on the seat. She glanced back at the squad car. The revolving cherries were still flashing.

Mrs. McCracken twisted around to observe her reaction.

"What," Tara asked the cop, still facing away, "no siren?"

Ryan grinned. "I considered it, but didn't want to scare anybody."

She liked that answer. She snapped her head back and poked her chin towards Mrs. McCracken. "Does he have a reputation for this sort of thing?"

"He does now."

That made Tara grin, too. Ryan chuckled under his breath.

"I'm sorry," he said. "I've seen you about town. I know that my brother mentioned me and I was worried that my dad might have plans to do so as well."

"What?"

"It's insane. Family. You can't live with them and, well . . . So I was hoping to meet you before they got on your case. Really. This is not standard procedure. I just wanted to say hi."

Tara was more than intrigued, although she wished she didn't feel so jumpy. He was a cop, which did not impress her, but he was also damned cute and this meeting smacked of being borderline off-the-wall romantic. "Hi," she said. She stuck out her hand, needing to do something. "I'm Tara."

"She's Tara," Mrs. McCracken jumped in. "This is Ryan O'Farrell, dear, Wakefield's finest."

Ryan took Tara's hand to shake but now was staring at the older woman with his mouth slightly agape.

"Oh dear," she said. "Did I get it wrong? You're Denny."

"No. You got it right. That's why I'm in shock."

"Oh my. I didn't even think about it. It just popped out."

"Hi, Tara," Ryan said to the woman he so wanted to meet, who'd not disappointed him as yet with a squeaky voice or a vulgar tongue or through any indication of innate stupidity. On the contrary, she seemed, on first impression, to be as bright as she was beautiful, and conducted herself through this odd meeting with humour and charm. Élan, even. "I'm Ryan."

"Ryan," she said, and finally slipped her hand loose.

"I'm free this evening, Tara, and I wonder if you might be as well. Short notice, I know. If so, I wonder if you would care to have dinner with me? I'm sure that Mrs. McCracken will vouch for my character."

"I will do no such thing," she stipulated. Over her shoulder, she added, "Such a pill in school, dear."

"But would you have dinner with him, if you were me?" Tara asked her, in a way teasing them both.

To gauge her reply, Mrs. McCracken looked the policeman over, then confided in Tara, "He's cute enough."

Tara, laughing, briefly buried her face in Mrs. McCracken's shoulder. For the first time she was embarrassed and emerged blushing. She covered herself by putting her helmet back on.

"Okay, okay," she said. "Fine. Seven? Pick me up outside Potpourri?"

"Delighted," Ryan said.

"Yeah," Tara said. She found both his grin and his renewed confidence attractive. "Delighted."

Mrs. McCracken was revving her engine. "Are we free to go, Officer?"

Grinning, Ryan waved them on their way. As they sped off and he walked back to his car, he stopped himself from pumping his fist in the air. But under his breath he did express, *Yes!*

■ ■ ■

FIRST IN, LAST OUT.

The rigs parked forward into a holding area, then the last truck to arrive was the first to back down to the loading station, and the first to then be free to go. Today the road was clear so they drove out immediately and Denny was the last to be loaded and released.

Dust from his predecessors hung in the air as he sped down the narrow gravel road. Light branches swished against the front bumpers and occasionally smacked his windshield.

He spotted a hawk at the top of a dead birch. Then the bird caught sight of him right through the windshield. In a vague way, he felt hunted.

At a straight section that formed a shallow valley, descending gently then rising, he began to slow. His habit was to speed up here but this time he geared down. At the top of the low hill, before his line-of-sight became obstructed by a bend and a dip, he spotted something, but didn't know what. The closer he got the more anomalous it appeared, as if some strange unearthly animal challenged him, then the image became perfectly clear but equally bizarre. In the centre of the road, in the wake of the three logging trucks that recently went on ahead, blazed a fire.

Denny rapidly double-clutched down through the gears. Then braked.

His rig lurched to a stop.

He waited as dust swirled up around his cab. He couldn't comprehend this. His diesel belched and coughed and remained boisterous in idle.

A collection of small dry branches had been piled and set ablaze.

His eyes darted to the right. He distinguished movement there. Then out of the woods strode a scantily clothed man, smoking.

In climbing down from his cab, Denny took his tire iron with him. He could make a show of nonchalantly tapping his tires but now held a weapon.

Skootch took up a position near and behind the fire and sucked on his joint. Denny went around and stood by his left front bumper and silently stared at him. Then Skootch flicked his miniscule roach into the flames.

"Nice of you to drop by," the tall, skinny, unclad man said.

"You're the one trespassing," Denny pointed out.

Skootch invested in an elaborate shrug, as though to convey his regal lassitude. "It's a free forest. So, Denny, you pitched around my third baseman. How come?"

"Pure hunch."

"Hunch, hunh?"

"I didn't like his haircut."

"Too bad. I wanted to see him hit. I still don't know if he can."

"Don't you? The game was on the line, Skootch. I played it safe."

"Probably a good call. I'm counting on you to play it safe." He parked his right hand under his left armpit. "Do you know who Stradivari is, Denny?"

The trucker made himself more comfortable. He couldn't risk driving over the flames until they subsided and he didn't have the means to extinguish them himself. He moved close to the centre of his truck and propped himself on a narrow shelf of bumper and crossed his arms. He deliberately let the tire iron hang down his side in a manner that left it visible but not otherwise threatening.

"You're holding me up, Skootch. I know that you have no concerns about time or money, but you're taking both away from me."

"Sorry to hear that, Den. This fire . . ." The man in the weathered vest and skimpy bikini-like bottoms waved his free hand as if the gesture constituted an explanation. "Spontaneous combustion."

"If that's your story."

"Sticking to it, yeah. Stradivari, Denny. Any thoughts?"

"Violins."

"Ah! Denny. You never cease to amaze me, man. Who would think that out here, on this dusty old fire road—which is aptly named today, don't you think—a trucker, a drinking man, a pretty fine third baseman to boot—great hit the other night, by the way, that was rank—"

"What do you want, Skootch?"

"Immaterial, Denny. What I want. He came into woods like these, do you know this? He walked through woods like these—"

"Stradivari."

"Antonio Stradivari, yeah, maker of the Stradivarius violin. Woods like these, Denny. Do you know what he'd do? This was the secret of his mad genius, this is why he was able to make violins that've never been duplicated for their quality or sound."

Denny waited.

"Do you want to know that secret or not, Denny?"

"I presume you'll tell me, Skootch, whether or not I want to know."

"Why would you *not* want to know this? Aren't you curious?"

He looked down, then up, smiling now. "I'm all ears, Skootch."

"He spoke to the trees."

"Sure he did."

"He talked to the trees, Denny. No mere tree hugger, our Antonio. He *asked* the trees, I kid you not, he asked who among them desired to be a violin."

"Volunteer trees would put up their hands, I suppose."

"Something like that, Denny. Something like that. They communicated back to him, and that's how he knew which tree to cut down."

"Kind of difficult for any of them to run away, I suppose."

Skootch stepped to one side of the fire to elude smoke.

"Among themselves, the trees chose who'd make the best violin."

"Save those stories for your groupies, Skootch. I'm sure your tales are worth a lot of tits and ass to you."

The tall, skinny man tugged on an earring, musing. "Wood is vulnerable, Denny. Trees are vulnerable. You should know this. Whole

196

forests can vanish with a lightning stroke. You know that much. I asked myself, just like Stradivari asked the forest, 'Who do I speak to if I want to protect what needs to be protected?' The answer came back, holy, irrefutable. 'Talk to Denny O'Farrell.' As if God was speaking to me, I swear."

"Oh, you talk to God now?"

"As if, Denny. As if. Same difference. I talked to the forest. And the forest said, 'Go, have a pleasant chat with Denny O'Farrell. He's your man.' I just want to remind you that even a trucker driving down a back road is vulnerable. I wanted to make that point. Tell me I've made my point, Denny, and we can clear this fire away. You can get on with your day's work, and I can get on with life."

In his gaze, Denny relayed a variety of emotional responses, many more subtle than his underlying agitation. "I appreciate the intervention, Skootch."

"Good."

"I'll give you this one. For old time's sake and because we both play ball. A man who plays ball can't be so bad. But if you ever threaten me again, I feel compelled to promise you that it's the last threat you'll make in reasonable health. Plus you can kiss the hardball season goodbye. Maybe someday you'll recover enough for slow pitch. Mostly, you'll be nothing but aches and pains."

"Don't be that way, Denny. We see eye to eye, don't you realize that yet?"

"On what, pray God Almighty, do we see eye to eye?"

Skootch quit the Napoleon pose and entwined his arms over his chest. Perhaps caused by the warmth of the crackling fire thin streaks of perspiration stained his cheeks. "Think about it. I believe that a forest needs to be protected, and I will do what I need to do when the time comes to protect that forest. Or any forest. You have similar concerns in your life, and you are willing to do what needs to be done. Your job, for instance. Providing for that big family of yours. Isn't that right? We see eye to eye on protecting what we believe is necessary. That makes us more alike than you know. It's just too bad that we disagree on what's necessary. Otherwise, Denny, we'd carry on as best friends. Don't you think so? Be honest now. I know that you're not the enemy you pretend to be."

Denny stood and stretched a little, not a stance that showed him to be itching for a fight, but neither was it a body language that indicated any backing down. "This is where I want us to agree, Skootch. I want that fire cleared away without you burning the woods down."

"Denny, Denny, I've come prepared for that." He stepped closer, bravely. "That's what I hope you'll take away from this meeting. The knowledge that I come prepared. I am prepared. You need to take that into your deliberations, whatever they may be. I'm not threatening, Denny. I'm just saying. For every action, there is a reaction. It's a law of physics and it's a law of the freaking universe. In life, there are consequences. You have to consider them. I know things didn't go your way last night, that that might cause you to do something rash. A rash O'Farrell is not a pretty sight to see. Think of this as a preemptive strike, my way of asking you to shape up and fly right."

The two men stared at each other. Then Skootch broke off the contact and went back into the woods. He was gone ten seconds and Denny was thoroughly mystified. He reemerged with a rake and a mid-sized fire extinguisher. First he broke the fire down.

"So it was the haircut?" Skootch asked.

"That was the tip-off. He's not one of your kind. That's why I walked him."

Then Skootch sprayed the timbers with white foam and the flames went out. Denny didn't wait for him to clear the charred debris away, although the skinny man seemed willing to do that, too. He climbed back into his cab and drove his rig over the smouldering fire and on into the shaded forest light.

He drove carefully, under his preferred limit, a deliberate device so that the anger ripe in his chest would not be steering this mammoth rig, nor would the full-blown temper inside him be stepping on the gas.

■ ■ ■

HOME, MRS. MCCRACKEN PULLED OUT her special paper from the drawer in her writing desk. Pastel daisies cascaded down the left margin. She was careful to make the date legible. "On such documents, Buck," she reminded her cat, "the date—whichever is the latest—is exceedingly important." She made notations on a pad beside her, then did a proper version, in elegant cursive, onto the sheet. When she wrote, "of sound mind and body," she warned Buck not to laugh.

15

A mere fingernail of gibbous moon would rise, but later, while in the interim the night remained dark. Clothing they wore blended with the deepening shadows. Riding on the bed of Denny's truck, Xavier Lapointe started out standing until Denny stopped and poked his head out the window to tell him that he made the pickup look more conspicuous that way, so he sat on the metal floor, only partially out of sight but drawing no particular attention to himself. André Gervais rode in the cab and repeatedly wiped his brow with the top of his ball cap then put the ball cap back on. Then he took it off again. Denny was expecting his pal to be talkative and hoped he might lighten the mood, but André, the aggressive gabber among them, turned laconic. They stopped outside Samad Mehra's house, where they witnessed their initial mistake.

The trucker twisted in the doorway to kiss his wife good night.

"Oh shit," André noted.

"How ignorant can a man get?" Denny pondered aloud and watched as Jocelyn Mehra gave them a friendly wave, which answered his question.

Xavier leapt off the back of Denny's truck to drive in Samad's. Denny rolled the side window down to call Samad over as he strolled across his lawn from his house.

"Hey there, Denny," Samad said. The man was self-consciously grinning, as though he was trying to get a joke he couldn't unravel yet.

"You got Alzheimer's now?" André asked him.

"Says who?" Samad asked him back. "Why?"

"What was that about?" Denny inquired. He leaned forward and André leaned back so that they could both to talk to him through the open passenger-side window.

"Huh? What was what about what?"

"Samad, your wife, she knows about this? You told me she wasn't going to be home."

"Don't be stupid. Her plans changed. We're going bowling, I told her."

"Bowling? Where exactly? Never mind that I don't bowl, but where're we supposed to go bowling, Samad, where nobody will see us? We can't be noticed because we won't actually be bowling."

The man shrugged, losing his grin, now worried about this inquisition. He glanced at the other two men, one inside the truck and the other back where his own vehicle stood parked, to see if they were understanding what he obviously did not. "In the city, I guess. What's so wrong with that?"

"In the city. Oh yeah? Joce must've asked you what bowling alley we're going to tonight—in the city."

"I didn't tell her that. What's the problem?"

"You don't know? Next time, kiss her good-bye in the kitchen. Or let us know ahead of time that she's still home."

"Fine! Bug off. Leave me alone. Anyway, what next time? There's not going to be a next time. Smart guy, what did you tell Val?"

"I'm doing extra maintenance on my rig."

"Oh." Samad seemed downcast. "That's good, Denny. That's a good one."

"Yeah, well. I should've gone over it with you."

This screwup, Denny decided, was not substantial enough to call off their gambit, although he wouldn't mind quitting on the spot and tossing their failure straight back in Samad's face. He stared out the window with his hands squeezing the steering wheel, then looked at Samad's worried sad-sack puss. The poor sod was clueless.

"Never mind," Denny said. "Let's go bowling."

■ ■ ■

IN HIS SQUAD CAR, RYAN drove his date home across the old covered bridge. They were having a good time, culminating in a playful intimacy at the lovers' leap on the opposite side of the river from the town site. Tara stopped him before they got too heated, so Ryan's expectations for the evening were properly governed. He'd be permitted to kiss her good night and allowed to take his time, but the final motion of the evening would be to say good night at the door to Potpourri.

Once on Main Street, though, the store close by, he suggested a nightcap, hoping to extend the evening.

"You're inviting yourself up? No," Tara said.

"Not what I meant. We could go to a bar."

She hesitated, but consented, and they drove past the gift shop to a nearby pub. The owner, usually an amiable guy, greeted them at the door with his hands on hips while shaking his head.

"What?" Ryan asked him.

"Ryan, seriously," he put to him, "do I need that thing parked outside my door?"

Both Ryan and Tara looked back, and saw the problem stirred up by a squad car parked outside a bar. Ryan was about to go back and move it when the owner chuckled and urged them inside. He was having them on. "Come on in. Enjoy yourselves. It's not like people are hanging off the rafters."

They entered, and Tara took note that wherever Ryan went in this town people seemed to like him, and that seemed to have nothing to do with his profession.

■ ■ ■

THE TWO FORD PICKUPS DEPARTED Samad's. Denny's led the way. He kept their speed down. He drove out of the keyhole residential development, out of the woods and onto the highway, then onto the narrow two-way into Wakefield proper. He stopped in the bumpy municipal parking lot on the edge of town and pulled into a spot on the gravel where he and André climbed out. He locked his truck using his key remote. They swung up onto the bed of Samad's truck and they both sat down and Denny tapped the side of the truck with his palm—Samad's cue to drive on. They headed back out the way they'd just come in and took the highway to skirt the edge of town, then they drove back in from the opposite side and in doing so approached the old covered bridge. By coming this way, they avoided driving through the centre of town. No one could say they'd been spotted there. Not one among them was a criminal or was ever an offender, but each understood what any crook instinctively believes, that no crime is worth committing unless it succeeds.

Denny wanted everything to run according to plan. More than anything else, he wanted to get away with this, but to do that he must expect the unexpected. He reminded himself to depend on the unknown as much as on any other factor.

Samad stopped near the bridge under a panoply of roadside trees.

Denny jumped down from the bed and Xavier skulked out from the cab looking miserable. He shot a glance at Denny, who nodded, then started walking uphill. The three men watched him go, climbing the grade to the bridge.

"Give him enough time," Denny said.

They knew to do that. Xavier walked across the bridge to control access on that side, and to signal them if someone was coming or to keep intruders away for their own sakes once the action commenced.

They didn't want to get anybody killed, especially not that.

On the truck bed, André rolled the forty-five-gallon barrel of fuel from the front to the rear, then secured it again with straps. He unscrewed the small cap on the top of the drum and inserted a manual fuel pump that screwed into the same hole as the cap and was deep enough to reach the barrel's base.

"Prime it," Denny instructed him.

André did so, and tipped the contents of a small bottle into the top of the pump. He revolved the lever until a little fluid spilled onto the ground. They could smell the gasoline now in the warm night air just as a breeze came up.

"You're an idiot, Samad," André said. He'd been holding the thought in and only now did he speak it, an outburst that proved he was nervous, too.

"Why am I an idiot?" Samad protested.

"Don't ask," Denny advised him. "You don't want to know."

"I want to know, but. Why am I an idiot?"

"We don't have the whole night to answer that question." Denny wanted to defuse any argument at this stage. He could kill André for bringing it up.

"Your wife knows who you're hanging out with tonight," André said.

"Oh," Samad said, as though he finally understood. Then he said, "So?" which proved he didn't.

"So tell her we decided not to go bowling," Denny decreed. He'd been thinking about this. "André told his wife he was going out for a drink, not bowling. And not with anybody in particular."

"Joce wouldn't let me drive if I told her that."

André uttered a little laugh.

"What?" Samad asked.

"Tell her I'm doing maintenance so we called off the bowling, we just forgot to tell you. Then you guys talked me into having a drink and you don't even know where we ended up. Some bar in the city. Tell her that because it's the truth. André, tell Xavier our new story when you catch up to him."

"Okay," André said.

"Okay, Samad?" Denny asked. He changed his tone. He recognized the problem here, that Samad was accustomed only to being honest, and was not at all practised in telling lies. He was less suited than any of them to criminal activity and had no experience at being either unscrupulous or deceptive. "See, none of us told our wives we were going bowling. None of us told our wives we were going anywhere with anybody in particular. Because the four of us are not supposed to be together tonight. Understand? There was no plan. Get it? No plan to get together. And tell Joce if she asks, or if the cops ask, that you were our designated driver tonight so you didn't have a drink. You just drove us to a bar and back. Okay?"

Samad was pouting, but he seemed to understand. "Yeah, sure," he said. Then he asked, "What cops? Your brother, you mean? Why would Ryan talk to us? He doesn't know anything."

Denny disregarded the question. "I'm going up to check on X," he said.

"Why would he talk to us?" Samad pressed on. "He won't, right?"

"Ryan might talk to anybody he can think of," André said, picking up on Denny's pacifying approach. "It won't mean much. It's his job."

Denny needed to be at a higher elevation to trace Xavier's progress. The bridge was 148 feet long, which took a while for a lumbering man to cross. Xavier was more than halfway over. He was not going slowly for him but not rushing either. Thankfully, no one else came along, and there were no vehicles. Late enough that the commerce of the town eased, yet early enough that the bars and restaurants weren't emptying out as yet. Denny pinched a mosquito just under his chin, then walked back under cover of the roadside woods to the truck.

He was thinking that if he were to do this over, he might not select Samad. He needed the fuel drum that he perpetually dragged around on the bed of his pickup, as if he was the kind of man who ventured off into the untamed woods beyond the boundaries of civilization to hunt or fish, either routinely or on a whim. Denny doubted that Samad hunted much and probably never fished, but he didn't doubt that Samad wanted people to believe that he did those things. Like everyone else, he was party to his personal insecurities. After he considered every angle, Denny knew that he couldn't ask any other person to carry a barrel of fuel on the bed of his truck, or do that himself, as it would be tantamount to a proclamation of guilt. He needed to rely on Samad, and now, as things turned out, on Samad's wife.

Walking back down the side of the road, he saw that he mistimed the moonrise, as an upper silver tip of the moon poked above a hilltop. Thin enough, therefore dim enough, to be of no particular consequence. Still, why did he mess that up? That should've been the easy part, accurately calculating the time of the moonrise. Now his confidence also waned.

He reached the others.

"Wait a minute or two—two, let's say. Xavier should be on the other side. Drive up to the edge of the bridge—"

"We know that," André said.

"I'm repeating it," Denny said, and he looked André in the eye and waited to see if he was about to give him any more lip. When André turned his gaze away and nodded, conceding, he said, "Watch for Xavier's signal. Don't you dare go across without it. You can't see what he sees over there. At that point, he's in charge, don't think otherwise. Samad, two things have to happen before you start across. You get Xavier's signal, and André says to go. Just one of those two is not good enough."

"I got it," Samad said. He was looking nervous. Perhaps the notion of two signals gave him hope that the whole operation might yet be called off. Denny supposed that everyone was secretly hoping for that, except, possibly, André.

They waited quietly then.

Denny wished that he still smoked although now was not the time even if he did. André still smoked, but not while he was hovering over an open drum containing forty-five gallons of gasoline.

Close to a minute went by when the headlights of a car appeared on their side of the bridge coming their way. Denny said, "Both of you get down, don't be seen," and he himself went around to crouch behind the truck. By looking under the chassis, Denny saw the vehicle, a small car, turn off, leaving them in the clear and in the dark once more. Denny returned to the driver's side of the pickup.

"Go," he said quietly, sternly.

Samad started the engine. André held on as the truck lurched forward.

Denny watched them walk up the incline a moment, then returned to the anonymity of the trees and scanned the darkened bridge.

■ ■ ■

IN HER FLIMSY WHITE NIGHTCLOTHES, Mrs. McCracken opened her outside door a crack to admit Buckminster. Unfettered, he slouched in, not certain that he agreed with her assessment that he was in for the night. She pulled the screen tight to the jamb to insert the hook in its eye, and even as she did so moths regrouped on the screen and a June bug out of season landed. Then she shut and latched the inside door, too.

"Done," she said.

Buckminster uttered an agreeable word and they both wandered through to the living room, where Mrs. McCracken returned to her cold cocoa.

"Something I cannot explain," she ruminated aloud, quietly at first, "about that girl. She intrigues me, Buck. I admit it. So few young women do. Really, I ought to harp. I'm inclined to harp, giving up a career like that, doing so little with a fine education. How odd, don't you think?" As she awaited her cat's reply, Mrs. McCracken was suddenly aware that she'd ceased talking under her breath and was now at full volume. She sipped more cocoa, then lowered her voice to a conspiratorial whisper between her and the feline. "But I sense that it's not tomfoolery, Buck. Her lot in life is to be a serious person who is also given to some distraction. Not an easy combination to live with. A rarity in this town, male or female, don't you think? But the rarest are the women. She is, undoubtedly, a serious person, with some distraction. Poor thing. I don't know what's to be done about her, having to bear life with such an onerous condition."

Buckminster circled his sofa pillow repeatedly, then quietly settled onto it. He yawned. Observed her intently.

"It's true. I really don't know what's to be done."

Finishing her cocoa, she set the glass down and listened to the tree frogs sing. Such a racket. She tried to hear right through their song, for in the heart of this night she was sensing a rhapsody so distant and refined that even the frogs ceased their chorus to attend. She listened.

"I know," she said. "It is that time."

She wasn't in the mood to go up to bed just yet, despite feeling sleepy.

Buckminster let his chin droop down. Momentarily, his eyes closed. As she sat there, hearing the ticking of her downstairs clock as the frogs went mute and detecting also a high, distant, inexplicable drone, Mrs. McCracken's chin also dipped forward. A ways off, down along the riverbank, a tied-up dog that she presumed, illogically, to be a mangy mutt barked thrice, the last sound to register with any acuity before she dropped off asleep in the comfort of her chair. The cat, across from her, also slept.

■ ■ ■

DENNY RAN, STUMBLED, THEN SPRINTED, breaking from the trees, shining a miniature flashlight, its beam dancing on the pickup's rear window. On the verge of shouting he restrained himself, noise a last resort. A risk to take only if they didn't see him. Samad caught the light slash across his mirror and braked suddenly, causing André to put a hand out to brace himself against the cab's roof.

"What the—?" André protested, too loudly for their circumstance. His words were cut off as he lost his balance and his chest struck the roofline.

"Keep your voice down," Denny hissed and continued his quick jog up to Samad's window. André bent down to listen in.

Denny took a moment to catch his breath.

"There's kids," he said.

"What?"

"Under the bridge. Toking up. I saw the flare from a joint."

"They're making out probably," Samad said.

"They better not be my kids," André said.

"That's not the point!" Denny flashed. "It doesn't matter whose kids they are. Or what they're smoking. We might kill them, you idiots."

"What do we do?" André asked.

Denny stepped onto the running board, clutching the inside of the doorframe and the outside mirror. "Drive across. Slowly. André, do nothing. Not now. Follow my lead when we're over there."

He took the time to think this through, but he was feeling lucky. This might have gone badly if he'd been late to spot them, or not seen the flares of their smokes at all. He didn't know if the others were feeling as he did now, but the seriousness of their work caused the blood in his veins, it felt like, to sink into his heels. Like a heavy tar. Then Samad stopped on the other side off the end of the bridge and Xavier didn't know what was going on as he walked quickly up.

Denny stepped down from the running board and whispered to Xavier, "Don't say a word."

"What would I say?" Xavier whispered back.

Denny stepped out onto the bridge. The three waiting men observed him in the breeze. A dim streetlamp down the road illuminated them, while shadows from the bridge's superstructure crisscrossed Denny. He didn't feel good about what he intended to do next, imitate his brother, but for several good reasons it was necessary. He toyed with calling the whole thing off because he was given an excuse now, this unbidden development, their risk factor increased. The gnarly, tight feeling in his gut and the blood pooling in his ankles reminded him that he was merely scared, and he argued with himself that to stop now would not be an act of wisdom necessarily, but one of fear. He could not halt what he was committed to do. He modulated his voice to be loud, clearly enunciated, authoritative.

"Okay, guys, I know you're under the bridge. I can guess what you're up to . . . what you're smoking. I can smell it up here. This is what we'll do. I'm driving down the road on this side and I'll wait five minutes. Then I'm coming back to check if you're still here. If you are, I'm bringing you in on a charge of vagrancy, assuming you've ditched your dope by then. Not much of a charge, but enough for me to inform your parents what you been up to tonight."

A girl's audible gasp.

On his way back to the pickup, Denny shared a quick word with Xavier, then he and André walked down the road behind Samad's truck as it drove off a safe distance. Concealed, Xavier watched the four youths flee, two boys, two girls, as they crossed the bridge to beat it back to town. Once they were gone he went under the bridge to check that everyone fled, then he came back up and signalled to the pickup that the coast was clear. Denny waited to give the kids time to completely vacate the area on the other side, and only after he saw them well down the road was he willing to cross back over.

This'll work out, he thought. A minor complication resolved.

This'll work out.

Yet the night was wearing on.

The moon rising.

They'd lost precious time.

■ ■ ■

HE USED TO SAY, "I'VE heard the whispers."

An acquaintance tested that refrain one time, asking, "What whispers? When? Willis, how did you hear these whispers? Nobody hears whispers that they're not meant to hear." The casual friend worked in his field, a shopkeeper also, although not from his part of the country. They met at the same winter trade shows from one year to the next and initially he was expecting something to happen between them but nothing did, and for a while he blamed the other man for this but later put the onus on himself.

"What do you mean?" he asked. He was slightly tipsy at the time, happily in an evening lull that held no particular fascination for him.

The acquaintance leaned forward. He was a plump, handsome man, with clear pores and cheeks so smooth anyone might believe he was incapable of growing a whisker. "Who exactly," he asked, "is whispering?"

Willis Ephraim Howard, Esq., learned something rather definitive about himself that night during the welcomed conversation: he was capable of fooling himself. He uttered that one declaration, *"I've heard the whispers,"* with such singular conviction and for such a long time that he convinced himself of its veracity. Confronted in a hotel bar in an American city—probably it was Chicago although trade shows blended together in his mind—he finally accepted that he'd never actually heard such a whisper. He collected no actual knowledge and not so much as a smidgen of evidence that anybody anywhere ever whispered about him in that way, currently or in the past. What he did was imagine the whispering to the extent that he came to believe that it was based on fact and experience, rather than on his own ingrained run-of-the-mill fear and gentle self-loathing.

The revelation made him giddy.

"I'm a fraud," he confessed. "A lunatic!"

"You're drunk is what you are," his gift store associate attested. "Oh, and something else." The man pushed himself back into the comfy leatherette sofa, crossing one leg over the other. He wore bright yellow socks with an Argyle pattern. Willis wished at that moment that he could dare to wear bright yellow Argyle socks.

He also yearned to hear what the fellow would say next, as he presumed he'd be uttering words he was hoping to hear. But the man disappointed him.

"You're curious," Willis was told, "but you're not keen."

And that, he knew, struck by the blow, was God's own truth.

Months later, Willis surmised that the line could serve well as his epitaph. The assessment did not apply only to the matter in question, his sexuality, but also to how he conducted himself throughout life. He was curious, but he was not keen. About anything. No longer drunk or giddy, he found the verdict to be unrelentingly depressing.

On rare occasion, Willis experienced sex with men, finding the forays, not surprisingly, messy, rowdy, troubling, mildly humiliating, unpleasant in a perplexing way, and yet rather exciting. He slept with women also, occasions that were even more rare, and he also found those experiences messy, but tepid, and although they were pleasant enough, which surprised him, he failed to be particularly excited. The arrival of a fresh young woman in his shop altered this perception, of himself if not of sex, for he sensed that the curiosity factor was not really his big thing anymore. With her, he thought, he could probably discover a genuine enthusiasm. She already demonstrated that her presence made him irrational, he practically gave away half his store to her, even if the space was more accurately defined as an eighth and in due time he was supposed to be compensated accordingly. He liked to think that it was not merely the sexual fantasy—although he also acknowledged that he often chose to deliberately kid himself. So the sexual fantasy probably did count more than anything else, he decided, but until he actually delved into that for himself what he enjoyed the most, what he was *keen* on, as well as being curious about, admittedly, was the aura of her presence. For that was it. He wanted to bathe in that aura. He wanted to bask in its evident light. He wanted to see himself reflected in the glory and the glow he felt when mirrored in her company. Half jokingly, he once defined himself as a rudimentary narcissist, yet somehow this woman accentuated his narcissism to an excruciating, highly sexualized degree. She elevated him by articulating his pain.

Tonight he dwelled upon this remarkable twist. The insight was delivered to his consciousness, as if by e-mail or by FedEx, about thirty hours previously while he lay in his bath, and he virtually wore the premise as a fragrance since then. Now, with some of the lustre gone, he thought things through. Weighed the evidence and decoded his logic. *What do I want out of this?* he asked himself. *The personal, the business side, either one, what is it I want?* He welcomed the introspection, believing that he was delving into what could prove critical in his life. *What will I do, or give up, to get it? Sex is out of the question, okay, she's not about to give me* that. Willis was proud of himself to be asking such penetrating questions, for at long last he was keen about the answers.

He decided to make a list.

Then, right away, to make two lists.

At the top of one sheet of paper, he wrote, *What I Want.* And at the top of the other, *What I'll Do or Sacrifice to Get What I Want.* Before he was able to add anything to his lists, he turned over the first sheet of paper and at the top of the blank side wrote, *Why I Want What I Want.* Now he was working with three lists. A side to one of the sheets remained blank, so he turned it over and stared at it awhile.

He flipped the sheets several times, and then he underlined each of the three titles with a cursive flourish. Yet, as each minute ticked by, he was drawn to the one completely blank side more than to the others, so he put that one on top. He didn't know what to write there, but assumed that a new and pertinent title would soon dawn on him.

When nothing did, he stood and stepped over to the opposite side of the room to his liquor cabinet. A broad choice. He chose a Bailey's Irish Cream that he poured into a favourite snifter, then sat back down on his sofa. He sipped, and curled up, tucking his legs up under him and crisscrossing his arms over his chest. He stalled, but knew what was coming next. *Give it a few minutes,* Willis Ephraim Howard advised himself. *This'll pass. We'll see what's on the tube tonight. This will pass.*

Rather than easily passing, his mood overwhelmed him, and Willis felt wretched. An abject ache in his chest gained intensity and although he knew what it was, just another onrushing accumulation of unhappiness, malaise, and depression, he worried that this was the big one, a heart attack that would drop him where he sat and rip him from his life and he'd be left with three blank lists and one blank page that even lacked a title, and regretted that these four sheets represented the sum total of his life. In the midst of his agony, that was the cruellest incision—that at the moment of his death, at the peak of his life, he wanted to inscribe what was important to him and was unable to do so, and that *blankness,* arriving at the very moment of his death, defined him, for at the crucial hour, that was exactly how he defined himself.

He wanted to survive just so he could put something down on the page.

Willis toppled over. No sudden stroke, no brutal attack, his heart was under no particular duress. His woe arrived by way of his own imagining. He was curious, in typical fashion, but not keen. Sexually, emotionally, even in a business sense, even when it came to plumbing his depths, he was merely curious. He lay in a circular huddle on the sofa and, as his anxieties politely let up, he shut his eyes and, comfortable again, considered just sleeping there. He thought of nothing to add to the pages despite a middling desire to do so. Perhaps, as time went by, he might be inspired to write something down. Or perhaps it was on the page already. The sum total of his life then, perhaps, added up to nothing. A big fat zero. In the interim, he'd put the pages away in a drawer, the blank one on top. Perhaps, perhaps, he'd see to them another day. Perhaps, that's what he needed. Another day to mull this over.

Eyes closed, he viewed a mental image of the young woman walking, chatting with customers, casting an intermittent smile in his direction. Willis swallowed hard, through a pain, a compression and a dryness in his throat. He didn't want to admit it, but he lived for those moments now, those inexplicable glimpses. It's not, he thought, that someone came into his life, disrupting it, but *something* came in, when the door was unlocked, the windows unsealed, when he wasn't looking and was caught unaware.

■ ■ ■

DENNY O'FARRELL WAITED IN A crouch. The bottom tip of the moon's sliver stood on end above a hilltop, visible to him now, and if he pulled himself upright the nadir would also appear. He stood, bending back a few branches and as he did so he turned his gaze away from the moon. Before him, the covered river bridge cast in the patina of faint moonlight stood stark and still.

As though breathing.

He listened to woodsy night sounds.

The river's rush. Wind in the trees. Bug flight and distant truck wheels on pavement. A gear change. The loud thrum of quiet.

Across the river, Xavier gave the all clear.

This time Denny issued no order. He simply nodded his chin.

The pickup drove its own length onto the bridge then stopped.

Old timbers released a sad creak. Then a croak. Then settled.

Samad waited, perhaps afraid to turn around.

From the truck bed, André Gervais spoke his command. "Go, Samad."

Samad liked that, in a way. Hearing his name gave greater import to his contribution. Then Xavier's repeated flashes encouraged him.

"Take it real slow," André counselled. Samad already knew to do that.

The truck moved cautiously forward.

With his right hand, André turned the pump's handle. Gasoline spit from an eight-foot hose, which he flailed with his left hand to release it back and forth across the floor of the bridge then up into the rafters. Before getting too far across he switched hands, then he called to Samad to go a speck quicker. By accident, he splashed himself and the truck.

They moved across the bridge, an easy pace, leaving a trail of stinking gasoline puddles on the floor and a sweat stain of gas on the side and upper timbers. Then Samad drove them off the bridge onto the pavement on the other side. He picked up Xavier thirty feet along.

"Let's go," Xavier, nervous, commanded. He jumped up onto the truck bed with André.

"Let's wait," André contradicted him. He was holding his arm, a trifle weary from pumping.

"Why?"

"I want to see this."

Samad did as well, apparently. With the transmission in park he opened his door and stood on the running board, looking back the way they'd come. He stared at the bridge, adored from the moment he arrived in this town. He played on it as a child and leapt from its braces as a teenager and watched the logs from the forest be guided down underneath it to the southern mills. Now it stood alone and abandoned in the dark. Sacred in its way. *Like a church, like.*

He saw a form—Denny O'Farrell—walk up the incline to the old covered bridge on the other side.

He watched him crouch down.

■ ■ ■

DENNY PAUSED.

He could smell the gas.

He needed to do this quickly, then disappear, yet he paused.

Then he struck a match against the flint on his matchbook and tossed it onto the gas-soaked timbers.

The flame flared on the wood before fizzling out.

He lit another match. This time it went out in a puff in midair.

The third match he used to light the entire matchbook, and set it down gently, quickly. Gasoline ignited in a soft blue line about three feet wide and burned as casually as a barbecue when suddenly Denny reared back from a sudden ignition. A sound like a wind shook him, and suddenly the fire encircled the interior of his end of the wooden trestle, then at panic speed it whooshed down the length of the structure. The heat seared him and he rolled himself away even as flames leapt back at him, and on the roadside Denny scampered to his knees, jumped to his feet, and retreated a short distance.

But he stopped, although this was against the plan. He turned around and looked back.

■ ■ ■

THE MEN ON THE FAR side dwelled momentarily in the thrall of the fire, before André shook himself alert and interrupted their rapture.

"Get out of here!" Gas, he realized, spilled on the truck, the barrel wasn't empty, he stank of gasoline himself, and a trickle followed them to this spot in a direct dotted line. The others now saw it, too, in the firelight. They never anticipated that the flames could surge across the bridge so quickly, as if in pursuit of them, and Samad scrambled in behind the wheel and drove for their very lives. Upon the crest of a gradual riverside hill, two hundred feet along, he braked, took a breath, and when his vehicle did not explode, dared look back.

The old covered bridge transmogrified into an inferno. Flames raged under the rooftop, blazed out through the side openings. Samad half fell getting out and stood on the running board to gaze over the roof of the cab. "Holy crap," he said quietly. He was thinking, *What did we do this for?*

Xavier meant to say something, but he and André stayed silent.

■ ■ ■

DENNY O'FARRELL MOVED DEEPER INTO the thicket, not to be seen in the brilliant glow of the fire. Across the river the truck had not yet fled. A mistake. The guys there were taking in the view, like tourists. The initial scorch still felt warm on his face, and he worried that his skin was marked by telltale burns—seared skin the only evidence a judge might require to throw away the key.

Burying himself low behind the shrubbery, tree trunks, and lowslung branches, he successfully reduced the amount of light that fell upon him, but he could not escape the flames' noise in his ears. That roaring surprised him. Not only did timbers grotesquely crack in the heat, but the fire's internal wind and the scorched air astonished him. Denny hid his face in his arms, to both hide and shield himself from the combusting frenzy.

The ferocity of the bedlam intensified, scaring him more.

When he looked up again, he saw that at least the guys across the river were long gone.

Denny sensed that he glowed. That he shone like a moonscape. Light the fire cast upon him radiated off his cheeks and forehead, he imagined, and within the thicket that concealed him, which itself might combust in an instant. If anyone looked upon him now, he believed, they'd see the fire not only mirrored in his eyes but burning there as twin torches. Suddenly, he was rudely shoved back against a tree. The knock came from a concussive burst through a section of the bridge roof. Flame and sparkling cinders whirled and ascended high into the night sky. For a moment that display lingered in his bones, he wished that he could just make this stop. He'd gone too far. He didn't mean to do this. And then, looking up through the leaves, he felt bewildered by how the flames transformed the dark.

■　■　■

JACKSON EUGENE WITHERS—FROM BIRTH, "JAKE"—PLUNGED his shoulder too heavily into the rear outside door departing a bar, consequently stumbling into the establishment's parking lot and looking more inebriated than he might have otherwise. He caught himself against a tall fence constructed for the sole purpose of hiding garbage cans from view. He sniffed a wayward scent. Straightening, Jake adjusted his ball cap and pulled down his polo, a ritual vanity that came too late. He was already spotted. He caught the covert attention of a police officer across the street and a short distance down in another lot. Jake pulled out his keys and climbed into his car, recently christened the Old Orange Shitbox by Skootch. As he drove away from the lot, Jake Withers was being followed.

Skootch's ball club played Les Tigres de Maniwaki that evening. The other team was mostly composed of mill workers, although their catcher was a burly import from the post office. They'd won handily, 6–zip. Handcuffed early by inside fastballs, striking out in his first two at bats, Jake was hit on the kneecap in his third. A Maniwaki plumber, a lefty, was losing his stuff by the seventh inning and Jake connected with a tricky squibbler down the third base line that, once the ball went fair over the bag, broke into foul territory, rolling under the infield fence for a ground-rule double. *A double!* Not only his first hit, but his first RBI, followed shortly by his first run scored.

A decent night. After a couple of beers in the company of his team-mates he wanted to get off on his own to soak it in. Or, perhaps, he'd drive back to Skootch's camp to see if any of the women were up. They might be. Talking away. Drinking. Smoking. Sitting by a fire. Maybe he'd go there. *Yeah.* Chat to some girl about his double that dribbled under a fence twenty feet from the third base bag.

He was driving arrow-straight down Main Street when his police escort, unimpressed by any evident level of inebriation, discontinued the surveillance. Jake noticed the headlights remove themselves from his rearview then instantly forgot about them altogether, his attention snagged instead by a strange glow through and above the treetops far-ther along. That impression faded, the sightlines blocked by buildings and a denser woods, but he kept looking to see if the strange light returned. Then it did, and he said, "Shit me," speeding up. Jake knew what it was before he got there but he couldn't really believe this and wanted to make sure. It could be a house. As he swerved too quickly around a bend he depressed the gas pedal. Fire. Red, orange, white, and blue. He continued to accelerate close to the burning bridge then braked hard and flung himself out of the car and raced on foot to the edge of the inferno as if he would find something there that he might do, or someone whom he might save.

He bounced on his feet like a prizefighter. Then Jake stood aghast before the fountain of flames, briefly stunned and marvelling at the shooting tangents. He just loved this fire. Its bedlam. His arms shot up and, as if he were some minor god kicked out of his lair by a rival lord, he bellowed, a guttural vexation and, perched on the precipice of the fire, he repeatedly spun in circles. He felt holy and mad and oddly exuberant. Twice he kicked the air with his foot chin-high. Jake dashed back to the car and his right palm landed on the horn and he left it there and he made hooting noises himself while the horn blared away. He was looking around for someone to hear, or see, or notice, and finally, back in the centre of town, he detected headlights. Right away that car was racing in his direction, cherries flashing blue and red on the rooftop, and a moment later the vehicle's siren wailed.

A few house lights in the neighbourhood popped on.

"Yeah!" Jake cried out, enjoying the reaction. "Yeah!"

He glimpsed through the trees and homes other vehicles that also flashed lights, which indicated another cop and probably that volunteer firefighters alerted by the cops were heading for their station. The car that tailed him a few minutes earlier skidded to a sharp stop.

The officer climbed out slowly, awestruck. "Ho-ly fuck." He audibly sucked in his next breath.

Jake nodded vigorously. He wholeheartedly agreed.

The cop got back on his radio but now the town was waking up. Shouts hither and yon and Jake speculated that phones were ringing off their hooks. This was news. This was an event. He looked back at the fire and thought it astounding, the most splendid and amazing sight he could ever hope to witness. For the first time since the last time he enjoyed sex, which was a very long while ago, he felt compulsively alive. The cop, considerably older than him, now stood right beside him, gazing at the fire as though he shared the same sentiment, and passion, exactly.

Before long, a soaring siren pitched in as the first vehicle in the Fire Department, a pumper, left the station.

■ ■ ■

THE NIGHT'S LAST KISS WAS warm, welcome, and it lasted awhile, although Tara, ever so gently, eased Ryan away with a light press of her fingertips against his chest. The two separated, yet stayed close, and were gazing at one another when a horn blared. Unusual at any time, but an annoyance at night. Ryan's police instincts were alert but he lifted Tara's hand in his to say a proper good-bye. They shared quick kisses and after the third, a police car raced past them, lights flashing. That ended their evening, and Ryan stepped back onto Main Street to see whatever the commotion might be, and saw the fire.

"Oh no," he said, stunned.

Tara joined him on the road. "What's that? A house on fire?"

Ryan whispered. "They've done it now. It's the bridge."

"Oh my God."

"I gotta go."

"Go," she told him, but Ryan was already running. His car was pointed in the right direction and he scrambled inside and tore off. A second later his coloured lights were flashing and moments after that the siren wailed. He was waking up the whole town. Every able-bodied man might be needed to fight this fire. He drove, and he couldn't believe a burst of flames, their height, that radiant orange plumage.

"My God," he prayed, because he needed a miracle here. "Please. Let it be somebody else. It's got to be somebody else."

■　■　■

THE CHANGE IN A DEPRESSED Willis Howard that took him from the calm of his television set late on a warm summer evening to a full-blown distemper was so swift, chaotic, driven, and arbitrary that he barely recognized himself and certainly not the vehemence that compelled him. He'd drummed through this rant before but never when he stood so precariously balanced on the cusp of such wrath, as though he was seized by a nausea so intense and crippling that it reduced him to a bodily reflex, one blithering scold upon another.

"MOTHERFUCKMOTHERS!" Language like that never crossed his lips and he felt that he jumbled them up somehow but he never spoke words laced with such venom. To merely hear any such utterance, offhand in a teenager's diction, or rough and senseless from the tongue of someone old and embittered, or a foul-mouthed logger, caused Willis to cower within himself, uncomfortable with the expression of crudity. And yet, he was the one uttering profanity and doing so having lost all modicum of self-control.

For they'd done it, the bastards. Always they got their own way, they ran the town and ran and ruined people's lives. Whether he was a child sucker-punched by a vile, rude boy or an adult contending with the animosity and gainful superiority of loggers, their slurs, their slights, which conceded no respect for the opinions of others and only niggling concern for the *lives* of others and what meagre attention they could muster came couched in mockery and disdain. No matter his station in life, the rabble reduced him, they brought him low. Damn loggers. Damn them to hell's bottommost sewer. Now they'd done it, burned *burned!* the old covered bridge that solicited thousands of customers nearer to his doorstep every year to spend their money in his shop and now they cut the town off from that resource so that their own precious resource *their goddamn trees* could be better served. They might as well have taken his own heart and soul but nonetheless his bank account along with a multitude of body parts and ripped that bloody stew from his entrails. *"FUCKERS!"*

He longed to burn each and every damned logger slowly on a spit with forks through their eyelids.

Willis Ephraim Howard, Esq., needed to pull on his shoes and tie up the laces before stepping out. On his front porch he could smell the old covered bridge, the smoke and more than a hundred years of sedate composure, faithful service, and pastoral peacefulness burning—history and ancestry, memory and fable, vanishing—a stench made disparate by the taunting lust of the fire seen from his eyrie above the treetops, and he heard the menace of the roaring, as though from the bellows of a great subterranean furnace. That roaring.

■ ■ ■

HIDDEN AMID TREES, DENNY SETTLED. The august fury of the fire spooked him, knocked him off his stump. He needed time alone to recover, to resume his posture, to remember why the action was taken, to recall that he'd been shoved into an untenable position. The fire entered a phase when the gasoline was consumed and the blaze retreated. A spontaneous lull. Tucked behind protective brush he imagined that the fire might simply go out, a charred remains the net result, the bridge still standing, still functional. His heart slumped then as abject failure loomed. Yet the fire fanned itself on a breeze, the heat imbued in the timbers assumed command, and the fire this time was no longer artificially inspired but fully legitimate as it fed upon the timbers, soon beyond control, the sage old wood wildly consumed.

This emotional slippage, from fear of failure to the restoration of the action's success, confirmed for Denny O'Farrell his own righteous intent, and while he took no solace in the vanity of the flames or in the destruction of the beautiful old bridge, he reaffirmed that this needed to be done and the weight fell upon him to stand as the man for the job. The bridge burned and he took no pleasure in that ecstatic flurry but reaffirmed his choices here.

Then that still, quiet reverie broke.

In a twinkling, as though the soul of his life buckled.

But it was not him. The bridge just snapped.

Denny spent his life amid the noise of harvesting timbers, so he knew the sound to be that of wood breaking. But he did not know how, where. The outcry came as concussive, like cannon fire, the initial stammer and dull thump of the shot followed by the rupture and chaos of explosion. A thunder, yet as quick as lightning, and that decisive. The render of the sound was accompanied by a chorus from the throng of spectators, both those nearby and those on the run to soon arrive. A reaction to the sound. Denny needed to see what occurred, and risked being spotted to nip through the woods closer to the river and the flames. He arrived at the riverbank in time to see what he never perceived, the near edge of the bridge, having broken from its moorings, falling into the Gatineau River.

The river will douse the flames!

In one illogical instant, he feared that the bridge might be saved by the river, and returned to its rightful position.

The rush of water carried one end of the burning carcass downstream, twisting the far side of the bridge so that the attachment points there were bent beyond their capacity to sustain the weight, breaking away in a slander of great guttural cries. Upright, one end a bow, the opposite a stern, the boat-like bridge artfully sailed upon the surface. The gargantuan flames appealed to the crisp black air, sparks rampant as though the river itself burned in sympathy, as this fiery proud ship sailed on down the stream.

Ashore, townsfolk were rapt.

Denny could move from his lair now, and in keeping with his plan join the throng. He'd set the fire but with no visible means to do so. And so he was free to mingle, to pretend that he'd arrived, like the others, from afar, to act the part of an astonished onlooker.

And he *was* astonished as the bridge slowly wended its way downstream, and in the current perfectly followed the contours of the shore. The sky lit up, the riverbanks aglow. He was not sure when his brother joined him, as people constantly milled around, changing positions to alter their perspective. He became aware that Ryan stood beside him.

The brothers exchanged a glance.

"I thought so," Ryan said. A moment ago he was asked by the shopkeeper, Willis Howard, if he intended to arrest his brother.

Denny minded his peace awhile. Then he said, "Hey, Ry, Dad said you were on a date tonight. How'd that go?"

Ryan remained beside him awhile, passively observing the fire. "I better not find out that my date was part of your plan," he said, "that it had anything to do with your timing." The two brothers stared at each other briefly, both unyielding, then Ryan walked off. He wanted to get the Fire Department—able volunteers who were allowing themselves to be mere spectators—on their toes. They needed to follow the bridge downstream in case it came ashore. He needed to avert that greater disaster, should the bridge set a forest, or the town, ablaze.

■ ■ ■

SHE HUMS TO DISPEL THE dark, her fright, this outlandish fire.

Unnoticed in its dark patch of firmament, a slim sliver of moon is eclipsed by a burst and roar as flames catapult into the night sky, illumining the broad bend of shore. Air erupts in a scintillation of light, while across the water hillsides glimmer a reddish hue. Some people are electric, a few are in a daze, awakened by the dirge of shouts, sirens, and ringing telephones as townsfolk swarm to the riverbank, most mystified, all stunned, to take in this apparent cataclysm in their lives.

Mrs. McCracken hums.

the beautiful the beautiful river!
Gather with the saints by the

Alone in the dark in her nightgown she seems particularly diminutive on this occasion. Perhaps more elderly, also, and more frail than usual, as if not being fully clothed accentuates the vulnerability of an older age. She sits upon a boulder in the shoreline park as the bright burning bridge slowly passes by, yet to thwart the gravitational pull of a dawning heartache her posture remains oak-straight. Did she ever intend to live so long to bear witness to an event this crude? A scurrilous act. *Arson. The culprits deserve not a single stitch of mercy. Not one stitch. Hang them.* She concludes what more than a few farther away are whispering, *Oh, they did it now. This time. Set the river ablaze. Those men. Those boys!* Her back taut, yet she feels herself go wonky, a trifle cockeyed, as if rather than being aroused from sleep she's been shaken from a groggy stupor. *The river, can you—? In flames. Right before our very own eyes!*

Sparks ignite on the crackling air.

that flows by the throne of

Her gaze remains transfixed upon the floating blue womb of the inferno and to her surprise Mrs. McCracken begins to feel strangely invigorated. She quits her song. Thoughtful now, somehow less furious. An odd idea crops up—*I might linger awhile.* She has not dwelled on such a thing in a very long time, there is simply no value to the exercise, but she is thinking now that she just might stay. Here. On earth. In this town. *Awhile.* For the first time in ages her life is possessed by genuine purpose, for she needs to ascertain how this conflagration will revise her study of the world, who might be uplifted, who brought low to lie seared or mangled or ruefully destroyed.

Oh my, she winces as the thought strikes home, *gossipy tongues will wag!*

The river. In flames. *Oh!* Burning. As though water combusts.

Overhead, ash drifts, settles on trees. Specks bloom crimson an instant, then cool on the palms of darkened leaves.

The old lady intermittently attempts to resume her hum.

Her new friend, such a perplexing young woman—*A vision that girl, oh!*—aglow in the river's firelight, also wears white on this night albeit with a fashion sense appropriate to her youth and beauty. *Yes! We shall gather by*—Tara approaches down the well-trammelled couples' path as if stepping on air, or upon a ribbon of shimmering dust. Arms meditatively entwined. She moves more slowly than the others who so urgently converge. Her heels kick up a shy trace of ash. *Why yes now.* Mrs. McCracken interrupts her hymn as a measure of boldness mixes with her familiar cunning, although she admits to an abiding confusion. Saddened by the grief of this hour, she still feels quite capable of looking forward. Despite a wish to remain circumspect, she smiles, and repeats, more as affirmation than as an afterthought, *Why yes now. You know? This might make a dollop of sense, in a strange way, in the longer long run.*

If Tara Cogshill arriving on the shore appears uniquely resplendent, perhaps angel-like, to Mrs. McCracken, then the woman sitting upright on a rock in her shimmering white nightgown, radiant in the glow of firelight under a canopy of undulating smoke looks positively otherworldly to Tara, as though transported from another realm. Amid the horde, she is the only person to have segregated herself off as solitary. The swirl of smoke that on occasion dips to touch the ground reflects a ruddy tinge of fire, and the woman's white gown mirrors the brightest flames off the blazing river.

Mrs. McCracken is watching her, Tara sees, not the fire.

Coming closer, she detects the blaze caught in the wash of those eyes.

Tara stands beside her while the old woman remains seated upon the rock. The younger one places a hand upon the senior's shoulder, and the frail-looking old lady covers that hand with her own.

They remain that way, gazing out.

Mrs. McCracken says, "My storm."

A reference that derives from a conversation they shared at the cemetery, but Tara does not know why she's mentioning it now, so asks, "Why say that?"

"Raine," Mrs. McCracken answers obliquely, "with an *e*."

Tara wonders if her friend has not lost her senses in the trauma of this event, or perhaps she's sleepwalking, in a way. Or she's merely being difficult or oddly sentimental or she's confused and disoriented. She's worried about her. The two women turn their attention back to the old covered bridge as it sails on downriver. "It's like the river is burning," Tara remarks, and given the flames' dancing reflections off the oily black surface that is exactly true.

"Yes," Mrs. McCracken agrees. "It's on fire, isn't it?" To Tara, she seems a long way off.

"It's like a burning ship. It's lying in water, in *water*! It's a fire on water. Amazing how it plain refuses to burn out."

"That makes sense," Mrs. McCracken contends. "It wants to carry on."

"How do you mean?" Tara asks, but she's a long way off herself and isn't really thinking about her question.

The older woman, though, takes it seriously. "The bridge," she divulges slowly as the thought takes hold, "would rather be a fire than extinguished."

And yet the old covered bridge, true to an ingrained dignity long nurtured, does eventually burn itself out upon the waters, quietly vanishing miles downstream into nothing forevermore.

II

RECKONING

16

Well-kempt, his home did show a few anaemic signs of ageing. Broad-planked oak floors, which he laid himself, and adored, for he felled the trees as well, reflected a patina only time could stain. Here and there the scuff of constant feet left them gently scooped. The north side of the dining room floor dipped to meet the wall, as though all material gravitated towards and down the riverbank and to the water on that side of the house. As if everything secretly drained away. For reasons that he could not readily decipher, although he suspected that either shadows cast by the tallest pines or meandering fair-weather cloud were the culprits, the room seemed a tad dreary today, given the brightness of the morning. As he hung up the telephone, he listened to a cardinal's clear whistle, high on the fir out back, which ordinarily might cheer him, and yet today the ensuing silence felt grim.

A phone call bid him come in from garden work, so now he washed his hands under the kitchen taps. He scoured his palms thoroughly and, looking up, was hooked by his reflection in a small mirror off to the side. So the house was not alone in showing its age. Alexander Gareth O'Farrell leaned back against the counter while he worked the towel, and continued to wipe his hands long after they were dry.

A neighbour called, virtually kicking herself with suppressed delight to be the first to fill him in on the details, such as they were. *They burned the bridge!* The tone of conversation shifted, and Alex believed she was fishing, to see if he'd stoop to accusing his son, which apparently was going around.

"Why on earth," he asked at last, still dealing with her news, "would my son burn the old covered bridge? Anyway, which son do you mean?"

"Not Ryan!" the batty neighbour retorted with some consternation.

"Denny is not a pyromaniac either. What are you insinuating?"

"I'm just saying. It's going to be difficult for Ryan, don't you think, if he has to . . . he may have no choice . . . if he, you know, investigates his brother. Do you think he will?"

"Will what?"

"Arrest him!"

No one slammed a receiver down, but the two extricated themselves from their discourse and hung up and that's when Alex noticed the age of the house and went into the kitchen to scrub his hands. He felt an odd subliminal relief that his wife was not alive to hear such distressing talk about her second child. If she was, Alex reflected, the report might've killed her.

If she was alive, he reconsidered along a different vein, *he never would have done it.* That's when he realized that he himself believed, on no evidence, just suspicion and intuition, that Denny was responsible.

He repeated his son's name twice aloud, both times softly. "Denny." A quiet, loving, forgiving sound. "Denny." This time rife with dismay.

Then he went around the house trying to locate his car keys, and after that drove into town. Assuming the tale was true, that the old covered bridge burned and sailed on down the river in flames, then he wanted to observe the gap for himself before he considered any subsequent move. He needed to observe the evidence firsthand, despite having been forewarned that absolutely nothing remained to be seen.

■ ■ ■

ARRIVING AT WORK, MANY of them late, truckers were advised not to start their engines. "You'll be going nowhere soon," the dispatcher's assistant let them know. Off and on they caught sight of the dispatcher through the window of his office, on the phone and pacing, and whenever he hung up he was obviously expecting the blessed thing to ring again. He was giving out no further information.

The men were remarkably subdued.

In pairs, a few of the younger guys balanced on a hefty log and endeavoured to wrestle one another off it. Denny considered the sport silly, given that the log lay flat on dry land. Float that thing in the river and then see who could stay upright on it and for how long. This is what they should have been doing with their lives, riding logs downstream. Any battle for supremacy then would not have been a mere logger sport but a life-and-death daily activity that determined their worth, and a skill that aided their ability to survive. Instead, number 2 diesel fuel ran through their veins and a few younger guys thought that balancing on a log *on dry land* meant something. Denny quashed an urge to yell, or even step right up to the fellow who apparently won that absurd contest and punch his lights out. He exhaled, to let his unbidden rage subside.

Older guys smoked and kicked around a few ideas about what would happen now, and out of that discussion one wizened, diminutive fellow started up a pool in which the object was to guess the date a new bridge would open to traffic.

"One thing wrong with that idea," Big Bill Fournier touted.

"What's that?" a sidekick asked.

"Who says a new bridge will ever get built?"

He spoke loudly, as though he knew whom he was talking to, but Denny didn't rise to the bait. For the time being, he let it pass. If Big Bill thought that burning the bridge was a bad idea, he could suck his own tailpipe, and Denny was on the verge of saying so. He'd offer to help shove it down his gullet.

Those few comments aside, the morning was remarkable for the lack of references to the fire. People kept their opinions to themselves, and no one was willing to publicly harangue, or celebrate, the arsonists, whoever they might be. By the same token, no one was so foolish as to speculate that the fire might have been an accident. Truckers knew what happened. They believed they'd be the beneficiaries, eventually, so it stood to reason that a few of their number were guilty of the crime.

Silence, then, was a form of thanks, rather than misgiving.

Denny came close to asking André Gervais for a cigarette but caught himself, realizing how bad that would look, the two of them huddled around a lit match. An image that snuffed out the craving.

The dispatcher ventured out at last and men came away from their logs and rigs and huddled groups to form a semicircle around him. Denny found himself in the front row. Not that it mattered a whole hill of beans, but he'd prefer being farther back. He respected the dispatcher, a muscular fair-haired man in his forties with a punched-in nose who'd never been a driver. He once worked in the woods felling trees until a bad back helped him graduate to a desk job, a task he performed well and with equanimity under pressure.

"Listen up, guys. I just got the word, okay? This is not my doing, so don't complain to me. We're going up north, east of Maniwaki. We'll haul timber there for the next few weeks until we get this figured out. The haul times won't be so bad, you should be able to get your loads in, except for today, because today we have to drive up. Tomorrow, you'll start up there in the morning. A longer drive to get to work for you guys, but that's just how it has to be."

"You mean we're leaving our rigs up there?" a voice inquired.

"That's it," the dispatcher said.

"Where exactly do we go?" Denny couldn't see Samad in the gathering, but caught the sound of his voice somewhere behind him. He didn't know why but wished he'd shut up. They'd not spoken since separating the night before, but he had lain awake afterwards thinking that Samad's wife, Joce, was the only person who could put the four of them together at the same time prior to the fire. He could not articulate why, but he just wanted Samad to stay completely quiet. In that way, to follow his lead.

"Be ready to bug out in twenty minutes," the dispatcher replied. "A company pickup is on the way. A lead truck will follow it. Then everybody, just follow the truck in front of you. I'll be in the pickup. I'm setting up in a tent for our spell there. What a joy that will be. Tonight, a bus will drive you guys back here to your personal vehicles."

Satisfied, the men began to disperse, but the dispatcher whistled for the resumption of their attention. Everyone returned to being quiet.

"One more thing, okay? We're going up there as one long line of trucks. Spread yourselves out for safety's sake so cars can pass, okay. Keep in touch by radio. Nobody goes off course, okay. Don't get lost. Understand?"

Few did.

"Look. Face it. We're not in everybody's good books right now. More than a few people are pissed off. I'll let you guess why, but we've received some threats already. At head office, and apparently, down at city hall."

"What kind of threats?"

A legitimate question, but it caused the dispatcher to examine his clipboard. He didn't want to reply.

Denny fully expected to remain silent himself, as he wished Samad had done. But after putting his hand up to get the dispatcher's attention, he repeated the question that another man initially raised.

"What kind of threats?" he asked in a quiet and calm voice.

The dispatcher looked at him, eye to eye, and reluctantly he shrugged.

"Crank calls, man," he said.

"What threats?" a stronger voice asked, now for a third time.

The dispatcher looked around. "Potshots. Fires. Shit like that there."

The men absorbed the unwelcome report. If somebody wanted to pick a fight, that was one thing, bring it on, but a shot out of the trees into a windshield was something to fear.

"They better be cranks," somebody near Denny muttered.

He was not alone in being surprised by what was relayed. Crank calls. Like everyone else he hoped that that was the case. He hadn't thought about dealing with anything more than that when plotting to do this. But everybody knew that plenty of sharpshooters lived in the hills.

■ ■ ■

AFTER VISITING THE SITE OF the old bridge, now a mere gap, a glimpse of the rapids, Alex O'Farrell needed a pick-me-up. As did others, he walked along the road to where yellow police tape and a few sawhorses barricaded the steep drop into oblivion. A visit that did not go unnoticed. Whereas others could look out over the stretch of water and not believe their eyes, he couldn't believe his ears.

"If you got something to say about me or my family," he finally challenged the flock of people behind him who were demonstrating a propensity for whispers and remarks, "say it to my face. Come on. Who's got the guts?"

He'd turned slowly to face them in a manner vaguely threatening, which he expected was enough to forestall any reply, while forgetting that he was no longer a young, lithe, and muscular logger whom people naturally feared to cross. That he might actually fight someone was nonsensical, and consequently a man even older than himself dared respond. "Did Denny do it or what?"

"How the hell should I know?" he fired back, then realized in an instant that that was not the reply his son might expect from him. But he had nothing more to add, and with two dozen people watching he walked off. For once he was grateful for his aches and pains from old logging injuries, as they prevented him from stomping away in a snit. Instead, he deployed a simple, if somewhat out of sync, amble. Elegant enough. Proud enough. He wouldn't call his stride a limp, but being self-conscious about his exit from the fray he admitted that he was probably a touch more disjointed recently, and hoped his hips were not on the cusp of giving out.

Time to see a quack, perhaps.

Although his car was handy, he chose to leave it parked and gave his legs and hips and restless sciatic nerve a workout. Never a man to just take a walk—he required a destination—he nurtured now a hankering for raspberry pie. Raspberry in particular, but he'd accept blueberry, and if he still remained bereft of a choice, an apple or maybe a rhubarb-apple would do. He wanted pie, that's what he knew. And if he happened to eat the whole damn thing by midafternoon he wasn't going to get on his own case.

This was a day to consume a pie.

So he walked across town to Potpourri, where he could pick up one of Mrs. McCracken's, as he preferred hers to the bakery's. Besides, if he went into the bakery he'd also buy donuts and cookies and then be obliged to actually give himself a good talking-to.

Due either to a mild absentmindedness these days or because he was disheartened and preoccupied, he completely forgot who was working down at the gift shop when, pie in hand, a waft of raspberry enticing his nostrils, he paid Willis Howard the discount rate for a day-old pie as Mrs. McCracken hadn't shown up that morning. "I was craving one of her fresh ones."

"I called," Willis told him. "She's taken the day off to mourn the bridge. Personally, I don't blame her, and anyway she was probably up half the night. You're celebrating, I suppose."

Alex stifled an urge to swat him. In an earlier decade he might have done just that. Instead, he turned to leave and at that moment, a woman emerging from the front corner alcove snagged his attention. She was quietly chatting with a second woman whom he knew from the bank. A light went on for Alex. He recognized the first one from the town meeting, the one his eldest had taken a tumble for, and remembered now that this was where she worked.

Ryan teased that when Alex saw her she'd literally take his breath away, give him a heart attack. The boy either didn't understand how things worked as time trudged along or he was trying to buoy his spirits, but nonetheless he did appreciate the look of her.

Reserved expressions and hushed voices between the two women revealed the subject matter of their discussion—what everyone was talking about, a burned bridge. Alex O'Farrell took five steps to leave, then hesitated.

He didn't want to go just yet.

Although he knew that he should.

Whoo-hee. A rare beauty in any town, but certainly in this one. Without realizing what he was doing he was staring as he did before, in a manner that even he might judge as inappropriate and inexcusable. But in one quick mental snapshot she both captured his interest and proved that he was not yet too old to welcome the phenomenon. Beguiled, he then seized on the mystery of what signified beauty. Somehow, when his senses were truly struck numb by a woman's presence, she was not someone he ever imagined. Anytime he conjured a certain style of beauty, and the woman of his synapses appeared on the street or on the screen, and even when she exquisitely fulfilled the dream, that sort of beauty was not as lovely as once perceived. Women who possessed the power to take his breath away or, as his son insinuated, give him a heart attack, were those who did not previously audition before his imagination. Surprise, then, was a big part of their look. The shock value of beauty, perhaps. As he continued to stare, Alex was also postulating that beauty was never about perfection.

He'd not bothered to think this through before, but was perfection with respect to beauty not a bore? Tiresome? Which is why a screen beauty at times was more enticing if she was muddied and scraped and wore a man's old shirt and jeans. Dolled up, forget it, that was trying too hard. This one was not dressed down, nor was she muddy, but she didn't try even a little nor did she have to, not with that skin. His chin flexed back as if deflecting a glancing blow. *Yes. Her skin.* The thought helped Alex grasp why he was not thinking *pretty*, or *cute*, although she certainly fit the bill to a T, rather *beauty*, and he was also thinking *rare*. As a film siren, some Hollywood dimwit might have altered the nose and enhanced the hair to de-emphasize her forehead, or committed the real horror, a boob job.

Luck was on his side, Alex decided, as the woman's client shook hands with her, shared a laugh, and departed just then. Oddly, the new woman in town knew to turn her head only slightly and tilt her chin just so, to stare right back at him.

Then she glanced at what he carried.

"If you've come here to share that pie, sir, you're in the right place."

Chuckling, Alex took a few steps closer. Further progress was stymied by a rack of gaily coloured hand-woven straw baskets from Argentina. He didn't think he should say what he was thinking, but did so anyway. "I wonder if my son fell for you as quickly as I just did. As I recall, I believe so."

At least she was taken by surprise also. She took a more analytical and anatomical survey of the fellow standing before her—she'd seen him once before, at the town meeting—and mouthed the name *Ryan*.

Silent as well, he nodded.

She lifted her hand over the baskets and they shook as he balanced the pie on the fingertips of his left.

"Tara," she said.

"Alex."

Then she crossed her arms and looked at him more closely.

"What?" he asked.

"That means," she assayed, "that you're Denny O'Farrell's father, too."

"The one guy everyone is talking about, yes."

"The bridge burner. At least, that's how they're talking about him."

"You know what they say about bad news. In my mind, the only news that travels faster is gossip."

"Would you like to come in?" she asked him.

A puzzling question. "I am in," he said finally.

She smiled. "To my part of the store. The side room."

"Oh. I didn't realize. Sure."

She went ahead while he backtracked and found the aisle that took him through the maze. Waiting for his arrival, she noticed his cane, merely slung over an elbow for the moment, and the laboured walk.

"Are you in much pain?" she asked.

"Only when it hurts," he admitted.

"Mmm. Looks like you need to loosen up. I know exercises for that."

"I garden," Alex said.

"Probably the worst thing you can do."

Twice he elicited a smile from her and each time she made him laugh in return. He detected a desire to keep doing so. "Can we eat pie here?"

"Only carefully. And that's no way to eat pie."

"I have to tell you. It's day-old."

"I know. Poor Mrs. McCracken. She's upset."

Alex nodded, not requiring an explanation. Then he looked around. "Hey, you've changed things up."

He didn't know why, but his expectations were overridden by a bizarre dawning compulsion, and he knew that he was going to buy one of her grandfather clocks. They did look quite splendid, lined up as dutiful sentries in sartorial spiffiness in a perfect row. He was tempted to salute. And then he did. That made her laugh out loud, so he did, too.

Then she said, quietly, "I wonder how Ryan's dealing with this. It can't be easy."

He shrugged. "I haven't spoken to either of them yet."

Alex saw that she found the admission curious.

"They're both working," he explained. Having seen for himself that the bridge was completely gone, he thought he'd visit Val, find out how she was handling all this, suss out if she knew anything. But he saw no reason to share that thought with this other young woman.

Tara directed her gaze to the tall clocks. "So, what do you think? Do you wanna buy a watch?" she asked, laughing.

Alex said, "Sure. Maybe. I dunno." He was spellbound. Not a good time to dicker.

■ ■ ■

THE DAY WAS PROVING TO be mild, a break from the lengthy heat wave, which Jake Withers appreciated given that he was called into Skootch's abode. An airless cabin on a hot day, an A-frame without insulation. In the winter he kept the stove burning wood nonstop, while in the summer his guests broiled. Skootch didn't seem to mind. As skinny as a greyhound, he wore scant clothing. He perspired as anyone else did but heat never seemed to bother him. The windows of his A-frame were left wide open and yet only the bugs entered—Skootch believed that humankind should live at peace with Mother Nature's creatures, including the blackfly and the mosquito—while fresh air stayed outside. The last time he was inside the cabin Jake Withers believed that he might melt, then be poured into a jug. This time, he guessed that he could survive okay.

The smoke didn't help, though. Skootch toked up as Jake entered.

He wore war paint. That's what it looked like to Jake. One broad black stripe between his nipples, and a second line under his eyes that slipped over the bridge of his nose. At first, Jake uttered a small laugh, believing that that might be appropriate. When Skootch seemed to not share in the humour, he censored himself, and sat on the floor across from the other man. Smokes, one of tobacco laced with hashish, another the grass that Jake peddled now, lay between them.

He crossed his legs in front of him and sat on a blanket on the floor.

"I thought we might have a powwow," Skootch said. "Talk things over."

"Sure, Skootch. Is something wrong?"

"Nothing's wrong, Jake. Do you think I'd invite you into my house if something was wrong? If something was wrong I'd invite you into the woods. Tie you to a tree. Stuff a rock down your throat. Scrub your cock and balls with poison ivy. Then release you. Watch you scratch the itch."

In alluding only to a potential threat, Skootch sharply heightened Jake's wariness and fear. "I just want to know if I did something wrong is all."

"You mean those errors? Reduce them. Get lower to the ball. Bend your knees. You've let yourself get stiff. As for your hitting, I've seen some signs. Your swing is loosening up. Contact will come, then the hits."

When Skootch passed the joint across to him, Jake accepted the tobacco and hash. He didn't do this stuff on his own, but he was polite, and rarely turned down these friendly gestures. He'd been raised to be polite, first and foremost. The tobacco scalded his tongue.

"Business-wise, your sales have been good, Jake. I have good reports on you. You're punctual. People have told me that. They like you. But I thought it was time that we chewed the fat a little. Y'know?"

"Sure, Skootch." The compliments made him nervous.

His host took a long drag, then exhaled slowly. When he finally evacuated his lungs, Jake received the smoke in his face.

"I'm going to increase your territory. Did you know that?"

"No," Jake said. "I didn't know that. Thanks."

"Someday I'll reduce it. That's the life of a salesman. You do well, your territory is reduced. Forces you to take blood from a stone to make things happen. Get me?"

Jake thought about it. "You mean, since my territory is increasing, that's a bad thing?"

"You're a rookie. You're just getting started. So I start you off small in case you don't work out. You get to cause less damage that way. But you're doing fine, no damage done, so I'm increasing your territory for now. Then, when you're making too much money and getting too big for your britches, I'll make you work with less. See if you can make more with less. Test your mettle that way, do you see?"

"I guess so. Yeah."

"Good," Skootch said. "Good. I run this ship like IBM runs theirs. Did you know that? Here's the thing, kid. I need you to keep your car."

"I'm keeping it, Skootch. It's running like a charm."

Skootch nodded, smoking, and closed his eyes while he inhaled. "Keep it that way. Invest in maintenance, Jake. This is my primary message today. Invest in maintenance. You're doing okay, Jake my boy, but you're going to make more money than your eyeballs can count. I don't want you driving around town in some Porsche or Alfa Romeo, picking up chicks. You don't want to pick up those chicks. Do that and we're dead. You'll be dead, anyway, but I won't let you take me down with you. You want a car like that? Keep it in some foreign country. But here, invest in maintenance. Your car is your disguise. Your disguise is your eternal salvation."

Jake nodded with some evident enthusiasm. "You don't have to worry about that. I know how to get around."

"That's important, Jake. I'm not sure there's anything more important than knowing how to get around."

Skootch opened up an aluminium case. Jake half expected him to take out something he would not like, such as a gun or a hypodermic for hard drugs. Hard drugs scared him. So did guns. But Skootch kept a variety of finger paints inside the case, and he twisted off the top of the orange into which he dipped the index and middle fingers of his right hand.

He traced twin tracks of orange across his brow.

"What are you doing?" Jake asked.

"What does it look like I'm doing?"

"I don't know," Jake said. "Putting on paint?"

"War paint," Skootch acknowledged.

"Yeah? We're at war now?"

"Yes, Jake," Skootch said. "We're at war now. That's another reason I don't want you driving around in some BMW or Lexus. Because we're at war. The Old Orange Shitbox keeps you safe. No Audi will do that for you."

Jake Withers waited awhile and then asked, "What war? Who with?"

"With the forces that are arrayed against the world, Jake. We're at war with our enemies. Who else? We are at war against the evil in our midst."

"Yeah?"

"Yeah."

Parallel purple stripes went down each side of his face, from high on the temple to just under the jawline. A slash of pure white was drawn from Skootch's lower lip, down under his chin, and over his Adam's apple to the base of his neck.

"Lean in, Jake," Skootch invited. "I'll paint you up."

"Yeah?" Jake said, tentative still. "What for?"

"For battle. Jake, come on, if you're going to war, look the part."

"I thought I'd make some deliveries today."

"Forget it. The roads are too dangerous for you now, Jake. Somebody might mistake you for a logger. Or worse. A tree hugger. Which is what you are."

Skootch painted the bridge of Jake's nose green then asked him to smile.

"Show us those pearly whites."

Jake did so.

"Hold that pose." Skootch fished out his cell phone from a scant pile of clothing on the floor and held it up to take Jake's picture. "There's plenty of girls here, Jake. I don't want you dating in town. I'm told you're not going with anybody from here."

"Come on. That's not really your business."

"Isn't it? Have you ever kissed a man, Jake? I mean, really kissed a man?"

"No." He was uncomfortable with this turn. "I'm not going to either."

"Good," Skootch said, then took his picture, then examined the result. "Then go out with girls from around here, Jake, so we can keep our eye on you, you know? Unless you want to go back to selling pavement."

Jake Withers was aware of the change forecast by this conversation. He considered his choices, what he should do. He accepted that the way things were going right now suited him, that even though he was not completely happy with the arrangement he could go along with Skootch. "What do you want me to do?" he asked. A query that indicated his compliance.

"Put on your war paint, Jake. Smear your face, your chest, your arms, your neck. I want to see what you look like in full battle regalia. Let me see my new young warrior. Then we shall study war, Jake. We shall devise tactics, our battle plan."

Jake hesitated, then he asked, "You mean like for baseball?"

This time, Skootch indicated that he did not mean that, but he did not say what he meant.

He watched as Jake applied paint to his skin. He nodded approval. He seemed to appreciate his natural artistry.

"Looking good. When you're done, I'm taking you for a long run through the woods. I've got some things to show you. I'll find someone who's superb with a needle. What you need is a loincloth. For today, you can wear one of mine. We have to toughen you up for battle, Jake. Understand me? We need to make a warrior out of you."

"I don't think I'm much of a warrior," Jake Withers demurred.

"Not yet," Skootch agreed. "Slip out of those clothes. Let's see what fits."

■ ■ ■

A DILEMMA.

Willis Howard sold a pie to Alex O'Farrell, forgoing the desire to shove it back in his face. He told himself that if it was a cream pie he'd do just that, but he knew that he was only kidding himself. He lacked the courage, and calculated that a man like Alex getting a pie in the face from a man like him would probably result in receiving a knuckle sandwich in return. As old as the elder O'Farrell might be, a blow from that man probably would kill him.

Anyway, he didn't have a cream pie so that was that.

The situation become more testy for him when he learned that Tara sold her first grandfather clock and that Alex O'Farrell was the buyer. He found the development difficult. She convinced him that she could outsell him when it came to the big-ticket items, and she just proved that to be true. He told her he sold one a year but hadn't actually sold one in over two years. He just liked having them around because they gave the store a sense of class. His supplier was willing to wait before he took the clocks back as he had more returns than he could handle anyway. So both the manufacturer and the shopkeeper conspired to pretend that they sold grandfather clocks for anywhere from seventeen hundred dollars to a little over four thousand. O'Farrell's purchase pretty much split the difference, costing just under thirty-one hundred. As well, she hadn't offered terms, which Willis never liked to do with the elderly as they often expired before their contracts, and put the whole thing on his credit card.

Amazing.

A fine development for his store, he just regretted that Alex O'Farrell was the purchaser.

"I thought you'd be more surprised," Tara said in response to his confounding attitude.

"His son—"

"Be careful now. I'm dating him."

"Not that son."

"—burnt the bridge, some say. I know."

"That family is not in my good graces right now."

Tara gave him a couple of taps on his left shoulder, which he found a tad condescending. "Two things, Willis. Innocent until proven guilty—"

"—everybody knows—"

"—and nobody is saying that Alex has anything to do with it. I haven't met Denny O'Farrell—well, briefly, in a storm—but he's a grown man. Are you going to blame the fathers for the sins of the children now? Isn't that ass-backwards?"

"What's ass-backwards is you dating Ryan."

"Excuse me?"

Sometimes he said more than he ever meant to release when in her company. She made him the opposite of tongue-tied. As if she oiled his larynx.

"Yeah. Okay. Sorry. Date whomever you want, it's no skin off my nose. But I don't know what he's going to do now. If he doesn't arrest his own brother, I can guarantee you the shit will hit the fan."

"You can guarantee that? And you won't have anything to do with pushing the issue either, is that fair to say, Willis?"

He yielded to a compulsion to open the cash register at that moment, just to hear it ring.

"Willis?"

She crossed her arms, awaiting a reply. He imagined that she was tapping a toe. Willis punched the drawer shut.

"I'm a citizen, Tara. I have my responsibilities. Everybody does."

"Responsibilities. That's a word. So is meddling. Are you sure you know the difference?"

Now she was mad, and did not wait for a reply. Willis was surprised when she bolted, returning to her alcove.

They remained separated for a while. A few tourists came and went. Finally, Willis went across to her space and leaned his hip against the doorjamb. "Listen," he said. "It's a really good sale. Congratulations. We'll have to agree to disagree on the other matter, but selling the clock, that's well done. Over the years he's been in this store probably fifty times. I think his biggest purchase was a ukulele."

"A what?"

"I'm serious."

Tara shrugged, accepting his willingness to heal their wounds. "It's a start. I hope to sell more clocks." Even when he was apologizing Tara found him creepy, and wished he'd go. "Anyway, you sold him a pie. If he was supposed to be persona non grata in here, why did you sell him a pie?"

"You're right. I'm sorry. I was out of line. By the way, that was also a good sale."

She wasn't following his thread.

"Someone buys a pie and then you help him eat it. And carve me a slice. Good one. We can sell more pies that way."

She knew that he was trying very hard to be funny, and ingratiating, but she chose to make this difficult for him and let his apology go by, only vaguely accepted. Just then, though, she saw her way out of this discussion.

"She's here. Look. Mrs. McCracken. With fresh pies!"

Willis glanced out the window, through and around the plethora of merchandise, as the older woman parked her Vespa.

"I'm surprised," he allowed. "I thought she'd be in mourning for the rest of her life."

Finally, they could agree on something. "Me, too," Tara said, but unlike Willis she was curious, rather than merely accepting, of this change in the woman's temper. The old lady bounded into the store as though she was celebrating.

"Do you know what the tourists are doing?" she exclaimed as she carried in a pair of lemon meringues that looked incredibly fluffy and light. She didn't wait for a reply. "They got off the train and went straight to where the bridge used to be. They're snapping pictures! Like never before. Basically, they're taking pictures of a *hole*. They'll go home and say to their friends, 'You'll never guess what used to be here.'"

"Why are you so chipper?" Tara asked. The leap from her misery the previous night did not seem either real or healthy. Tara felt then that she should not leave her side, eventually walking Mrs. McCracken home and staying on for a late-night cup of tea. The revolving lights of assorted emergency vehicles intermittently flashed on the windows of her home while they sat together.

"Willis, do you understand what you must do?" Mrs. McCracken demanded, ignoring Tara a moment. "Sell everything bridge. Postcards—triple their price—T-shirts and those, what do you call them? Hoodies! Dreadful word. Anything with a bridge on it, they'll buy."

"If they ever show," he complained.

"Oh, they'll show. You can't look at nothing forever."

"Anyway, it's only for a day or two. The novelty will wear off. With no bridge there will be no tourists."

"Exactly! So let's change that."

"Mrs. McCracken—" Tara attempted to intrude.

"Oh, don't look at me that way, I have not lost my senses. I am overcome, overcome I will say, with a thought. I have been enlightened, sweet girl, and now fate and I daresay my legacy awaits."

Her spirit was so infectious that Tara was not only sporting a smile but she and Willis managed to share a laugh together. Her indefatigable presence somehow dissolved their spat.

"Okay. So what gives?"

"We won't give up!" Mrs. McCracken looked from the man to the woman and raised her hands in a gesture that was meant to indicate that the mysterious was nothing if not obvious.

"On—what?" Tara asked.

"The bridge!" Mrs. McCracken kept looking from one to the other as though they were drawn into a contest and her job was to anoint the winner. She feigned impatience, when neither came through, and smacked her lips. "The old bridge is to be rebuilt. We will have a new old bridge!"

"Seriously, Mrs. McCracken," Willis Howard said, "and I've never asked this question of you before—although once or twice I might have been tempted—but have you been drinking?"

"Oh, don't be an idiot! Four o'clock is my hour, not a moment before!"

"The covered bridge is gone, Mrs. McCracken. It's not coming back. The government will now build the fast highway bridge the loggers want and that's the end of it."

"That's not the end of it!" she fought on.

"I have to agree with Willis," Tara put in.

"Oh, goodness, you're both as idiotic as my grade ones! Of course, the government will build the highway bridge, and it will be ugly and it will be a monstrosity and there's nothing to be done about that."

Tara was on the verge of interrupting her, but settled for a puzzled look as Mrs. McCracken carried on.

"The government will not build a new covered bridge. They can't afford it. They don't have the expertise. Neither the loggers nor the highway department will be in favour. But we, ladies and gentlemen, good citizens of Wakefield, we shall build a new old covered bridge all by ourselves."

Both Tara and Willis Howard were loath to burst her bubble, and so delayed, but Tara soon ventured, "And how do we do this without, oh, I don't know . . . money?"

"We raise it!" Mrs. McCracken beamed.

"With bake sales, I suppose," Willis deduced with evident scepticism.

"And lotteries, and an appeal, and car washes by the kids, and—"

"Do you have any idea what an old bridge like that costs? The wood—"

"We're surrounded by forests!"

"The labour alone—" Tara said.

"Volunteers! Think, people! You're not thinking!"

She cast her eyes between them as though waiting to congratulate the first one to get it. Yet her two listeners shared a glance and failed to return her enthusiasm.

"You're not thinking positively," Mrs. McCracken noted. "We can do it," she encouraged them, although the lack of support seemed to have reduced her own belief. "People built that bridge, not government, and people can rebuild it without outside help."

"Do you have any idea," Willis Howard asked, "how many pies you'd have to bake and sell to pay for it?"

"Oh, don't be such a party pooper!" she taunted him.

"Mrs. McCracken," he said, "there aren't enough years left in my life to raise that kind of money, let alone in yours. As for volunteers, you can count on me to hammer a nail, but it won't be pretty or efficient, and if you want me to raise a beam to the rafters . . . sorry, but forget it. It's not going to happen."

Quick to rise, her enthusiasm now rapidly ebbed. Tears sprouted in her eyes. "I just don't want to quit," she said quietly. "I don't want to lose. I don't want to be defeated."

She sounded so heartbroken that Tara Cogshill took a deeper breath. She fell silent, hopeful that Willis Howard would do the same. He chose instead to have the final word. "I hate them, Mrs. Mc-Cracken," he said. "I hate them for what they did. But the bridge is gone. It's not coming back."

The old lady held her hands to her chest, as though she wanted to weep but could not, her pain too grievous to endure.

■　■　■

HE LED HIM THROUGH BRAMBLE and over loose stones, along rocky river streams and up short, steep hills that winded him, through forest and glen and a farmer's field in fallow lanced by a hot sun so that he perspired, smudging the war paint on his flesh so that he did not look human, yet he was alien to these woods and a stranger on this path. He followed Skootch, hoping that this was the right thing to do and also out of fear. Skootch had on his skinny sandals, but bereft of proper footwear Jake Withers settled on baseball cleats for this trek. Sometimes they proved to be adequate gear, yet useless on stone and being relatively new they were giving him blisters. So he suffered. His feet, his lungs, his thighs hurt. His skin was scratched and bled and at the sight of blood Skootch whipped him with a pine branch, driving him to the ground, then cackled as Jake complained and at moments in his own way begged.

He pleaded for Skootch to stop running and when he did stop mosquitoes and deer flies swarmed and he wanted to get a move on. Skootch was testing him, he knew that, but he did not know why. He chose this work, this livelihood, with this man, and so he ran through the woods with him, virtually nude, panting, bleeding, dizzy from the exertion and the heat. Skootch panted, too, but he only laughed at the bugs and blood, the heat and the scourge of the underbrush.

Jake collapsed once, and Skootch bent over him, breathing heavily, too, hands on his knees.

"Do you know how rich you're going to be?" Skootch asked him.

He did not.

Skootch bent down on one knee, close to him. "Whisper. In my ear," he said, "how much you'd like to make in a day. Give me a number. Each and every day. To make this worthwhile."

"I don't know," Jake said. He didn't.

"Think about it. Then whisper in my ear."

Jake thought about it and then he whispered in Jake's ear that he'd like to make a thousand dollars a day.

Skootch nodded, and remained bent on one knee. He placed a sweaty hand on Jake's slickened shoulder. "I can't let you make that much money, Jake. Once in a while, maybe. Not every day, day in, day out. If you made that much money you'd buy foreign cars and who knows what kind of woman you'd want to bring home or what kind of trouble you'd let rain down upon us. So no. You won't make that much. I won't allow it. But you will make enough, Jake, and women in our camp will surprise you, if only you give them a chance."

"I'm trying to give them a chance. I don't think they like me."

Skootch laughed. "Women, eh?" he said. He put his head back and hooted. "Woo-wee! The games they play! Imagine that. Playing hard to get in this day and age. You show them, Jake. You've got it in you. I see what you're doing now, what's your plan, and I have to tell you that I am relieved."

"My plan," Jake said.

"Yeah, letting them think you've got something on the side, back in town. That'll get them thinking. They'll fret and get wet. Are you loyal, Jake?"

"What? Yeah. Sure."

"You won't make a grand a day, I can't allow it for your sake or mine, but especially yours. Are you damn loyal anyway?"

"I said yes. Yeah."

This time when Skootch put his hand on his shoulder the fingers worked into his muscles, hurting him. He noticeably recoiled.

"Because if you're not loyal I'll slice your earlobes off right here, right now. They're a little large."

"With what?" Jake asked, and he smiled. He thought he was making a joke, rare for him, although his jokes had a habit of going awry.

"With this," Skootch said, and he produced an impressive hunting knife in his opposite hand. He placed the blade gently under Jake's chin and Jake fell back farther and lay flat on the ground, panting, searching about. They had run through the woods, over streams and up hills, and Skootch, close to naked in his thong and his sandals, wasn't carrying a knife. Now he did, and Jake Withers was desperately afraid of him.

"Skootch. Come on."

He leaned over him. He smiled as Jake's breathing grew erratic.

"Are you loyal, Jake, my boy? Are you now?"

Jake nodded in the affirmative.

"Yeah? You'll do what you're told? You'll make your rounds? You won't cheat me out of so much as a dime? I've got a ton of mouths to feed, Jake. You're going to stick your dick into some of those mouths I'm feeding. I don't want you to rip me off."

"I won't, Skootch. Come on. I'm loyal."

"Yeah? So I can stick my dick into you anytime I want? In your mouth? Up your ass slowly?"

"Come on. Don't talk to me like that."

"Don't tell me what to do or say, Jake."

"You're not that way."

Skootch laughed. "You don't have any clue what way I am, Jake. No clue." He removed the blade from the young man's skin but he did not move away from him or let him up. "Relax. I'm talking in metaphors, man. Don't you know metaphor? So, metaphorically, Jake, will you take it up the ass for me or not? I'm asking you that in a friendly manner. I really want an answer, though."

Jake did not want to reply but he knew that he should. "Yeah," he said. "Sure."

"You will, yeah?"

"Metaphorically, yeah. Of course. I'm loyal."

Pulling away from him finally, letting him sit up, Skootch sat on a patch of grass himself. "Some people think I'm a hard-ass, Jake. But am I really? I want my people to be loyal to the man who makes them rich and who takes good care of them around the clock. Honestly, do I ask so much?"

Jake chose to brush twigs and dirt off his sweaty skin.

"Do I now?"

"Course not. We're loyal, Skootch. That's not too much to ask."

He nodded to indicate that he was satisfied, and stuck the knife upright in the ground.

"Where'd you get that?" Jake asked him.

Skootch looked at the knife. The intensity went out of him, and he seemed abruptly disinterested in their circumstances.

"Sporting goods store. Hunting section. Why? Do you want it?"

"Yeah? No, I mean, where'd it come from out here? You didn't leave the camp with that."

"We haven't left our camp, Jake." He looked at the young man, then with his chin inscribed a broader territory. "What you see around you, the whole of the forest, this is our home. It's our divine encampment, Jake."

Jake nodded, and he wondered about a variety of things, and he wanted this day to end soon.

"Come on. Catch your breath. I'll show you something."

Skootch left the knife in the ground. Jake found that strange and looked back several times as they walked on through a thicket when there seemed to be many easy routes to follow. Then they broke out onto a small clearing that was surrounded by the thicket, but here a rock outcropping restricted the vegetation and Jake gazed at a rectangular wood box with a lid.

"Open it," Skootch instructed him.

He was flapping his hands at mosquitoes tormenting his neck and a deer fly trying to land in his hair. But he opened the box, which was about a foot deep and fourteen inches wide and about two and a half feet long. Inside were rags, empty bottles, and jars filled with liquid.

"When you come out here, bring matches. You got the fixings for Molotov cocktails. Do you know what they are, Jake?"

He nodded. "I don't get it," Jake said.

"Go back and get the knife," Skootch told him.

"The knife? I don't know if I can find it."

"Try."

Jake went back through the thicket the way they came and picked up a route that seemed familiar. When he came out to the area where they were sitting earlier he couldn't find the knife, although he saw where it had stabbed the earth. Skootch came up behind him, having leisurely followed along behind.

"I don't get it," Jake said.

"We didn't come alone," Skootch informed him. "Come with me."

They walked. This time he took an easy route, but the farther they went along the quicker became the pace. Skootch could walk so quickly that Jake needed to break into a trot from time to time to keep up. They emerged onto a gravel road, and Skootch walked along it for a while and then returned to the forest. He stopped, and they waited in the bush.

"Have you been listening?" Skootch asked him.

"To what?" Jake asked.

"That's my point," Skootch said, and he tore off across the road, bent over like a soldier hoping to elude gunfire. Jake did the same.

They walked through another section of standing timber and this time they came out to an area where a young woman whom Jake recognized was looking away from them through a set of binoculars. She was a very rounded girl who seemed athletic for her ample size. Something in the way she stood and sweated in the sunlight caused Jake to think that. Her hair was pulled straight back to a ponytail and she squinted quite severely when she turned and looked at them, holding the binoculars high in both hands. She wore shorts. Her white tank top with broad shoulder straps was damp with sweat and Jake could make out the ring of her left aureole very clearly and the soft jut of the nipple.

She raised the binoculars again, which pushed up her ample cleavage, as he and Skootch came alongside her.

"No trucks?" Skootch asked.

"Nary a one. Anywhere."

"I never heard a single diesel today."

"What's the deal?" she asked.

"They've moved their operations. Probably to Maniwaki. They've got a smaller job site up there."

"There's a few pickups around. That's about all they left behind."

Skootch appeared to be thinking.

"No, let's stick to Plan A. We'll be patient. They have to come back here. They can no more abandon these woods than we can. Jake?"

"Yeah?"

"Do you know Belinda well?"

"Yeah. Hi, Belinda."

"Hi."

"What I mean is, do you really know her? She likes you. Did you know that or did that skip your notice?"

He was embarrassed. He hoped that Skootch wasn't going to humiliate him in front of her. He noticed that Belinda was smiling sweetly, that she was not embarrassed by this, and then he accidentally glanced at her nipple. Her breasts were so large. He'd never been with a big woman. He steered clear. He was thinking that it might be interesting in the right circumstances, if she liked him well enough.

"I'm going to leave you two lovebirds alone," Skootch informed them. "We'll pick this up later, Jake. When you're done with him, Belinda, guide him home. The poor boy will only get lost out here."

"No problem," she said. Then, just as he was leaving, she passed him the knife. Skootch was about to take it when he changed his mind. "Put it back where you found it." He held his hand up high to Jake. They hooked their thumbs together and clasped hands. "Loyalty, Jake," Skootch breathed in his ear. "Loyalty is its own reward. You'll see."

"Loyalty," the younger man repeated, then he was suddenly alone with Belinda as Skootch disappeared into the woods.

She laughed.

"What?" Jake asked.

"You look really weird in that loincloth thingy. Not to mention the fucking war paint. What've you been doing? Playing Tarzan?"

"It's what Skootch wears," he protested.

"Yeah. Skootch. Consider the source, man."

Jake managed to smile. "Yeah. I guess. Tarzan. Something like that." He didn't want any attention on his loincloth, but Melinda was looking and then she stopped smiling and lifted her shirt right up and over her head. She wore nothing underneath and her breasts he saw were large and plump and so big and really sweaty. He stared. Her nipples were huge. She placed her left hand under one large breast and raised it up.

"Why don't you just take that silly thing off?" she suggested.

Jake found nothing to say. The size of her nipples impressed him. The one grew as she kneaded herself.

"The loincloth," she added.

"Here?" Jake wondered.

"You know a better place?"

Her right hand started to slide underneath the cloth while he flinched and considered what to do.

"Good lump," she noted.

■ ■ ■

RYAN O'FARRELL BOOKED OFF, BUT he did not drive the squad car home, a privilege afforded him by his rank, and he did not change out of his uniform. Instead, he drove up to his brother's house, parked on the street rather than the driveway, crossed the lawn, and knocked on the screen door. The wood door behind it was wide open. He could hear his nephews' voices rise from the backyard, and the next time he knocked he banged the door louder.

Valérie was coming to see who was there. He knew it was her, but looking through the screen into the dimness of the house he could not evaluate her expression or attitude. She wasn't really paying attention and had only the screen to open, but as she did so she was surprised to see Ryan.

"Hi, Val." Quietly.

She looked at him, then looked across her lawn at the squad car, then she chose to step outside and let the door slap shut behind her. She was carrying a dish towel.

"The front door, Ry?"

He looked sheepish for only a moment before he gathered his resolve. "I need to talk to Denny. Maybe it's better that we don't have that conversation in front of the kids."

"So you're being considerate."

"I guess so, yeah."

"Do you see his truck in the driveway?"

Ryan didn't need to look. "I do."

"Then he's home." She folded her arms across her chest, the dish towel dangling from a hand. She scrutinized him with some degree of venom but Ryan did not relent, then suddenly she did. "Ry. Talk to me first."

"Sure." He shrugged.

She stepped to the edge of the small porch. "How bad does this get?"

What he took to be venom, he saw now, was that but also a mixture of hurt, worry, anger, bewilderment, and fear.

"You're not saying he did it, are you?" Although he asked a question, he continued very quickly so that she wouldn't have a chance to answer. "Because I don't want you to say that, no matter what. Especially to me, but not to anybody, ever. Not even, and this is important, not even to Denny."

"What are you saying?"

"Because you'll have to convince yourself otherwise if you expect to have a chance here."

"Ry—"

"Do you want to keep your husband home, looking after you and the kids, or do you want him in jail?"

"I want him home!" she burst out. "What a stupid question. Ryan!" But she wanted to say a lot more besides that, only Ryan wouldn't let her.

"Then listen to me. Think differently and in a hurry. It's about the only chance you've got."

"Are you going to arrest him?"

Ryan looked down at the porch deck, then away, then back at her. "Val. It's not going to be me."

She held his gaze awhile. Her eldest was calling for her from the backyard when they both heard Denny's voice demand his silence.

"SQ," she said, meaning the provincial police, la Sûreté du Québec. The skin on Ryan's chin flinched, as if to confirm this.

Val exhaled, nodded, then did her best to get across a smile. "Good. Good. Okay. I didn't want Denny to have to deal with you."

"They're not going to give him a free pass."

She smiled, and opened the door. "It doesn't matter who they send," she told him. "Whoever it is won't be smart like you, or tough like you. Thanks for chatting. I'll get Denny away from the barbecue. And thanks."

"For what?"

"The front door."

Ryan paced the porch awhile, and finally sat on a railing with one foot on the floor and the other raised. He heard Denny's boots coming down the hall but he didn't look up until they went still. Denny remained inside the house, looking at him through the screen.

"Officer," Denny said.

"Denny."

"What can I do for you today?"

"I'd like you to answer a few questions."

"You can't ask me a few questions while I'm looking after the barbecue? You can't ask me a few questions over dinner? We have to be out here? We're having Atlantic salmon tonight, Ry. I know you prefer Pacific but it was the best we could find on short notice."

"So you knew I was coming."

"If I were a betting man, Ryan. Why don't you come around back?"

"Why don't you step outside right here? We might get into something, Denny. I don't want to do that in front of Valou and the boys."

Denny O'Farrell nudged open the door and stepped outside. He went to the opposite railing and leaned on it with his palms, his back to his brother. Then he turned around to face him.

"We have to work in Maniwaki now. That's a drive up. A drive back."

"I'm not asking you if you burned the bridge down, Denny."

"Didn't you already?"

"Because if you didn't do it and you say you didn't, I might not believe you, and we don't want that, right? But if you did do it and you say you didn't, that'll make you a liar. So I don't want to put us in either situation."

"What if I didn't do it and I say I did?"

"Do you really want to shit with me, Denny? Today?"

The younger brother minded his peace.

"I'm just here to inform you of something."

Denny shrugged. "Inform me."

"Brother to brother," Ryan said.

Denny shot a harder glance at him. "I'm listening."

"Burning the bridge is not some misdemeanour. If it's arson, then that's a major crime. Even so, I might be allowed to investigate, but not when the value of the loss to property is so extreme. The SQ assumes that the job is too big for any town cop and they take over the case. They'll take over this case, Denny."

Denny considered the news. "Well, good," he said. "Brother to brother, I didn't want to put you in an awkward position. Such as having to investigate me for no good reason. Just because there's been some rumours."

"Brother to brother, I'm still going to be in an awkward position. If you didn't do this, you have nothing to worry about. If you did, I'm not going to let you take me down with you."

They waited awhile, both quiet in the warm air. Denny chose to break their silence. "I don't see why you can't stay for dinner now. We're done talking, right? We haven't thrown any punches."

"Not so far. Thank you, but I can't stay. I've got a date."

Kicking up dust with his heels, ambling down the road, came a figure both men recognized at the same moment. Denny sighed.

"Have you talked to him yet?" Ryan asked.

Denny shook his head. "I just got home."

"Good luck with that."

Denny kept his eyes on his father as his brother stepped off the porch and started across the lawn. "Hey, Ry," he called to him.

Ryan slowed his pace, then stopped walking as he turned. The movement was familiar to Denny, something he'd seen from him throughout their lives together, and these days he noticed the same physical motion repeated in his two small sons whenever they were reined in by a parent. A slouch undermined his correct posture, indicating a total lack of desire to talk. "Yeah?"

"You don't want to stay and help me out here, do you?"

"Hell, no. You got this one on your own."

"Just so you know," Denny admitted, and while he did not look at his brother directly he wanted him to feel a certain intimacy in his words, "I feared talking to you more."

This time Ryan checked down the road at their father approaching.

"Denny, maybe that's something you don't quite have right. Maybe you don't get everything. Not every time anyway."

As he turned away, Ryan flicked his wrist, a mere halfhearted wave, and walked back to the squad car. On the street, he initiated a broad, over-the-head wave to his dad, which was returned, but the old fellow was still too far off for him to wait. He had a date and needed to change and get ready. He was glad for that excuse on many levels. Ryan glanced at his brother, briefly, before he drove off, just as Denny was going back inside.

Walking down the road, Alex O'Farrell just wanted to rest. He wished his older son backed up to say hello, if for no other reason than to give him a ride the rest of the way. He didn't understand this weariness all through his bloodstream. He didn't appreciate this aggressive grinding pain. Against his better judgement he was going to be good to his younger son tonight, not only because he wanted to eat, but later on he might have no choice but to ask him for a lift back home.

17

On their first date, Tara fiddled with the two-way radio in the squad car on route to dinner, acting like an eleven-year-old brat and playing the role to the hilt. Upon vacating the restaurant, tipsy, saucier than ever, she installed herself in the backseat, unable to leave as no interior handles for doors or windows existed.

"It's a squad car," Ryan protested, mildly at first, hands on hips as he stood upon the pavement. He could not willingly participate without being drawn utterly under her influence where, he feared, he might find himself awash. "In a public parking lot. I can't neck with you in the backseat if that's what you're hoping for. Is that what you're hoping for? People will notice."

"So?"

"They'll gossip. We'll be in the papers."

"Great! Not to mention, Ry, if you climb in here with me and close the door, neither of us can escape until we're rescued. Won't that be exciting?"

"Yes." He considered it, totally tempted. "And no."

"What do you mean, no?"

Essentially, she was waving around the prospect of public humiliation as her trump card. He was stuck on the pavement while she grinned at him from inside, delighted by his dilemma.

She poked her tongue out at him. Then showed him a little more thigh.

"Come on out," he said, trying not to sound plaintive.

"Make me," she parried. Tongue, literally, in cheek, she added, "One way or the other."

He could easily get silly in her company. Ryan countered, "I'll turn on the siren and walk away until you do come out."

Good chess move. This guy was proving more interesting than expected. "Arrest me," Tara challenged him. "Take me to the jailhouse."

So he closed the door on her and climbed into the driver's seat.

"Are you serious?" Her eyes, already large, seemed to expand as she gazed through the protective screen. He started up the car.

"Consider yourself under arrest, ma'am."

"Oh, now it's ma'am? And I thought our date was going so well. For a first date, anyhow."

"The lights are too bright at the jailhouse. Instead, I'll show you what we do with our incorrigible prisoners."

"Goodie."

She talked a lot, brushed her hair, and checked her look in a compact as he drove across the old covered bridge, then up a long hill to a roadside lookout above the beauty of the Gatineau. A lover's dark leap. Teenagers preceded them there, two couples in one vehicle, who spontaneously departed as the cop car pulled in. Then Ryan got out and opened the trunk. Tara had no clue what was on his mind, especially when he pulled out rope.

He opened the rear door opposite her.

"Sex toys? On a first date? Seriously, Ryan?"

When he used the rope to tie back a door to a tree, preventing her from locking them in, she laughed, and performed a mock scream when he crawled in beside her. She had no escape, wedged to the opposite door, and even though she intended to be playful she was suddenly intensely aroused by the desire in his eyes.

She liked that.

He kissed her, and she loved the seductive control that governed his passion as well as the fullness and softness of his lips. He was a good kisser. Ryan surprised her when he touched her intimately, and they both got giddy.

His hands seemed everywhere and not everywhere enough at the same moment. Briefly, she allowed him to slip back her bra with his thumb to take her left nipple between his lips.

What life can be. If only.

Tara prompted them both to surface.

A pretty fine first date, she assayed. She told him so while they searched each other's faces, but she did not tell him that this romantic gazing felt compulsory rather than spontaneous and was the only time during the evening when she did not feel at ease. Then, as though he knew that, he kissed her eyelids shut, and this silence and gentleness and darkness was lovely, too.

For their second outing, Ryan borrowed a friend's car. No more police vehicles with shotguns and radios to keep her preoccupied, and in any case he desired a modicum of elegance. His pal forgot that his three girls were due at ballet class, so while he promised Ryan the car, it was missing when he came over. The friend tracked his wife down and in a massive violation of procedure Ryan traded the squad car—on condition that his wife and daughter take it straight home from class—in exchange for the Camry.

He wasn't late, yet cut it close when he drove up to Potpourri, frazzled and edgy, to pick up Tara. No door to knock upon or bell to ring, access to her apartment was only through the locked store, so she was waiting on the railway tracks by the side of the road in a pale blue print dress with a scattering of polka dots above the hem of varying hues and sizes. In her hands she held a small black clutch. The light of the setting sun tinged her skin. In a trice he feared that he might slip into the danger of hyperventilating or succumb to some fumbling ailment equally embarrassing, or with any luck just be utterly tongue-tied. Parking, he fully intended to get out and in a gentlemanly flourish open her door, but lickety-split she hopped in, leaned across, and gave him a peck on the side of his mouth.

"Hi!"

Glumly, he stared.

"Ah, earth to Ryan. Hello!"

A laugh broke across him and he recovered. "You look gorgeous," he said, and put the car into drive.

"Thanks. You, too." She had that knack, to get the upper hand. Ryan noted that this was going to be a perpetual challenge. "Where to?"

"We have a table above the falls." At a stop sign he shot a glance at her. "At the Old Mill Inn."

"Good. I stayed at the Old Mill when I first arrived."

"Then you've eaten there already. Okay, I'm officially disappointed. We could go somewhere else."

"Hey, no, it's a great spot. Anyway, I only ate at the bar. On a barstool. Like a hooker. I didn't want to sit at a table by my lonesome. Too conspicuous. Men would admire me, wives hate me. I'd feel a trifle ill, frankly, to dine alone in a place like that. Akin to putting myself on display in public. So great, I'm delighted to dine properly with company. Do we have a view?"

"We have a view."

"Perfect. So how's tricks, Ry? Have you put your own brother in jail yet?"

She was needling him, he could see that, but still, there'd be no escaping this new and troubling circumstance in his life, although he fantasized otherwise.

■ ■ ■

A LOVELY EVENING, THE AIR on the lengthy outdoor balcony warm, the meal fine, and their chitchat hummed along quite naturally. Ryan was satisfied that the date was going well and kept a running score-card—so far, a positive tally. His qualms about dining out locally faded. Too many inquisitive eyes and straining ears being a concern. Yet the restaurant catered first to clientele staying at the inn overnight, then to tourists accommodated elsewhere but desiring a gourmet meal, and finally only randomly to cottagers and full-time locals. As far as he could tell, not a soul present was looking to tamper with his privacy. No one knew him.

"The SQ will spare you the trouble," Tara noted. Her vantage point took in the waterfall, a cascade mesmerizing in its continuous muffled thunder and sense of an endless moment.

"That possibility occurred to me," Ryan admitted.

"Okay," she said, embarking on a change of subject.

"Okay what? You're thinking something."

"Last time. First date. When I declined to catalogue every last titbit of my life history—"

"You refused to tell me anything of consequence."

"—you threatened to check me out."

Ryan raised one shoulder and lowered the opposite, a shift he performed several times, as if to emulate a teeter-totter seeking a balance.

"You did," she insisted.

"What I said was, specifically," he modified, "that pending your own detailed revelation of what you've been up to in your life, and in anticipation of that, ah . . . for lack of a better word . . . report, I was prepared to do my own study. If there's any black marks I don't know, if you're an embezzler on the run, I can find that out, being a cop."

"God, you're so tangled up on nuance, you'd think you were the lawyer." The way she smiled seemed wonderfully flirtatious. "So did you? Check me out? I bet you did. Or did the bridge business interfere? What did you find out? A whole whack of lies, I bet."

"So you admit it then." He was surprised by the revelation previously kept to herself. "You're a lawyer."

She briefly poked her tongue out at him. "Am I?"

"You're being sly, Tara. That's not how this is supposed to go down. You're supposed to tell me about your deep dark past."

"What do I get out of that again?"

"You get to ask whatever you might want to know about me. And I'll be obliged to answer. That's the deal."

"See. That's where we have an issue." Dessert was finished and the dishes cleared. They were on to coffee and Grand Marnier.

"Of course you do." That Ryan was enjoying himself showed. Determined to make things happen, he also felt comfortable in her company, and they both graduated to freely kidding each other. "From you I expect nothing but roadblocks, at least when it comes to personal stuff."

"Whereas you're an open book, right?" Unexpected, the retort caught him slightly off guard and Tara swooped in to take advantage. "So spill. You and your previous ladies. What went down with that?"

Ryan suppressed a worry. Over appetizers, she surprised him when she mentioned meeting his father and selling him a grandfather clock.

Odd, as his father bought almost nothing in life that he couldn't eat or wear. The two shared a pie on the stoop of Potpourri, on the husband's bench. No plates, just two plastic forks and the raspberry pie. They dug in. "We had a blast," she teased him. At least, he hoped she was teasing. "A bit like being on a first date. Except Willis came over and tried to ingratiate himself, the bugger. He wanted a slice, but he wouldn't eat from our communal plate." She rattled him then by recounting that on the stoop of the gift shop, in full public view, she gave his father a yoga lesson while Willis Howard watched.

"Yoga," Ryan noted. He was imagining her gyrations.

"He needs to loosen his hips and glutes."

"You got my dad to exercise." She might as well have told him he'd agreed to go bungee jumping.

"Twisted him up like a pretzel. I warned him. He'll be sore tonight. Watch. Tomorrow he'll feel better. He'll be back for more."

She knew how to keep him dangling on a string, the impending fall over a gorge not unlike the one alongside them.

"Of course he'll go back for more. You're a beautiful woman! Even if you crippled him, he'd be back for more."

The compliment mixed in with what he said wasn't lost on her, but she did defend herself as well. "I didn't cripple your dad."

They both smiled.

"You said me first," Ryan challenged her. "Why me first?"

"It's not you first. You investigated me. Whereas I haven't given you a second thought. So I've already been scrutinized. So it's *your turn*, see?"

He was about to acquiesce but thought better of it. "It is so *not* my turn. You sneaky devil! You pumped my dad for information! You already know more about me than I'd ever want you to find out."

She nearly slipped one past him, only to find out that he was sharper than anyone she previously dated. As if, perhaps, he could handle her.

"Actually," Tara demurred, "I only have your dad's version of events."

"And he's cagey. Like me. Or, rather, I'm like him that way. So you didn't get any real dope."

She turned serious. "I guessed that. I wondered why that was, what's the big secret."

"Meanwhile, my knowledge of you comes from outside sources."

"An impasse," she acknowledged.

"So you first," he decreed.

"Think so? Why me first?"

"Because I have nothing to say of interest. Brokenhearted boohoo stuff. But you. A rising young lawyer in a major law firm, who quit, not as anyone might think, after losing a case, but after winning a big one that most people considered unwinnable. Instead of riding that tide, raking in the dough and accolades, you quit. Why? Disillusioned? That old song?"

She played with her snifter, and while she cast a smile his way a few times it was not with any sense of happiness. He could tell that she was preparing herself to bend, to reveal more than she might initially have intended.

"As for my illusions, Mr. Smart-ass Policeman, I was disabused of them early in life. So, no. Not disillusioned. It's much more . . . standard shrift."

He waited, his expression slowly losing its swagger.

"Disenchanted," she said.

He waited still. He saw that she was not up to being coy, but was quite serious for the moment. "How so?"

"Mainly with myself, truth be told. To say that I suspected that I did not like winning might be true, to a point, although I didn't understand it at the time because, you know, I'm pretty damned competitive. Always have been. For a while that's all I had to go on, but I knew there was more to it. Ry, the only way I can explain this—not just to you, but even to myself—is step by step. I've done this before—explained it—with Mrs. McCracken. So I know how. Step by step. First, I was asking myself, 'What's going on?'"

"Meaning?"

"Meaning, what's going on with me? Tired of winning makes no sense. A preposterous idea, really. Borderline insane. I lived with the concept for a while because it's all I dredged up. Step two, it hit me that I still loved winning, just less so when I deserved to lose. That kept me going for a few days, mulling it over. In the past I'd won cases for clients who were assholes and it occurred to me to quit then, except that that seemed lame. Why let those types drive me out? I stayed on, but less happily. Step three, I found out I could win cases when the lawyers across the aisle were . . . thorough enough, and sufficiently anal-retentive that it could be honestly argued that they did their job, they just lacked the mental *elasticity* to keep up. When I thought it over, a so-called unwinnable case sometimes was like taking candy from a baby." She let her voice trail off.

"You weren't sufficiently challenged."

She shook her head slightly, to indicate that that wasn't it either.

"I never wanted to be a lawyer in the first place," Tara told him, her voice quiet now. "Took me a while to admit that, though. I just never decided on anything else. Daddy's profession became mine, by default, in a way. In school I found out that I enjoyed the law, a good portion of it anyway. And I'd always loved winning. Winning made me want to win again. I wanted a streak. Then I was home one night by myself. Relaxing, but feeling, I don't know, vaguely uneasy. To cheer myself up

I had a drink, but I also spent time adding up what my billable hours and my commission for the big win were going to be, roughly. I would have to do that accounting in a few days anyhow. I started to calculate forward. What could I expect to earn over the next year, decade, and finally, over my lifetime? I looked at the final number. Then adjusted it to be more realistic, which brought it up even higher. Ry, it scared the living daylights out of me. And I wanted it. For the first time. The wealth. Oh yeah. The fame, too. Very cool. The power. Totally enchanting. And a tiny, wee, infinitesimal voice said to me—I can't stress how faintly that voice spoke, a microbe, as if it was an atom on life support—'So, babe, it's now or never. What'll it be?'"

"You call yourself 'babe'?"

"Sometimes." Her deeper pause indicated that more was forthcoming, and from a depth. "I realized that it wasn't about winning or losing anymore, if it ever was. The thrill was gone, if it was ever really there. Here's the thing—I wasn't living any part of my life through my own choices. My life was hectic, but orderly. Lots of pressure, but safe. Mapped out. No chaos. Nothing rapturous. Failed relationships in part because they were never great and they couldn't be great because they could never be separated out from the career, to think otherwise was just silly. My life was my career. Period. Not only was I doing what I didn't particularly want to do, and never really chose to do, but I was being, day in, day out, a person I didn't want to be. My life wasn't working and it wasn't going to work. I finally saw that this was as good as it was going to get, it was built in, no escape routes anywhere. Truth be told—I wish I could claim otherwise—my flight wasn't part of some tirade against the law. I got the law. Being successful wasn't about winning and losing, and certainly it had nothing to do with right and wrong."

"What else is there?" Ryan sipped from his water glass. "You've taken away the high road *and* the low road."

"What's left is billable hours, Ry. And a tolerance for a level of boredom that could break an ascetic's will. Persevere and the whole deal gets even more boring. An old classmate of mine defended criminals. Not one who came to see him was innocent, he claimed. No such thing. I'm a big girl, I can accept that. But it began to dawn on me that that held true in my world as well. My job was to be an arbitrator between grievance and greed. I got that. Except, grievance was not located on one side of a case and greed on the other. They both commingled. The victimized were on the beaten-down side of certain actions, but they weren't themselves *innocent*, they were also *culpable*. Work this out, but it's not about winning and losing, or about being right or wrong, or justice and injustice, or even about being powerful or impotent. For me, it came down to figuring out how one aspect always mixed in with the other." She'd been looking away, but sought his eyes now. "If you will, like fire on water, like a burning bridge. Doing what's wrong in order to alter the landscape and then trying to fix it. I was the bean counter, the one who rallied arguments in order to better obfuscate the truth, or to support the hour's lesser stupidity. I was the one who—*successfully*—represented this set of greedy bastards with a grievance against that set of greedy bastards with a gripe. And I was going against anal-retentive legal teams lacking the mental elasticity to at least make things interesting. So, yeah, after a long, dark night of the soul that lasted a week . . ." She let her voice trail off.

"You quit. Just like that," Ryan said. Admiration tinged his voice.

She squinted a little, and the smile forming along the edges of her lips evident enough that he grew worried.

"You crazy?" Tara inquired. "You think I'd surrender my law career to a dark night of the soul? After all that torturous work? Get real, babe. That's not what happened."

He knew he resided in the palm of her hand, desperate to have it all explained to him.

Tara used a pinkie finger to break the surface of her Grand Marnier, then moistened her lower lip with the fluid, and tasted it with her tongue. "When I did leave—and actually I never decided to leave, I just up and left—"

He settled back in his chair. "Up and left," he repeated.

"Un-huh. How that happened is another story."

"Oh, it's another story."

"Which I'm not telling at the moment, do you mind much?" That teasing laugh again, but she quickly returned to being serious. "The hardest part about it, Ry, I didn't want my split, my flight, to be naïve. It had to be real. To feel real, anyway. I was throwing a big part of who I was down the drain, truth be told. I was so far removed from anything that felt real for so long, I guessed whatever I did had better be extreme. Toss everything away. Back to square one. Re-create it all. My very own personal end of the world. My very own personal rapture, even. That's what I was craving, in a way. Some sort of exceptional reality. Some sort of light. If not a rapture, then a rupture. A change."

"So you hopped an old steam train to Wakefield."

She smiled brightly, lighting up the room for him. "I'd have preferred a freight, riding the rods, but what can you do? I came in style. An old pickup took me from Halifax to Ottawa and when it broke down, lo and behold, there stood the Wakefield choo-choo."

"So this was never your destination."

"Yes and no. I was following a thread that indicated my destiny. Not exactly bread crumbs, but I'll say no more about it. But destiny, not destination, that's the key. That's what I was chasing. Complicated enough for you? I burned my bridges—pardon the reference, Ry—and here I am. A poor girl selling grandfather clocks to granddads. Cool, huh?"

Ryan found himself enamoured of her story, and it jived with his own scant investigation. Except she held back the most important part. Intuition told him that she wasn't giving that part up anytime soon. She trusted him with a few facts, but he had still to earn the more intimate, more privileged, information. And yet, when he received a modicum of encouragement from her, he chose to confront an issue head-on. He knew that she was lying, in part, and he found this rough to handle.

"What's wrong?" she asked.

He wasn't adept at hiding much from her. "Your father, my study showed, is a professor of microbiology in Halifax. He's not a lawyer."

Guys trying to make her would have let that pass. She liked that he had the backbone to bring it up.

"Just checking, Ry. To see if you did your homework." As he continued to stare at her, she chose to come clean, removing the tongue from her cheek. "Okay. I didn't mean my father. For a while, not that long really, I had a lover. He had a nickname. You know, a term of endearment."

"An older man."

She shrugged. "Somewhat. Whatever. It's in the past. He wasn't ancient. God, the look on your face. Is this a problem?"

Ryan deduced that she kept him working, that every hurdle led to another. He expressed at least a level of consternation in several gestures and expressions that might more commonly denote a stressful labour.

"That's not the problem," he decided. "I don't think so anyway. I may have to see how it settles. But . . . your story would have led anyone to think, and me to think if not for my research, that you referred to your father. The reference made your career path seem more legitimate, in a way."

First she smiled, then she placed both elbows on the table, intertwined her fingers, and rested her chin upon them.

"My career path remains," she countered, "legitimate. But on the honesty ledger, are you so forthright and honest yourself at every turn?"

"It's early days as far as getting to know each other goes. I've been ripped in the past."

"Your poor boring past," she stated, once more throwing him off. "For God's sake, Ry, you're on a date. You want to criticize me for a figure of speech?"

"Calling your ex-lover 'Daddy' is not a figure of speech."

"Ryan, don't take this the wrong way or anything, but you're so full of shit, you reek."

He laughed. Her knack. He'd not want to be opposing counsel in a courtroom with her, but if he was learning anything, it was to show no fear. "Okay, I'm curious. How do I take that the *right* way?"

"Ryan O'Farrell, true or false. If a murder occurred in this town, by law you would cede authority to the SQ. They would investigate, not you."

She was waiting for an answer, so he said, "That's true."

"With respect to any major crime, however, either the minister of justice would have to direct the SQ to take over the case, or the local police could choose to make a formal request for the SQ to do so. A request, by the way, they are not permitted to decline. I have not seen the justice minister on TV lately—"

"I made the request," he admitted.

"Which means?" she probed.

"Which means what?"

"You did not merely lead me to believe—which was what I did with you, I admit, which is what you're so upset about—

"I'm not," he began, and finished his thought, "upset," but he was already conceding that he was exactly that. Upset.

"—but, Ry, you specifically told me that the SQ was obligated to take over the investigation of a major crime, that that was the case whenever the dollar value was so high. In other words, you lied to me. On only our second date. You lied. Not only a big lie but a really elaborate one, too. So, Ry, what do you have to say for yourself now, oh Mr. High and Mighty Bullshitter Cop?"

She feigned talking sweetly to him, yet he considered himself roundly condemned. "Yeah," he said. "Well, that's true. I admit it. I lied."

He felt stuck. He matched wits with her to this point in time, but now found himself bereft of a response. He was surprised and more than mildly relieved when she chose to bail him out.

Tara sat back, perfectly emulating his posture, one hand down on the chair, the other on the table. "Hey, Ry. I know what a pickle you're in. The town is waiting to see if you'll hang your own brother, and if you don't, they're prepared to lynch the both of you. Bringing in the SQ quiets the naysayers, and yet . . . if they know that you did it on your own, people will think that you acted to take yourself off the hook, that you sold your own brother down the river. Because, you know, that's pretty much what you've done, in a way. So instead, you made it look as though you have no choice. Of course, you want your brother to think that way, too, that you have no choice."

"That's one side of it," Ryan murmured. He was hanging on by a thread.

"And how can you explain to anyone," she continued in a single stream, "let alone to me, that you're far more intelligent than that? Who knows in this town how smart you really are? Ry? How crafty? You keep that to yourself, don't you? Your dad says so anyway and I think he's right. If you tell people that you brought in the SQ because as the local authority you will remain an informed party, and from that position you're better situated to . . . oh, I don't know—help? . . .

your brother? . . . well, why do that? Telling everybody your reasoning is never part of the plan, is it? People won't be able to keep up anyway, right? So you trust that you can tell your little fib and get away with it. As far as anyone can see, your hands are tied. The SQ is on the case. Nothing you can do about it. Trouble is, that means lying to me, too. How's that working for you so far?"

"You talk a lot," he pointed out.

"So interrupt."

He put up his hands, partially in surrender, partially to help mould a new idea. "Tara. Ah. How does this play out, do you think?"

She looked at the finger he was wagging back and forth between them. "You're talking about me and you? You're changing the subject? Now? I don't think so."

So he leaned into her. And placed his trust in her hands. "People in this town are ready, as you say, to lynch my brother. If not literally, they'll do what they have to do to make him pay. They're being somewhat overly emotional about it right now, even a little extreme."

"Granted," she said.

"But, if outside investigators come in, suddenly they'll clam up. They'll mind what they say. Their threats, their lies, their exaggerations, the rumours they've concocted to be facts, the shreds of information they've reconfigured as elaborate conspiracies, suddenly will vanish, because this town will not shovel shit onto one of their own to outsiders. No matter who, no matter the crime as long as it's short of murder, and I'm not even sure about that. We'll eat our young, but we won't force-feed them to outsiders."

Tara was getting this. She was impressed. "So you bring in the SQ and suddenly the rumourmongers shut up."

"They're run to ground. It's my way of making this town shut up, so a proper investigation can take place, not a rush to judgement based on hearsay and rumour and innuendo. And rage. And past grievances. My brother catches a break this way. If he's guilty, he's guilty. But now it won't be a bloody lynching."

She admired his passion, startled by the intelligence behind the intensity. She was in trouble here, but she was routinely in trouble whenever she took up a fresh romantic interest.

Something else, as well. This guy devised his strategy on his own, he could risk no confederate. He probably did a lot of that. He was well liked in his community, but he had to be a lonely man.

He continued to try. "So how does this play out? After the big fib?"

His words, his look, his smile, conspired to make her laugh a little. "You're talking about our kiss good night later on? Because only that is up for grabs, pardon the pun. It's still on. But that should mark the limit of your ambitions for the evening. You lied to me, bro. You gotta be punished for that."

Consciously ramping up his charm, the intimacy of seduction, he lowered his voice yet another notch. "Now about this kiss. Can it linger awhile, at least?"

A fleeting blush betrayed her, in its way a form of concession.

She leaned towards him as well, and lowered her own voice, and covered his hands in hers. "See, sweetie, this is the deal. I'm complicated. You're not. You fall for complicated women. That's your problem. It does you in. Your dad says so, and anyway I can see it in you. I don't fall for simple strong guys like you. I prefer crash-test dummies. Maybe it's time for a change. Who knows? But, whenever I have a dalliance with a straightforward nice guy, it turns out I'm too complex for him. So the deal is, we're wrong for each other, so wrong, and you should know that and get it through your noggin at the outset. I'm not getting on the fast track to disaster here. Even though I'd survive. Would you? Odds are, no. So don't rush it."

"If you think we're so unsuited—"

"Why bother?"

He nodded.

"I got a crush on you, Ry. Okay? Not stop-the-presses or anything, but I do. I'm old enough to know that there will always be another handsome dark stranger farther on down the road who'll seek me out. So. There's that. Why risk hurting someone I'm finding out I kinda like? Because I'm finding out that I really kinda like you, Ry, and I can't dismiss that, and because . . . you're a bastard, you know, but damn it, despite your country-hick status, aren't you just about the smartest man I've met? Who's my age anyway. And doesn't that fucking appeal. Am I right or am I fooling myself? Let's just say, I'm willing to stick around and find out. But here's the kicker, Ry—I hope you can tell I've thought about this—I'm holding out. That's a conscious decision. This isn't going to be easy for you. If things go badly, you can thank me later. If they go well, and the odds are they won't, then at least I'll have learned something along the way."

Ryan was not convinced that she was as complicated as she claimed, or that he was as straightforward as she judged him to be. Yet they'd arrived at a threshold. What lay beyond was worth pursuing in his mind and heart, so he wasn't sure if he should argue the case just yet. But he did.

"Give me an example," he suggested, "of how you're so compli-cated."

"You poor lamb," she said.

"Just one example."

She mulled that over. The question was fair, she considered, and to answer was fair to him. "Okay. Just one example. I think your father is hot. I don't mean cute, or that I admire his rugged good looks. I think he's attractive. At least to me. Hot."

He wished he never asked.

"Restroom," Tara announced, and unwound from her chair. Then she leaned over him while standing and indicated the endless cascade of water into the gorge below. She whispered, "Down there, where the water slows, where it's deep enough to have a dip? My first night here, I swam in the moonlight. Nude. Think about that while you're moderating your ambitions for the evening."

While she was gone, Ryan called for the cheque. Waiting, watching the steady tumble of smooth black water, he grinned. He knew that she was perfectly correct in one instance, and wondered if his father told her things about him that tipped her off. Complicated women were his undoing a few times in the past. He thought that he won her over for a moment during their discussion, but as always, she could not part company until she attained the upper hand. A compulsion with her, he gathered. A complication. He chuckled silently to himself, knowing that he didn't mind. At least, for the time being, not yet.

18

Belinda proved kind to Jake through a good portion of the night, until he fell into a deep, remorseful slumber. He accepted that he had lost his life. Later he awoke intermittently, both exhausted and restless. To readjust. She slept in such odd positions, mainly on her tummy, with her mouth askance emitting a strange clatter and blast. Several times he had to shove her off him—a foot once, an arm, her breath from his face—but he gathered that this is what people did when they slept together, especially in a bed that drastically sagged in the middle, bodies harnessed by that sad gravitational pull. He'd never previously slept overnight with a girl while reasonably sober and the enterprise proved surprisingly revelatory to him. Once he was afraid he couldn't breathe, and failed to figure out if he was having a bad dream or if he was quietly suffocating against the press of her back.

In the morning, Jake was awake for a while yet didn't budge, couched in her comfortable softness and oblivious to the world. He considered going for a piss, only to crash and snore. Then he was wide awake, startled and disoriented to discover that he and his new girl were not alone.

"Skootch? That you?"

In the morning shade in a corner of the room the tall man seemed to levitate inches off his seat, his hands as high as the top of his nose at rest on a walking stick. Flies alighted upon his skin. Although he seemed immune to their trespass, Jake Withers did catch him blow one away with a gust of breath.

"Dude, put some clothes on. Mother of God, you're giving me a hard-on just looking at you over here."

Hastily, Jake yanked up a sheet, a motion that gave Belinda cause to stir.

"What're you doing here?" he demanded.

"Waiting for you to wake the fuck up, what do you think? Trying to resist masturbating myself." He tapped his stick four times, a hollow-sounding beat. "Do you do that, Jake? Cast your seed upon the dark waters, like a sailor boy? Across the dusty earth like some randy farmer lad?"

"Fuck off."

"Oh my. He's got his dander up. Anyway I agree. Enough dilly-dallying. You slept so long a fellow might think you never been inside pussy before. Let's get a move on, man. We're sailors today."

"What?"

"You heard me! Get dressed."

"Get the hell out of the room first," Jake insisted, the sheet wrapped tightly around his midriff.

"What? Are you Presbyterian now? Get up!"

"Get out!"

"Jesus!"

Jake wasn't sure if Skootch was storming out or just doing a pantomime of storming out, but momentarily he heard him opening the fridge door and shaking cereal into a bowl, so he couldn't be in any genuine bad mood. He dressed quickly and Belinda was awake now, not the least concerned about her nudity as she stretched her arms and yawned, then grinned. "Kiss me," she said. Then she picked grit from an eyelid.

He kissed her anyway.

"Mmm," she said.

He didn't know if she was referring to their time through the night or the morning peck but either way he accepted her murmur as being complimentary.

"Skootch is here," he said.

She examined what she'd scraped from her cornea. "What's he want now?"

"Maybe just breakfast."

"He'll want more than that. He always does."

Jake was pleased that she put something on as she got out of bed, before padding across the floor in her bare feet to tramp outside to the communal outhouse to pee.

"Kid!" Skootch was yelling, so he ventured out to the kitchen.

"What do you want, Skootch?" Jake asked him.

"We're sailors today. Have you seen my raft?" He was all but nude and scratching the back of his naked right thigh.

"What raft?"

"Upriver. Not far. A short hike for a fit man. We'll sail her merrily downstream into town. Me and you. Moor her up there. Consider it a project."

"Oh yeah?" Jake shook out cereal for himself, Cheerios, although as he poured the milk he felt the urge to urinate intensify. He started into the cereal and caught a dribble down his chin just as Belinda returned. A cat slipped inside in the nick of time as the ill-fitting screen door thunked shut. Belinda topped up the cats' bowls while Skootch bored in on a second helping. "How big is this raft? What kind of raft?" Jake asked.

"It's fucking enormous," Belinda attested on her way through to the bedroom to get dressed. "Why are you moving it, Skootch?"

He answered with his mouth still full of Cheerios. "Because I can." He chewed and swallowed, then explained. "Occurred to me in my sleep. Call it a revelation if you want. The bridge is gone now. So I can sail downriver as clean as a whistle. There's no structure to stop me. Except for deadheads."

"Deadheads?"

"Logs stuck in the water from the old days. Know any sea chanteys, boy?"

Belinda came back to the bedroom entryway, where a light curtain hung in lieu of a door. Struck by a thought, she said, "The rapids."

Skootch winked. "Don't worry your pretty little head about anything so trivial as the rapids. Thanks for your input, though. So sweet. But Jake will see us through! He sure looks like a river rat to me. Doesn't he to you?"

Skootch was positively beaming, and Jake wondered what Belinda would say, whether or not he looked like a river rat to her, too, as he stepped outside to piss on the forest duff.

■ ■ ■

THE PLAN, INITIALLY, FORESAW SETTING up shop in the centre of town to catch tourists disembarking from the train. Mrs. McCracken went so far as to erect a table under a sun umbrella, then sit on a folding chair to await the locomotive's telltale toot. Yet before the train arrived, she abandoned the strategy, and decamped to the road leading up to the old covered bridge which was no more.

An inspired move.

Sitting alone in the railway yard she began to feel foolish. Hot under the sun, she felt her confidence ebb. Something did not seem right. She gleaned that she would probably come across as an old kook on a mission, and not in any way that she could turn to her advantage. She'd find it necessary to pontificate and argue, relentlessly urging people to sign her petition. How else would she keep the throng from slipping away, *to have their fun,* or from avoiding her altogether? At the bridge entrance, on the other hand, she need not say a word. The silence of the missing span would speak for itself and for her cause. As many tourists per day as once tramped upon the old relic now visited the austere vacant space, for the fire made the national news and the site—where nothing remained to be seen—was suddenly a landmark for prurient interest.

On her table, Mrs. McCracken placed stones with enough heft to guard her collection of photographs against the breezes. Pictures of the bridge in flames. She needn't initiate a word as the minions arrived. They gazed upon the vacant space and the river. They checked out the snapshots in her collection. They smiled, and read the petition with interest. They signed, while she sat comfortably under the protection of trees and did little more than smile.

She was further inspired. As the train made ready to depart, *that* was the appropriate time to set up shop by the locomotive. By that time of day, word would have circled around. Visitors would be less suspicious, more friendly. Some might urge their travelling companions who'd not signed to do so. What's more, while they were waiting, she'd sell pies. And lemonade. And make a mint.

Locals contended that her idea was absurd, that no level of government in a million years would rebuild the old covered bridge to re-create the very problem they were failing to resolve. And doing it privately was financially ludicrous. The wood alone would cost millions, the labour, thrice that. Yet outside visitors were both more open-minded about such matters and less influenced by garish opinion. They wanted the bridge back. They thought it was a grand idea. They were willing to sign a petition to make it happen. Especially because the old lady seemed so sweet.

While they were at it, a number of travellers, just before they climbed back on the train, surely would purchase her lemon meringue. Her strawberry-rhubarb. The apple crumble. Mrs. McCracken felt giddy with the joy of her idea. "Nothing ventured, Buck!" she advised her cat after her first foray by the bridge, for she was giving herself an hour off before returning to the rail yard. "You watch! More than nothing will be gained."

■ ■ ■

"DOES IT EVEN FLOAT?" JAKE asked.

"I think so," Skootch speculated. "Though it's been a while."

The raft, about fifteen feet square, supported three levels of shambles stacked one on top of the other. A banged-up kitchen stove and a ceramic toilet with its lid a-kilter stood out in plain view. The deck was littered with baseball bats and ropes and children's toys and a set of aged downhill skies without the bindings and what appeared to be a small car's axle. The edges of the planked deck were rimmed with slices of frayed truck tires retrieved from where they'd blown out on highways. A flag of a foreign country Jake could not identify flew on a leaning wood mast erected in pieces and bound together. Scraps of wood, junk pottery, and bicycle parts were piled in what might charitably be called the bow. The first storey of the teetering plywood shack growing out of two-thirds of the raft housed sleeping quarters. A mattress slept inside. The room reeked. Above that level, up a wood ladder hammered to the outside walls, a space purported to be a den, although it could serve as a kid's playroom as only small fry need not duck the low ceiling. An old sofa and an even older armchair and a simple wood bench toppled onto its side welcomed adults who slouched in, but any such visitor, Jake saw, first stepped over a litter of junk. On the outside, black tarps were fitted as eyebrows above the windows, which could be lowered into place during a storm, although Jake guessed that the interior would then feel much like a coffin's.

The ladder ascended to the roof, what Skootch called the sunporch.

Broken-down old patio chairs were strewn about up there, the webbing on one busted clean through. A squirrel skittered off as they arrived.

"We can sun-bake in the nude!" Skootch exulted.

"*You* can," Jake corrected him. Then he asked, "So it doesn't float?"

The forward edge of the craft rode upon mud.

"It might. Probably it floats. We won't find that out until you go."

"Me? *I* go?"

"Look. Somebody has to meet you with lines to grab her as you sail past. Otherwise you'll sail on down the river and never stop. So that'll be me. I'll volunteer. Because I know ropes. I'll moor you to the shore in town."

"That's only if it floats, if it gets that far and through the rapids."

"You can swim, can't you?"

Jake could not deny that he could swim.

"But what if I can't catch the line you throw me?"

"Then I'll throw you another! Anyway, you'll catch it. Know why?"

"Why?"

"You won't have a ton of choice. It's catch a line or sink, Jake."

"Shit," Jake said.

"Okay," Skootch concurred. "We'll fix her up some, make her

look pretty, then you'll sail her down the beautiful Gatineau River into Wakefield."

Every engine onboard—and there were several, Jake calculated, as he looked around—appeared unattached to any fuel source, and in any case heralded its shabbiness, already culled for critical parts.

"With what form of propulsion?" he inquired.

"The current, Jake. You told us you saw that bridge sail away? If a dumb-assed burning bridge can sail downstream, imagine what a raft can do! A houseboat built for the purpose! You'll be our riverboat captain, Jake. Think of the adventure. The whole town will watch as you surge through the rapids, they'll cheer as you come ashore. You'll be a local hero, boy. You'll make the news."

"As long as it's not on the obituary page," Jake said.

"God Almighty, I wish I was you," Skootch attested.

■ ■ ■

LATE AFTERNOON SETTLED UPON THE town. Nothing seemed at risk to Ryan Alexander O'Farrell as he drove down Main Street. Tourists were dispatched back to the city aboard the steam train, and the evidence from the day confirmed a creeping worry: the train wasn't booked to capacity. The lack of a covered bridge perhaps eroded the visitors' numbers, a trend likely to worsen as time went by.

While Ryan received the official count from the train's conductor, no one else noticed the 16-percent drop in passengers. Tourists remained ubiquitous throughout town, and the corresponding fall in revenues would only show up over time. If the numbers indeed went further down, then passions might rise.

He drove out of town into a keyhole residential development, where he spotted Samad Mehra in his trucker's garb, mowing the lawn.

Ryan stopped the squad car in front of Samad's house and donned sunglasses and a trooper's hat. He did not do this routinely, but he wanted to strike a badass pose.

Spotting him, Samad turned nervous. Conspicuously, he cut the power to his lawnmower, and as the engine sputtered to silence he was searching around, as though contemplating a mad dash.

"Hey, Samad," Ryan said. Stopping in front of him, he put his hands on his gun belt.

"How's it going, Officer?" Samad asked.

Ryan coughed up laughter, surprised by that remark. "Officer! You never call me that."

Samad was nodding and Ryan half expected him to bow. "I don't know what to call you."

"So then you know why I'm here," Ryan said.

Samad looked away, then nodded yes, then shrugged, unable to decide.

Ryan helped him out. "You're right to think that this is an official visit. You're a smart man, Samad."

"What's up?" Samad asked. He kept glancing back at his house to see if his wife was watching, or if she would be out soon to help.

"I'm trying to add up how many guys it took to burn down the bridge. Any guesses? There's Denny, you—"

"Me!" The man seemed apoplectic, and clamped both his palms on his chest.

"You carry that extra fuel for hunting. So it was you and Denny—"

"He's your brother!" Samad cried out.

"What's your point?" Ryan asked.

Samad looked clueless.

"Nice lawn," Ryan mentioned.

"Thanks." Samad gazed across it. They both did.

"Do you fertilize?"

"Oh yes, believe it, I fertilize. I weed to exhaustion. Joce, she won't let me use chemicals. Not even the legal ones. I keep the grass thick. That solves my problems. No creeping Charlie. My neighbours? Dandelions. On my lawn, not too many. Did I tell you? You can go look. Go. Look. My fuel barrel is full."

"Say what? Your fuel drum? You mean on your truck?"

"It's full."

Through the dark glasses Samad could not be certain that Ryan was glaring at him, but he felt uncomfortable looking back at himself reflected on the twin lenses. They were mirrors and he wanted to tell him so. "You know what that means, don't you, Samad?"

"What does that mean?" he asked.

"You filled it up after it was emptied. I'll check, but I don't expect to find your truck on a video gassing up. I won't find a credit card trail."

"No, no. You are right. You will never find that."

"Because you're a smart man, like I said. You located a full forty-five gallon drum out in the woods somewhere, didn't you, at one of your old job sites? Filled it ahead of time and then refilled your own from that, so nobody's suspicious. That's good. On the other hand, that makes this entire episode premeditated. That's bad. Isn't it, Samad?"

"No. Yes!" He shrugged helplessly. "I don't know. Wait. I don't understand you, Ryan."

"You went there after the bridge burning and refilled your drum. To make it look like it was never empty. But only a really dumb cop would fall for that one. You don't think I'm that dumb a cop, do you, Samad?"

The suggestion mortified Samad. "No, no, you're a smart cop, Ryan. Officer. Officer Ryan."

"So André Gervais was the third guy with you. Who was the fourth?"

The trucker started to say something several times but no coherent word emerged. He finished with another elaborate shrug. Then he said, "Your glasses, they're like mirrors."

"Look, Samad," Ryan confided, "I really want to thank you for respecting me. You're an honest man. You've helped me out a lot today. Thanks."

He turned to leave. Samad called him back and Ryan faced him again, hands still on his hips.

"I didn't tell you anything!" Samad protested.

"You didn't deny that it was Denny and André, Samad. I want you to know how much I appreciate that." He walked towards his car.

"Wait a minute!"

Ryan kept walking.

"Hey, wait a minute! Wait! Ryan! I didn't tell you anything! I didn't do it, Ryan! None of us did! We didn't burn the bridge. It wasn't me! It wasn't us! It's just a rumour! I swear it!"

Ryan didn't salute him exactly, but he touched the fingertips of his right hand to the peak of his cap as he climbed back into his vehicle. Samad looked crestfallen, holding his hands out, palms up, as though imploring him to listen to reason as the policeman drove off. He looked as though he was ready to drop to his knees.

Driving, Ryan checked his watch, wondering how this would time out. His next stop was at the home of André Gervais, as he expected that the man was not the first on Samad's call list. With luck, his arrival might be equally unexpected. Ryan was surprised when, minutes later, he strolled up André's walk to find him also working hard during his off-hours. A busy bunch of guys. André was hunched over a series of loose pipes, wearing a welder's mask and holding a blowtorch.

André watched him walk up, immobile except to push the hinged mask onto the top of his head, then nodding when Ryan got close. This time the policeman left his sunglasses in the car, judging that that ploy wouldn't work on this man, and anyway the sun was setting lower in the hills and trees.

"Hey, André." Ryan chose to speak French. "I guess you better put that down. I wouldn't want to get the wrong impression."

André turned off the torch and removed the mask altogether, which he tucked under an arm. "Putting in a backyard faucet, for the pool."

"You have a pool?"

"Aboveground. A crappy vinyl thing. What's up, Ry?"

"I talked to Denny first, André. I owed him the courtesy, you understand. You know who I talked to second."

André didn't. "Who?" he asked.

"Your weakest link."

Rising from his crouch on sore knees took an effort for the large man. "Okay. Do you want to make sense anytime soon?"

Ryan sighed, moved to his left, then back. "Four of you were out that night. Must've been. One guy to drive the truck. One guy on the pump, another on the hose. Denny was alone on the town side, so he struck the match. That makes four. You. Samad. Denny. I'm guessing Xavier. Four. Right?"

Slowly, feeling some aches and pains, André bent over and picked up his torch-ignition device.

"You're barking up the wrong tree, Ry. Just like everybody else in town. You shouldn't listen to idle talk like that. Dumb-ass gossip is what that is."

"You'll agree with me on this point, André. I was right to go to Samad before you. You're tougher, no question. But help your friend out here. If it wasn't Xavier, just say so." He looked right at him, gauging his reaction. "So Xavier was the fourth. I thought so. Thanks."

"I didn't say that," André insisted.

"You didn't have to. You didn't say it wasn't him."

"How am I supposed to know? I know nothing about it."

Ryan already turned to leave but now, confronted by what he assumed to be a lie, retraced his steps. "Samad drove the truck. Woof. You sprayed with the hose. Woof. Xavier ran the pump. Woof. Denny lit the match. Woof. How am I doing, André? Close enough maybe? Am I still barking up the wrong tree?"

André turned his torch back on and snapped the flint. The torch ignited and between them that bright light burned and they listened to the wind of its velocity. This time Ryan was the one to nod to the other as he took his leave.

∎ ∎ ∎

DENNY WAS SITTING ON HIS porch awhile, sipping beer, silent and brooding as the evening settled. Val ventured out once, drying a salad bowl in her hands.

"I just noticed the calendar. You have a game tonight. Did you forget?"

He looked up only briefly. "They can play without me sometimes," he said.

She observed him closely. "I'll remember that in the future," she said.

She went back inside and later called in the kids who were playing in the front yard where they caught more of the late-evening light. Momentarily, Boy-Dan came around to the back and repeatedly pounded a ball into his outfielder's mitt, as he was allowed to stay up later than the other two who took their baths first. Denny resisted the urge to ask him to be quiet, but Boy-Dan seemed to get the message anyway and quit the mitt pounding, and after a few minutes he went inside without being asked.

Darkness enveloped the yard when Valérie came back out. "Company," she announced.

He was expecting cops. "Who?" he asked.

"Hickory, Dickory, and Dock, who else? Do you have beer out here?"

He gazed back at her without comprehension.

"Your fucking partners in crime. They're coming around the side."

The remark was the first they shared concerning the fire. Ryan warned her to make a point of knowing nothing, and she kept her own counsel, and Denny was scared to death that she might confront him, for then what would he say? The truth? A lie? Either recourse seemed fraught with grievance and risk.

Denny held a deep breath, then released it slowly. He glanced at her off and on. For as long as he knew Val, she possessed a foul tongue. They went to the same schools together, but being three grades apart kept them from meeting until they were both out in the world. He met her, finally, over a pool table, and seven of the first nine syllables out of her mouth were curse words. He didn't know it back then but she was going through a hard time. Her father, a logger, left the family home. She was an adult by then but three years later, after they'd been married for a year and a half, she told him that she was the reason her dad left. She kicked him out, leaving the house to her and her mom. And then she married Denny, leaving her mom on her own, which caused a steady stream of guilt to flow for some time, before her mother moved back to another logging town where her sister was widowed and her mom and aunt lived in houses side by side across from the house where they were raised. "Happy," Val once said, "as they can be. Two clams." Which did not mean, she explained to Denny, that they were as happy as they should be.

He asked her then if she was happy. She answered that a lot of people have thought a great deal about how much a child inherits from the parents, "psychological and DNA and stuff like that," and that she had a mean streak in her that she got from her dad, "although he wasn't so bad really, he just talked like a sailor for no reason and everything that came out of his mouth was a complaint. I got tired of him. I probably wouldn't kick him out today, now that I'm older, wiser, but even today I'd just ignore him." And she confided that she had a sad streak in her that she got from her mom, "but I don't get depressed like her, hardly ever, her problem is chemical and I don't have that." Then she said that a happy streak that ran through her was uniquely her own, she couldn't say where it came from, but that he could rely on it because she had throughout her life so far and never been let down.

"Yeah," he told her on the porch. "I got beer."

Val closed the door behind her quietly as she went in, to not wake the kids upstairs as André, Samad, and Xavier came around the side of the house. Xavier went to the trouble of offering his hand, which was odd, although Denny shook it, while the other two made themselves comfortable on porch chairs and cracked open beers. Xavier then went down to the lawn below them and sat on a picnic table bench, facing out at them from the table, using the edge of the tabletop as a backrest. He chugged from his bottle.

"We weren't supposed to meet up, remember?" Denny reminded the three.

"We can't pretend we're not friends," André said.

"That's more suspicious," Samad concurred.

"People already know we're friends," André said.

"I know," Denny said. He sipped. "Yeah. Even Samad knows that much."

"What do you mean, even Samad?" asked Samad.

"Give him a break, Denny. Your brother skinned him alive tonight."

Denny looked up, curious about this turn. Xavier nodded to confirm that the comment was true.

"I'm not used to being interrogated," Samad complained.

"Interrogated!" Xavier quietly scoffed, and took a long pull on his beer.

The others weren't laughing. "So what happened?" he asked. He held the neck of his bottle between two fingers.

André seemed angry. "Don't underestimate your brother, Den."

"I don't," Denny assured him.

"He sold me down the river," Xavier maintained.

"Who did?" Denny asked.

"I did," André admitted.

"Wait a minute," Denny said. "You—"

"Basically, he made me say the fourth guy with us was Xavier. He gave me no choice. Either I said that or I said nothing. So I said nothing. Which gave us all away. I never knew he was such a hard-ass shit, your brother."

Denny waited for more, but nothing further was forthcoming, so he assessed what they'd told him. Took a deep breath.

"He's going to fuck us over, Denny," André said with conviction.

"He buttered me up," Samad confessed. "Then he barbecued my butt."

"My brother's not so tough."

"Rein him in, Denny. Rein him in or we're screwed."

"I got screwed," Xavier commented, "by fucking Samad and André, my amigos." He chugged his beer. "I don't know what's going to happen when he talks to people who don't like me."

"Guys, you're missing the point," Denny contended. "Ryan helped us out."

"You're missing the point," Samad decreed, an assertive statement for him. "My butt he barbecued. He stuck a thermometer up my ass to make sure I got done to perfection."

"For God's sake, Denny, we could do hard time for this if your brother doesn't let up."

"Actually, he was doing us a favour," Denny maintained.

"He wasn't doing me no favours," lamented Samad.

"Especially you, Samad. He was pointing out our flaws. Especially yours. Xavier, didn't he talk to you?"

"Not yet."

"That bothers me."

"What do you mean, our flaws?" André asked him.

"Ryan's not on the case. The SQ is taking this one up, because the bridge was so valuable. That makes it a major crime. When the property damage is that high, the SQ has to come in, the local cops bug out."

Denny drank from his bottle and for the first time that evening, the beer tasted good. He knew that he was figuring something out. He was guessing that he finally had help, and was surprised by the source of that assistance.

"Oh shit," André said.

"Provincial Police," Samad said. "I will be a Butterball."

"You guys don't get it," Denny stressed. "Ryan showed us what to do."

"He did not indicate no such thing like that to me," Samad insisted. "You are the one who does not get this." For the first time he shouted, *"He spread butter on my ass. Do you get that, Denny?"*

Probably Valérie was listening all along. In any case, she poked her head out to say, "You will not raise your voices. My kids are trying to sleep. They will not hear you talking because you're going to be quiet. The next man who raises his voice goes home." Not waiting around for anyone's acquiescence, she shut the door.

Samad apologized to Denny. "Sorry, man. But he did not help me out."

Xavier seemed to understand. He drew himself in from his sprawl on the bench and sat up straight. He noted, "He has to cover his own ass."

"Of course he does," Denny agreed.

André seemed to draw an understanding as well. "I can handle the SQ, but Samad . . . ?" He let his voice trail off.

Denny and Xavier nodded in concurrence.

"What about Samad?" Samad inquired. "I can handle SQ."

Denny tapped the base of his beer bottle against Samad's thigh. "You're too nice a guy, Samad. You have no experience at being a lying shit at heart, not like the rest of us. So handle this," he instructed him. "An SQ cop *interrogates* you, asks you a question, you say, 'I wanna talk to my lawyer first.'"

Samad looked around at his friends. "We got lawyers now? Who?"

"I don't know who," Denny fumed. "Do I look like somebody who knows lawyers?"

"So how come Ryan never talked to me?" Xavier wondered.

"He knows you were with us," added André.

"Thanks to you," Xavier reiterated.

André got mad but managed to keep his voice down even as his resentment leaked out. "I told him sweet fuck all but it didn't matter. Tell him nothing, it's still like you gave away the password to your on-line bank account."

"The point is," Denny intervened, feeling hopeful for the first time in a couple of days. He was seeing the light at the end of the tunnel and hoping that it wasn't a train. "Everybody says sweet fuck all from now on. If the SQ claim that they got us on video, they're lying. Whatever line they string you, it's not live bait, no. Don't fall for it. You had no idea what you were up against before. Now you do."

"How come?" Samad needed this explained.

"Because my brother gave you a dry run, Samad. He's not investigating the case. It's not his case. He gave you a taste of what it will be like, a chance to do better next time. So do better next time. What will you say?"

Samad thought it over. "I want to talk to my lawyer first. A lawyer I don't have, but maybe I will have one soon."

"Not that last part. The first part is fine."

"I don't sound guilty?"

"Do you want your ass barbecued or not?" Denny pressed him.

"Not."

"Good. If a cop says you sound guilty because you want a lawyer, tell him that people in town are telling lies about you. You need to protect yourself against those rumours and lies."

"What rumours? What lies?" Xavier asked him, assuming the role of an officer.

"I want only to see my lawyer. First, I want to find one, then I want to go see him."

"Same goes for everybody," Denny said. "But look, there's one more mistake you made tonight. Do you know what it is?"

No one had a clue.

"Ryan questioned two of you, and right after that you three came running over here to see me, putting the four of us together. Don't do that, okay? When the SQ calls, and they will, don't call each other up, and for fuck's sakes don't run to me. If it was the SQ who talked to you tonight, and they didn't know who the fourth man was, or the third, or the second, they would know now, just by following one of you here and seeing who else showed up. Remember, we don't know who the SQ will talk to first, second, or third. No contact afterwards, until we see each other on the job, like usual. Okay?"

They agreed that next time they would do things properly.

In close unison, the three visitors polished off their beers and this time each shook Denny's hand. Xavier and André nudged his shoulder, and Samad shared a knuckle bump with him. When it seemed that they might take too long, Valérie came out onto the porch, and they said their final good-byes to her as well and went on their way. Val sat in a chair close to her husband.

The night air was lovely, the darkness pervasive now.

They sat together in silence awhile.

"Kids down?" Denny asked.

"Oh yeah," she answered. "Denny," she started, but her impetus stalled, and she waited awhile.

Denny spoke next. He braved the threshold he'd been unwilling to cross, to include her. "I'm sorry about this, you know."

"Are you? Does it do any good, being sorry?"

He didn't know what to make of the question, and felt his defences rising. So he gave it time to let a visceral reaction pass.

"At this point, Denny," she went on, "regret doesn't mean much. I might lose my husband to a prison cell. My children will be without their father for who knows how long. With no income, the house will be gone, and then what?"

"Val, I don't think that—" He meant to say that he did not believe that things would come to that, but she stopped him short.

"That's right. You don't think. You believe that everything will work out in the end. Well, you know, I've always loved you for your optimism, Denny. But I never thought I was married to a criminal, and now, apparently, I am."

"Val."

"I hate this, Denny." She spoke quietly. "Do you get that? Are you hearing me? We're in danger now. We're in big fucking trouble. No matter what you intended, or what you expected, it wasn't this, but this, this is what we've got."

"Val. Listen."

"No, Denny. I don't want to hear it. I don't care what you want to say. Just fix this. Somehow, some way, before our lives get washed down the drain, fix this. Do what you have to do, but for fuck's sake, fix this."

A great breath expired from her, and she slumped forward to let it just go, to allow her grievances and pain and worry to slide loose. She just couldn't bear it anymore, this descent into an oblivion that she foresaw as inevitable but which Denny was denying as even remotely possible. In this matter, she knew she was right and that he was misguided. She wanted to get him to face reality or everything they both cared about would be forever lost. All that might be lost anyway.

"Old Mrs. McCracken," she let him know, "started up a petition today to build a new old bridge."

"That won't fly."

"People are angry, Denny. When people are angry, strange things happen. You, more than anyone, should know that."

Finally, she rose from her seat, leaned across to kiss his forehead, then left him there. Denny stared out into the night, wondering why his body felt so turbulent, how a pain without any physical origin could so intensely gnaw through his arms and torso.

■　■　■

As DENNY BLINDLY STEPPED INTO the ambient dark of his bedroom an hour later, he came upon Valérie still up, her body curled in the light of a streetlamp and contorted on the small bench seat by the window. Her fingers clutched the toes of one foot. He suspected that he might be in for another scuffle, but her mood had undergone a sea change.

"I'm sorry," Val said. He stood beside her. She put her feet down on the floor and rested her head against his tummy, and he held her there awhile.

Then he sat down next to her as she slid over. She used a handy tissue to dab an eye, then a nostril.

"I don't mean it," she said. "You can't fix this. If you can, you will, but saying fix this . . ." She raised and lowered her left arm. "The guys put that kind of pressure on you when they wanted the problem with the bridge fixed. Look where that got you. You did something incredibly dumb, Denny. So I'm not saying fix this."

"Because you don't know what the hell I'll do."

He meant to add a dash of levity, and perhaps succeeded, yet she found truth in the statement. "That's right. I don't know what the hell you'll do."

She reached out a hand, which he clasped.

"I'm guessing you thought this would go away, that nobody would say boo, nothing would happen. Burned bridge. No proof. That's that. Let's move on. Let's build a fancy new one. Maybe that'll happen. Why not? Nobody saw you do it, right?"

"Just out of curiosity," he asked, "how come you think I did it?"

"You'd've told me by now if you didn't. At least we have that much to rely on. You're not up for a lie of that magnitude. Not with me, anyway. I hope you're up to it with the rest of the world."

She grew concerned when he did not reply.

"No heroics, Denny, right?"

"No heroics," he reassured her.

"It's hard to imagine how this will work out well. If it works out badly, I'll have to get a job."

"Come on."

"I will. This is what I'm facing, Denny. The kids . . ."

312

"What about the kids?"

"Never tell them the truth. Promise me that. Right now they're sticking up for you among their friends. They'll be devastated. Boy-Dan's already disturbed. I guess he's heard some things. I mean, I don't want you to lie to him, but you can't let him down right now. You can't ever say to him that you did it. He'll be so disappointed in you. Please, Denny. Promise me."

"Sshh, shh," he motioned, and took her back into his embrace.

"It's not just that. Their disappointment. Denny, if they know the truth, they'll say it. If they say it, you're doomed. We'll be wrecked. For sure, Denny."

"Okay," he soothed her. "Let me talk to him. I won't lie but I won't tell him anything. I'll come up with something."

"He's got questions. You're away all day. You don't hear this stuff. But you should hear his questions."

Denny was avoiding the kids when he got home. In part, because they were looking at him strangely, and were unusually silent. They kept their questions to themselves in his presence, afraid, perhaps, of accusing their father of doing something bad. That just seemed so impossible, so unreal. He didn't know what to say to smooth things over.

"I'll work it out. That much at least, I'll work it out."

"Denny, you can't. That's the point. You can't work this out. None of it."

They held each other, and squeezed, until it seemed that one or the other might slip off the padded bench. They undressed with an overt weariness, and managed their ablutions under the bathroom's bright light before they collapsed into bed in the dark. The night seemed especially quiet, a distant raccoon fight the sole interruption. Denny detected the change in his wife's breathing, glad to know that she was able to sleep tonight. She slept only fitfully of late. She was exhausted.

He thought that he might be capable of doing the same, but his mind refused to slow down. The night of the fire skimmed through his mind, and Denny sensed that thinking about it might cause the memory to unravel, to twist, turn, and snap undone. What happened could not be reversed. He still couldn't believe how that bridge broke off and fell into the river, staying upright, and how it floated away. What happened to the bridge, he was beginning to fear, just as surprisingly, could happen to him.

19

From the moment he awakened, Ryan was nettled by an urge to go fishing. He supposed the desire was born from a forgotten thread in a dream, or subconsciously he just wanted to be away somewhere, yet the notion persisted and occupied his fantasy life on through the morning. Gazing out his office window, he was indulging in some imaginative casting and feeling disgruntled that that was not going to happen anytime soon, not in the real world anyway, when an American sedan pulled up. Two men stepped out.

"Cops." He spoke under his breath to the empty room.

They weren't in uniform but he concluded that if those two guys weren't SQ detectives they were hawking broadloom. Since nobody sold carpet door to door these days the investigation of the bridge fire was officially under way.

He regarded the men as they crossed the parking lot and approached the entrance to the police station. Of average height, yet with large frames, he counted one as overweight while the other, equally heavy, struck him as muscular and reasonably fit. The more robust sported either a Mediterranean complexion or a particularly notable tan, but given his profession Ryan didn't believe he put in the necessary hours on a beach or in a tanning salon. This one wanted to move more rapidly, slowing his pace only to suit the other, an indication that the superior rank belonged to the portly cop. Both detectives already looked bored and the day was barely off the ground, which suited Ryan's overall strategy. In his experience, outside cops in a new town with only one case on the docket habitually were undermined by boredom, which in turn led to inertia, which fostered an inevitable carelessness.

A woman in her thirties happened to be departing the premises as the visitors lurched up the walk, which elicited a smile from the detective with the olive skin and brokered one in return. Stepping aside graciously and with some flourish he gave her room to pass, then let his eyes follow her gentle motion. In the wake of that mildly flirtatious exchange, the second man with the higher rank came across as grumpy. He scowled. Before entering the building, he succumbed to an obligation to tuck in his shirt dislodged by the movement of his protuberant belly. A job that clearly irritated him.

Ryan O'Farrell, consciously taking a deep breath to help him relax, pressed a button on the intercom. "Francine, two SQ just arrived. Show them through, please." A moment later he pressed the button again. "Francine? Are you there?"

Silence.

He stood to fetch them himself from the corridor.

■ ■ ■

TARA CAME TO EXPECT DISPUTES between herself and her partner at Potpourri that required debating a master of the passive-aggressive repertoire. Yet she failed to catalogue a major sore point between them. She suspected that he was of a mind to be ornery on every issue, to wear down her resources, perhaps, and to lay claim to a perceived notion of dominance. While his insecurities ran amok, she believed that his recent run of prickly opposition to every suggestion she brought forward was part of a larger scheme, and to combat that design she needed to scope out his overall plan. What, oh what on earth could he be up to? He didn't want her gone, she gathered, although she conceded that her confidence in that opinion might be misplaced. As far as she could tell he wanted to remain in business with her. What he might be after, then, was to formally shape and limit her contribution. Or at least position her influence in such a way that it better suited him. To what end remained a mystery.

She dearly hoped that it was not his intention to propose. *Crikes!* Hard to tell with that guy. That was the one possibility that would wreck everything.

In retrospect, she grasped that she ought to have anticipated his attitude to her latest project. As with most of their disputes, she could muddle through the specifics with him, winning lesser contests while still not seeing the broader canvas of what the stakes entailed. Tara took the initiative to encourage local artisans to drop by and pitch their wares, only to hear that Willis Howard carried on a running feud with every craftsperson whom he deemed, with disdain, *local*. She extracted from him that he accepted the necessity of artists in their line of work, but in his estimation no one living within a hundred-kilometre radius of the store could possibly be adequate for their enterprise. Even someone marginally beyond the border of that circumference was cutting the matter too close for comfort.

"Willis, what's up with that? You can't be serious."

"Why would anyone," he argued, exhibiting a strapping self-assurance, previously concealed, "with even a smidgen of talent, live near here?"

"Seriously? Extrapolate that line of thinking throughout the world, Willis, and no artist would live anywhere."

He was adamant. "If you're a great artist, move somewhere. Anywhere. Somewhere better. You can, you see. You're not tied down."

"So, it's not that you subscribe to the theory that the only good artist is a dead one—which, you know, has some prevalence in the world—but in your rationale the only good artist is one who's skipped the country."

"Artists can live anywhere on the planet, that's my point. If they're any good, why live here?"

"I hate to break it to you, Willis. Any craftsperson who can afford to pack up and move to the South Pacific—is that your fantasy? The Gauguin thing? Or does it have to be a New York-London-Paris–type thing? Anyway, that person doesn't sell their stuff here. We don't have the clientele. And nobody, anywhere, is a better artist by mere virtue of living somewhere else."

"You don't understand," he complained, and she agreed, she didn't. "Local artists come by."

"They—come by?" At least he was trying to explain. "Okay. So?"

"To see if I've sold their stuff. Then they want to show me how to present their work. Where to put it and how to light it. They want to rearrange my store and instruct me on what I should say about their wares."

"They want their work in the window, I suppose," she said, and she was bending, beginning to detect his point. "Of course, that's one of your gripes against me. I want to rearrange things."

"This is different. No matter what I do for them, I don't do enough. I'm taking too big a share, I don't appreciate art, I don't know retail, I'm a neophyte, or a troglodyte, I don't understand colour or design or I'm not original enough, or forceful enough, I'm a stick-in-the-mud or I've got one up my rear, I should be shot for merely breathing or for not taking their advice, at the very least I'm forced to listen to an endless litany of grievances followed by a harangue of heavy-handed suggestions. So I banned them from my store. Outright. The exceptions are those who seem timid—although you still have to watch out for those ones, too. They have tricks up their sleeves, I've noticed."

Tara didn't mean to laugh but she couldn't help it. "Okay. I get it. You *do* have a point. But I can't choose an artist based on his or her level of timidity. I forgot that we discussed this a while back." She leaned over the counter, content now to further forge their alliance. "I'm to deal with the artists, that's our arrangement. Which is what I'm doing. But you have to let me choose them, and with the exception of a few who might not be worth the trouble, I'll base my judgements on the merit of their work. If they come back through the doors to complain, they will address me, and I'll take care of them. I'm not afraid to spank an artist."

Willis remained up in arms. "Who decides, I want to know? Who can judge what work is good, what isn't?"

"I can," she told him. "At least, I will. It's my store—you know what I mean—my section of the store. So I'll choose and after that, either the public will accept them or reject them."

"It won't be your only problem."

She was enjoying his endless protestations now. She let herself be amused given that he could be exhausting otherwise. "What else, Willis? What am I missing now?"

"They're drug addicts."

"Yeah, well, me, too. So there you go."

At least he possessed the wherewithal to discern that his own chain was being royally yanked. "Fine. Make light. It's your funeral," Willis pronounced. Despite that, she could tell that he also enjoyed the exchange.

"Maybe so," she forewarned, "but it'll be yours if you don't get cracking on my lemonade machine."

"About that," he intimated.

"Now what?"

"You heard that Mrs. McCracken started selling lemonade at the train station? I was thinking to let the old biddy keep that monopoly to herself."

"*A*," Tara stressed, "this is a business and we are in competition with many other businesses. *B*, she only sells lemonade for an hour before the train leaves. *C*, I will make better lemonade than her and if we put her stand right out of business that's not our concern. *D*, I will also be getting her to bake and sell more pies, so you don't have to take her welfare into consideration. Okay?" She didn't wait for Willis to answer. "Okay," she confirmed, thereby retiring him from the debate. He was foot-dragging on the lemonade issue and she wanted him to feel her displeasure.

"Fine." He went off in a quantitative huff. She judged it a seven on the Richter scale.

Tara no sooner returned to her nook, happy with her performance in battle, than her peace was interrupted by Alex O'Farrell coming in with a woman who was, she guessed, approximately his age, perhaps five years older. Out of the corner of her eye she saw that Willis was now edging his way back, positioning himself to eavesdrop.

"Alex, hi. How are you?"

He seemed to give the question more than casual consideration. "Not too bad," he said, as if the conclusion surprised him. "Like an old pair of jeans, that's how I am. Looser through the hips and thighs. Sciatic nerve pain—markedly reduced. Ah, this is a neighbour of mine, Marley Buchanan. Marley, this is who I told you about—Tara."

"I have a broomstick thicker than you," the woman said.

"Ah. Okay. Hi," Tara said. The new arrival's physical demeanour seemed strong and stout enough to intimidate a plough horse. This woman could snap her, she believed, like a cracker. "Do you fly on it?" Only after the words popped out did she realize that she may have issued an insult, but the woman took the comment as intended, laughing along.

Then Marley Buchanan explained, "You fixed him up pretty good."

Tara looked from one to the other, unaccustomed to being at a loss.

"So we'll pay you, we decided," Alex told her.

"Excuse me?"

"To start a class," Marley filled her in. "We need a class."

Tara hadn't previously considered it, but then, why not? Given Willis Howard's disapproving stance a short distance away, arms folded defiantly across his chest as if this new matter was even remotely his concern, the idea sounded both interesting and viable.

"We have more friends," Marley assured her. "On our street alone."

"We'll top the class at five, maybe six," Tara piped up. "I won't travel. We'll do it upstairs. Okay?"

Shaking his head, his disapproval noted, Willis Howard wandered off to tend to his ongoing inventory assessment. That's the last thing he needed he was going to tell her when he caught an opportune moment. The last thing. People coming over to do *yoga*. Thumping on his ceiling.

■ ■ ■

EVERY TIME HE SPOKE HE smiled. Ryan was surprised by how quickly he took a liking to Detective Vega. The man's card proclaimed his first name to be Enrique, but his friends, he said, called him Quique. He asked Ryan to do the same.

"Mexican," Detective Luc Maltais let him know. "A Mex who's never been to Mexico, if you can believe that."

"I'm Irish. Never been to Ireland yet. Someday, maybe. You ever been to France?" he asked Maltais.

"My people've been here awhile," Maltais told him dryly, as though to suggest that the question was not relevant, a sourness to his tone. "But yeah, I been to France."

"My people have been here awhile, too," Ryan quipped, "not that that adds up to a mountain of marshmallows." Ryan judged Maltais as a cop who wore a chip on his shoulder for so long he forgot why. The glum disposition was so comfortable and ingrained that it could no longer be jettisoned without a prefrontal lobotomy.

"I was conceived in Mexico," Quique mentioned. "Born in Quebec City. So he considers me a transplant."

"I consider you worse than that," Maltais lamented, but left it there. Ryan could see where, over time, he might get to enjoy this guy, too. For an old cop he seemed okay, and really only looked a trifle worn. His curmudgeonly disposition, while prevalent, seemed theatrical and not genuinely derisive.

In two cars, the three of them drove down to inspect the area where the bridge once stood and stared out across that vacant gulf. Nothing pertinent remained to be examined, but the newcomers grasped the dimensions of the space. By looking over Mrs. McCracken's photographs, they appreciated the magnitude of the fire.

"Who was first on the scene?" Maltais inquired.

Although he expected the question, Ryan chose not to answer on the spot. Both SQ officers looked at him and he wanted that, their interest. He was courting their curiosity to help him guide their progress.

"You don't know?" Vega checked with him. Notwithstanding a kindliness to his voice, he expressed disappointment in Ryan's silence.

The three men moved away from Mrs. McCracken to converse in private. At their backs, by the train station, the steam locomotive puffed away, having arrived a while ago. Passengers were still organizing to take the shore path, then scale a short hill through the trees to the site. Ryan warned the officers to expect that parade—Maltais resented that a crime scene was now a tourist attraction.

"One of my officers got here early that night," Ryan recalled. "Second on the scene maybe. One other man was here before him. Forgot his name. He's not somebody well known in this town. My officer will remember."

"You didn't interview that one other man?"

"Me? My officer talked to him. At the time, things were chaotic."

"I'm sure. Since then?" Vega inquired.

"Not my case," Ryan reminded him. "If I interview people ahead of time, that might contaminate your investigation, no?"

The officers agreed with that but seemed disgruntled also.

"About that," Vega said.

"We don't get this," Maltais confirmed.

"What don't you get?" Ryan asked. But he knew.

"Why ask the SQ to take over the case? You can't get that many big-ticket crimes up here. I'd think you'd put up roadblocks to keep us out."

Ryan prolonged his silence, which further secured their attention. Fish on a hook.

"What?" Maltais pressed impatiently.

"A rumour's flying around town," Ryan told him. "You'll hear it. It's not based on anything. I'm not aware of any witnesses. It's only hearsay. A guy mentioned as a potential perpetrator—"

Ryan let his report hang in the air awhile.

"Yeah?" Vega prodded.

"—is my brother." Ryan raised his hands. "Conflict of interest. If I don't get him convicted, people will think I let him get away with something. That he's innocent won't enter their heads. If I convict him . . . let's say that I agree with most folks. I'm not the person to do that."

"So is he innocent?" Vega inquired.

Ryan deflected the question. "It's like I said, I'm not investigating the case. I didn't ask him."

"Why do people think differently?" Maltais wanted to know.

"He's a logger. Probably one of their leaders. Loggers want a new bridge. They were frustrated it didn't get built. That's well known."

"So they had a reason to burn the bridge," Vega noted, and nodded. He seemed to have the background. "Your brother included."

"My brother—his name is Denny—he fought for a new bridge through legal channels. Guys like him, in my estimation, aren't the hotheads who turn into arsonists. So I'm guessing it was someone else. Someone with his own reasons. Someone who's got a criminal streak in him. There's a lot of loggers in this town and some of those guys are hotheads. My brother? He's a worker, a family man, he's never committed a crime. I don't see why he would now."

The cops nodded. They could see his predicament, caught between family and the local population.

"Makes sense," Maltais mentioned. "I'm going to ask this little old lady over here, see if she has an opinion on the subject."

"Fair warning. Don't call her that."

"What?"

"Neither little nor old."

"I'll keep that in mind."

The other two tagged along behind him.

Mrs. McCracken was pleased to show her photographs again, to give them a detailed visual account of the fire. When asked who she thought was involved, she declared that the only possibility was outsiders.

"Why's that?" Maltais asked her.

"It's simple. Even a logger who wanted a new fast bridge, even that man grew up here. Any man who grew up here adored the bridge. Ask him, the policeman, if he didn't love the old covered bridge."

Nodding his chin, she virtually forced Maltais to do so.

"Officer O'Farrell," he asked, speaking to him in English for the first time, "were you in love with the old covered bridge?"

Ryan admitted that that was probably true. "Kissed my first girl on it." A reply that seemed to seal the deal.

"Do you think his brother loved the bridge?" Maltais asked.

"Ryan?" Mrs. McCracken queried.

"I'm Ryan," Ryan said. "He means Denny."

"Of course! If anyone loved that bridge it was Denny!"

"How do you know that, ma'am?"

"He was a student of mine. I know him! Once a year I conducted a class right on the bridge, a field trip for my grade twos. Everybody loved that bridge. Everybody! Except," she reconsidered, "obviously, an outsider. A malcontent. A n'er do well."

They thanked her for her contribution.

Ryan was about to lead them away when he noticed Detective Vega separate off to stand on the ridge above the water. He seemed transfixed, staring upriver, in a distant daydream. He craned his neck in an expression of curiosity and befuddlement.

Ryan called to him. "Quique?"

"What the hell is that?" Detective Vega shouted back.

Ryan returned up the hill a short distance to gain the same perspective, while the other cop, Maltais, chugged along as well, willing to move when he felt an urgency to do so. The two stood beside Vega, each man trying to make sense of a perplexing sight. Ryan O'Farrell broke their silence by swearing, but he could no more explain what he saw than could the visiting cops.

A weird floating contraption, its base burying itself in the rise and fall of the river so that it resembled the rear of a dilapidated city tenement more than any houseboat, a squat tower churning in the waves, tore away from rocks lining the opposite bank into which it collided and, spinning in a prodigious circular motion, plunged down the slope of the rapids.

Across the deck skidded items only loosely lashed down while belts and ropes bound a jostling array of percussive pots, pans, and thudding *things*—clothes and suitcases and battered furniture, toys and sports equipment, tools and half-executed carvings and sculptures—as fruits bashed about in slings and tormented chains thrashed sundry bicycle parts and internal combustion engines in whole or in ruptured chunks, while other debris, wrested free from their pins, plopped into the water to either disappear or to accompany the tower, swaying, heeling, careening down the rapacious current.

Initially, the fellow on deck appeared to be in charge, a captain of this tenuous ship, hustling to get a single long oar to break the water's surface and effect some modicum of steerage, but that proved a short-lived assessment. The man was thrown about himself, once right off the edge into the drink and only a quick grab of a fortuitous rail—an upright crankshaft embedded in the deck—kept him attached, and he pulled himself back up only to be slammed into the side wall of the vessel's three-storey cabin by a sudden, violent lurch. He reached for a line that inadvertently caused a tangle of rope to land on his noggin. By this point the barge entered the full chaos of the churning rapids, its viability and balance in doubt, and while trying to extricate himself the man veered on his bottom and crashed headfirst into the remnant of a six-cylinder motor that was sliding along more slowly. He was sufficiently stunned to spend the next several seconds attending to his wound before he was catapulted forward as the raft slammed into the quiet water at the base of the drop and its pell-mell thrust was suddenly aborted. A big wave rose up around the raft, and the floating barge settled while the intrepid captain hung on. Down on his knees, he clutched a cast-iron house radiator, and as it became apparent that he'd conquered the wildest section of the river, he drifted down to a prone position on deck, let his arms fall freely, and just lay there, bleeding.

Both SQ officers looked to Ryan O'Farrell to check his reactions.

"That guy," he said. "On the deck."

"Yeah?" Maltais asked.

"That's him, I think. Pretty sure. First guy to the fire. Same guy."

The current held the raft—and they saw now that it was intended to serve as a raft—in its influence. Attracting a crowd along the river-bank, including many disembarking from the steam train, the vessel ambled downriver conning the shoreline. An elderly person in a walker could move equally as fast. Mrs. McCracken, up for a better view having missed the action, travelled more quickly than the boat.

The SQ officers exchanged a nod, which Ryan encouraged. "I never saw that he had motive before," he said. "Now I do."

"What these eyes have plainly seen," Mrs. McCracken stated, and the men concurred with the sentiment. "What I've observed go down this river in recent days," she added, and they agreed with that unfinished remark as well.

"Gentlemen," the local officer announced, "you can come along or excuse me, but I'm off to see what's up with that houseboat."

The men chose to tag along.

"You call that a house?" Mrs. McCracken scoffed as they readied to depart. "Not I. Do you call it a boat? I cannot. If it's not a boat and it's not a house, how can you call it a houseboat?"

Ryan indulged her. He spoke over his shoulder. "What do you want to call it then?" Stopped at his car, he awaited her reply.

She thought the question through. "To call it an eyesore is to pay that contraption an unnecessary compliment, one it clearly does not deserve," she declared. "Plain and simple, it's an aberration. If anything should be burned on the river . . . If you have half the brain I think you do, Officer O'Farrell"—she turned away to gaze out over her beloved ravine, perhaps affected still by the missing bridge and seeking, on some level, revenge for that—"sink it."

■ ■ ■

HER FRESHLY BAKED PIES WERE cooling nicely upon her return to the quiet of her home. Mrs. McCracken decided against taking a lemon meringue into the late-afternoon sun—it might go squishy, soaking the bottom crust. Her apple crumbles would be fine, packaged in boxes for transport on the slow train.

Things were not going as splendidly as hoped. Not a single passenger made it up to the old entrance to the vanished bridge today, compelled instead to watch a ridiculous floating contrivance get lassoed off the town's riverbank and pulled ashore. So her petition did not fare well. Still, later on, the attraction of pies and lemonade ought to draw people to her stand. "The day," she whispered to Buckminster, "remains to be salvaged."

She was feeling, after giving her cat a brushing and a treat, then settling back into her chair, in need of salvage herself. After taking an uncomfortable turn, she elected to struggle up from her spot and over to the sofa, where, should the need arise, she could spread out. Catnap. She set the alarm clock kept handy for such occasions so as not to oversleep, and when her queer intestinal queasiness developed into dizziness and an odd attitude down her limbs, she concluded that she was in for a wee spell. She extended her limbs. She would give herself a good lie-down.

"I've earned it," she declared.

Soon she felt better. Anxiety dissipated.

"Inner ear, my Buck," she informed the cat, her diagnosis for the day. She did not suspect that he shared her worry, but he came over to ensconce himself alongside her forearm, an intimacy she welcomed. "That one came on quickly, dear," she informed him. "A wee nap, as we know, is the best remedy for whatever ails these old bones."

She did nap, and fell asleep both quickly and deeply. When her alarm sounded in an hour it seemed too soon, and a long way off, and she took a while to respond to her cue. Mrs. McCracken opened her eyes and surveyed the space. She noticed Buck across the room, that rather than nap himself he was keeping a watchful eye on her from his favoured chair. She tried, but failed, to get up. She fully intended to be cross with herself and with her predicament, but discovered that she was unable to speak. The incessant alarm annoyed her no end. She shut her eyes, thinking that a further moment of quiet might help. She again felt somewhat queer, and again failed to speak when she tried. She knew what this might mean. That conclusion instigated an intense moment of panic, of terror, which she brushed aside as quickly as it advanced. She reminded herself that she was a strong person who held herself to a high standard in the face of calamity. She told herself that if this was that dreaded thing, then this was it, and she might as well face whatever came next. A stroke might kill her, but it might not, and she must ready herself for either alternative. She wondered who might be by to see to her. Might she be missed? And then, finally, and it seemed that she was never able to fully achieve this moment before, or not for some time, she relaxed. She let that endless fretting dissipate, just go.

She might have been pleased to know that, since she didn't supply Potpourri with pie that morning, Tara Cogshill ventured out to visit her stand by the train platform. When Mrs. McCracken still did not arrive, Tara suffered an inkling, and the walk was a short one over to her home. She knocked on the outside screen. The cat meowed. Tara went in. She saw the elderly woman on the sofa and heard no sound. She wanted to call Ryan, to have him check on her. It's not as though she ever . . . but she pushed the thought away. She called out to her, softly at first, then more firmly. Mrs. McCracken appeared to be sleeping, eyes closed, one hand up under her jaw for support. Tara went over and touched the woman's cheek. Instantly, her hand jerked away. Then she let it rest on the old woman's temple. Her friend had not been gone so long. Her skin felt warmish cool. Tara would say to Ryan, after she called him to come over and wrapped Buckminster's blanket and toys and his litter tray to take him away with her, that the death must have been peaceful.

20

A flicker ticked across his mind.

Shadow simultaneously dimmed the windowpane in his fitful sleep. Denny flinched.

Cloud smudged the moonlight shining through leaves, a shimmer created by the flight of a dashing nocturnal shade, that tinkering in his craw, a flicker which, now gone, left him in some subliminal distress. An ethereal crimp that he endeavoured to put out of his head. Yet the thought, undefined, returned on its own wing. He would need to confess to himself and argue the matter through, to begin by acknowledging that he indeed entertained the notion that *the old bat's dead, which makes her idea for a new old bridge deader* and yet, a residual instinct failed to release him from an abject worry.

In part, he didn't mean to call her an old bat, and regretted that, too.

Sorry. You were a real sweetheart. I bet nobody's called you that for a while.

He remembered a time, during Christmas holidays, returning from an outdoor skating rink. He was about seven or eight, as he recalled. Mrs. McCracken was coming his way and he just got scared. She frightened him, her authority, her austere countenance intimidated him, to run into her outside of school without the safety of others around was terrifying. He thought about crossing the street to avoid her but knew that she'd give him heck for not crossing at the corner, but then her feet went out from under her and Mrs. McCracken landed on her backside in a wink. Denny stood still for an instant, too surprised to react, but when she experienced a hard time surfacing he raced over. "Ohh," she was saying, "Oh my." Tears derived from the shock of her pain. The two of them worked together to get her back on her feet and then she asked him to please help her home.

She walked with a deep limp and sometimes when her left leg took her weight she exclaimed, "Ow!" He went all the way home with her, the woman steadying herself by keeping one hand on the little boy's shoulder.

Once she was in her door she thanked him, dried her eyes and wiped away a few sniffles on a tissue, and looked as though she was going to be all right. The best she could manage was a cautious shuffle, though. Denny waited at the door to see if she could sit, and when she did, a question simply jumped out. "Where's your husband?"

She looked at him from her sofa, still red-eyed.

"Everybody calls you Mrs.," Denny explained himself.

"Gone to his rest, Denny. Much too early, gone to his rest."

Denny said, "Oh." Then he left the house and ran a long way home until he was out of breath. He walked slowly the remainder of the way, wondering about being at rest. The memory of the day impressed him for its clarity as he considered that Mrs. McCracken was finally at rest herself, and thinking about it, he continued to fidget and fret.

The next morning, sleep-deprived, he showed up for work after the drive north to his new harvest field to learn that he had reason to be out of sorts. A fellow driver named Roy with whom he rarely shared a word, yet who seemed remarkably sympathetic towards him, told him that with Mrs. McCracken gone quite a few people were rousing themselves to support her cause. His wife, Roy said, told him so.

Glum, Denny O'Farrell thanked him for the heads-up.

And smiled as he walked away.

Oh, sweetheart.

He should have known. Just because old lady McCracken passed on didn't mean that she actually was going to leave town, or leave him alone.

Good on you, McCracked, Denny muttered to himself, perhaps out loud, before he thought to bite his tongue. He really didn't want to encourage her. *You old bat.*

■ ■ ■

FROM A DISTANCE, SOMEONE MIGHT assume that Skootch remained oblivious to the very scene he so diligently created the day before. Tidying up his raft from the chaos of its rambunctious descent through the rapids, he remained chagrined by the loss of a few items overboard. As he kept no inventory and possessed only a rudimentary memory of such artefacts he was feeling their absence as a vague and generic loss, rather than as the diminishment of any specific need.

Yesterday, under the noses of two visiting cops, Ryan O'Farrell, and a crowd of onlookers, he reamed Jake out for the material losses. Then the three policemen talked to a shaken, soaked, bleeding, and seemingly disoriented Jake Withers. They wanted to talk about the old bridge, and what he'd seen. He'd left the bar early that night, he told them, after a single beer following his ball game—he'd hit a double, he said—because he didn't want to drink a lot and drive, and what a beauty of a lie that was. Skootch positively beamed with pride. That's when Ryan asked him to step off the raft until the interview was over, and then he was going to talk to him about *all this*, meaning the dilapidated raft. Jake went on to tell the police that he saw the fire and blared his horn and saw nothing and no one else. A cop was the next person to the scene and that was that, the bridge burned. The cops were noncommittal in their responses, and wrote down his personal information, but ashore Skootch guessed that Jake was doing just fine from the titbits he overheard, and why shouldn't he shine? Right through the interview he was sticking to the simple truth.

Then Ryan approached Skootch on shore. "So what the fuck is this?"

"My yacht," he explained. "A public riverbank, Ry. Anybody can moor here. To save you the trouble I already checked. There's no law against it."

"Not yet," Ryan said, then he carried on with his new SQ pals.

Now, a day later, assessing the rearrangements to his gear, Skootch put together a plan. He selectively differentiated between the changes which were beneficial to his accommodations and those which ought to come undone. Half the time he couldn't remember where his stuff used to reside anyway, so a number of objects ended up in fresh locations, such as a swizzle stick stuck in the maw of a clay marmalade cat, and a banjo, stripped of its strings, hanging from a pot rack that was stepped on its side and strapped over a window as an awning. Busy with the housekeeping, he wore only the skimpiest of genital thongs over which hung small flaps, front and rear. Casual viewers compared his attire to fig leaves, and one wag among the many who observed him commented, "I think I can make out his figs." His long legs and astonishingly lean torso were baked to a reddish clay after the summer's exceptional heat. Calves, arms, and shoulders were nibbled by bugs but he showed no remorse, whereas a few people observing him were wont to scratch the itch, and scratched themselves in sympathy. Children—boys in particular, but a few girls also—formed the core of his rapt audience, yet he paid no one heed as eventually he retired to his penthouse balcony under the sun. He took his ease on a warped and ragged patio divan while reading, many noted—as if such a thing was incomprehensible for a man of his appearance and reputation—the morning newspaper duly delivered by a paperboy.

Someone pointed out that he was studying the business section.

When an attractive young woman emerged from the lower grotto, the whole of his visible world, so it seemed, gasped. A sufficient reaction that Skootch looked up, to see what on earth just transpired. Children stood with their mouths agape. One exclaimed, "There's two of 'em on that thing!" The boy's dismay was countered by a stern look from Skootch which dictated that he be left alone, but as he did not insist on it, or actually say so, folks lingered awhile.

■ ■ ■

"WHY ME?" HE BEGGED.

Jake Withers and the other tree huggers nestled in the woods, concealed by foliage, tormented by bugs. Before them lay a clearing, dusty and remote, where truckers a short distance from their rigs gobbled lunch.

In attire not so dissimilar to that of his mentor, Jake Withers bristled at the suggestion that he was a gutless maggot. He wanted to know why he could not be assigned to the group who were going to spray-paint trucks, that seemed the lighter chore. Instead, he was assigned to the firebombing brigade. Now he wanted to know why he was selected to commit the first defiant act by throwing the first torch. Not being rewarded with an answer, egged on by the unsolicited rebuke of those who swarmed beside him—*"Why are you such a gutless maggot?"*—he took a breath, struck the rag of his Molotov cocktail in the small fire at his feet—*"Are you man or vermin? Prove to us you're one or the other!"*— and fuelled by his rampant fear he ran. Raced the burning wick to the parked logging truck where he hurled the gasoline-filled bottle, accurately enough using his third baseman's good arm, a mere toss across the infield. Just like that, liquid flame swam over the truck and its cargo of timbers and Jake fled back to the safety of the woods and to the wonder of his new and unsolicited life.

After him, more cocktails arced through the air, like cannon fire of old, though silent. The miscreants hurried back to the refuge of the forest, where they paused to watch the flames lay siege to the three fully loaded rigs. They waited. And waited still. They were disappointed, for the fires did not impress them. Raw logs, the timber not yet hewn and still green, do not readily ignite, they found out, their dismay palpable. After their planning and the thrill of execution they earned only the shouts of truckers who'd been enjoying the quiet of the hour at a picnic table to amuse themselves. But no great flame. No incendiary romance.

Until something happened.

A logger would later explain that his vehicle carried three jerry cans of gasoline to service a generator in the field, that they were strapped to the rear of his cab. In the acute heat, they ignited and in succession exploded. First the cab caught fire, flames licking through the open windows, seats suddenly engulfed. The intensity of that heat combined with the Molotov fires created a localized inferno. Somewhere in its systems a gasket on a diesel line or a section of rubber hose melted, and so the fire welcomed a steady leakage of fuel to cook the rig. That one truck would be destroyed, and Jake Withers and his crew of ragamuffin, self-proclaimed ecoterrorists celebrated their trophy.

He anointed this as the grandest day of his life.

Jake had no clue how it all transpired, how he was transformed into this new being, nor did he care.

His heart stammered in his chest. He'd never known such exuberance. He could not believe what he did. Neither could Belinda, who took his face in both her hands and kissed him, hard on the mouth, her tongue digging up into his palate. Then they both ran. They scooted. They leapt roots and swung from a convenient branch to propel themselves farther on their way. Like playful jungle chimps. They ran and tumbled and laughed and scampered through the native woods. After a while, along with others, they stopped and bent at the waist to catch a breath, then hoots and a few happy hollers lifted them on their way again, gambolling through the mottled sunlight to a benevolent freedom.

■ ■ ■

ATOP HIS RAFT, CHAMPION TO the vista he surveyed, Skootch heard sirens unfold from the fire hall, first, soon from the police station also, as the first responders charged off. An audience turned away from him to trace the sounds. He noted the direction the emergency vehicles headed, on into the woods, their sirens eventually fading, and returned his attention to the sports section of his paper, studying box scores from last night's Major League games.

■ ■ ■

HOURS LATER, AT A HARDWOOD planing mill, Detectives Maltais and Vega relaxed by the forest's edge. As the next truck drove in they observed it park. The big engine rumbled and shook and issued a gush of air, a whale surfacing from the sea, before it lapsed into silence. Maltais worked a kink from his shoulder blades. The driver climbed down from the cab and moved off while a forklift swung around to claim the prized load. Both detectives gazed across the dusty compound to a small administrative hut where the sun reflected brightly off the door's small windows. An inspector there stepped out to give them a nod, their signal that the driver they wanted to speak to had just pulled in.

The driver, André Gervais, uncapped a bottle of water and spread himself out upon a picnic table's bench, his arms running along the tabletop, his knees apart so that his inner thighs could catch a scant measure of coolness. He saw the two men amble towards him, they seemed in no hurry, and knew who they were before they showed their badges to prove it.

"Son of a bitch," André said.

"How's it going?" Detective Vega asked him. "A hot one, eh?"

"Hot enough," the trucker agreed. "Been hotter."

"Some summer. This heat. The humidity, eh?"

Maltais chose to take a load off, sitting down on one end of André's bench. "I'm Maltais," he said. "The Mex is Detective Vega. You're André Gervais?"

The trucker sputtered his lips in an attitude of nonchalance.

Vega gave him the benefit of the doubt. "Tough day?"

He shrugged. "Tough enough. We drive farther now, with the bridge out. Make less. It's the same heat, though." Then he looked directly at the man questioning him. "Other things made this a piss-poor day. Maybe you heard."

"Yeah, we heard," Vega said.

"Speaking of the bridge," Maltais remarked. "What do you know about it?"

"Me? What am I supposed to know?"

"How did it catch fire?"

"How am I supposed to know that? Some tourist tossed a smoke, I guess."

"Why a tourist?" Vega asked. He remained standing, and very slowly paced in front of André.

"People from around here know better, I guess."

"Do they? Where were you when it burned, may I ask?"

André looked up at Vega. He'd never physically feared a cop, and in a way admired policemen who were likely, from time to time, to accept a challenge from men who could probably kick their arse in a brawl. Maltais was too old and too fat to fight, but this other guy looked as though he could make it a contest. Not that he had any intention of fighting anybody, but as a matter of speculation he wondered who'd win that tangle, if guns and badges as well as loggers' hobnailed boots were set aside.

"I guess you got a right to ask," André said. "It's your job."

"That's true," Vega confirmed, as though the idea just now occurred to him. "It is."

André chose to be cagey. "How come you're asking me questions? You're SQ. I mean, how come our local cops don't talk to me?"

Vega seemed set to answer but Maltais cut him short. "We're on it. You don't need to know more than that. Where were you when the bridge burned?"

"At home, I guess. In bed."

"Is that right?"

"Yeah. I guess that's right."

"You're only guessing?" Vega queried. "I'd think you'd remember."

"How come?"

"Big night. Big event around here."

André wished that Ryan O'Farrell gave him a more lengthy interrogation. He might be better prepared for this one. Then he remembered that he was not supposed to be home, but out with the guys, on account of Samad's wife saw them leave together, but it was too late to change his story now. Under pressure, he reverted to his original tale, screwing it up. He wished he could restart this interview.

"I was at home. In bed."

"You're sure? You didn't come out to see the beautiful sight? Lots of people did."

"I would've, I guess. But I was asleep."

"You guess?" Vega inquired.

"What?" He supposed that he could change his story later and just say that he didn't remember at first. Why not?

"You guess you were asleep?"

"Yeah. Yeah, I guess so."

"Lots of guesses."

"Anybody see you there, at home?" prodded Maltais.

André just stared back at him and chose not to answer. Then he said, "What is this?"

"People saw you in a bar downtown," Vega informed him.

André looked up at him, squinting into the sun. "That was before the bridge burned maybe. Like way before. Before I went home."

"My point. You weren't always home. You left the bar when?" Maltais pressed on.

André brought his legs together, thought a moment, took a sip of water, then crossed them. "I dunno. I finished my beer. Then I walked home."

"Walked!" Vega announced, as though he couldn't believe it. "Then you hopped into bed and fell asleep."

"My wife was with me. You want details? Positions? What is this?"

"What's with the attitude?" Maltais asked.

"What attitude? It's your attitude. Christ, my truck got spray-painted today. Look at it! Other guys got theirs firebombed. You should be out arresting tree huggers, not talking to me about some fucking bridge."

"You didn't like the bridge? I thought local people loved that bridge."

André resorted to more water.

"When did you leave the bar?" Maltais insisted on finding out. "What route did you take home?"

"I didn't write down the time. I took the long way home."

"No hurry to get into those positions, huh?" Maltais noted.

André glared at him. Timbers were coming off his truck and the three men watched that raucous procedure. Then the two policemen stared back at him as if they were still expecting a reply. "Look," André fumbled. "The long way home is flatter, see? I still got to go uphill but the long way is more gentle. Not so steep, see? It goes along side streets. I take a path through the woods, so no, nobody saw me, there's no point asking."

"That's okay," Vega assured him, and put his hands in his front trouser pockets. "We weren't going to ask."

André sipped more water, squinted up at him. "Why not?" he wondered.

"For the reason you said," Vega responded. "There's no point."

The two cops simply gazed at him, implacable, as his eyes went back and forth between the two. Maltais made a show of departure, grunting as he shoved himself upright. Enrique Vega seemed to be churning an idea around in his head, though. He said, "Tell me about these tree huggers, Mr. Gervais. Mean bastards, are they? Nutcases? Fanatics? What can you tell me about them?"

André would rather let loose with a spiel but he checked himself. "What do I know? I guess they're some kind of fanatics," he indicated.

"More guessing," Maltais said, and stifled a yawn with his fist.

"It's just an expression," André declared with more than a trace of frustration at last apparent in his voice.

"Why do they want to do that, do you think?" Vega asked. "Attack logging trucks? What's their purpose in life overall?"

"Beats me." André shrugged. "Ask them when you find them. Like you said. Nutcases."

"Do you think your truck was targeted for that paint job? I mean, yours in particular? Any special reason for that?"

"That I can't say," André told him, sounding miffed. "Ask the tree huggers. Anyway, who said mine was targeted? Probably random, no?"

"So you're saying that they don't know who it is they're going after?" Vega continued to press him. "You're saying they didn't have a clue it was you?"

"I guess that's what I'm saying. I don't know them, why should they know me?"

"That's what I'm asking. Do they know you for any particular reason?"

Vega froze him with the question. André thought it through logically. He was not targeted because the other trucks that were firebombed or spray-painted weren't driven by men who had anything to do with burning the bridge. But he only knew that because he knew who burned the bridge. He could not explain that, he had to play dumb. He was not supposed to know who, if anyone, burned the bridge. Nor who didn't.

Maltais and Vega exchanged a glance. They just caught him out. The suspicion meant nothing in terms of reliable evidence, but catching him out once meant that they could do it again, and probably at will.

André finally remembered what he was supposed to say. "I'm sorry, but if you guys keep asking me questions about a goddamned burned-out bridge for some fucking shit reason then I want my lawyer present."

"You got a lawyer?" Maltais pointedly asked him.

André nodded. Then he shrugged as though to contradict the nod.

"Are you in trouble often?" Vega inquired with a confidential inflection.

"You want him present?" Maltais tacked on.

André remained mute.

"What do you want to call a lawyer for?" Vega continued in that quiet voice, as if they were old confidants. "You know they charge by the half minute, hey? At least they do in the city. I don't know about this backwater. Maybe by the minute, but still. Have you got something to hide?" Vega prodded.

"I'm not hiding nothing. But . . . rumours get going around in a small town, stupid gossip. I got to protect myself."

"From gossip."

"I don't want to be railroaded here."

"By us? We wouldn't do that. Why would we railroad a truck driver? These rumours, what do they say you did?"

This time he possessed the gumption to sustain his silence.

"Well," Maltais postulated, and spoke to Vega, "I doubt they're saying he firebombed the logging trucks."

"I agree with you on that one," Vega said.

"I doubt they're saying he spray-painted foul language on his own cab."

"What did they write on it, I wonder? That's your truck over there?"

André nodded.

"Look. It says, 'Fucker trucker.' God, are these people poets? 'Bridge burner bastard.' Why would they write something like that? Do they know something we want to know? Maybe they're trying to tell us something."

"It says that on every truck they painted. Four different trucks."

"Well then," Vega concluded, "maybe those four drivers are bridge-burner bastards. What do you think?"

André felt the temptation rising to just hit him. Which he worked to quell.

"Thanks for your time, sir," Vega said, and offered a friendly departing wave. "We'll meet up again, I'm sure."

"Only with my lawyer present," André let him know.

"Amazing," Vega commented to his partner. "Truckers in the world today, they have lawyers."

"On fucking call, I bet." Maltais gave his head a forlorn shake, as though he could barely contemplate such a bizarre development in modern life.

■ ■ ■

RYAN WALKED BACK AND FORTH in a half circle before a small outdoor table in plain sight, mystified. Then stood still. Watching him, Tara waited. Amusement lurked within her glance, her expression something of a mask to him.

"I'm flummoxed," Ryan declared.

"*Sheesh*. That's a word," Tara noted.

He might have pronounced on a number of matters. Or mentioned that he wanted to kiss her so badly he was just about willing to do so in public, and in full uniform, damn the fallout. He was thinking that she looked so beautiful to him at that moment he could sit down and write a letter saying so—writing, rather than saying anything out loud, to give himself a better shot at lining the words up properly. Her hair, her eyes, her cheeks, her skin . . . He'd expand his use of the language beyond anything previously accomplished. Her look so mesmerized him at that moment, despite the amused expression, accentuated by how sunlight through the overhead umbrella glowed on her forehead and on her nose. A band fell directly across her wrist as if she wore light as a bracelet. He wished that he felt free enough to say so, but she also confounded him, especially now, and so he added only, "I'm perplexed."

"How come you're so flummoxed and perplexed, Mr. Policeman?" she teased. She knew how come.

"You know I'm busy."

She was sitting on the railway platform at Mrs. McCracken's old table under the deceased woman's aged sun umbrella. Before her on the table she exhibited the photos of the fire Mrs. McCracken collected and below these presented the woman's controversial petition. Ryan was driving by when he noticed the crowd she attracted, and wanted to know why.

"Indigents," Tara said, "take up valuable waterfront property with floating junkyards—"

"Only one. There's no need to speak in the plural."

"He has a young woman on board now. Maybe more than one."

"Shit. He would."

"You don't have a city ordinance to affect his removal."

"Not yet."

"Meanwhile, wild woodland children are assaulting logging trucks with Molotov cocktails. Foreign police officers have arrived to investigate who burns down bridges around here. Oh, I'm sorry. I misspoke. I used the plural. So far only one bridge has been incinerated. But even with one bridge burned I assumed you were busy. I didn't expect to see you for even a minute. So. You know. You get points. I'm glad you made the time."

He studied her. She called herself complicated, but he was thinking that she was just too smart for her britches—or at least for the light yellowy floral-print sundress she wore. He wished they'd advance to where he could expect permission to remove it in private. While the soft turn of her small breasts under the cotton granted visual enchantment to him, standing above her an achingly sharp glimpse of a trio of freckles along the visible inner edge of her left breast ruptured his brainwaves. An aneurism. He needed to plant his gaze on her eyes, but she was taunting him, he could tell, as his own eyes wilfully bounced around like a pair of impudent scoundrels.

"What are you doing?" he asked, and tried to sound gruff.

"You can see." So. She knew he was looking.

"I know, but you know what this means. You're putting my brother in jeopardy."

"Am I?"

"You are," Ryan insisted. "People are lining up against him. More than ever since this so-called war—"

"Everybody's calling it that, aren't they? War. It's Denny O'Farrell's fault, they say."

"Exactly my point. Tara, this doesn't help."

"Doesn't it? Are you sure?"

"Tara, stop! You know it doesn't!"

"Do I?"

He fell silent.

Backed up.

He advised himself to remember that she was sharp. She liked to believe she was complicated. Even though she decamped from the profession, she could still be as slippery as any clever lawyer. He took a moment to think it through.

"This helps?" he asked. "My brother?"

"Yes! Maybe it does."

"How?"

"I can't tell you that," she said.

"Why not?"

"Because you don't want to know." Their parry and riposte eroded his patience quickly, so he was pleased when she finally broke from cryptic, single-phrase responses. "Ryan, if you knew, you'd be compromised. So you can't know. Or, to put it another way, you can't be informed, or told outright. But if you were to solve the puzzle on your own, then keep it to yourself, that might be okay. Yeah. I think that might work out all right."

He gave the petition a second quick study. "You've named the bridge."

"Unofficially, yeah."

"You have actually named the bridge?"

"I don't have that authority, Ryan. It's only a suggestion."

The Alice Beauchamp McCracken Memorial Bridge.

"With a name like that, who in this town wouldn't sign?"

"Don't know."

"Beauchamp?" he asked.

"That was her name."

"People will line up to sign this," he speculated.

"You think?"

She might actually put together an impressive petition, more so than Mrs. McCracken herself, alive, could manage.

He was no further ahead.

"Is this some sort of a grief thing? I'm just asking. I mean, are you okay?"

She smiled fully then, as though to acknowledge the tenderness in what he was trying to express. "I'm fine! It's true, I'm very sad. And you're right, I'm doing this in Alice's memory. But you should trust me—I know what I'm doing."

So he was being baited and she wasn't going to help. He got that part. "Okay," Ryan said. "All right."

"I know. You're busy."

"I am."

"Yeah. I am, too. Okay. So. Bye for now."

He looked at her again, then down at the petition. He was hoping that this might be a test, of his own acumen, or of his ability to keep up with her and, after a fashion, impress her. He guessed that she was probably betting against him. Still. That petition. How could it be helpful? The girl he was dating was agitating for a new old bridge, a cause that would keep the burned bridge going as the talk of the town instead of letting it die a natural death and help keep his brother front and centre as the town's freshly minted pariah. As far as he could tell, she was working on the wrong side of the issue.

"You realize," he added, "that this is a completely futile idea, right? A new old bridge. If there's one thing I agree with the loggers on, it's that."

"Really? Come on. Think. You know it's not futile."

In keeping with her custom, she finagled the last word. Ryan tilted his chin and raised his eyebrows, and was about to smack his lips together when he made an oval of them instead and blew out a slight kiss. He actually managed to surprise her with that, which pleased him. With a grin, he wandered off back to work, still perplexed but sensing that more remained to be revealed. *On every front,* he thought, *on every damn front.*

■ ■ ■

STRUGGLING TO FIND THEIR WAY around an unfamiliar town, the pair of SQ detectives were unable to speak with Samad Mehra until that evening. When Samad turned into his driveway after work they were waiting for him. Before he parked, the plainclothes officers were already climbing out of their car on the street. His wife, Jocelyn, watering her exterior flower boxes at the time, scurried down the steps to intercede on behalf of her man. She didn't want those city detectives getting their hooks into him.

Water sloshed from her bright green can.

"Sir," Maltais, the older and heavier of the two, announced as he ambled up the paved driveway. He adjusted his pants and shirt to fit his body inside them properly. "SQ. We'd like to have a word with you, if you don't mind."

Samad was not yet out of his truck. The door was open, his feet on the asphalt, but he leaned back to fetch his lunch pail. "Talk to my lawyer," he said.

"Our own police we have!" Jocelyn continued to scurry towards them, water splashing. "We don't need to talk to you!"

"Actually, ma'am," Vega said, and gave her a wide grin, "you do."

"You are trespassing here! Get off our property!"

The two cops looked at her, then down at their feet to study where the property line might logically be drawn. They shrugged, and took four steps back onto the public street.

"Fine," Joce Mehra confirmed. She was a round woman, fairly short, with well-trimmed hair. She wore glasses, the frames dark and thick, that suited her face well. While her accent was distinctively Indian, specifically from Delhi, suggesting that she was raised there, her clothes were conspicuously Western, suitable for any suburban housewife. She wore designer jeans with a sleeveless white top. "You are standing on my street now. I am standing on my property. Now you cannot drag me off my own property!"

She stopped running, and stood between the men and her husband on the driveway, defiant.

"Who's dragging?" Maltais inquired dryly. "Detective Vega, have you been dragging this woman around?"

"No, sir," the somewhat younger cop attested. "I never drag people, sir."

"I'm telling you," Samad wanted to make clear, "to talk to my lawyer."

"Call him up," Maltais challenged.

Samad wasn't sure what to make of that suggestion. "Why should I?"

"You have no warrant. I am betting this," decreed Joce.

Maltais took his time to gaze at the barrel of fuel on Samad's truck, long enough to get Samad to turn and look at it also. "We'll get one," Maltais said.

"I will scream when you start the dragging," Joce forewarned. "Neighbours will hear. They will come by. They will take a video."

"My advice," Vega said. "Dig up that lawyer."

"Drag a woman by her hair!" she exclaimed. "You should be ashamed."

Vega couldn't contain a chuckle as the two cops headed on their way.

"The video we put on the YouTube!" Joce let them know.

She believed that that was the threat that drove them off, for the officers did leave the vicinity. Both Joce and her husband stared at the road long after the officers' car vanished.

"Samad!" Joce hissed under her breath.

"What?"

"Fill up the tank with the gasoline. Do this quickly." When he did not jump to her bidding, she snapped, "What are you waiting for? An eclipse of the sun? Go now! Do you want me to do it for you? Why? Why do you want the mother of your children in jail? Why, Samad?"

"Joce, take it easy. The fuel drum's full. We thought of that already."

"Who is this *we*?" she fired back at him. "Who is this *we* thinking for you, Samad? Who put you up to this? Was it Denny? Don't tell me! I don't want to know. You cannot think intelligently for yourself, Samad. Was it Denny?"

"You just told me you don't want to know."

"Who wants to know such terrible things? Was it Denny, Samad?"

"I need to look up lawyers in the phone book," Samad said.

Abruptly, and, to Samad, inexplicably furious, Joce chose to stomp back into the house, twice waving one hand above her head to let her pique be known. Water wept from the spout of her watering can, leaving a trail that Samad dutifully traced on his way to the door.

■ ■ ■

AS DUSK APPROACHED, RYAN STROLLED down to the riverside and leaned against a tree trunk. The angle of his view under the foliage took in a wide bend in the river and Skootch's floating encampment. He observed the man cook on a castaway charcoal grill, then settle in to enjoy the meal with a companion. Light laughter skimmed along the river's course. Ryan moved across to a boulder that jutted above the surface a mere step off the embankment and sat, curled his legs up under himself, and somewhat frog-like whiled away the time brooding. Darkness fell. Lamplight flickered on aboard the raft. While he wanted to believe that he was doing some serious thinking here, as that was his intention, Ryan concluded that no clear thought drifted his way on the evening air.

Eventually, when it appeared that Skootch's friend was busy with the dishes, he walked on down to the raft, pulling out a small flask from his hip pocket. "Share a nip, Skootch?" he called up, as the man ascended to his rooftop aerie.

"Officer, you think me a ravaged whore."

"Take another look. I'm not in uniform."

"A cop in jeans is one sexy look, Ry, don't you think? What's in that thing anyway?"

"Single malt. Permission to come aboard?"

"How can I resist? Ask Samantha for cups. Bring them up with you."

He didn't need to ask as she heard the request and supplied him with matching mugs—Ryan supposed that nothing else on this boat could possibly match. Her broad grin emphasized a sumptuous and somewhat beguiling earth-mother persona. He climbed the ladder while dangling the mugs in his right hand, and up top settled onto an upturned crate and liberally poured the whisky. Skootch leaned back on his sketchy patio divan. Cooler air had yet to drive him to clothes.

"Thanks for this treat, Ry. How's it going with you in the world?"

"Life is interesting enough, Skootch. You know that."

"Rare times, Ry. What more can a man ask for? Rare times."

"Cheers."

"Cheers, copper."

Ryan let the note of mockery pass. Possibly, Skootch considered it friendly. They both exhaled through their mouths, indicating appreciation for the whisky and its bite.

"So," Skootch wondered, "are you here to evict me? Because I don't believe you can, not legally."

"You know the law, as always. Legally I cannot, so I'm not here to evict you. If that day comes you'll have ample warning. Council sessions, public debate, and on the day of your removal, TV cameras, I imagine. You'll see to it, I'm sure. You'll make us both famous."

"You get to play the villain. The big bad cop."

"And you the wild kook."

"The sad-eyed victim, Ry. I'm rehearsing my part."

They both seemed cheered by the prospect, and laughed in harmony over their roles. The responsibility naturally fell to Ryan to change course.

"So, Skootch, a man has to wonder, and I have to ask, what's brought you into town?" In the candlelight he licked his lips and, like a boxer warming up to his opponent, feinted with his chin. "Upstream, you had it made. More peace and quiet than most men can tolerate. The tranquillity you relish. Proximity to nature. Solitude. Big bad cops, not to mention the vile public, leave you alone."

"I've opted for the bright lights, Ry. A change, for sure. But change comes upon us. I spotted an opportunity and seized it."

"How so?" Ryan asked.

Skootch scratched the tip of his nose first. Then scolded him. "That part's obvious, Ry. A smart guy like you. The bridge is gone. *Pfft!* It's no more. Suddenly, I got no impediment to gliding my raft downstream."

"You realize," Ryan counselled him, "you can't go around saying that."

"Why not?"

"Think about it."

His eyes shifted around. "I'm thinking. I still don't follow you."

"Motive. You gave me one. To burn the bridge. To get it out of your way."

Skootch now stood keenly focussed on Ryan. He remained still and silent longer than Ryan considered necessary to create an effect. "Dear friend," Skootch summed up at last, "not a soul on earth will make that deduction. Or, may I say, that accusation. We know who burned the bridge, don't we? Don't we? I have no proof who—*individually. Specifically.* But it was loggers. We both know that and we probably know which loggers. I for one do not go around burning beautiful relics which ought to be preserved through eternity and everybody, and I mean *everybody*, knows that. I am the protector of such creations, as

I protect the forest, and the river, the very air we breathe. I am not the destroyer. I don't pollute. The loggers, you know this as well as I do, as a body they're the destroyers. They're the polluters."

"Nice speech. Really, Skootch, you should be a politician."

"Maybe. Or maybe that's what I secretly am. I'm just not into elected office so much. Something about the accepted dress code."

Ryan altered his tone to press his query, wanting this foray to be intimate rather than accusatory. "Ever think, Skootch, that maybe you failed? You set yourself up as the protector of the bridge, you even came to me to talk about Denny, and now the bridge is gone. Where were you when you were needed?"

"Excuse me, but if I'm not mistaken, Officer, you're the one charged with upholding the law and maintaining order. Keeping the peace, shit like that. Where were you on the night in question? Wasn't that your job, not to mention, forgive me for saying this, but aren't you your brother's keeper? You were forewarned."

"I failed in my duty. No question. But did we both fail, do you think?"

Skootch weighed Ryan's admission and his query. He hoisted his cup and sipped with evident pleasure. "Right you are, Ry. We both fucked up. I wasn't around when that bridge met its fate even though I knew, ahead of time, that it was doomed. I regret my absence. But I won't beat myself up too badly. Nobody can be everywhere at once and who can imagine, let alone prepare, for each and every contingency in life? Neither me nor you. I absolve you of your sins, Officer O'Farrell"—Skootch broke into oratorical gusto and performed the sign of the cross in midair—"as I absolve myself of mine. *Mea culpa. Mea big time fucked up.* Thanks for the whisky, by the way. It's yummy."

Ryan sipped as well, and uncapped his flask to top them both up.

"A quasi–Irish Catholic boy like me, even one raised by a Presbyterian Scottish mom," he said, "appreciates absolution. So thanks. But the thing is, Skootch, I'm not sure if you're in a position to absolve me of my sins. But I know for a fact that I'm not in any position to absolve you of yours, given that it's my job to keep the peace and, as you say, uphold the law."

"The frigging law. I'll never understand what possessed you to take the job, Ry. Were you stoned at the time? On a binge? Brokenhearted, maybe. You've kept your footing on shifting sand, I know."

"I'll never understand why you took up your profession either."

The man chuckled, and spread open his arms as though to indicate the river, the town, the surrounding forests and hills, and the last trace of evening light. "This magnificence," he questioned him, "yet you wonder why?"

"I enjoy it, too, Skootch," Ryan pointed out to him. "As much mine to enjoy as yours. Except, admittedly, for this pile of junk."

"But I have the *freedom* to enjoy it, Ry! You dress up for Halloween each day and strap on a gun in case somebody wants to shoot you. Your attire claims you, it defines you. As does mine."

"Touché," Ryan conceded.

"Not to mention, though you chide me for it, I figure if there's a half-dozen women in my life I won't be bitten so badly if one decamps in the middle of the night. I rue the loss of an infielder more."

"You got me there, too," Ryan said.

They let the night prevail then, surrendering to the gathering ambiance. Bats and nighthawks skittered above them on a mosquito hunt, and below them the windless surface of the river was broken intermittently by patrolling fish, nibbling at the toes of water bugs and ditched flies.

"Whatever happened to us?" Skootch asked. "Is that the question posed at this hour?"

Nodding, Ryan concurred. "Time goes by. Hey. Speaking of time, it's sad about Mrs. McCracken. She used to keep us both in tow."

"Yeah. I loved that old chick. Arrogant as sin, though. She told me one time that she refused to give up on me. So I told her that I pray for *her* every night. Man, that rotted her socks. Teed her right off. How come she was so old from the day she was born, though? I don't understand that about her."

Ryan reached up under his shirt's collar, yawned, and scratched his shoulder. He was still yawning as he began to talk. "She always wondered why I never arrested you. She actually suggested, seriously, I think, that I sink your boat, although in fairness, I don't think she knew it was your boat."

"Sweet old dame. I wouldn't put it past her to sink me herself, if she was still around. Do you have plans along those lines, Ry?"

"Not yet. But I could sink you, Skootch, in more ways than one."

Time to resort to the whisky.

Skootch chose a rather solemn tone, for him, when he asked, "Why haven't you? Long ago I ceased to believe that it's just for old times' sake."

"Here's to old times," Ryan said. They clinked mugs, and drank.

They revelled in the quiet of the night awhile longer.

"As boys, Ryan, we thought we'd ride this river one day, float the logs downstream. That's before it hit me what an ugly thing a hewn forest can be, and wanted no part of the work. Before you got religion and became a cop. But I miss it some days, the dream. Do you? I still go to bed at night sometimes and imagine myself on a log drive. It's an old-world dream. Before clear-cutting and contaminated rivers. But it was a good dream, while it lasted. You miss it?"

Ryan took up his tone, this bend in the river of their discussion. If Skootch wanted to be nostalgic with him, he was willing to go there.

"Sometimes. Sure. Like you say, though, our worldview didn't have a snowball's chance of holding up. We got knocked off our plank by life, Skootch. If you want to move logs today, drive a truck. That's a far cry from being a raftsman."

"Yet here I am. Living on the river. At least for a spell. And you, Ry, do you want to cut the crap?"

He nodded and sipped. "Okay, Skootch. If you want me to. This morning three logging trucks were firebombed. A few others were spray-painted. There's not a person in his right mind who doesn't think the tree huggers are behind the sabotage."

"Tree hugger," Skootch parlayed, "is a derogatory term. You may continue to use it, just as I will continue to say, for example, logger fucks, but I just want to make that point, you being a civic official who really should mind his tone."

"Duly noted," Ryan complied. "Let me remind you, I'm not in uniform."

"You will be tomorrow. Sabotage, also, is a discretionary word."

"How about *you* cutting the crap, Skootch? You play with language, but . . ."

Skootch looked away and back, nodding slightly. The nod felt defiant now, even threatening. "Fine. Violent acts of protest, and some minor vandalism, occurred today, initiated by a person or persons unknown."

"The crap, Skootch."

"At the time I was sitting on top of Ol' Smokey here, in plain public view, eating my curds and whey. What the fuck is whey anyway, do you know?"

"I thought so," Ryan said.

"Thought what?"

"You made a public spectacle of yourself in order to establish a

357

rock-solid alibi. You were saying, you've wondered why I haven't put you away yet."

"Are you suggesting that old times' sake doesn't cut it? I like to think that whatever it is you imagine I might be doing that requires my being *put away*, in your words, I have not given you one shred of evidence to sustain the charge. Am I correct?"

"If you screw up, you're done. You're toast. You'll be under arrest. You're right to think that way. And you're right to think that you do a remarkable job of covering your ass. There's another aspect to this, though."

"Do tell."

"I prefer the devil I know, Skootch."

"You don't honestly think of me as a devil, do you, Ryan? Not you."

"Likely, your replacement, if it comes to that, will be an ugly thug up from the city who keeps a pistol in the glove box of his SUV and a semiautomatic in the trunk. He'll have biker pals. He'll keep people in line by beating the shit out of them with a baseball bat that's never met a ball, or by executing them somewhere along the riverbank and burying them in mud. Things will change without you, Skootch. You have your own methods of maintaining internal order. I prefer them. There's not a good-sized town on this continent that doesn't have buyers and sellers of illicit drugs, so I'm not going to kid myself into believing I can stamp out the problem or make it go away. The best I can do is keep the ancillary problems under wraps. Your methods help with the internal order around here. Until now. And now it's time that we consider again the internal order, for the benefit of everyone concerned."

Twice Skootch appeared set to respond, and twice he swallowed his words, washed down with another sip of whisky. He had more to think about here than anticipated.

"So this discussion is about internal order?" he wanted to clarify.

"It is."

"Hmm." Night fully collapsed upon them. Their platform remained lit by a hurricane lamp and a few candles in pots, and by streetlamps a distance off. They could see each other well enough. "This is also about Denny," Skootch construed.

"You don't want a war between tree huggers and loggers. Neither do I."

Skootch sat up so that he was sitting astride the divan. "Ryan, I care for the forest, the river and the air, and for the planet. That care, of course, has to be financed. So I learned to attach myself to what really counts in life and I don't give a shit for stuff that doesn't matter no matter what people think. Except, of course, baseball, but baseball matters to me. As it does to Denny, which is why I'm so fond of him. Him and me, we started that league. Us, we decided on hardball, none of that fastball shit. But there's a cost, Ry, a payment extracted from those who denude and destroy. I warned your brother not to destroy that bridge."

"Thoughtful of you, Skootch."

"He did not heed my warning."

"So a truck was destroyed. Let's say by a lightning bolt from heaven. So tit for tat. This is where it ends."

"If the loggers are satisfied with that, then fine. But you and I both know they won't be. If it's a war they want, it's on their heads."

"Regarding your internal discipline," Ryan said, trying to find traction.

"This is about Denny, right? Will you at least admit that?"

"You said so yourself, you don't know the individuals involved. No one does."

"Except the individuals themselves."

"I haven't heard anyone confess, have you? But let's say the loggers are up in arms, which is not a stretch. Let's say that for your sake, Denny's sake, my sake, the town's sake—my God, even for the forest's sake and the river's—let's say that if the loggers saw some retribution exacted—"

"Upon tree huggers?" Skootch asked.

"Upon the firebombers—then is there not a good chance that hostilities might cease? On both sides?"

In the silence that ensued, Ryan knew that his brother's close childhood pal was weighing the options.

"Denny is still on the hook—"

"Not necessarily."

"The SQ is investigating, I heard."

"That's the problem, you see. I'm betting that they don't want to stick around. It's not their turf. They don't give a shit. They'd rather get back to their friends and families and favourite watering holes. Maybe they golf, I don't know. Life here is a motel room and restaurant food and their per diems don't pay for the best places. Here our cheap places to eat and sleep are, well, cheap."

"And the golfing sucks."

"They want to find a legitimate suspect to lay a charge against and beat it."

"But not if it's Denny."

"They don't care if it's Denny or not. As it happens, I do."

Ryan stood up to depart. He said what he came to say, and dared go no further.

"At least you're not a choirboy," Skootch remarked. He reminded him, "I've only asked one thing of you, Ry. I respect you too much to ask for special dispensation, or a blind eye, nothing like that. One thing only I've asked. Remember what it is?"

He couldn't recall initially. Then something cropped up.

"You have got to be kidding me."

"Why? This is going to cost me," Skootch negotiated. "I should be compensated in return, no? It should cost you something."

"You're persistent. I'll give you that. God."

"Just," Skootch mollified him, "to the end of the season—and the playoffs. No long-term commitment."

Ryan saw no easy way out, and so consented with a nod and took his leave. He climbed down the ladder and on the lower tier the youthful earth mother smiled as he leapt off the raft onto solid ground.

"Good night," she said. "Come back soon." The moon, just rising above the hills, shone upon her face and bounteous cleavage. But he'd spoken his piece, and would not return.

■ ■ ■

PARTIALLY CLAD, DENNY AND VAL fell asleep in each other's arms. They'd had a few drinks. When his alarm woke him Denny found his socks pulled off his feet and his belt buckle undone, but otherwise he still wore his lazy-day jeans. Up during the middle of the night, Val changed into her PJs, and now snoozed soundly through the alarm. Denny tapped it off, then fell back asleep himself. Jerking awake further on, he was already late, and a little annoyed when Valou, minutes later, knocked on his bathroom door. He swung her up into his arms and gave her a bumpy ride.

"You're a pork pie!" she called out. How could the child, any child, be so awake so early, with so much energy and life while he possessed so little? Of his three kids, she was the least concerned about the troubles in their household, and for that, at least, he was grateful.

"You're a pork pie with a lemon nose and jalapeño peppers in your teeth."

"You're a pork pie with Buffalo wings for ears and a . . . a giraffe with a liquorice pipe in your belly button."

"Now you're just being silly," he said, and put her down. "It's a silly game, but you can't start off silly."

"Why not?"

"Not enough fun that way. It has to work up to being silly. Daddy needs a shower this morning, sweetheart. Use the toilet downstairs, okay?"

"Aw."

"New rule. Come on. I'm late. Scoot! Look at poor mommy. She's still asleep. Go quietly, okay?"

She was surprisingly obedient and Denny entered his shower where he felt achingly tired and deeply gloomy.

He already booked off a couple of hours for later in the morning to go to Mrs. McCracken's funeral, but when he got downstairs he phoned in to say he would not be back until the afternoon. He drove into town to look up the only lawyer he knew and was outside the man's office when Joe Pavano showed up for work, parking his Austin Mini. He followed Joe through the doors into the modest law office.

The sign on the door called him Giuseppe.

Joe was in before his secretary. Typical behaviour. Always the nerd.

Denny deemed that the lawyer was not ageing well, despite a level of prosperity he and his peers would never know. Not just the balding hair and the expanding waistline, but the bags under his eyes were overly pronounced and he detected a slight wheeze to the man's breathing. They both fathered young children—perhaps Joe's were wearing him out before his time.

"Good morning, old buddy."

Giuseppe Pavano gazed at Denny in the doorway to the office as though he did not recognize him. Finally, he said, "My secretary doesn't make appointments this early for anybody."

"Yeah. I came in on my own. Checking things out. It's been a while, Joey boy, how's it going?"

"I haven't heard that for a while. People call me Joseph, if they're not calling me Giuseppe, or Mr. Pavano."

"We go back to the good old days. I sure as hell won't ask you to call me Dennis."

"What's up, Denny? What can I do for you?"

He seldom was made to feel unwelcome, anywhere, and in this instance his irritation rose quickly, snaking through him. He didn't see why Joe Pavano should have anything against him and supposed he'd turn out to be another poor slob who loved the old bridge more than life itself. One of those nut bars.

"I might be in the market for a lawyer there, Joey. So I thought of you. My old pal. Who else?"

Joe Pavano waved him through to his office from the outer greeting area. His visitor sat in front of the broad desk and looked at pictures of Joey and his wife and kids. The man had more kids than Denny remembered, and he thought to make a joke about turning off the tap: *Holy cow, Joe, how do you get any lawyering done with all those diapers?* But he held his breath. He sensed that he might sound desperate, and enormously uncomfortable, being here.

"We go back a long way," Denny reminded him as the man fitted his girth into a black leather high-backed executive chair. He attributed the desk to being an Ikea piece as the fittings were familiar. Maybe he wouldn't cost so much.

"Yeah, we do," Joe agreed. "We go back to when you pulled my pants down behind the dugout so the girls could laugh at my fat ass."

"That happened?" Denny asked. He wanted to laugh.

"I don't intend to represent you, Denny."

Suddenly he did feel desperate, and grasped that he had never felt quite so forlorn before. "Joey, come on, bygones, right? Harmless fun. You don't want to carry a grudge, right?"

"Sure I do. If you have a problem with that, too bad. But Denny. Come on. I do general practise. Family law, estate planning. If you want a divorce, I'm your guy, although I tend to prefer the wife's side. Criminal law I don't do."

"I didn't tell you why I'm here."

"You burned the bridge down, Denny, everybody knows that."

"Everybody knows squat! Fuck you! You're a lawyer! You can't just spit out something like that. What about judge and jury? What about innocent until proven guilty?"

"You'll be charged unless your brother pulls a fast one. And found guilty."

"Well thanks for nothing anyway." Denny got to his feet.

"You're welcome. But here." The lawyer scratched words on a pad, then tore off the sheet and handed it to him.

"What's this?"

"Major crime, Denny. Arson. A financial loss that can't be over-stated. You'll need a city lawyer. These people can suggest a choice of names."

Denny turned the sheet over in his fingers. "Okay. Thanks. Sorry about the, you know, the fat-ass thing. Do you think I can find a good one? Lawyer, I mean. Can a guy like me catch a break, do you think?"

"Depends on what you can afford. You'll probably need to put up your house and truck for collateral."

Denny stared at him a moment. "I could lose my truck?"

Joe Pavano touched the fingertips of his left hand to those of his right, and nodded. "Not to mention your house. That's if you win. Losing will mean jail time. What do you think that will cost you?"

Denny sensed what Giuseppe Pavano saw, the blood draining from his face, although he felt it leave his body altogether. He entertained negative scenarios in this, but never went this far along or imagined the more frightening ramifications. His wife tried, and failed, to get him to face up to what was happening. Now it was all hitting home like a sledgehammer.

"Joey," he whispered.

"I prefer Giuseppe, actually, now."

"You have to help me, man."

The lawyer indicated the sheet of paper in Denny's hands that listed the relevant agencies to call. "I already have. Good luck with all that, Denny."

21

The movement commenced as imperceptible, developed into a trickle, then evolved into a steady migration. Officer Ryan O'Farrell noticed the early risers on the roadways, but deluded himself, believing that the few motivated to be early were excessively earnest rather than prescient. They proved to be both. A steady flow became a river of human and vehicular traffic into town and he finally got his head around the logistical problem that was rapidly developing. He accepted that assigning a single officer to handle traffic control for the funeral was a mistake.

Out on the highway well beyond the weedy north end of town, a dilapidated but popular service station drew down its broad garage doors and locked up. Scribbled on cardboard, a sign taped to the front window read: BACK IN 3 HRS. Similar signs were stuck on the moribund pumps. The owner, two mechanics, and a gas jockey drove off the premises in a single car. Behind them travelled the beat-up vehicles from the camp down the road operated by Gordon "Skootch" Skotcher, and behind the relics in pickups and company

Jeeps drove loggers, both truckers and woodsmen. Mill workers were the last in from that direction, en masse. They travelled into town where government offices remained open but the bakery was shutting for the rest of the morning and where, to the dismay of a few but to the surprise of none, the town's main supermarket posted a sign on the banister at only five minutes after ten to announce that its doors were closed.

Tourist shops awaiting the daily train lowered their blinds.

As the evidence mounted, Ryan reacted to his problem. The rookie assigned to traffic would soon be overwhelmed, so he called others in from their rounds and roused two men off shift to report for duty. He confirmed his predicament driving past an artery already crammed with cottagers and city folk and perhaps a few from farther afield. He put on his revolving lights and used the road's shoulder to squeeze past the jam. By the time Ryan reached the church, the parking lot was already bursting capacity and cars were lining up chockablock down Main Street, some partially on lawns, others slouching into ditches. He noticed that the minister was more attuned to the situation than he'd been, as amplified speakers were set up on the front steps. If not the whole world, then a good measure of this part of the visible world was planning to attend Mrs. McCracken's service.

Ryan didn't guess that the woman of his current dreams, Raine Tara-Anne Cogshill, was safely ensconced inside the sanctuary, driven there by her business partner after locking their shop's doors. At her insistence, she and Willis Howard were on hand early enough. Tara wanted to set up a table for her petition to rebuild the bridge, and assigned a teenager recently hired to work in the store to oversee accumulating signatures. She and Willis were now squashed into a pew about a third of the way down from the narthex, along the aisle. Conversations percolated around them, louder than elsewhere as many in this particular group were hard of hearing. Through no design of their own and in the absence of any planning, the pair was seated smack-dab in the centre of a brigade of elderly ladies, spinsters and widows, many of whom arrived by van from the local nursing home six blocks down. They pealed with commentary, laughter, news, and artful gossip.

Tara giggled to herself a few times. Would she ever be one of these? She could not imagine it—neither the clothing nor the hairstyles nor the chat appealed, never mind the hysteria—yet she pondered also if any of their ilk once lived lives akin to her own.

She looked around her. She could not imagine that either.

They blew in from another culture, from different weather.

She was struck by their attire, as though the fashion style was intended to celebrate a flamboyant old-biddy flare while paying homage to the customs of grief. Small black bonnets denoted a funereal consideration, but these were outnumbered by summer bonnets on the tops of blue- and red-rinsed hair. Gauche broaches and purses and bright print dresses stood against dark colours to coordinate with the transient gloom. Summer gloves were plentiful. So playful and dear were the flaunting colours, ruffles, and tucks that Tara could scarcely differentiate whose voice belonged to whom as her ears surrendered to the maze and squawk, the open doors permitting not only a welter of breezes and perfumed scents to slink inside but also eliciting a tonic of chatty spiels.

"I imply no such thing. You misunderstand me, as is your wont. I said—I repeat myself, dear—I only hope that someone who has something good to say knows how to say it. That's the gist of what I mean to say."

"Why won't they know good things to say—"

"Stop being such a ninny!" an admirably spry lady of ninety-five chided her younger sibling, a dour-looking woman of eighty-eight. Tara affixed their ages using her best judgement and, she believed, a benevolent benefit of the doubt. They might well be older.

The younger chose not to be bullied. "Why wouldn't they have good—"

"Because people don't know how to talk in public, you silly galoot."

"Why don't they then?"

"Because they never learned! You have to learn how."

"I'll tell you something. Alice knew how. Alice could speak in public."

"Alice," the senior sister concurred, "knew how."

A third voice with a cranky trill to her timbre queried, "Wasn't she a teacher? Didn't she teach?"

"Good grief, where've you been for the past fifty years? Of course she taught!"

"Then she can talk."

"What?"

"She's a teacher. She can talk."

"Of course she can talk! We *know* she can talk. That's half my point. But she's not going to do any talking today, now is she? I just hope that whoever does do the talking today knows how, that's what I mean to say but I might as well be talking Swahili to this pew!"

"Is she a teacher then, the one?"

"What? Who, dear?"

"The one who'll do the talking? I hope it's not the preacher himself. He's not a good talker, that fellow. Doesn't he just mumble so."

"I don't know who's going to do the talking. I live in the same home you do, although perhaps you haven't noticed. Nobody tells any of us anything. I only hope that if someone has something nice to say he knows how to say it."

"It might not be a man," a friend cautioned her.

A new voice opined, sagely, "Man or woman, I hope I can hear them."

"Just turn up the volume, dear," another advised.

"Oh, not yet. Not yet. You're shouting so."

"I don't understand. Why wouldn't someone have something nice to say? Alice was a nice person."

"Doesn't matter if she was nice or not," a new voice interjected. "She's dead. People speak well of the dead at funerals. Most of the time anyway."

"Listening to that man mumble is like listening to a crow gargle."

Tara didn't really want to share a glance with Willis Howard, but at a certain point it became inevitable, and sure enough they both muffled giggles into their palms. They need not have bothered with the subterfuge, as the women around them were oblivious.

At the end of the service the women nearby were agreed that the speakers—several presented themselves—spoke well.

"I liked the part about the pies especially."

"The part about the kindergarten kiddies had me in stitches."

"I noticed."

"I liked hearing about the day her young husband died."

"Oh, you would. You always choose the saddest tales."

"Not always."

"Yes. Always."

Tara was unsure if she did not appreciate the saddest stories herself. She found that she was less complimentary towards the speeches that washed over them for an hour than were the other women, but she chose not to be critical either. She did find in each talk a snippet or two that conveyed the spirit of the woman she grew so fond of in a short time. She particularly enjoyed the logger who related how the old lady ran over his toes one time on her motorbike. When he objected, Mrs. McCracken retorted that since he was wearing steel-toed boots, what did it matter? "Just watch your step," she warned him, "the day you wear sandals. And sandals and socks, you'll rue the day."

At least she warned her victims beforehand.

The group collectively known as tree huggers, Tara noticed, were not represented by a speaker, yet their presence was acknowledged and they were thanked for the homemade wreaths created partly of wildflowers. On the way out, she overheard a remark suggesting that at least a few of the flowers might not have been so wild, snipped, perhaps, from local gardens. "To think I first blamed the squirrels." Tara smiled. She was here to commemorate Mrs. McCracken's life and to honour her passing, and did that, but the community in which she landed was making an impression on her once again. Among others, she questioned whether the town might never fully recover without the grand old dame.

By the parking lot, Willis Howard fell into a conversation with a group of men while Tara visited the petition table. She didn't notice Ryan O'Farrell slip into the space next to her, until he spoke.

"This is really not fair." He seemed cross.

Catching his meaning, she stood her ground. "The Alice B. Mc-Cracken Memorial Bridge idea is taking hold."

"Are you the one behind this?"

Tara did not recognize the woman's voice addressing her, and turned. "Yes," she admitted.

The woman confronting her was approximately her age, and quite attractive, although her gaze seemed overtly combative, her brow in a crunch.

"Tara," Ryan said, "this is my sister-in-law, Valérie O'Farrell. Val, this is Tara Cogshill."

The woman was obviously steeling herself for battle, although the formal introduction stymied her offensive somewhat. Tara wondered if Ryan was intentionally stepping in for that purpose.

"Oh," Val said. "So you two are dating."

"Hi," Tara said, conspicuously friendly. She saw Val give her a full-body scan but refrained from returning the favour.

Val was momentarily tongue-tied and started in with less intensity than she might prefer. "You're new here. So maybe you don't understand everything, but something like this," she argued, "it has complications."

"I've tried to tell her that." Ryan shook his head. While he agreed with Valérie's side in the matter, he didn't want her going off half cocked, which he feared she could do with some drama and little persuasion. The evident tightness around her eyes and the clenched jaw reflected Val's inner temper. She was managing to control herself. Several times she looked from Ryan to Tara.

"Do a better job of it," she warned him quietly, essentially warning them both. She let that settle as her only parry for the day and brushed past them.

Briefly, Tara raised her eyebrows, a private, and intimate, communication with Ryan, which acknowledged the close call. She then followed Val's trajectory, seeing Ryan's brother for the first time that day in the midst of his children where they waited in the parking lot. The view subdued her, and she said, "Handsome dad, isn't he?" She recalled the night he gave her a lift in the rain, how striking he looked then, how sexy. "Good-looking family. I guess this isn't the best time to tell your sister-in-law that I'm anticipating the complications she's worrying about. I'm counting on them. She should, too."

"Please don't get into that with her. She won't know what you're talking about any more than I do, but she'll have a lot less patience than me."

Inexplicably, Tara smiled. "Patience," she asked. "Is that what you call it?"

"What do you mean?"

"What you feel for me. Patience?"

Caught out, he permitted a chuckle to escape, pleased that she was willing to flirt. "What do you want me to call it?"

She started this but wasn't willing to be drawn in any further.

"Ry, I'm going up to the cemetery for the internment—"

"Why?" he asked point-blank, too quickly, as though he questioned her right to go there.

Now Tara, too, was confrontational. Her expression changed. "Remember the day you so gallantly stopped Mrs. McCracken for speeding just so you could chat me up? Incidentally, that's still in your favour. We were coming back from the cemetery. She brought me up there." She softened, and felt herself softening, as though the memory of Mrs. McCracken returned her to the events of the day. "I don't know why, really. But who else did she bring to the gravesite specifically to visit her husband's grave and her own future plot? You? The old ladies inside? I'm betting no. For whatever reason, she chose to bring me there, Ry, me, the outsider, so I'm going up there now. I was about to suggest that we see each other afterwards—"

"Okay. I'm up for that." Ryan clasped the proffered straw.

On the one hand, she wanted to curtail the offer, now that she was miffed, yet she also wanted to repeat his choice of word, *up*, and considered it, until she felt a blush coming on. Any innuendo could easily travel beyond the flirtatious and signal, possibly, the collapse of her will in their mutual joust, but in any case be more than she was willing to express in a chaotic parking lot after a funeral. She still wanted to round up Willis Howard to get him in line for the solemn drive up the mountainside. So instead she said, "You know where to find me," and cordially touched his wrist, and they both returned to their tasks.

■ ■ ■

WIND, SNUFFED IN THE VALLEYS, sullied the mountaintop. Women battled to keep their hair and hems in place, while men clamped hands over grey tufts to preserve a semblance of grooming and pulled closed their lapels. The minister's buoyant words suffered in the stiffer gusts. Despite the difficulties, dust came to dust, and ashes to ashes, and Tara's heart, really for the first time through the morning, slung low. *Death.* She could remind herself that it came to everyone, that every creature ever to step upon the earth either died or had that moment coming, as did those as yet unborn. Whatever time she would know after her death she probably knew something similar before she was born, be it nothingness or *somethingness*, so really, what was the difference? The fear, the dread, she supposed, and the unknown, composed the difference. When dread was allowed to knock on the door, when she permitted herself to anticipate the end, to speculate on whatever came next, she suspected that no matter what came next it was nothing new—*just new compared to yesterday, or maybe not even*—she quivered. Internally, she quaked. She wished, in a way, that she could attend a funeral—she'd been to a mere half dozen as an adult—without thinking about dying herself. *That's Alice in that box. What if she wants out? What if I want out when my time comes? But that's not Alice in that box. Girlfriend, tell yourself this—that'll never be you. Your chunk of change—okay. Your old now useless lifeless bod. But not—me.* She wished she could just think about Alice, and as easily as that commune with her. But death, as happened at these things, got in the way.

In departing the cemetery, Tara cast her gaze across the windswept lawn of the departed, and over the robust hills. A river flowed a long way below in the valley, invisible from above save for a portion of its darkened gulley. Clouds on a scud. *You can see forever if you can see an inch, dear Alice.* A good choice of burial plot, as a prime minister who'd been a Nobel laureate deduced before her. Alive, Alice envisioned this, the sight lines, the intemperate winds, the trees, the sheer expanse of vista, the immaculate, changing skies. Alive, this seemed a good place to be, a decent spot to stow her last material possession, her lonesome old impoverished carcass, a good place to lay it down gently within a beautiful earth.

She spied, one gravestone over, the maternal family name. Alice's middle name. This time, the translation hit her. *Beauchamp.* Good field. Beautiful field. Close enough to *wake field*, in a way, to be spooky. As if she was born for a fine grave such as this, and here.

Tara did not know what she was going to do with her life, what the future might stimulate, what adventures and travels might arise or where she might die and when, or with whom, and she knew that it would be nothing but silly to forsake the whims of fate to cause this fresh inner desire to come true, but she did feel that she wouldn't mind being buried here—*ashes, though, not the whole damn body, cremate me, please, the worms*—when her time came. She'd be content to join dear Alice on this slope. Did the grand old lady not suggest it?

No rush, though. Just saying.

And perhaps that was it, this careless intimacy with her own death that put her awash, instigating feelings both romantic and more private than she wanted them to be, a lustiness gathering steam and taking precedence. *Sex and death, whoo boy.* And a need, reborn, for love and frolic. She stepped off the grass of the cemetery onto the gravel road and she felt herself weakening, warmish, damp and at least inwardly wild. *Willis, this could be your lucky morning,* a joke to herself as he drove her off the mountain of the dead. A joke she banished the instant it surfaced to focus instead on *my policeman. He's in uniform right now. Looks good in uniform, doesn't he? Oh mercy, I want him. I want him to want me. Holy! Girl, girl, get a hold of—*

■ ■ ■

OFFICERS MALTAIS AND VEGA BOTH signed a petition to restore the old covered bridge and have it named after Alice B. McCracken. Neither thought the effort was anything but impractical and a bit dopey, and both were aware that as officers of the law they were expressly forbidden from signing petitions or publicly taking a side. But they needed a measure of traction in this town. They came up against a public that refused to have anything to do with them. People clammed up. The detectives remembered the old lady with some fondness, although she was no different than the rest, but in supporting this petition, others might think better of them, loosen up a little. Talk. At the funeral they spotted Denny O'Farrell and followed him and his family home. They already knew where he lived but catching him in was proving difficult. This time they parked along the curb just as his truck came to a halt in the driveway.

When Denny clambered out of his vehicle, he spotted them stepping out of theirs. His wife said, "Den." He calmly instructed her to take the kids inside. She did. He wandered down the driveway and met the officers at the edge of his property.

"Some people in this town," Maltais said in English, "want us to talk to them on the street. Like we might contaminate their grass or something."

"I don't even know who you are," Denny said.

"Sure you do. But you're right. We haven't been properly introduced."

"We're not here to piss on your lawn. We're friends of your brother," Vega said, but he didn't extend his hand. He reached into his pocket as Denny was essentially forcing him to do and pulled out his badge. He held it up and the shield glinted in the sunlight. "Vega," he said.

"Maltais," the other one said and he also showed his badge. "Do you have any more formalities in mind?"

Denny said, "Pardon me?" A way of questioning the man's attitude, but then he broke from that poor start and invited the policemen into the backyard for a beer. He wanted to demonstrate that he wasn't afraid of them, and not antagonistic either. He wanted them to know that, whether or not it was true.

"It's early," Maltais noted.

"I was at a funeral," Denny said. "That can build up a thirst."

"We're working," Vega pointed out.

"You're friends of my brother, you said. So you don't have to call it work. Come around out back, guys. We can sit at least."

Maltais agreed to sit, and perhaps to drink beer. Vega shrugged in partial agreement. "We were at that funeral, too."

"You were? Why?"

"We met her. Mrs. McCracken. We liked her. We interviewed her."

"You interviewed Mrs. McCracken? She probably shook you down."

Vega smiled. "Maybe that's why we went to the funeral, out of respect." Each of the three men knew that that was a lie.

"Come on back," Denny encouraged them. "There might be food, too."

They moved more slowly than he did, which caused Denny to look back a couple of times to check on their delay. Vega, his suit jacket open, walked with his hands in his trouser pockets and his head up, looking around as though gathering impressions. Maltais cinched his belly with a single jacket button, which did appear on the verge of springing loose. He directed his observations to the ground. Denny's first instinct was to dismiss him, perhaps because he appeared slovenly and depressed, but his second thought was to scratch that opinion. The man's nose to the ground that way, he looked like an overweight bloodhound, droopy of flesh and bleary-eyed, but a bloodhound as an investigator was not someone to ignore. From his testicles up through his gullet, through his lungs and heart and windpipe, Denny felt fear inexorably rising.

Val was ahead of him. She put out the beer and salsa and chips. Then she went back inside but Denny knew she'd be listening in. He twisted a beer cap off and handed the bottle to Vega.

"Okay without a glass?"

"No problem. Thanks."

"I could get a glass."

"In a backyard, beer is best straight from the bottle."

Maltais agreed and accepted his beer and Denny rushed to untwist a third cap and to swallow. He was not certain if the beer helped him relax but it felt good to quench his flaring thirst.

"So was it worth it?" Vega asked quietly.

"Excuse me?"

Neither man answered him. They sipped their beers while Denny took another long pull.

Then Vega said, "I mean, you could get ten years. More or less. I know it's not worth that. But the stress. The worry. Even if you get away with it, was it worth it?"

"I don't know what you mean," Denny said.

"I'm sorry to hear that," Vega told him.

Denny took the bait. "What are you sorry to hear?"

Vega shrugged first. "Because that's what a guilty man would say. A guilty man says, 'I don't know what you mean.' Both the innocent man and the guilty man know exactly what I mean, but only the guilty man asks me to repeat the question or tells me that he doesn't understand it. Did you know that?"

Denny said that he didn't know that.

"There you go. You see?"

"I don't see anything," Denny said.

"You don't know how a guilty man responds, no reason why you should, so you said no. Plain and simple. You didn't say to me, *I don't know what you mean*. That time, you gave me an answer. *No.* Now, if I say, was it worth it what you did, and you're an innocent man, you would say . . . well, you tell me, what do you say, if you're innocent? I'll give you a second chance."

"You're playing games with me."

"No, I'm not, and you just failed your second chance. Ten years you can get, Denny. Maybe an even dozen."

"You'll lose your house," Maltais added.

"Your family."

"Maybe not his family."

"Maybe not your family. But your house."

"Your truck."

"Both trucks. Maybe fifteen years."

"Fifteen?" Maltais whistled in mock surprise. "That long? Wow. Your good life. Gone. Your friends, they'll enjoy the new bridge." Maltais rubbed the fingers of his right hand under the thumb. "They'll make the big bucks."

"But not you," Vega told him. "Counting down your time."

Denny drank some more. "So what would an innocent man say?" he wanted to know.

"Ask the innocent. But since you agree with me that you're not innocent, he would not say what you just said."

Val came out onto the back porch and she crossed her arms. "Okay, that's enough," she said.

The three men looked at her.

"We're having a hard time with wives on this trip," Maltais noted.

"They keep kicking us off their properties."

"Nobody's kicking," Val said. "But you are playing games and that's not fair. This is serious. Ask serious questions. We have the rumours to fight against. We can't do that if you play games."

"Where were you the night of the fire?" Vega asked her.

"Me?"

"It's a serious question."

Her eyes shot to Denny and back. "I was here," she said.

"I believe you. Was your husband here?"

She needed the bulk of her strength not to look at Denny again. "No," she said. "I mean, he was, of course, for dinner, but then he left."

"You see?" Vega said, but she didn't see and he wasn't willing to tell her what she was supposed to see.

"That doesn't mean he did it," Val protested.

"Of course not," Maltais said.

"But if everything you say is true—" Maltais pointed out to her.

"—it probably means that you didn't do it yourself," Vega finished the thought. "You're in the clear yourself, but of course, we never suspected you. But it also means that you can't say if he's innocent or guilty. Unless he's admitted it to you, you probably don't know. If he's denied it to you, well, that doesn't mean much, does it? So the point is, you're not a witness. We accept that. So if you don't mind, we'd like to talk to your husband alone, ma'am."

She lingered, and looked at Denny finally. He nodded, and she went back inside. Denny was touched that she didn't slam the door, and he took that as a signal to stay in control of himself just as she was doing of herself.

"Rumours and innuendo. Interview games. Seriously, guys, what else you got? I mean, I doubt if you guys could care less if I'm guilty or innocent—"

"That's cynical, Mr. O'Farrell."

"—you only want to know if you can pin this on me or not. So I don't care if you think I'm guilty or innocent, and I don't care if I act innocent or guilty because I don't know how the innocent or how the guilty act. Psychological bunk to me. You know it won't hold up in a court of law—"

"I've always noticed," Vega interjected, "that only the guilty ever mention a court of law."

"Oh, fuck off with that. What do you have? What evidence do you have to even be talking to me? I wondered, at first, why you never came to talk to me, because I know what people in town say. But now I get it. You wanted to build up your evidence first. To have something on me. Fair enough. So here you are. It took you a while, so what do you got? Speak now or bug out, that's what I say."

"Or bug out?" Vega repeated.

"You see? I could say now that that's what a cop would say who didn't have any evidence. A cop who was talking to a guilty man, who knew *why* he was a guilty man, would have pinned back that guilty man's ears by now. Instead, you just repeated what I said with some kind of mock alarm. So, yeah, bug out. Since you've got nothing."

"Your house. Your trucks. Maybe your family. Even if it's only five years."

"Threats? Yeah, you got a lot of those. I'm waiting to hear some evidence. You don't have any. And do you know why you don't have any evidence?"

"Why, Mr. O'Farrell? You tell us."

"Well, maybe because somebody else did it. Maybe that's why.

Now leave, please. Feel free to take your beers with you or chug them down. Or hell, drink them at your leisure. But gentlemen, this so-called interview is over."

Maltais stepped close to Denny. He stopped staring at the ground to gaze at him. Denny returned the look. Those weepy bloodhound eyes. He knew he should fear this man, for what he could see, for what he could sniff. Maltais whispered, as though imparting a grave secret, "We may have a witness. It's okay to let your brother know. He might be unreliable, our witness. We think he has something against you, so it's possible he didn't really see what he says he saw. So you see, we're actually *not* trying to pin this on you, Mr. O'Farrell. We'd rather not. Unless you did it. But if we can't break this witness down, then you go down. Nothing we can do about that. Nothing you or your brother can do. So you get sent to hell and maybe you never come back. A lot of good men don't. So don't piss on my pant leg. You're living in hell right now, I can see that, I can feel that. It might turn out that we're the only hope you got in this hell of yours. So watch where you piss if you know what's good for you, Mr. O'Farrell."

Denny stared back at him, and for the first time in the conversation he was both conflicted and confused, as though he didn't know himself whose side he was on. "And you're into being my only hope, because of my brother?"

Maltais scratched his neck in an upward motion, using the backs of his fingernails. He thought about the question. "I don't really know your brother. Not that well. No, what you don't get is this. We understand. We really do. We know that you're not a criminal. Maybe you committed a criminal act, and the courts won't look kindly on that. Nor will we. But you're not a criminal. If you burned that bridge, we have reason to believe—in fact I can pretty much guarantee—that you're not likely to be stupid enough to go burn another one."

Vega moved in close as well and Denny wanted him, in particular, he didn't know why, to go away. "We want to get back to hunting criminals. Not the foolish workingman who did something wrong," he said.

"So we can help. You know?" Maltais continued to whisper, as though, Denny was thinking, he wanted to make sure that Val was not part of this discussion, that this was strictly man to man. "That's what we're saying. You'll still do some time. But maybe you can get your buddies off, they might help with the family expenses while you're gone, maybe we can talk with the prosecutors, you know, to clear this up pretty quickly and give you, a family man, a workingman, with no priors, no likelihood to reoffend, an even break, a sharply reduced sentence. A couple of years maybe. It's worth thinking about."

"In other words, since you have no evidence, you want me to confess."

"We may have a witness. Hell, we probably have one, I'm sorry to say."

"Your brother," Vega added, "will get wind of it sooner or later. So you'll know for sure we're not bullshitting you."

"So what we're saying is," Maltais scratched his neck, then brought his bottle up for a sip, "you've got to think about being *strategic*, Mr. O'Farrell. A hardened criminal, I'm not going to give him a break. A family man with young kids who made a mistake, he's got to own up to his responsibilities, face the music, but you know, he can be strategic, he can make this work to get the best possible outcome. I've said enough for now. But think about it, Mr. O'Farrell. You can save your friends. People won't forget that. And you can ease the pain for yourself, too. I believe that. Good-bye, and thanks for the beer. There's a little left in my bottle but will it be okay with you if I just put it down on the stoop?"

Both cops seemed to be waiting on his reply.

"Yeah, sure," Denny said, and he remained where he stood as they moved away, put their beer bottles down, and shuffled off around the side of the house. He was still standing there when Val came back outside. She crossed her arms, and this time leaned against a supporting post for the porch roof.

"So," she said, "what did they say?"

Denny wasn't prepared to look at her just yet. "They want me to confess."

"Did you?"

"No. They just want me to think about it."

He seemed strangely distant, his voice his own and yet so oddly pitched.

She went to him, and when she took him so gently into her arms he seemed to stagger against her, and she believed for a moment that she was the one holding him upright.

22

Just when she hoped he would, Ryan tucked his head into the store.

"Ah. So you do know where to find me!" Tara greeted him.

"Maybe I'm here to buy something."

"Like what?"

"I don't know, like, paperweights?" He cast a look around the store to check out the possibilities. "Or canvas shopping bags with an imprint of our dearly departed Old Covered Bridge."

"We're making up new ones showing the bridge on fire. Or I am. Willis is opposed."

Disembodied, working in a drawer around his ankles behind a counter, Willis Howard parried, "I will not exploit our tragedy."

"He's ethical," Tara mentioned. She sipped from her coffee mug.

"I have extra duty tacked onto my day," Ryan told her. "So, you know, I booked off for a break."

"Nice. You're not here to arrest me then?"

In adolescence, a girlfriend's attempts at coyness came across as snide, so early in life he hated coy. Tara was teaching him otherwise. "Care for a late lunch?"

"Train's in!" Willis Howard called out from behind the cash, where he ensconced himself to continue eavesdropping. "Busy time coming up!"

"That's why we hired Lise," Tara chimed back. "You'll be fine, Willis."

"I've got people coming to see me, too, later."

"Hush." Ryan looked ready to pistol-whip him. She whispered, "If you really want to piss him off? Have *lunch* with me upstairs."

One look and he guessed that the invitation might be a ploy. Struck by lightning, mute, he nodded.

"Gone fishing!" Tara called out and was heading for the side stairs, around the corner and somewhat out of sight, before Willis could fulminate a response. Ryan tramped behind her, and the moment he entered her suite she shut the door behind them and they kissed.

At length.

When she opened the door briefly Ryan thought that she was checking to make sure her business partner was not peeking through the keyhole, but she was letting the cat out.

"You have a cat now?"

"Buckminster," she explained. "Mrs. McCracken's. She likes to wander the store."

He took her hand in his.

"Seriously," she said, and indicated her kitchenette, "I do have food. Bread. Cheese. Crackers."

He didn't answer but kissed her awhile instead. Then he ran his mouth down one side of her neck and up the other to nibble a lobe. When she broke free she touched his jawline with her fingertips, flashed a smile, then stepped away and slyly undid the top button on her jeans. She let him consider that event a moment. Then she slid the zipper down, shoved the jeans to her thighs and wiggled to drop them to her ankles. Her underpants, he saw, were removed with the same flurry and kick.

"How much time do you have?" she asked. He didn't hate coy anymore.

He checked his watch. "Two hours. Nearly. About."

"So," Tara inferred, "a quickie."

"Two hours?" he mildly argued before detecting that she was still teasing. She stepped her feet out of the jeans, leaving them on the floor. The hem of her robin's egg blouse hung low enough to assure her modesty, then nothing below that but lovely bare legs. His hands went to his own shirt buttons. A more conventional start, he knew. After his shirt, his gun. Tara turned, he caught a glimpse of her derrière, then she spun onto the narrow captain's bed, up on her knees and facing him holding a small decorative cushion before her sex with one hand, the other hand rising, suggestively, until her chin rested on the curled digits while the littlest finger poked her mouth. Unadulterated girlish coquette. Brash, though. He wasn't sure what to make of her now.

"Don't worry," was her advice, as if reading his mind. "I'm no little girl, sir. Just helping you get charged up."

He undressed more quickly. "No worries there."

"So I see."

His shoes gave him trouble, the laces needed to be untied while she giggled at him, then he chose to be less conventional than he may have been in a previous life. He stripped naked, the last item off being his damned watch, and when he approached she was expecting him to remain standing, but he went to his knees, to the floor, and she gasped as he guided the cushion to one side as though opening a curtain and with the utmost tenderness kissed her thighs.

Ryan slipped his tongue as low as he could go under her pubis and she adored this man and put her head back and the sounds she emitted let him know how much.

She felt herself opening, as he grazed her with his tongue.

He unbuttoned her blouse. From the bottom up. A slow, thoughtful ritual, conducted in utter silence and reverent, while she held the weight of his cock from underneath with one hand and stroked its upper surface with the other. Nibbling her lower lip was an involuntary reflex now, not guile. She let go to permit him access to ease the blouse off her back and arms, except that he used it to trap her wrists in the fabric awhile as he kissed her, her arms pinned behind her, then he let her finish the removal herself and undo the front clasp of her blue bra, which she slipped off her shoulders and gently, teasingly, let slip to the floor. Tara lay down then, her arms modestly crossed over her breasts, expecting him to lie his fine body on top of her. He surprised her by raising her left calf to his touch and kiss, and slowly his lips drifted upward, pecking at her skin, until the two of them lay prone together, side by close side. Skin to skin. No longer could she restrain herself, although she seemed afflicted by an incongruous shyness amid her desire. He was the more astonished one as she initiated their rhythms, their coupling, this sudden desperate shared joy, this happy outrage of cries and squeals and wilful moaning. A passion tripped up by laughter repeatedly. At first she was urgent, near frantic, fearing perhaps that he might soon be spent, but her confidence in their motion gained with his, and only when she called out and he was stifling her gasps with his fingers to restrict public awareness of this rampage did the pace quicken to a level that broke a near bellow out of him and she was the one laughing her head off now and trying to stuff her wee fist between his teeth.

He ended up mauling her elbow while he writhed and she giggled.

Lying together, recovering, grinning in a cartoon Cheshire way, she was somewhat tempted to say, "I love you," and open herself to that adventure and to all that it might promote, but unable to trust herself in her present euphoria she said instead, "Willis will be incorrigible now."

Ryan said, "I won't be able to face him."

"He'll be pleased," she replied, "to have that power over you." They kissed again. Their tongues playful together.

His kisses closed her eyelids with such sweetness she sighed.

They lay quietly awhile.

The way Ryan sucked in a breath caused her to intuit that he had something to say. Perhaps something serious. Tara snapped her eyelids open and placed a forefinger over his lips. She didn't want to hear any such words now, not when she wasn't willing to say them herself, not yet, not here. Maybe sometime. Maybe never. Somehow she communicated that, that this was another of her complications, which he accepted, and they just kissed and touched lightly. Then she said, "Do you really have to go, really? Or was that just more of your imbecilic hick-town small talk."

"If it wasn't absolutely critical," he told her.

She believed him.

Tara took a very deep breath. "So tell me your plan," she invited.

He gazed at her, his head supported by his hand and upright forearm, his elbow on the bed. He knew what she was talking about. "Will you tell me yours?"

She nodded. "You first, though."

That again. He took a while to begin.

"I know," she said.

She could not possibly know his plan and he looked at her quizzically.

"To tell me," she explained, "you have to trust me. I know that."

So he told her. He trusted her. The story was difficult to bear in a way.

"It's because it's family," she said when he reached the end. She asked, "Right? You're not always such a bastard, are you, Ry?"

"Does it matter?"

"Of course it does. If you're up to becoming the father of my children—"

"We're having kids already!"

"I didn't notice anyone roll on a condom, did you?"

"I assumed—"

She placed her forefinger to his lips, laughing lightly at his sudden consternation. She was always able to catch him.

"Baby, you assumed correctly," she said. "But. You know. I feel like I'm in this. To find out where it leads."

They gazed at each other. She didn't want him to say anything, but he did, "So am I," and then she was glad that he spoke and was succinct. But she didn't want him to say anything more just yet. No mush. She needed to come to terms with this on her own first. Words right now would affect her only as silly.

"It's because it's family," he admitted. "I'm not always such a bastard." He was trying to make light but she could tell that this hurt him, that this was going to cost him.

"He's lucky, Denny is, to have a brother like you," she whispered.

"Not so much. When this is over, I'm going to kill him."

She laughed. She believed him, too.

"Actually, something's up. One of many compromises. A deal. I suspect that I'm going to break Denny's heart, in a way that really will hurt him. We'll see." She was mystified, but he said no more. "So what's your plan?" he asked.

She told him.

His affection for her didn't come with a gauge, yet he cherished her even more. At the very least, he revelled in this, the idea. The chance it presented.

"So," Ryan summarized, as though he needed to draw them a chart, "I'm the notoriously good guy, who's going rogue, and you're the notoriously bad, cynical, *complicated* girl who's doing what's right. And beautiful, really."

"Finding our true selves, do you think?" She meant to be funny.

"Not such good news for me."

"You'll adapt. Well. You have to." She sensed that she could say something then. "So I guess this works, huh? Me and you, I mean. In a way. Sort of. Maybe."

They kissed, and she liked that he kissed her at length even in the aftermath of their lovemaking. That was so nice.

Then he said, "You have to do it sooner rather than later."

"Do I? Why—? Are you—?"

"I am," he told her.

"Today? Sure," she promised. "I'll go see your brother."

"He might be working."

"Then I'll talk to Valérie. If she's out, I'll talk to your dad."

"Maybe," he said, and he was ruminating over something, so she let him hold his pause awhile, "just talk to Dad first. Let him bring it to Denny himself."

She nodded. That might be smart. Leaning way over, she snatched her underpants off the floor and fiddled for the leg holes while he ran his fingers along her spine.

"Hey, Ry, now that we know that sainthood is a distance off for you—"

"You're going to hold this over me, aren't you?" But he was kidding, too. Ryan swung his feet onto the floor and leaned over to clutch his clothes and pull them up in a bundle.

"Next time, and in future times, you know, like these, you will talk dirty to me, won't you?"

The upper hand. The last word. She just could never let that go.

When he glanced back, Tara poked out her tongue at him, loving this.

Sitting behind him, she looped one arm over his right shoulder, the other around his waist, and pressed against him. She kissed the back of his neck, then rested her cheek against him. He felt her twin nipples, in particular, touch his back, and closed his eyes and concentrated on her nearness and delayed their departure awhile, the two of them just breathing, sitting there, skin to skin as though no skin existed, unwilling to budge.

Buck commenced scratching at the door.

Tara said, "You still have some time. Ryan. Make love to me before you go. Really make love to me, Ry."

He did.

23

His task, Ryan speculated, was the easier of the two that needed to be accomplished. Tara's assembled upon a higher moral ground, yet could prove to be much tougher. For him to successfully execute his plan, he had merely to be a bastard. Play that bit part. In so doing, forgo his integrity as an officer of the law, relinquish his sense of himself, and, while he was at it, damn his soul to a flaming hinterland of hell—although he admitted that that might be jutting over the top, a tad. Tara, though—she was being counted on to transform the world and that was not an exaggeration. By a landslide, the more difficult mission. He gathered his courage from that.

Ryan bided his time in a hollow off the edge of the northbound highway, his vehicle tucked out of sight in a thicket and ready to pounce.

Earlier, in Tara's company, he made a joke about killing his brother, but the crime Denny committed was nothing to sneeze at. Ryan wrestled with the notion that he might have done the same if he'd worn Denny's work boots. Or not. He was uncertain and would never know.

Something had to be done about the bridge, that was evident, and help did not appear to be forthcoming. But to burn it down? Man. *Especially* when his older brother was the town's top cop—putting him in a sticky position. Someday, maybe in Denny's backyard, they'd have words about it all. Just not yet. Although on that front, he was handed a way, by Skootch, surprisingly, to get even. So in the end he might be able to work through a desire to strangle his kid brother.

Serves him right. I'm going to come through, too. He'll hate me for it.

He was a cop, he knew the law, but he did not condemn his brother, not when he was on the verge of doing worse. At least, what could be construed as worse. *Morally, yes, worse.* He didn't have a peg leg to stand on, and from a legal point of view both legs were hobbled, and him without a cane. It's not as though he could ask anyone to rule on the finer points of jurisprudence. *Your Honour, which do you think is the greater trespass, burning bridges or abusing your authority as a policeman to perpetrate a grave injustice?*

Perhaps Tara could make that ruling, except that she knew his plan and while she didn't exactly approve—how could she?—she was okay with it.

She understood.

Oh. Tara.

To trust someone with your hopes and dreams, and with your baggage, that was one thing, but with your moral decrepitude, that was something else. Again, over the top, he knew, but still. A whole other world opened for him, for them, and now he was going to do this. Nothing in life was ever simple. Or simple enough. At least she knew now that he was a complicated person, too.

Which seemed to count with her, for some reason.

He had to be complicated enough to suit her, to maintain her interest.

An orange Dodge reared over a hillock in his side-view mirror. Ryan checked the radar gun. The bastard wasn't even speeding. Which figured—nothing was ever easy when you wanted it to be.

Ryan O'Farrell started the engine on his squad car as the Dodge sped by at the legal limit. Before he moved out from his spot amid the trees, he rubbed his face with both hands. A postcoital sleepiness delayed him, but that was mere excuse. He was now going to do something he should not do. That he didn't really want to do. That was flagrantly wrong.

But he decided to do it. Though he hesitated.

He had a choice. He knew that. But his mind was made up.

Ryan took a deeper breath, his last as a relatively innocent man, and steered his vehicle onto the highway. He stepped on the gas and surged forward. To announce his descent into the morass of corrupt humanity with appropriate fanfare, he popped on his revolving lights, and then for good measure, the siren. *Ready or not. Here I come. Sorry, buddy. Over the top, perhaps, but our lives just took a turn for the worse. Yeah. Both our lives. But mostly yours.*

He raced after the garish bright orange Dodge. Driving a car that colour was reason enough for an arrest. When the orange blob tried to outrun him, Ryan got mad, and commenced a high-speed pursuit.

■ ■ ■

TARA DID NOT DOUBT THAT Willis Howard cosseted a legitimate complaint, but she also knew what he did not—that she was willing to make it up to him another time. Even though she'd skimped on her duties in favour of robust lovemaking upstairs and so was behind on things, her next task took precedence. The opportunity to put her plans into motion had arrived. Her turn to act. She called Alex O'Farrell. They arranged to meet by the riverside. Expecting to tangle with Willis's righteous ire on her way out the door, she was bewildered instead by a scenario not anticipated.

Willis was busy talking to two men.

She'd seen them about town and knew who they were. Everybody did.

SQ detectives.

Everybody in town refused to talk to them in any meaningful way.

Apparently, Willis Howard didn't receive the message.

What Willis could possibly relate to the policemen Tara did not know, but she was alert. With swift clarity, a whoosh, she allowed that she and Willis could never resolve their differences and simply be friends, or become happy business partners forevermore. She readily detected in his marrow an inner malevolence, and most of the time this is what she most trusted to locate in him.

"Willis, I have an appointment. Gotta run."

"What? I'm busy myself right now. As you can plainly see."

He huddled with the detectives by the clay pottery stand she recently redesigned, adding the works of local artisans. Funny, that he chose that spot to conduct his subterfuge. *You fucking Judas.*

"Lise can help take care of things," Tara sang out.

Lise was dusting the upper shelves.

"No, she can't. She doesn't have a clue. Hang on for an hour."

"I have a clue," Lise objected.

"Can't," Tara let him know. "Muddle through, Willis. I know you can. See you!" She didn't want to add, but did anyway, "I'll make it up to you." At that moment she caught the interested glances of the police officers, and bolted.

Her larynx felt raw, ripped, even though her screaming had pretty much been silent. Rapturous, her only word for it. That second joust with Ryan took her where she'd not been before—*Hey, Daddy-o, you were fine, we had some times, but geez, let's face it, you were old, sweetie. I just found out there's a difference*—and now she strolled along on her own two feet feeling a seismic pummelling through her limbs and joints. She was so far gone for a few moments that she might have let out a telltale scream, which would have Willis Howard pounding on her door wondering if she'd just been murdered, or, knowing him, wanting to interrupt, to prohibit such wanton joy within earshot. And she did scream, she couldn't help herself, only she had no voice by then, no sound escaped her, although her throat hurt afterwards.

A small mercy, the silence of my scream. Tah.

She felt it coming. Ryan did well by her, he had good hands, good instincts, *I adore his penis* although that wasn't what did it *and it wasn't only him* or sex after abstinence, which was part and parcel, too. Her own pent-up fright and enthusiasm for her new life, Mrs. McCracken's demise, the spectre of death, *fleeing, quitting the profession and now, suddenly,* in her life, a guy. Romance, perhaps like never before, swayed and surged inside her and she could hold nothing back, nothing she could sequester for next time, or another time. Somehow she landed in that room seized by a greater wonder and urgency than she was ever privy to before and never fully imagined.

Whooshes!

She was overcome.

A confluence, she was guessing, that may not easily return.

Tara ambled down the winding couples' walk, quickly at first, then she measured her steps as though to counter the river's flow. As if treading water. She wore low heels, comfortable enough but the pointy toes were an ill fit for the stone and dirt surface, and the breezes that scuffed the mountaintop during the hillside internment ceremony were now rambunctious in the valley of the town below. As if Mrs. McCracken still wanted, and expected, her say. Along the way stood the monstrosity of a barge, or whatever it wanted to call itself—a slum built on a rusted stack of oil cans, it looked like—and she didn't want to go that far down the shore to pass it by, so she detoured across the grass to the water's edge and sat where she could keep an eye out.

She'd been wantonly and basely sexual with men before, but never, she reflected, never so spontaneously crazily passionate and nuttily delivered out of herself. Never so beguiled. Never so happy. She revelled in the difference. Thought back to exquisite details. The intimacy. Her own inner storm. She felt atilt. An axis bent.

Then she saw Alex coming over. He already spotted her. Tara worried that after what just occurred she remained as exposed as when she lay naked and virtually expiring, which is what it felt like, on a bed. Her nerve endings popped through her skin, she felt flushed and compromised, certain that the crafty old guy with a reputation as a philanderer in his day would identify her state of being. He would know. Guess, anyway. She took a deep breath, blew it out, combed her breeze-tossed hair with her fingers, and urged her rational self to return to base camp. He couldn't possibly tell. How could he possibly tell? *He can't possibly tell!* She waved to him, and the old guy, having doffed his cane, waved back.

He was still fifty feet away and she could tell that he could tell.

Get a grip.

He hugged her as she greeted him, kissed both cheeks, and sat upon a boulder. She smiled, checked him out, and guessed that he feigned being oblivious to her bliss. A gentleman. In his company, she could breathe more easily now.

Tara could guide this conversation to where she meant it to go, across to its sombre concerns and deft tactics.

"Look at that thing," first, Alex pontificated. "A floating rat's nest. You don't happen to have a pail of gasoline and a match, do you?"

"So that's where Denny gets his predilection for arson."

"Well, my God, look what burns, a beautiful old bridge, and this is left standing? Maybe we should start a trend."

"Or maybe we should, you know, fix things."

He gave her a long look. She was a natural beauty, no doubt there. "How are you and Ryan doing?"

"Oh, fine. Why do you ask?" *Don't you dare answer that question.*

Alex looked away awhile, then seemed to grow preoccupied with the laces of one boot. "Is that what you called me down here for? To fix things? I thought you wanted to wrench my hips back into place."

"Are they out of whack? You're walking with a hitch, I noticed."

Looking at her, he smiled. *You dare smirk and I'll—*

"Life is a hitch," he said. A simple aphorism, meaningless in some circumstances, emotionally fraught in others. Then he asked, "What does 'fine' mean exactly?"

Ryan must have been a mess after his previous lady to provoke this everlasting concern among his loved ones. "You're worried that he's lost? That he won't recover this time? Okay, here's the bulletin you've been waiting to hear. I'm totally, like, into the guy, okay? So maybe I'm the one who's lost. I'm the one who's hanging by a thread. Maybe him, too. But I'm right there with him. So far, we're in it together."

He hoped for something from her, some consideration, an indication, and never expected the honest spiel. He was both taken aback and impressed.

"Okay," he said. "Good."

She apprehended then that she'd inadvertently advanced her cause for the afternoon, that the moment needed to be seized. Tara did not want her powerful attraction to Ryan to be part of this, but now the two pressing aspects in her life, romance and action, were inseparable. Perhaps, she reconsidered, as it should be.

"Ryan's in trouble, Alex. Because of Denny. So he's going to do what he has to do. I'm not going to tell you what he's going to do but you won't like it when you find out. *If* you find out. Know that there's nothing you, Denny, or I can do about it. By now, shall we say, it's water under the bridge."

"Okay," Alex said. Waiting.

"He's going to fix things for Denny. You'll like that part, but you know, it's not even for Denny. Reading between the lines, if this was only about his brother he'd probably arrest him and let him do his time."

"If it's not for Denny—" He stopped himself, as though he answered his own question even before he got the words out.

"Right on. The kids. And Val. He doesn't want this to fall on them. So he's doing what he has to do. The family is ninety percent, I'd say, and the town the other ten percent."

"Okay," he said. Whatever it was, he understood that part. For him, the grandkids were paramount, and he knew that Ryan loved the town. He figured his son was doing this at least partly for himself, as well, but there was no point in trying to split that hair.

"Now we have to help. To make this come out right."

"What's that? Burn that barge, I hope."

He knew right away that the joke didn't work. Rather than apologize he waited.

"Alex, we have to change the culture. How people think. How do I explain this? People are against Denny and whoever burned the bridge, which is perfectly understandable but we can't let that animosity stand. We have to change their minds so that they are for us, in a way, but for different reasons, and we have to do it soon. Right away, in fact. We have to do that by changing how people act. At least, what they do. And specifically, what they do next. That's where you come in."

He didn't have a clue what she was going on about, but already it seemed impossible. On the other hand, she always seemed to be about impossibilities. Fixing his bad legs, that was impossible. Reviving his eldest son, less impossible. Taking over Willis Howard's store, now *that* was impossible. He tapped his cane against the surface of a stone submerged under the earth between his feet with only a portion of its broad granite back showing. He tapped the stone as though gently awakening the earth. "Let's see. You're consulting with me because I represent that culture you want to change. The retrogrades, shall we say. The old men of the woods and the river and the young men of big industry, big machines. The polluting barbaric dim-witted unclean hordes."

Tara smiled. She really liked this guy. "Yeah, I'd go that far in my description. Further still, but really, I couldn't say it any better. The polluting barbaric dim-witted dirty hordes. I understand that you're their great poobah, a legend in your own time, the loggers' great mythic leader. How come you don't have a statue of yourself down here?"

She got him to laugh, at least.

"Yeah. Legend. From when I cut forests down with my bare hands, then commanded the river to take the harvest to market under my feet. Barbaric, to use the world's resources for what they were meant to be used for."

"You nearly killed the river doing that, Alex. You nearly wrecked the forests, too, but for now look at the river."

"You're a tree hugger? One of those?"

"Not a hundred percent. But I believe in protecting the environment, and I believe we have to support it or die. But just consider the river. Except for that monstrosity, why are there no boats on the river? And it's a given that that thing is not a boat."

Alex watched the river flow awhile. Even as he stared, his expression changed. When he spoke, he gazed at her.

"The deadheads," he said.

"The deadheads," she repeated.

"I love this river, Tara. That's what people don't understand. I hate that we did it any harm."

"Be careful. People might think you're a tree hugger, too."

"We can't navigate the river—"

"Because?"

"—because the goddamned deadheads will rip holes in the bottoms of our boats, tear the props right off our outboards. We killed the river for boating, for swimming, for fishing. It's still choked with all our debris."

"Exactly."

He stood, and heaved himself up from the boulder. That one leg looked unnaturally stiff to her. Oddly bent. He was beginning to understand what she was getting at. "There was never a reason to do anything about them. An impossible job. Now? Do you think—? There's enough?"

She shrugged. "You're the woodsman. I haven't done a calculation. But a lot of waterlogged timber is floating just under the surface. I've done my research. It's still good wood."

"I could have told you that. Saved you the research."

"Alex, Denny has to bring this forward himself. I won't even say it out loud myself. Not until he does. It has to be him. You understand why?"

He mulled through the obstacles. He nodded, to indicate that he understood. "You want Denny to say it. Right time, right place. But also, if you're working some sort of, what do you want to call it?—conspiracy?—with Ryan, then nobody can be seen to be putting words into Denny's mouth."

"Or else it won't work. I see where Ryan gets his smarts."

Alex foresaw problems. "There's more to this than what Denny can do."

"For sure. Tasks for everyone. The whole town, in fact. That's the point." She caught his glance. "Including me. Including you. I'll provide the legal expertise, among other things, because you're going to need that. You have to get the old guys on our side, because the young guys will respect their opinion. If they think it's just tree hugger nonsense, then everything's lost. Your son—both your sons, really, but Denny's the one who has to address the loggers. How tough is that?"

"Nothing but tough," Alex acknowledged.

"If he doesn't win them over, it won't happen. If it doesn't happen, then his life in this town, even if Ryan gets him off, will be, you know, difficult. To say the least. As well, without this, if Ryan does get him off, then Ryan is also toast as a cop in this town. He can beat the system but he can't beat public perception."

Alex tapped his cane a couple more times against the earth. "I get it."

"You said conspiracy. Okay. But miracle is more like it. So you'll talk to Denny?"

"Talk to him? I'll convince the bugger."

"We need him to be wholehearted."

"He will be."

"This'll take years."

"He'll make the time. It's either that or spend it in jail."

He was already moving off, ready to proceed.

She called him back. Gave him a little peck on his whiskered cheek.

Alex issued a small appreciative nod, a token of thanks, and studied her. "You know, if not for Ryan seeing you first, I would've come after you myself."

"Oh *gawd*! What a bloody family. Go. Scram! Get out of here!"

They both liked that, this familiarity. This cordial rub between them.

Alex shouted down the riverbank before he left. "Hey, Skootch! Skootch!"

Rising from his divan, Skootch gave a noncommittal wave.

"You're next! You're next, buddy!"

Unaware of what to make of this reproach, Skootch persisted with his friendly wave.

"There'll be no more fires," Tara forewarned.

"Lightning strikes happen."

"I'm not telling you this, so you're not hearing me."

"What?" He ceased his quick retreat. "You're not telling me what?"

"He's helping."

Questions about that dawned on him, but he didn't know where to begin. "With the deadheads? We don't need him."

She shook her head in the negative.

"Tara, what are you not telling me that I'm not hearing?"

"He's helping Ryan."

"Skootch is?"

She didn't answer. He got it then. Or got enough to alter course. Or understood the bare minimum—matters were afoot, and he was to stay clear.

"See you," Alex said, and trod off.

He was gone about fifty feet before she shouted after him, "We have to work on that left leg of yours!"

Without turning, he saluted with his cane to acknowledge her healing enterprise. And walked on.

■ ■ ■

RELATIVELY QUICKLY, HIS QUARRY QUIT the chase, although not as soon as Ryan hoped. At the very least, he could nail him on refusing to be pulled over.

Jake Withers did turn his Dodge to the side of the road, sparing himself greater trouble, and Ryan O'Farrell unclipped his holster as he tucked in behind him. Before he got out, he called to his subordinate down the road to tell him that the chase was finished and to carry on in their direction with caution. He didn't need the help, but he wanted a witness, and so he waited for the other cop to arrive.

His name was Henri. Older than him, he was experienced, a steady hand if not necessarily the brightest bulb on the dash. Henri enjoyed highway work, so that's what Ryan assigned him. Nothing out of the ordinary, then, for Henri to be part of this caper. Such details might prove important, depending on how the matter evolved.

The other officer parked in front of the Dodge and Ryan lumbered out of his car, taking his time, really. He removed his pistol from its holster and held it down at his side. Jake Withers was nervously looking back at him with his window lowered, anxious to explain himself. "I just panicked back there for a second. You surprised me, man. I got spooked. I wasn't speeding, was I? Was I speeding? Maybe I lost track of the limit. Thought I was doing fifty."

"Eighty," Ryan said.

"Eighty! No! Oh! You mean kilometres."

"You're not old enough to remember miles per hour. Put both your hands on top of the steering wheel, sir. Right where I can see them."

"This old car. The speedometer. It's still in miles per hour."

"Put your fucking hands on the steering wheel now!"

Ryan stood by the rear bumper and aimed his pistol through the glass.

Jake Withers complied, instantly this time, and shut up.

He was scared.

Henri opened the door to his own car and aimed his pistol at the driver. Ryan moved up alongside and checked the rear seat, shot a glance into the front, then opened the door and told Jake Withers to get out.

"What's wrong, Officer?"

"What did I just say?"

"I'm getting out."

He climbed out and Ryan turned him and told him to put his hands on the rooftop and he frisked him. He patted down his ass and his crotch and his thighs and calves. The man's pockets were empty except for his wallet. Henri came over aiming his pistol at the man's face and Jake Withers began to sweat and shake a little. Ryan pressed the young man's forehead against the roofline then pulled his arms down one at a time and cuffed his wrists behind his back. With his right boot he kicked the guy's feet farther apart so that he was spread out awkwardly and balanced leaning forward against the car's frame.

"Get the keys," Ryan said calmly to Henri, who put his gun away and reached inside and snatched the car keys from the ignition.

Jake Withers kept up his complaint. "I wasn't speeding."

"Don't pin your hopes on that. You refused to pull over when apprehended, when requested to do so by an officer of the law who was flashing lights and sounding a siren."

"I just panicked," he whinged. "I didn't know what was going on. I got taken by surprise. Really, that's all."

"Shut up. I'm taking out your wallet, sir. Checking your ID and licence."

"Take the money. I don't care."

"Excuse me? Did you hear that, Henri?"

"The bribe part? Yeah, I heard it. Stupid fucker."

"Let's not be foul-tongued," gently, Ryan chided him.

"Bastard insulted me," Henri reminded his boss.

"Oh geez," Jake Withers said.

"Do you want to keep talking?" Ryan asked him. "Maybe up

the ante on attempting to bribe a police officer? Really impress the judge?"

Jake thought about it. "I got nothing to say," he decided.

"Cat's got his tongue. Finally. What's this envelope?" The envelope was small and stuck out from his wallet.

"Pictures," Jake said.

"Family photos, huh?" He took a quick peek. "Oh my God. Jesus Christ. Is this—are you kidding me?—is this *you?*"

Jake took a glance back. "Oh shit," he said.

Ryan flashed them at Henri, who returned an inexplicable snort. He tucked the snaps away in his shirt pocket. "Henri, check the trunk, will you? After that the glove box."

"No!" Jake Withers cried out.

The two policemen looked at each other.

"No?" Ryan tormented the driver. "No? Are you saying that you specifically do not want us to look in your trunk? What do you got in there? A body?"

"No," Jake said. And quietly, as though he actually knew how pathetic he sounded, he added, "Nothing's in there."

"Henri," Ryan said, "we've got a hardened, experienced criminal here."

Henri smiled and played along. "How do you know that?" He crossed his arms and pushed the weight of his ass against the car.

"Because he knows that if you don't want a cop to check your trunk just insist that nothing's in it. That way the cop will believe you and forget about it. Only experienced criminals know that trick."

"He knows the ropes, this guy. A real pro."

"Check for a body in the trunk, will you, Henri?"

"Yes, sir."

Henri opened the trunk. For some reason, in perusing what he surveyed, he took off his cap and tucked it between his left elbow and his rib cage. Then he whistled, a long descending note to indicate that his findings impressed him.

"Whatcha got?" Ryan asked. He held Jake Withers against the car with his left fist pressed into the young man's back.

Henri put his cap back on, an odd gesture, then bent over and ruffled through the items there. He straightened up to report a treasure trove.

"Sir, I got what looks like a shitload of marijuana."

"No!" Jake Withers protested.

"Quite a few kilos, it looks like. I got other drugs. Could be coke."

"What? That's a lie!"

"Bags of other stuff. Could be anything."

"Best guess?" Ryan asked.

"H, maybe. I got other drugs back here. I'm thinking crack, also."

"A pharmaceutical wonderland," Ryan said, and he double-checked the man's ID. "Mr. Jake Withers. Are you a druggist?"

"That's bullshit! Bullshit!"

"Sir?" Henri asked. His face did seem oddly grave.

"Yeah?"

"I got the makings for Molotov cocktails back here. Gasoline. Bottles and rags. I got six sticks of dynamite. I got serious firepower here, sir. Rifles. Pistols."

"What?" Jake Withers asked. He was squirming against the car, driving his forehead into the roofline again.

Ryan changed his tone. "What is this? Who are you? Are you a fucking terrorist or something? You planning a mass murder, something like that?"

"You're crazy. There's nothing there. You're yanking my chain."

"So you say there's nothing there?"

"Marijuana, maybe."

410

"Oh sure, cop to the dope, not to the weapons and hard stuff. Is this your car, sir?" When the young man didn't answer right away Ryan bore his fist more intensely into the young man's spine as if it were a drill. "This your car or not?"

"Yes! It's my car, fuck."

"Did I catch you driving it or not?"

"What? Don't I got a right to drive my own car?"

"Then let's take a look at what's inside it, shall we?" Ryan suggested, and pulling the other fellow back by his shirt collar he shoved him towards the rear of the vehicle.

They both looked into the stuffed trunk, at the prize cache.

"I've got incendiary devices," Henri said.

"That's bullshit!" Jake yelled, not comprehending what even his eyes did plainly see.

Ryan pulled him back by his hair, speaking directly into his ear. "You been firebombing trucks, Mr. Withers? Have you now?"

The man didn't answer. He gasped from the hair pulling. Ryan didn't slacken his grip.

"Henri?" Ryan asked, quizzically, as though the notion only struck him that moment. "Tell me something. Weren't you the first person at the bridge the night it burned?"

Henri was hesitant. "The first cop," he answered. "The second person."

"Right. Didn't you say somebody was there before you?"

"Yes, sir."

"A redhead?" Henri didn't volunteer anything more, looking at Ryan in an odd way. Ryan inquired outright, "Is this him?"

Ryan let go of Jake's hair so that the young guy could look the officer straight on. Henri nodded. He put his thumbs inside his gun belt and made an emphatic motion with his chin. "Oh yeah. He's him. Definitely."

■ ■ ■

ATTACHED TO THE FIRE HALL, the police station stands as proudly contemporary, even spiffy, the finest modern building in town aside from the luxurious funeral parlour. The architectural plans originally designated three rooms for interrogations. Ryan nixed the idea, suggesting that the region would have to undergo a crime wave of epic proportions for the department to require the use of three rooms at once. Two would be fine, "because sometimes two guys get into a fight and we need to interview them separately. Same thing with domestic disputes. If we need more than two the perpetrators will just have to cool their jets until we're ready for them." And so the third room was transformed into an officer's lounge, with a coffeemaker, a sofa, a small fridge, and a table which ordinarily, no matter the time of day, had the sports section spread across it. Ryan brought Jake Withers, and eventually his lawyer, into that space, as other officers processing an altercation that ensued from a minor traffic accident occupied both rooms designated for the purpose.

He didn't want them, as it turned out, to cool their jets.

"Coffee?" Ryan offered the lawyer. Jake already had a cup going, his third.

"Coffee," the man said, sounding as though, rather than accept a cup at face value, he was granting it careful consideration. He hung his overcoat—warm for the day so he carried it across his forearm—over the back of a chair. "Sure," he decided, and upon further reflection added, "Thanks."

"We called up your client's former employer," Ryan mentioned while he poured.

"Former?"

He waited for the lawyer, wanting the process to be on the up-

and-up. Jake Withers contacted the firm in the Gatineau Yellow Pages with the largest advertisement, but the man they sent looked straight out of law school with a nervous expression and a tentative demeanour. On first encounter, the man's striking features were his diminutive size and a perpetually moist upper lip. Height should not be a consideration, Ryan wanted to remind his prisoner, as the man's physical bearing clearly disappointed Jake Withers.

"Your client claimed that he came to this part of the world to sell asphalt, counsellor. Apparently, he doesn't work for that particular firm anymore—the Rathbone Paving Company—although for some strange reason he tried to convince me that he did. According to company records, they set him loose in the field and have never heard from him since. Not even to say, 'I quit.' They're asking for their catalogue and samples back, by the way."

"Fuck 'em," Jake Withers commented.

"Asphalt," the lawyer said. Ryan was beginning to wonder if he could speak in full sentences. So far, he'd restricted himself to single words only, although he did appreciate the man's brevity.

"He was supposed to sell people on the idea of paving their driveways."

"Driveways?" the lawyer asked his client.

"People around here," Jake railed. Then he stopped talking and looked at Ryan O'Farrell.

"Go for it," the policeman invited. "Tell us about people around here."

He clammed up. He chose to say no more.

"Evidence?" the lawyer, whose name was Réal Desjardins, asked him.

"His fingerprints match those taken from a shard of glass, a remnant of a Molotov cocktail used to firebomb a logging truck. Molotov cocktail materials in the back of his car are consistent with glass bottles used in the truck attacks. Dynamite. Weapons. A few with their numbers filed off. Kilos of weed, some hashish, a bag of crack, and a considerable fortune in cocaine were found in the vehicle he was driving. Which is registered to him. We don't know where to start with so many charges. The drug amounts are too significant for personal use only, so qualify for the charge of trafficking. Several types of illegal drugs, so several counts. And with respect to quantities, the same"—he slowed down to make sure the lawyer got this part—"holds true . . . for the heroin . . . we found."

"Heroin?" the lawyer asked, but he was looking at his client.

"Yep," Ryan answered when the mute Jake Withers did not. "H carries a sentence, hey? In this part of the world especially. On city streets, sometimes a gram gets a pass. Out here? In bulk? Uncut? No, sir. If we have nothing more than the marijuana rap he might get a suspended sentence at worst. But H? Serious stuff, Jake. Serious time. You and your lawyer should talk that one over. While you're at it, I've got another meeting. There may be a further count. Running down the evidence on that as we speak. Tell him about it, Mr. Withers. While I'm gone, tell him what you've been up to lately. I'll be back in a jiff."

He departed the makeshift interrogation room bound for the men's locker, where he scrubbed his hands for no reason. He combed his hair. Then he went back to join the other two.

"Here's the thing," Ryan said. He sat down. "A bridge got burned—"

"How many times do I—? I didn't burn that goddamned bridge!" Jake reiterated, his voice dry, as though he was rapidly losing interest.

"I know, just like you don't have heroin in your trunk and you don't firebomb logging trucks."

Quietly, he maintained, "I didn't say that."

Ryan ignored him and spoke to the lawyer. "We've got your client on the drugs and the firebombing. That's open and shut. The bridge burning is trickier. So I want to propose a trade, if your guy is interested."

"Trade," the lawyer mused, as though the concept was new to him.

"If he cops to the bridge burning—"

"I didn't burn the fucking bridge!"

Ryan looked between the two men. "Please advise your client to stop saying that. It's pissing me off. He can cop to the arson, in which case I'll just not bother to press the other charges. For the arson he gets, what, first offence, three to five years? Maybe a few more? I'll encourage something to his benefit with the prosecutors. Tell them he's helped on other crimes. Not that he has. Or, he can maintain that he never burned the bridge and go down for the drug offences, and the firebombing, do ten to fifteen, minimum, and pray to God the judge lets the sentences run concurrently."

"The prosecutor," Desjardins said. Two words. Positively loquacious.

"She doesn't need to hear about drug charges. They'll vanish. But we have a problem in this town. People are upset about the bridge. Your client did it. We have a witness, a police officer actually, which makes him highly credible, who puts him on the bridge at the time of the fire. The only person in sight, in fact. We have Mr. Withers's history of firebombing, which we can now prove. We have witnesses who will testify that he rode a raft down the river after the bridge was burned, so he has motive. He wanted to get rid of the bridge for his own yachting purposes and blame it on the loggers. But do this quickly, counsellor. I have SQ detectives in my office and the prosecuting attorney is on her way." He spoke directly to Jake Withers then. "So you can do fifteen years, twelve, maybe even nine, if your lawyer has game, with good behaviour, or you can start with three to five, probably a few more, if you cop to the bridge, then get it knocked down to eighteen to forty-two months if you behave yourself. You're much more likely to get early parole if all you are is a bridge burner. Your choice."

Jake mulled it over while his lawyer and the policeman waited. "You want me to go to jail for something I didn't do."

"Have it your way. If you prefer, we'll send you to jail for what we know you did do. Only for a much longer time. Mr. Withers, your lawyer will set you straight on this. Bad guys count themselves lucky when the more serious counts get knocked down and they get to cop to the lesser charges. You're getting one hell of a break here."

Jake was clinging to a final hope. "I didn't put that shit in my car. But I can tell you who did. I can testify about who really pushes drugs in this town, in the towns around here."

"You mean Skootch?" Ryan asked, and smiled, which crushed the young man's spirit. "No secrets there. Thanks but no thanks. We need him where he is for a while. But I'll let him know about your request."

Despair hit home. Jake chewed on his scant choices. When he consulted his lawyer, the man nodded his chin, then Jake did that also, agreeing.

"Okay. Now let's hope I can make this happen. Hang on. In your case, Jake, you're not going anywhere. Both of you, help yourself to the fruit and the cookies. I'm going to send an officer in to take your written statement, your confession to burning the bridge. Are you okay with that?"

"Guarantees?" his lawyer asked.

"I'll write that letter myself."

They were in agreement.

He departed the room.

Only the lawyer chose to munch on an apple.

416

Jake Withers slumped on the sofa and placed a hand over his eyes, waiting to confess.

■ ■ ■

DENNY O'FARRELL COULD CRY. MAN enough, he would. The twin lamps in the room were turned low, and he was glad of that, preferring that his teariness go unseen. Val moved in closer to him on their living room sofa, and placed an arm around his lower back as Denny slumped forward. She rubbed the muscle of his near biceps with her opposite hand. Whispered, "You can do this, Denny."

He could. His personal darkness gave way to a beam of light and now good fortune shone upon him. He doubted that he deserved it, which tempered his elation. Nonetheless, he was not going to reject this chance, this turn in the road. Denny nodded with conviction. "Yeah. I can do it. I will do it. Sure."

Alex sat in the big armchair opposite them.

"It'll take some sacrifice," he cautioned his son. He found the scope of this, the ramifications, more than daunting. Here he was, a man sliding into an older age, and this might become the exceptional undertaking of his life.

No one bothered to mention the obvious, that the sacrifice stood as minimal compared to extended jail time.

"Hell," Denny said, "it's a challenge, right? So it'll take some balls. Big deal. I've got a pair."

Alex wanted to make sure that he understood, that in the euphoria of the moment his son did not underestimate the matter, nor take the enterprise lightly. "You will meet some resistance. Be prepared for that."

First he looked at his dad, then at Val, and rested a hand on her thigh.

"Bring it on," he said, but gently, with a quiet resolve. "Look, I brought this on myself. And on both of you. If I can undo that, then I'm prepared for whatever it takes. The sacrifice is mine, okay. But I'm not going to use that word. What I'm going to do is keep my family together. That's not a sacrifice."

"As I see it," Alex considered, "we need everyone to pitch in. The whole town. But you have to do more than your part. It's on your shoulders. I know you get that much. You have to convince some people, maybe inspire others, maybe fight with a few, keep things going when folks feel like quitting, when things don't go right. That you can do. But. Also. You've got to be patient, Denny—not your best attribute, *impatience* got you into trouble in the first place. Hell, if you waited five or ten years—"

"We don't have five or ten years, Dad."

"See what I mean?"

Already he was shown to be deficient for the task at hand, and Denny took a breath. He nodded, admitting that he had his shortcomings.

"You're smart, you just don't always choose to be."

"Yeah, I know, Dad, but—"

"—and this is the hard part, Denny—" Alex stopped, and gazed at his son awhile, interrupted in his thinking by another voice, other words, distinctly his deceased wife's, and while he might have been tougher on him if left to his own devices, that separate notion altered his tone. Alex went quiet, while feeling himself sagging under the breadth of this, the weight. "Denny, you're going to have to be wise for a change. We know you're a good guy, and I love you to death, but *goddammit* if you aren't half kid and three-eighths crazy."

A laugh burst from Denny, an involuntary reflex. "That's what Mom used to say about you."

"Yeah. And that's my way of saying that you're too much like me.

You like to fart around—be good, be kind, have fun, and push the boundaries. Sometimes a little, sometimes a lot. This time you overdid it. Let's face it, Denny. This is serious fucking business. That new girl in town, she's come up with an idea, but you have to make it work."

"Will this be enough, though? It might help with the town. But what about those hard-ass SQ guys? They'll lynch me if they can find a way."

Both Val and Denny looked to the family patriarch to see if he could summon any hope where apparently so little remained.

"Here's the thing, Denny. Just between us, and I don't know the details myself—except I'm told that I won't like it—but Ry is saving your ass. He's putting himself on the line for you. That's another reason to come through."

The news hung in the air awhile, and partly Denny did not speak because he couldn't.

Alex also had trouble finding his voice. "In other words, son, no more farting around. So help me on your mother's grave—"

Denny's lips were quavering and his emotional wreckage was no longer hidden. Valérie caressed his back as he bobbed his chin and dabbed an eye.

In absorbing his dad's comments, he wasn't buying into the whole of the lecture—he was already past getting himself into this sort of muck and mire again—but neither was he going to react against any portion of the commentary. He had this coming. Other people were going to want a piece of him who'd be a lot more harsh than his father, mean and full-on cruel at times. So the part about being patient and wise could begin right now.

Denny nodded in the affirmative.

The three of them did.

Alex said, "Okay, so can a man get a beer in this dump or what?"

Val smiled at him. Alex was embarrassed by her gaze that conveyed so much tenderness. "Thanks, Dad," she said.

"Yeah, yeah," Alex said. "It's not my idea anyway. I'm just the messenger."

"You know," she said softly, "Mrs. O'Farrell might not even recognize you now. Her river-rat husband, so wise and thoughtful. She'd be damned proud of you, Dad."

"Just don't tell her, okay? I like to keep her on her toes." Alex knew that more tears would flow if either of them said another word. So he just wagged his chin a little and gave his cane a wee tap against the carpet.

"Ry's new girl, Tara—let her know, okay?" Denny requested. "Tell her I got the message." The girl he rescued from the rain after a baseball game—who could guess that that slight act of consideration—but really, he thought she was hot, so did it even count as kindness?—would be returned a hundredfold and then another hundredfold. She was smart, with a good head and a savvy idea. A stranger, imagine that, understood them so well. She hung out with Mrs. McCracken. Maybe some of the old coot rubbed off on her. He stood. "Yeah, big shock wave over here. We got beer."

■ ■ ■

PECULIAR, PUZZLING, THE REACTION THAT he received from the detectives when he told them he solved their crime, that he was holding their bridge burner in lockup, a confession in hand. They seemed incapable of understanding him. Something was not working and his mind raced to grasp what he might have missed.

Then they told him.

"We have a witness," Quique Vega revealed.

"What kind of a witness?" Ryan O'Farrell asked.

"The kind of a witness who says your brother did the bridge burning," Maltais filled in. "We told your brother, he didn't tell you?"

Ryan doubted him.

"He says your brother had help, our witness, but can't name the others."

"We also have kids who were under the bridge right before the fire," Vega tacked on. "Chased away, it turns out, by someone they thought was you. Because he said he was you. So maybe it was you. They didn't actually see the person, though. But we've noticed that you and your brother sound alike."

Ryan was thinking quickly even as he absorbed the blows. "If somebody who scared them off told them that he was me, then they'll think it's true. Doesn't matter what the impostor sounded like, as long as he was male."

They were in his office, Ryan and Maltais seated, Quique Vega choosing to stand, occasionally pace. Maltais leaned so far forward for a moment that his elbows touched his knees. He knitted his fingers together. "In a court of law, I admit, a lawyer makes that argument and, with most juries, wins it."

"But in this room," Vega put forward, indicating that he and his partner discussed these points, to the extent that their thinking freely flowed from one to the other, "we're policemen, we don't need to make that distinction."

"I'm just saying," Ryan said.

Quique Vega liked to pick up things. Photos in their frames. An old award won at a high school swim meet. Past mementos. Nothing dramatic, as though Ryan lived a rather tame life.

"Sure. Sure. I know," Maltais said, as though he felt a need to soothe him. "The sound of the voice is circumstantial at best, maybe unreliable. But we have a witness, you see. Someone who attests to your brother's guilt."

Ryan nodded. "A witness. Okay. That's significant for sure. But I have a confession. By the person who actually did burn the bridge. Or attests to it, as you say. The confession is being written up and signed as we speak."

"This is a credible confession?" Maltais asked him.

"The guy's own lawyer is present."

The two detectives shared a glance.

"Who's the witness?" Ryan asked point-blank. He was guessing that they wouldn't tell him.

"Who's the confessor?" Maltais asked him back.

"His name is Jake Withers. You've seen him. He was the dopehead who sailed that raft down the river, remember?"

"And the first man to the bridge after the fire," Vega recalled. Ryan noticed that he never put anything back in exactly the same spot. The mementos of his past were being rearranged. So he wasn't a likely or possible friend, as he was doing it to irritate him.

"Did you interview him?"

Vega reported that they did.

"And?"

"He said he didn't burn the bridge. He was adamant about that."

"That was then. Now he says he did it."

"Why?"

"We have his fingerprints off glass from a Molotov cocktail from the truck fire. So he has an incendiary background. We found fire-making material in the trunk of his car, including guns and dynamite. Some of those charges will go away as long as he cops to the bridge burning. I gave him that in trade."

"Which charges go away?" Vega wondered.

"Well," Ryan said. He shrugged. "Every charge does." He was glad now that he didn't mention the drugs to them. Not yet.

"So he has an incentive to be our bridge burner," Maltais said, and after that the two men simply stared at each other awhile and the silence between them felt fertile and rife. "And as we know, you have an incentive to make it so."

"I brought you in," Ryan reminded him.

"Sometimes I wonder why."

Ryan didn't want to push him on that, didn't what to know what he might have deduced. "Who's your witness?"

"Willis Howard."

"Oh, for heaven's sake!" Ryan stormed.

"What? He's a credible witness. A respected member of this community. A businessman. What's your problem?"

"He's a notorious prick!" Ryan fired back. "And—"

He wasn't quite sure what he wanted to say.

"And what?" the one he liked, but less so lately, Quique, asked him.

Ryan studied the man. Time to be convincing. "He's hated my family since he emerged from the womb. Plus he hates, he despises, loggers. The whole industry. Ask anybody. He wants the industry shut down so that we can become a tourist outpost with no big business, the whole district impoverished while he rakes in the cash. Seriously, ask anybody. Of course he wants to hang the bridge fire on a logger! He hates loggers and he hates the forestry industry and he hates my family in particular."

"So you said. Why your family?"

"Because we represent— My dad— Except for me, we're loggers. Famous ones, even."

"Loggers can be famous now? Like rock stars? I never heard that."

"Around here, my dad, he's like a legend. Mythic, even."

"Mythic," Maltais repeated, his mockery subtle.

"Find out something new," Vega said, and shrugged.

"Mr. Howard's home is well situated with an excellent view of the bridge," Maltais pointed out. "The former bridge."

"So why didn't he come forward sooner if he had such an excellent view?"

This time they hesitated, and Ryan knew then that they already asked that question without receiving a satisfactory reply.

Quique Vega finally sat. Detective Maltais gently rubbed the knuckles of one hand in the palm of the other, thinking. Ryan clutched the forward portion of the arms on his chair, and the three men looked at one another in turn.

"I guess," Maltais broke the impasse, "we should interview your guy."

"Any objections if I talk to your witness?"

The visiting officers mulled it over silently. Ryan wanted to chide them for being telepathic, but this was no time to make light. "I guess that'll be fine," the senior detective decided. "It's your town. Your people. Just don't, you know, threaten him, or bribe him. Nothing like that."

What was meant to be a joke didn't sound like one.

Vega smiled, an attempt to dispel the obvious erosion of trust.

He detected barely perceptible eye communication between Maltais and Vega, giving him permission to add something. Ryan folded his hands, waited.

"The thing is," Quique Vega stated, "you've got a confession, but we have to ask ourselves, did your guy have time to do the crime?"

Ryan didn't want to answer, for the simple reason that he did not know why the question was being asked. "I don't see why not. He could have taken his sweet time as far as I can tell."

"Not really," Vega informed him. "We interviewed your officer."

"Henri," Maltais recalled.

"Henri," Vega repeated. "Now, he was outside a late-night bar, waiting to see if any drunks came out and got behind a wheel. He followed your guy."

"Did he?"

"Yes, he did. He says so. But he gave up on him. Your guy was driving straight as an arrow within the speed limit. So he broke off his tail. He says it was only a minute or two later that he heard a car horn blaring away and right after that he spotted the fire. So your guy didn't have much time, did he?"

He was reeling. God, he hated lying, and forced himself to keep his eyes on one cop or the other. "Well," he mulled, "I'll want to ask my guy about that. See what his timing was. See if he was in the car that Henri was following."

"Only car there."

"I know. But he's got legs. He could have walked."

"His car. If somebody else drove it there, who's the accomplice?"

"No, no, like you, I think he drove the car," Ryan cut in. "I'm not saying he didn't. Molotov cocktails. That's his thing. He'd have them in the trunk, just like he did when I picked him up. Throw a few of those, takes seconds, and that old wood, a hundred years old, after a hot summer, those old slats and timbers go up like a tinderbox. In no time flat. The evidence, the glass and all that, sails down the river."

"Is that what he says?"

"I want to go read his confession."

The officers again exchanged a silent communication, evaluating him.

"Why don't we all go read it?" Maltais put to him.

Ryan fought hard not to squirm. He paused while his thoughts raced and the collective dust in the room settled. The others could tell that something was forming in his quick mind. "How about," he proposed, "if I go read my guy's confession, probe some more, see how his

425

story stacks up? Do that first. He's my witness right now on unrelated charges. I want to make sure he's solid before I pass him over. I'm giving up other charges, after all, I can't let him go unless the case is solid. You've given me some doubts, so let me go over it once again. In the meantime, you guys can revisit your witness. See where he's at. See if he doesn't want to revise his view of the world. Then we switch."

The three men mulled the idea for a few silent ticks.

"Why?" Maltais asked finally.

"Like I said, I need to make sure he's signed that confession, that it makes sense and it's a good one," Ryan explained. "If it's not valid, then I have to bring back the other charges on him. So I got to make sure he's crossed his *t*'s, dotted those *i*'s. Push him about the timing, see if he can't nail that down."

"Because you know, I wouldn't want you filling in the blanks for him. Nothing like that," Maltais said.

They squared off in combative attitudes, but Ryan broke from the posture quickly. That was a dark gopher hole, nothing to be gained going down it. Instead, he opened his top desk drawer. "Let me show you something. You interviewed him, you probably think he's a straightforward young man."

"We do. Maybe not too bright," was Vega's assessment. "But he did look like hell that day on the raft. Not too straightforward then. Going down through the rapids, though, anyone would look as though they just took a stroll through a car wash." Maltais reached over and accepted the small envelope Ryan passed to him. He opened it, checked the photographs inside, showed them to Vega.

"This the same guy?" Vega asked.

"Same guy."

"Where'd you get these?"

"Out of his wallet. That's his truck-burning costume, apparently."

426

The snaps showed Jake Withers nearly nude and wearing grotesque war paint over his face and body. The images depicted a sordid or violent or at least a messed-up young man, the impact such that the SQ detectives appeared to relent. Impressions they'd formed about the suspect were thoroughly dashed.

Still, they hesitated.

Ryan acknowledged that he was missing something. For some reason, they were not inclined to believe him. If they were going to bend, they needed something to take away. Proof would be fine, nothing better, but in lieu of proof, they needed something.

He sat back, gave himself over to his talk.

"You know, off and on, you guys mention my brother. I know why. It's a conflict of interest for me, no question. But you do understand what's at stake here, don't you? A bridge was burned. People want to pin that on the loggers, but they're the ones whose livelihoods are impacted by that, in a negative way, at least in the short term. So maybe it wasn't them. Right now, they have no bridge. The next thing that happens was logging trucks get firebombed. Some people think that that was retaliation, or maybe it's just made to look that way. No matter what, do you really think that loggers are going to take this sitting on their asses? Really? We've got a war brewing here. Environmentalists on one side, and some of those people might be ecoterrorists and drug dealers, and loggers on the other side, and some of them may even want a piece of the drug action. Nobody's squeaky clean here. If I don't get this under control in one hell of a hurry, you're going to be back here, only next time it won't be for an arson. We'll have dead bodies in the woods. People beat up and lying in the gutters. More than a few. A war, guys. Yes, in this dinky town. We've got a chance to stop it in its tracks. So unless you want to move here and be solving killings for the balance of your careers, let's proceed wisely."

Both men observed him awhile, and never did check with each other.

"Okay," Maltais agreed quietly. "We're not here to inflict our will, Ryan. We just want a resolution. Of course, we want a good resolution. The right one."

"That's why I asked you in."

"Oh sure, that must be why."

Maltais and Ryan fell into a locked gaze, as if they were slipping back into their mutual distrust and recrimination, until Vega intervened, standing. He put his hand on a small decorative wood box in which Ryan kept coins, keys, and paper clips that were seldom required, and slid it over eight inches. The other two cops took their eyes off each other to watch him do that. Vega said, "We're agreeable, Ryan. Once more around for good luck, before we take steps. But you know, you have to know, eventually it comes down to burden of proof."

"Of course."

Code. He knew he was lying about some things, but not about everything.

Without further formality, the SQ detectives departed the office. Ryan waited. When he saw them outside through his window, strolling towards their car, he got on the telephone. He had essentially no time to get Jake Withers to change his testimony and line it up properly regarding the timing, and no time at all to get Willis Howard to recant his lies. He couldn't do both on his own at the same instant, and needed help.

24

Perfect timing. Tara would have kicked the shoppers out of the store herself, except that the final dregs of a steady drove of tourists were departing just as she got off the phone. She waited a few seconds longer for them to leave without inflicting any roughhouse encouragement. Then Tara locked the store's front door and flipped the window notice to read CLOSED/FERMÉ.

She needed time. She had none, Ryan explained, because the SQ detectives would be suspicious if Willis Howard changed his mind after he talked to him. So she had to do it before they got there. They were secretly baiting him to do it the other way, but that way would fail and they'd get to pin his ears back then, maybe destroy him. So she had to do it for him.

"Do what?" she asked.

"Change Willis's mind."

She was alone in the store now with Willis. As defiant, as surprised, or as dismayed as he may have wanted to sound, when he spoke he came across as subliminally petrified. "Why did you lock the door?"

"Why did I—? Why did I lock the door? Willis, I'm going to strangle you, or slice an artery, or at the very least kick your balls in repeatedly—why do you think I locked the door?"

"Excuse me?"

"I don't consider it fair that the whole neighbourhood be forced to listen to your endless screaming and caterwauling, do you? Because, you know, you are going to scream and caterwaul, Willis. Soon."

The way he shot his glance around the room, anyone might think that he was looking to flee. "What are you talking about? Are you kidding me? I don't think you should talk to me in that tone of voice, Tara."

"I'll talk to you any way I choose."

"No, you will not. What's gotten into you?"

Sequestered behind the rectangle of countertop that protected his cash area, with the big sign suspended above his head that read WILLIS EPHRAIM HOWARD, ESQ., he perhaps spoke more bravely than if bereft of the fortification. She couldn't get to him easily, and if she did fly over the counter to try to seize him by the nape of the neck he'd have an opportunity to flee through a gap out the other side, perhaps run into the streets and holler for help, and where, if she managed to grab him, he could at least publicly plead for mercy.

"Willis Ephraim Howard," she said, as if reading his name off the sign. She added, "Fucking esquire."

"What's gotten into you?"

"You've done it now, haven't you? Screwed everything up. Including our business. We're supposed to be business *partners*. Why didn't you tell me you planned to sabotage everything we've been working for? Everything *you've* worked for throughout your entire screwed-up life."

She deployed this knack of catching him then keeping him off

430

guard. He was trying to teach himself to counteract her ingenuity and properly defend himself, to stop her from always getting the superior hand. She was never this extreme in staking a claim over him before, but now, having some experience with her tactics under his belt, he believed that if he had any hope in this discussion—or furore, or battle, or whatever was about to transpire between them, *murder*—he needed to fight back. He pretended to know precisely what she was talking about, although that was difficult when he stood so avidly in the dark while she was so clearly entrenched upon her warpath.

"You should talk," Willis Howard challenged her. "Who's got the more screwed-up life? Me or you? Do you want to take a vote? Open the door. Come on. Let's have a public debate on the subject."

"You sycophantic, conniving, deceitful—you know what? I don't have to go through the dictionary. There's a word for you."

"I'm not sycophantic. I kowtow to nobody."

"You fucking liar."

"And I don't lie. Stop swearing. I didn't know you were on meds—are you off them now?"

He could come to enjoy this.

"Or maybe I'm wrong. I was thinking *imbecile*, but perhaps the word for you hasn't been invented yet. Maybe you're just . . . *Willis. Willis. Willis.*"

He rejected her refrain and exaggerated enunciation. He warned her, "Stop that. Shut up."

"*Willis.*"

"Shut up! Open the door, Tara. I don't know what game you're playing but we are not closed to business."

She laughed. "Seriously? Do you really want the whole world to hear this? Anyway, the cops will be here soon. I suppose we'll have to open up for them."

"What cops?" he asked, and the question felt weak on his tongue, he wished he could have it right back. "How do you know that?"

"Ah, Willis, *your* cops. The ones you've been lying to. The ones you're being *sycophantic* with. The SQ, asshole."

He swallowed, which she noticed.

"Willis," she began, and let the volume of her voice drop several notches, so that it felt conspiratorial, "you've screwed everything up. You are single-handedly going to turn the town against you, and by extension against us and this store. You have just driven us straight into the ditch with your lies and distortions. You never saw *anybody* burn the old covered bridge."

Somehow, she knew what he was saying to certain people. Her cop boyfriend. He tipped her off. Bastard.

"You've got it wrong," he fought back. "The town won't be against me. They've got this old regime going, don't talk to outsiders, but it's time to grow up. To join the world. They'll thank me, once the story comes out. Everybody knows the loggers did it. What the police are begging for and what this town needs is for someone to say who. I'll say who. I have the courage to say who."

"Courage? You think you're going to be some kind of hero? That's the idea? You want to call the snivelling, slimy, wormy old grievances you haul around in your rectum your courage? You're mistaken. You don't know what's going on, Willis. To be fair, not many do. But there are plans in place to get the town out of this jam. You prefer war between loggers and tree huggers? Or between loggers and . . . yourself? That's what this town and this business needs? Think about it. It's simple. We need the bridge back. It'll be back if you shut up. But there'll be no new covered bridge if you lie to the police. You will have prevented that from happening, and everybody will know. They will know who to blame for tearing this town apart. War will ensue. People will get beat up. They will hate you for that, Willis, and hate your store, if you speak your lies in a court of law."

"I saw what I saw. That's not lying. Mine was a perfect view of the bridge."

"You mean you saw a perfect opportunity to pin blame on someone you don't happen to like. Why? Because I'm going out with his brother? Is that what upsets you?"

"I don't have to listen to this." He wanted to break from the ramparts behind the cash, but couldn't decide on an exit. One opening led straight into Tara, the other would make it appear as though he was on the run out the back way. Trapped, he looked confused, turning this way, then that, undecided.

"Oh, but you do, Willis. Do you know what I did for a living? Before I joined this illustrious enterprise?"

"No, I don't. I just presumed you were a hit woman for the mob."

"Ha-ha. Funny. But close enough."

"Nonsense."

"I was a lawyer. A litigator. I still am. So talk to me, Willis, or I'll excoriate you on the witness stand and I promise, once I'm done, not a soul in this town will ever speak to you, let alone cough any morsel of business your way."

He stood still. Clearly astounded. "A lawyer."

She scoffed. "I bet you thought I was a whore. Something like that. A high-priced call girl, maybe? Or am I flattering myself? That's why you never asked. Well, maybe I was a whore, not far off it, but not quite as you imagine. On the witness stand, *Willis*, I'll slice into you to a depth you can't begin to measure. Oh, it'll be nasty. Not a pretty sight. What was he wearing, Mr. Howard? Oh, don't be silly, every guy wears a ball cap in this town. How could you tell what he looked like in the dark? You watched him from *inside* the house? Are there no reflections on your glass windows? You can identify a man's features, under a base-ball cap, in the dark, through reflective glass, not to mention through trees, at seventy yards? Really? Would you care to repeat that perfor-mance, Mr. Howard, you with the eagle eyes, under similar conditions? A controlled experiment, Mr. Howard. We'll parade people you know on the lip of the old bridge, at night, with scant moonlight—hell, we'll spot you a full moon—and let's count how many you can pick out that way. Here's a tip. I won't play fair. I'll dress women up as men, and when you name a Linda as being a Mike, I'll make you the laughing-stock of this town, this county, this region, this province, this country. My advice, move to Costa Rica, far enough away from your shame. Hey, know what? You can be an intermediary down there for local artisans. Send me up a few trinkets for the store, which, by the way, I will own outright after you're forced to sell. And sell cheaply. To me."

Willis Howard chose not to speak, which may have been wise at that moment. Out the front window he saw the SQ officers drive up and park across the street. Tara followed his gaze, and noticed that her time was short. She needed to wrap this up.

"Or, Willis, you can forgo your conspiracy and keep your store, compound your business even, because that's part of an overall plan to which you are not privy, as yet, although I will want you to take on a leading administrative role." She knew to not only threaten him, but to tempt him with an exchange, an arrangement, and never mind that she might regret it later.

"A leading role, in my own store."

"Not the store. The bridge. The town. We are going to develop this town, Willis. The next fifteen seconds is insufficient for me to give you the details, but the project is large and you will be asked to administer the books. Be a fund-raiser. You'll be a more significant public figure than you've ever been, and you'll be seen as standing on the side of the angels. So either you are on side, on my side, or you commit perjury on the witness stand and probably do jail time for that, plus receive the enjoyment of being publicly eviscerated. I will rip you apart and steal your store. So decide."

A policeman found the door to be oddly locked, and so knocked.

"I guess he can't read," Tara said, waiting, continuing to stare at him.

"I don't know," Willis said. "I've already told them—"

"Look feeble. I know you can manage that. Make yourself seem undecided. Baffled. Here's a tip, Willis. The person who actually did burn the bridge? He confessed. He's not the one you wanted to see charged. Stick to your story and you'll look awfully bad and probably bury yourself even before I get the chance. That's why the cops are here, to find out why you lied to them. So tell the truth. You hate the loggers. The O'Farrell clan. You got carried away. They've given you a hard time over the years and you're probably sitting on a stack of legitimate grievances dating back to kindergarten. But Willis, this is not the time that you get to beat them down. If you try, I pity you."

"Answer the door, please, Tara." Willis tried to sound stern.

The cops were knocking.

"They always win," he complained.

"Decide," quietly, she commanded him.

III

REDEMPTION

25

On a Saturday morning in midsummer, Dennis Jasper O'Farrell drove his beloved blue Ford down to the riverbank and parked off the community walking path on a grassy slope. He took a few moments to gaze across the water, both hands pressed to the steering wheel. Miniature waves, frolicking in a wily breeze, sparkled in the sunlight, hinting at their power to induce a trance. Momentarily lost to his reflections, Denny studied the vacant space where the old covered bridge once stood.

After a while he stepped down from the cab, proceeded to the rear of the pickup, and lowered the tailgate. From the truck bed he hauled tools—a cant hook, a crowbar, a peavey, a timber hook, and a pair of log carriers—which he placed in a neat row on the ground. While a poor workman might blame his tools, Denny believed that a good workman granted them exceptional care. Climbing onto the truck bed, he lifted heavy chains that he dropped into a single heap alongside his equipment on the ground. Next, he gathered lengths of rope, stuck his arms through the hoops they formed, and jumped down.

Pairs of pedestrians slowed their progress to observe him. Individuals may have wondered what he was up to, although one elderly gent could not care less, as any diversion to his daily routine was most welcome. Vehicles were not commonly permitted to park on the lawn and a couple of old-timers discussed this aberration as though it mattered. Their debate grew heated for a spell.

Close by, high on the roof of his raft, Gordon "Skootch" Skotcher lowered the financial section of his morning paper to his lap in order to watch Denny lug gear across rough terrain amid the trees to where waves lapped the shoreline, a distance of some thirty feet. He made several trips. Once all the tools and chain were brought down, Denny returned and opened the passenger-side door, pulling out a one-piece fly fisherman's wading suit, the leggings affixed to the boots, the jacket zipping up the front. More people were watching him now as he squeezed into the cumbersome outfit. He returned to the shore walking with something of a waddle, and without a rod, reel, or hook on a line, stepped into the river.

People discovered straightaway that he wasn't there to fish.

Instead, he circled a length of chain around a deadhead, pulled the loop taut and flung the bitter end towards the shallows near shore. One end of the log stuck out two feet above the surface, the other sunk in mud at a thirty-degree angle to a depth unknown. He tied rope to the chain and came back ashore to knot it to a stout tree that overhung the waterway. The log hadn't budged since last winter's ice broke, but now lay doubly secured. For what reason, no one knew.

Then Denny undertook to float the heavy timber.

He got under it and heaved and used his peavey to try spinning it and pulled and pushed and grunted with considerable exertion. He tried it from one side and then the other. All his efforts seemed in vain. Still, he struggled on.

Over time, his labours elicited advice.

"Denny. Denny. Try a chain saw. Cut the damn thing into sections first."

"Oh yeah," a second wag commented. "That'd be smart. Put on scuba gear. Start up a chain saw underwater. Say a prayer for the poor fucking fish."

"No worse off than what he's doin' now."

"Lease a 'dozer, Denny. That'll do the trick."

"Try a crane first. Lift it straight up that way."

The discussion expanded as the number of onlookers increased.

"My advice, if you asked me, I know you didn't, but if you did, I'm just saying, if you asked my advice, I'd tell you to just give up. Quit."

"Listen to the man, Denny. That thing's waterlogged. The tree won't float."

Denny groaned and pushed with his shoulder and wrestled the timber as though it was a creature from another world bent on his destruction.

"Who knows how deep it dug itself in? That could be one mighty trunk."

"What's wrong with you, Denny?"

"Why are you doing this again? Anybody asked you that yet?"

Dozens had, and the man knew it, too. Denny paused to take a breather. The day was not that hot and standing to his hips in cool water he was reasonably comfortable despite his toil. But this one log required more than the sum total of his strength, and more help than his tools could muster.

Still, he returned to the labour undeterred. More people were coming by and the growing crowd attracted others. Finally, a logger whom Denny only vaguely knew suggested, "I got a pickup with a front-end winch on it, Den. Want to try that?"

Nothing else would do, and Denny said yes, with thanks. The first words he spoke since entering into combat with this log.

"Hang on. I'll be back in a few," the man let him know.

■ ■ ■

HAND IN HAND, TARA AND Ryan strolled along the shore path. They stopped near the scene of Denny's activity. Tara chose to sit on one of the park's boulders, positioned as strategically as a landscape architect might locate a sculpture, serving lovers to sit upon, children to play upon, and daydreamers to absently admire or even stroke. During the river's fire, Tara found Mrs. McCracken seated upon this very rock, having resorted to the stone in her dismay and sorrow, a memory that comforted her now.

Ryan kissed her, then they nudged in closer to each other.

"Look," he said. He did not mean for her to gaze elsewhere, rather, he was directing her attention upon himself. He did not usually indulge in this sort of preamble.

"What?" she asked him.

"I have a story, too," he explained.

"So if you tell me yours, I have to tell you mine, is that what this is about?" She smiled and squeezed his knee.

He shrugged. "Look," he said again. "No deals. I'll just tell you mine."

"Okay," she agreed. She expected little more than a tale of woe about his love life. Bless him, he was a simple man.

"So, my first big crush came early. If I fell for this girl later on in high school, maybe we'd write a different chapter, but that's something I just like to imagine, I guess. Anyway, kids' stuff, too early to be anything but hapless. I should have tried again a couple of years later, but the first experience was so fraught with ineptitude and embarrassment that I wasn't ready to go there. But I never really stopped being attracted either, so I did try again, only this time we were all grown up and in our twenties."

He intended only a brief pause to organize his story, but Tara seized the chance to offer up her own speculative shorthand. "So she broke your heart."

He smiled. "She didn't give me that chance, at least not to be deeply heartbroken. Over before I could blink. Since those innocent days of high school she became what even you might call a complicated girl. In every way. Take that to mean whatever you want because she lived up to the billing. Neurotic in so many ways I couldn't keep track. And a party animal. Always into the latest thing no matter what it was. Pretty, though. But one date with me and the public attention that that fanned, which wasn't so sensational, really, warned her not to get involved with a cop. Certainly not this cop. She didn't want to be in the public eye, or seen as somebody expected to be a do-gooder, like me. I noticed on our first date that the bottom of her purse was littered with twigs and seeds and I said something. Which was dumb. No big deal, but our second date consisted entirely of her explaining to me why there was never going to be a third date. But there was a third, and a few more, I was a bear for punishment, but it kept coming around to the same issue. I was into her, she wasn't reciprocating, while she was crazy and I wasn't. So I was getting the message but not acting on it and then she lowered the boom. Not quite a broken heart because early on I'd come to the conclusion that we were impossible. But it was a ride and then, you know, afterward I did feel bruised. I missed her. But the problem was, I came out of it feeling discouraged, in a real way, especially seeing that my job diminished my chances with certain girls. To counter that disappointment, I got involved with someone almost right away, the first girl who would have me, and this time it was with someone I should definitely have left alone."

"Because it was a rebound?"

His expression was noncommittal on that. "If I took my time, I might've figured things out sooner rather than later. By the time I caught on, I was in too deep. Not to be mean, but *she* was mean. Hard to detect, at first."

Tara thought to add a lighthearted remark, but a cautionary intuitive notion caught her tongue. He suddenly seemed quite far away.

"Her name was Maria—the girl I had the schoolboy thing for. She was killed in a traffic accident, driving to Hamilton to see a friend."

Tara leapt to the story that Mrs. McCracken told in the cemetery over a young woman's grave. She tried to pull up the name on the marker in her mind's eye. "I'm sorry, Ryan. For her, of course. For you. Did Mrs. McCracken tell me about her? Something about a delayed autopsy?"

Ryan nodded. "Ten years ago. You should have known Mrs. McCracken then. A firebrand. I helped her out a bit. Gave her my counsel on some things she knew nothing about—jurisdiction, protocol, what you could say without being hauled into court for slander, that sort of thing. She thanked me for that, then she thanked me for helping her out the time she cracked her head on ice. I didn't know what she was talking about, and she thought I was demented for not remembering. But one day I had a flash. I checked with Denny. Sure enough, she was mixing us up. *He* had helped her, although he said he didn't know she cracked her head, only hurt her hip. I think that was the first time she mixed us up, but since then she's never kept us straight."

Gently, Tara stroked his forearm.

"So what happened with you and your new girl?"

"Never meant to be. We weren't happy from the get-go. Certainly

I wasn't. We fell apart, as though, after Maria's death, I had no reason to be with this other woman, since I'd only gotten involved with her on the rebound from Maria in the first place. Stuff surfaced at home. What we kept on the side reared up. Recriminations all around. Antipathy. She said a few things I'd call slander, that's for sure. I found out what it means to be a compulsive liar. In one sense, it was just a breakup, but in another it was so messy and mad and so damned *public* that it wrecked me. I still can't believe I stayed so long with someone so controlling and so basically *unkind*, to me and to everyone else. I lost confidence in my choices. So that's all there is to it. Small-town heartstrings. No biggie."

Tara looked at the man she once considered simple, who was not only that but also more complicated, and injured, than she'd surmised.

■ ■ ■

A SECOND PICKUP PARKED ILLEGALLY on the grass. No one actually complained, and as it happened the community's top policeman was sitting on a boulder nearby with his girlfriend, so most people assumed that this activity, whatever it might be, had merit or, at least, was sanctioned.

Skootch climbed down from his aerie in his usual scant garb.

And went closer.

He watched as two large, muscled men lugged a winch cable down to the shore. Denny affixed the cable's hook to his chain. People were commanded to stand to one side, and they acquiesced. Denny himself stood off to one side in the water as the winch took up the slack then strained against the weight. Little occurred. Perhaps nothing occurred. The waves lapping around the timber made it difficult to agree if the timber shifted at all. A few thought so. Most did not. Denny took up a cant hook and while the winch pulled with its full force he tried to turn the log at the same time. The task appeared hopeless and he might have given up on this first log when the timber suddenly released from the river bottom and slid free as smoothly and yet as slowly as an arrow being nudged back out from its target.

The timber was not so waterlogged as many supposed, floating just below the surface but an inch or two higher after Denny scraped off excess mud. Like an alligator out of its climate, the old wood lurked in the stream, a dark, menacing, and inexplicable thing. Few observing the ritual understood the purpose of this battle, but they gave a timid cheer anyway, and Denny received a scattered round of applause.

He accepted their approbation with a smile.

When he moved down to the next timber closest to him, the crowd grew more fervent in its demand for answers.

"Oh, come on! You're not at it again!"

"Just say why, Denny."

"What's this all about?"

"Denny! Hey, *Denny*! What are you *doing*?"

And so he told them.

He announced, "I'm building a new old covered bridge."

Most of the men on shore simply stared at them, a few with their mouths slack, while the women's tendency was to look at the men, as if they could or should explain this, then back again at Denny.

"Skootch," Denny requested, "toss me one of those ropes, will you?"

The man did so, and Denny lashed the floating timber to the shore then removed the chain around its bark. He dragged the chain over to the next log and secured it, and this time when he went to fetch the winch cable he found that four others formed a line to pass it to him and that the driver of the vehicle was altering its position slightly to improve the angle of attack. Everyone automatically stood back this time without a word being said as the winch took up the strain and this time, after seemingly being stuck as stubbornly as the first, the log launched out of the water with a surge and collapsed back down with a terrific splash that caught Denny full in the face. That gave everyone a chuckle and the smallest kids were beside themselves with laughter. Denny was grinning, too, but he had work to do and indicated with his chin that he wanted a line again and Skootch tossed him another length. A perfect throw. Denny lashed the two big floating timbers together with just the one line securing them to the shore. He then heaved himself up and sat on the logs, taking a rest. People observed him. They were quiet a minute. While the current held this small raft in place, Denny slowly, always careful to secure his balance, stood upon the two trees, the first logger to stand upright upon logs on this river in a generation.

"You can't," a woman addressed him, "rebuild the old covered bridge."

He heard her very well, but failed to verify exactly who spoke. Denny was preparing his reply when she added an important addendum to her point.

"Not by yourself."

He was glad to concur. "Lady, after my work this morning, I'm inclined to agree with you on that wholeheartedly."

An older man proved more severe. "It's a harebrained idea."

"Why?" Denny asked him back, but he did not await his reply. He forged on with a prepared argument, contending, "This river is jammed with deadheads, don't you see? Boats can't navigate, our kids can never swim here. As it happens, they can't jump off the old bridge anymore either, since there is no old bridge. And when the government builds the new one, the traffic will be fast and furious. Nobody, not even kids, will want to play on it. So the river has gone useless to us, but only because we choked the life out of it. Pull these deadheads out, and there are thousands, and thousands, shave away the outer wet, what you get inside is beautiful, clear, sound timber. Do you know why it's so beautiful? It's been seasoned but that's not all. It's such damn beautiful wood because it's all *free*."

Denny moved back judiciously on his logs to let them manage his weight more evenly. He was cautious, for to topple into the river now would not only make him a laughingstock but more important scuttle his plans before they were given a proper airing. He spoke louder when he spoke again, perhaps cognizant not only of the people lining the shore but of those sequestered in the woods and of those farther back on the grass or strolling by on the couples' walk. He wanted his voice to reach as far as his brother and Tara Cogshill sitting on a rock, not to speak to them necessarily, but to make use of their presence there to gauge the distance he needed to project his voice.

"The wood lying in this river is everybody's wood, right? No one else has claimed ownership. The forestry industry has ignored it for years. But as we found out this morning, no one man or two or three can pull out a single log. Not without help. But if we help each other, then we can harvest this wood, and with that lumber we can build a new old covered bridge. It's not a harebrained idea at all, although I once thought so myself. The two biggest costs to building the bridge are material and labour. But the river can be harvested for our timber, and if the whole town is willing to pitch in, the people will supply the labour."

Bystanders continued to stare out at the man standing on the water as though he meant business. They couldn't look away from him.

"You mean like volunteers?"

"Yes, but don't say it that way. I'm not asking you to join the army."

448

He got the laugh he wanted. Then a voice mentioned engineering costs and legal feels and administration expenses of various sorts and he was going to go on with his dismal accounting when Denny interrupted him, not to argue but to agree. "As far as the milling goes, you're right, it's costly, except maybe we can ask a mill to do it for free as a worthy donation and maybe it just might. We can arrange the work to be tax deductible. Fund-raising will be necessary, there's no getting around it. But we have people in this town, I suspect you're one of them, who can take that on and be successful at it. Think about this, folks. We can build a new old covered bridge that can stand where the old one stood, only this one might remain for centuries after we're gone, so long as no hotheads set it on fire. Nowhere on this earth is anyone building old covered bridges anymore. We can build ours the old way, with old tools and mostly old methods. Old materials only. To partake of that, to help build such a thing, I don't know about you, but to me that sounds like a once-in-a-lifetime opportunity, and personally, as you can plainly see, I'm onboard with it."

Somebody asked, "I thought you loggers wanted a fancy bridge, a four-lane job or something like that."

"Yeah, we do. And the thing is, we're getting it now, because no bridge exists and the government has no choice but to build one. They have to keep the road open. But that doesn't mean we can't build another one that's a replica of the old bridge but doesn't serve trucks or buses or cars anymore. It no longer needs to. We can build one that's damned nice to look at, too, so we can all be proud of it and proud of this town."

Denny knew that he was tempted to say, "proud of this town again," but that implied old grudges, many rightfully held against him, that he preferred not to resurrect.

On shore, most people harboured the thought that he had destroyed the original bridge, that he was one of the bastard hothead

449

loggers. For that reason they withheld any immediate approval, but as they mulled the project's feasibility they also considered its import. What dawned on many of them was that this could be a way to broker the very peace they were having so much trouble imagining. On different levels they knew what Denny was doing, and saw that he benefited, but they did not necessarily, or uniformly, disapprove.

■ ■ ■

RYAN AND TARA OBSERVED THE proceedings from their distance. Sometimes they heard Denny quite well, more often his voice was carried off on the breeze, or was muffled by a chatter of leaves. Knowing the gist of it, they preferred to grant him the space and time to begin his recompense on his own.

Ryan stood on the boulder briefly, then leapt down again.

"What?" Tara asked him.

"He's standing on the logs. The way they sink under him, he looks like he's walking on water."

She smiled. "Denny's no Christ figure."

"Around here, who is? I'll hand it to him, though, he has a flair for the dramatic. The bridge when it burned, who's seen anything like that? Now this."

"The oratory's not half bad either. Watch out, Ryan. He might run for mayor some day. Be your boss."

Ryan chuckled at the thought, but admitted he'd vote for him anyway.

Seated, Tara reached out her hand. Her boyfriend, standing, took it in his. This time, responding to her glum expression, he was the one to ask, "What?"

"Want to know what happened to me? How I got here?"

"Sure I do. But I wasn't trading before, with my story."

"Maybe you were. Maybe you weren't. But I'm ready now. Anyway, now that I know you're a whole lot more complicated than I thought, I'm more comfortable letting you in on this." To help him be more comfortable with that, she playfully stuck her tongue out at him.

He sat beside her again and placed an arm around her side to tuck her more closely to him.

"Don't worry," she assured him. "It's only strange. I'm shy about it but you won't want to arrest me. I'll come across as goofy. Worst case, you'll think I'm off another planet and want to ship me back there."

"Okay," he said. "I'll keep NASA on standby. Tell me."

She gazed down the river first, as though to find certain rhythms and connections to her memories. "I was aware, and my older man was aware, that our time was up. I loved the sea, I always loved the sea, and I first became involved with him when I was crewing on his yacht. We raced. Usually just outside Halifax harbour, around the buoys, but on occasion we were on longer races, and this one time, heading home, we put into a small harbour along the coast to duck a storm. I noticed a man there. A very handsome young man. Standing on another boat. A fishing boat. So virile-looking, so Marlboro man–looking, I admit, I went a little weak in the knees. He was repairing nets as the sky darkened and lightning came our way. A sight. I could tell that the attraction was spontaneous in both directions."

"I've experienced that. With you."

He tried to make light, but Tara paid no attention. Yet the sound of his voice seemed to interrupt her train of thought, as though she was projecting herself back in time and now was abruptly returned to the present. She kissed him, a peck on the cheek, perhaps to remind herself of the company she kept.

"I bought a little red truck for myself, really old, nothing much more than scrap metal really. Full of rust holes, but it got me around town. I could have afforded more but I didn't need much. I was a downtown girl, I walked to work, so the truck was perfect. Frankly, I thought it was cool. I thought I looked cute in it. Cute in a good way. Okay, sexy, whatever. So I checked the nautical chart just to find out the name of the harbour I was in, which I committed to memory, and about a week later I drove back in my little red truck. The gorgeous man wasn't there. I made four trips before I found him."

"Persistent."

"In love with an impression of a man. When we met, impression and reality diverged. I went through with it anyway. In making the break from my old guy it was easier to say that I'd met someone else. I know that sounds bad. It was bad. It was. I knew it from the start. Still. I liked the guy enough."

Ryan was relaxing into the story, as he was beginning to feel that he might not have a rival out there of mythological proportions, which was worrying him. He drew slow gentle circles on Tara's back.

"So we had a thing. He was a fisherman. A lot of those guys have educations now. Not because they need them. But they go to school, graduate, then go back to what they grew up doing and love. Fishing. I loved that about him. Primitive work but a degree in English lit. Sometimes I went out to sea with him, usually I stayed home. Did my own work. Went to visit him in my little red truck when I felt like it. I knew I was hurting him and I knew I was suiting myself. But I got the breakup I wanted from my old guy and at the same time I wasn't completely high and dry, if you know what I mean. So I stayed on."

Ryan easily imagined her driving that poor boy mad.

"But then one day I went to see him and he wasn't back when he should've been. A big storm was making landfall. Bigger than the one that brought us together. Apparently he'd gone out farther to help another craft in jeopardy. He radioed in that everybody was fine, but the rescue kept him out in the storm longer than was safe. So. You know. I was worried. The rains came, and they were unbelievably fierce. I parked my truck facing the sea to wait for him and the waves, crashing the shore—I was mesmerized and petrified to the core. People urged me to come back into town to wait, but somehow, I just couldn't. I didn't want to. I knew what this guy faced from time to time and there I was, seeing him only at my convenience."

Laughter broke from the shoreline where a repartee ensued between Denny and many of the onlookers taking an interest in his proposal. Denny was reeling them in, for he really was on a fishing expedition.

"Did he make it back?" Ryan asked.

"He stayed out at sea a lot longer. I got reports. The second boat was in tow and the storm was intensifying. People told me that the waves hitting the shore always look far worse than they are in open water, and that might be true but they were big and I was scared. I ate in my truck, I slept in my truck, I peed in the wind and the rain and got soaked while the waves created these giant plumes all around me. I don't know what it was, Ry, but at a certain point I got it that things were going to change. Not just with this pleasant but bogus relationship I found myself in, but with me. About how I conducted myself. How I moved through life. Even my work. It wasn't merely the relationship that was bogus, you see. And that's when I really felt it, Ryan."

He waited a moment. "It?" he asked.

"The storm. The wind and rain, the huge crashing waves." She turned to look at him, to make sure that he understood this part. "I felt the storm inside me. Not outside. Inside. I became that storm. Or that storm took me over somehow. Entered me. Whatever. I felt it. The storm was determined to claim someone, that's how I was thinking about it, that's what I believed then and I still do. Instead of taking my lover and his boat, that storm took me. Never a day goes by when I don't feel the wind, or the calm afterwards, or I don't feel the waves, or the ripples afterwards. Whatever I do in this world, I'm partly that storm. It's in me now.

"See," she added, after a pause. "Complicated."

"Okay," he said, but she knew that he did not wholly understand. Moreover, that he could not. Still, he repeated himself, "Okay."

"Do you know what the most amazing thing is? I told Mrs. Mc-Cracken, and that old gal, she understood me. She totally got me."

Tara required a moment to collect herself then, and Ryan granted her that. He kept his questions to himself, trusting that she was committed to revealing those things that precipitated her arrival in his life.

"When the storm abated, word came that radio contact with the boat was lost. Probably just electrical, people said. No SOS was sent out and I was informed that one would be sent automatically through an emergency signal if the boat went down. A GPS thing. So people were confident in a way, but nobody knew what was going on, and if the boat didn't have electronics . . .

"Then a heavy, heavy fog set in. That frightened me as much as the storm. I stood on a rock, Ry, a lot like this one, actually, and I had a conversation with myself. I needed to—I didn't know exactly—but essentially I needed to make amends between myself—and I'm now part storm, part wind, part *Raine*, it's always been my name—between myself and with my better intentions. We'd become estranged, me and my better intentions. I promised . . . I don't know, the wind, the waves, the fog, the sea, *God* . . . I promised that if my fisherman made it safely home I would give him a night to remember, then I'd climb into my truck and do him an even bigger favour. I'd drive away from there. I didn't have to wait long either. His battered boat motored in the moment the fog lifted, the rescued boat in tow, which felt so miraculous.

I wept, and then, for once, I chose to live up to my instincts. The very next morning I hit the road."

Ryan absorbed her story, pleased to hear it. She seemed pleased to have shared it. After a few moments, he asked, "So after that you came straight here? Where's the truck?"

"It's not easy to break away from a life you've put down. So, no, it wasn't straight here literally. But in emotional terms, yes. I was done with my old life. I made sure that I came away with very little. Except that I was passing through northern Maine when I sought shelter from a much milder storm. In a downmarket bar I met this witchy woman. That's what I call her. She was a trauma room nurse, in fact, but she had affection for her drink and a yen for telling stories and a witchy demeanour. We enjoyed a laugh a minute. At the end of our evening, both of us plastered, she told me that I was to drive until the truck gave out, but that was not where I should remain, that I'd regret it if I did. From there, I was to find the end of the line before I stopped. I had no clue what that meant. I asked her ten times to tell me. But not until my little truck gave out and this town's cute little choo-choo rolled into the station close to where I was sitting on my hands wondering where to go next did I suddenly get it. When I found out that the train went to the end of a line, only to turn around and come back, I imagined that I'd found my destination. Maybe even, as luck would have it, whatever fate has in store for me. A garage took the truck off my hands and I bought a ticket. So there you go, Ryan. I'm a bit nutty. But that's how I got here. And here I am."

They sat in silence for a considerable time, each reliving the other's story, and picking up bits of dialogue from the shore.

"I was wondering," he said, perhaps merely to change the subject, but it was not entirely that, for the time was upon them to speak of difficult things and perhaps to seal their arrangement, "if there's not a lawyer around somewhere, anyone you might know of, who might lend some time to a poor sap in jail. A kid came to this town selling asphalt and he'll be leaving in a paddy wagon with a one-way ticket to prison."

She needed a moment to think through the ramifications. "It's possible, Ryan," she pointed out to him, speaking slowly, "but our complicity—"

"I know."

"Everyone's— It won't wash off. Or burn away like the bridge. The truth still has to be suppressed. And he was, in his own right, a criminal."

"I know. But he didn't do the crime he's going down for. I arranged it that way. After the damage has been done, can't we help somehow?"

Tara indicated Denny, who was out in the water wrapping chain around another deadhead, aided by people ashore. Nothing further needed to be said. Everybody was going to have to pitch in around here in order to change just about everything in their lives.

26

Sundown marks an early impression upon a valley town. Cascading hills darken while the opposite sides of their peaks are dyed with a fresh smudge of pastel colouring. Shadows expand across the forest, yet the face of a sheer stone cliff shines with a diamond glaze. Returning from a long day's labour, a driver passes through the steep gloom governed by heavy foliage into blinding sunlight, then follows a twist in the road where the light rapidly flickers, jumpy amid the leaves.

A clarity consumes the air. Evening remains on the verge, as the warmth of a summer's day in early September lingers.

Dinners are wolfed down. Many men dispense with the formality entirely, pack a sandwich and a beer and return to their vehicles. In numerous homes a debate ensues. Older boys want to tag along, to be part of this. "It's a school night!" mothers contend, an objection that for once carries faint merit. Girls vie to break the rules also, and in the end their moms join in, anyone who can wield a hammer or nudge a shingle into place who isn't fearful of heights, or fears missing the occasion more. The opportunity won't come again, not in this time nor in any other. A word is uttered: *history*. Tonight, history will be fabricated as the sun goes down, as hillsides glimmer with a reddish hue. Later on, under a waxing gibbous moon, as a wry dalliance of stars reflects on the silvery, oily black river below them, people of this town will labour through a night that casts a lurking judgement on their lives.

So they drive, yet more arrive on foot, traipsing down to the river's bridge for reasons they hold to be both complex and personal. Old pals embrace. Perpetual foes greet one another with a glance, their truce repaired for this project. Young ones seek each other out, then fidget, awaiting their chores. The elderly also hang back. Unable to wield tools or haul materials up a ladder, they gladly converse, lend their opinion, recall sad things and glad things, and speak of other people. Sagely, they nod with a sense of the evening's wonder, then go still, overcome for a bit, moved by their luck to be alive to experience this moment. Conversations resume, lift upon air ascending from the warm soil into the evening's cooling grace.

Although it's rarely mentioned, everyone sees again in his or her mind's eye a vagrant night in this place, when the river sorely raged with fire. Less than a gracious memory, yet an imprint inextricably embedded within them all.

Ghosts attend. For some as reminiscence. For others, as a tangible presence or two, attached to those who fell along the way, yet who deserve to be here. A few spare a moment's thought for one who slumps alone in his prison cell. No one's innocence has been spared. The dead, then, the broken, the joyful, the familial, the earnest, and the warring factions who are bound together now by common enterprise, all justly receive their instructions, then climb, take up their hammers and begin to pound away.

Twiing! Twiing! Th'wonk!

Across the rooftop of a covered bridge, hammers rise and slam down. As the last light of the day winks upon the rush of water below, and on into the moonlit dark, every man, child, woman, and friend, enemy, saint, or deviant, the victorious with the defeated and every revenant on a visit, in bright, holy rhythm begins to pound, needing to fix this, to make their world whole again.

The finish is too close now to quit and wait for daylight, and the hours after work and dinner have brought in so many more reserves who tonight are especially keen. The crisp crack and *twiing!* of hammers on nails is all a body can hear, the dull *th'wonk!* on wood as nails strike home. Doing this the old-fashioned way was Alexander O'Farrell's idea, a suggestion picked up, proposed, and carried through by his son Dennis. Nail guns not permitted. Whenever it has been both feasible and economically viable the bridge was constructed using methods from a bygone era, and tonight, aided by a few gas lamps and the moon, the workers can see well enough. Not a soul complains and no flattened thumbs are tossed into the resplendent rapids below.

They hammer in the haunting, breezy dark.

Twiing!

Echoes roil on down the riverside.

Th'wonk!

Then, quite abruptly, the crew of volunteers goes still. No hammer is swung. As though each man and women experiences a similar reaction or is receptive to a mystical cue at virtually the same instant, they stop working. A cough. A shuffling as people alter positions. Muffled conversations. Yet a sudden quiet, just like that. The tribe of workingmen and -women quits hammering and instead chooses to gaze in near silence upon the constellations above in their lazy, blinking strut, or upon the river below in its artful surge. Everyone takes a breather. While the moonlight has washed out a few stars, men and women still crane their necks, while others chose to lie upon their backs and gawk, skyward, in their tiredness and in their awe, for would ever such a time occur again, to be out hammering nails on a rooftop at night creating a work of art under the wild sacred heavens while a river gambols beneath them?

"I know why we stopped hammering," Denny O'Farrell comments. As do others, he breathes heavily from his exertion. Now eleven, his eldest, Boy-Dan, received permission to stay up this late to help, for as Denny and Alex explained to Val, the opportunity would not return even in the lad's lifetime.

"I'll bite," his dad, Alexander, says. "Why?"

"Because we don't want to finish."

Alex considers that awhile. Then says, "Not a day goes by in my life, Denny, when I don't wonder who or what sired you."

Boy-Dan thinks that that is too hilarious and says so, and laughs, while Denny merely grins, taking no offence.

No one needs to explain himself or herself to another. Of course they desire to finish building the new old covered bridge in the place where the original stood. For more than two years now they have enjoyed the benefit of a new highway span upstream, and this faithful replica will be merely decorative, prohibited to vehicular traffic, enjoyed by those on foot or on bicycles or, to the consternation of a few, on skateboards. Lovers will kiss on the bridge, even get married on it, and children will run and skip and gaze down at the rapids. As summers return and the tempest of the river subsides, adolescents will leap through their fears to plunge into the cool waters below. Another brave generation of whelps. Tourists will snap photographs and bask in the aura of another time when beauty and tranquillity engendered solace from lives of hard labour, sacrifice, and periodic woe. They want to finish the bridge because this has been an undertaking for the ages, to live for generations as lore, as pride, as adoration. Volunteer loggers fished from the river the old timbers left behind by the logjams of old and the sawmills agreed to hew the wood and plane and cut timbers, so that the wood for the new old bridge, its trestles and braces and walls and even its shims, comes only from logs culled from the Gatineau, and at no cost. As if the old bridge, its ashes in the water, gave itself back. Loggers, mill workers, tradesmen and carpenters, barbers and chefs and clerks and accountants carted and sawed and hammered and riveted into place each beam and post and support and plank, and the whole town raised the money when cash was necessary for the engineering costs, principally, and also for paint and the legal and accounting fees and for taxes and hardware and for the rental of cranes and trucks and other pieces of heavy machinery whenever a donation of equipment proved deficient. Now they are shingling the peaked roof, the final step in the enterprise and a task to which the community has swarmed, loggers and tree huggers alike, businessmen and tradesfolk and artisans and housewives and retirees, children, too, firemen and bakers, bums and bankers, everyone anxious to be on the rooftop to complete the task and if it goes on through the evening into the den of night, so much the better. So of course they want to finish, but Denny and no one else needs to explain why no one is in a rush to have that final nail hammered home, for everyone desires that the bridge be built yet no one wants their activity to conclude.

This is the crucible of their lives as a community.

Blessings and their ample shortcomings are etched onto the frame, knitted into the hatch of tresses, and bolted, knotted, painted over, and made to look pristine. That last moment can only arrive with sadness, and too soon. With pride and yet regret.

"Dad," Denny says, knowing full well that his own son sits beside him also, "not a day goes by when I'm not proud of the fool who did."

Three generations of O'Farrells fall back into the communal silence. They have much to reflect upon. Denny feels the substantial dark ache that lies submerged in his chest as he considers again the stranger lodged in a prison cell for the crime that he, Dennis Jasper O'Farrell, instigated and committed, and he will suppose that his father will dwell on that poor man, too, often. He hopes that his son has no inkling of that aspect, and never will. He presumes that his brother remembers the fellow as well, that not a day goes by when the name Jake Withers fails to cross Ryan O'Farrell's synapses. Each of the three, Ryan, Jake, and Denny, play third base. They have that in common. He understands the countervailing theory, that the boy did wrong, went bad, that he could have stood trial for crimes that boasted of longer sentences, that it was only a matter of time before he was caught and convicted for those serious felonies and that in the overall scheme of things he was probably done a favour. Maybe, but Denny knows also what is right and what is wrong, and while building the bridge has been the right thing to do, putting a man in jail for a crime he did not commit is wrong. But he and everyone else did it anyway, the right and the wrong, and then just let it go at that.

That is who they are now, he knows. Who he is.

They live with the knowledge daily.

And persevere.

Attempts to get Jake out came up short. Denny reminds himself often that he could just confess, set the man free that way. But he made his choice years ago, and carries on.

He likes to think that such events and lessons compel him to be a better man, but he believes also that he should have been a better man when it counted, as there isn't much he's willing to do now about the past. Except to do his job, raise his family, and erect the bridge to help undo the wrong he committed the night he cast the old bridge upon the waters of the Gatineau River in flames, so fiercely roaring.

Although the word offends him, Denny sacrificed for the new old bridge. Innumerable weeks passed when he gave more time to the bridge than to his job or family. Now he is seeing it finished, at last. Some have talked that the privilege of hammering the final nail home ought to be his. He doesn't know about that, but believes that if his hand raised that hammer it would also be gripped by many, not by himself alone or even by a few. By a boy in jail, for sure. By his brother, who landed on Skootch's ball club that summer, replacing Jake Withers at third base, and who virtually single-handedly beat the Blue Riders in the playoffs with his bat, breaking Denny's heart. Ryan still plays third for the hated Wildcats, who are mostly tree huggers and criminals, raising a few eyebrows, and regularly outhits his younger brother. Ryan deserves to grip the hammer for the final nail, also. And his dad, a true king of this river, and Val, who saved him, and people he didn't much like, such as Willis Howard who kept the books. He grew to respect what a demanding job that could be, although he still doesn't like him but the feeling is mutual, so who really cares, and of course Raine Tara-Anne Cogshill, his sister-in-law. She goes by Raine now, switching her first name rather than her last when she got married, that girl just did things differently. But she gave them the idea to rebuild the bridge themselves and held up the legal end. Part of her new law practise, which she parlayed into becoming the logging company's local lawyer. She and Ryan moved into Mrs. McCracken's old house, left to her by the old lady herself, and there's another one who definitely would place her hand on that hammer—Alice Beauchamp McCracken, in whose memory the bridge would soon be christened.

She might even manage to hold the final nail. At least he couldn't damage her ghostly fingers if he missed.

Men who carried out the arson with him would also hold that hammer, André, Samad, and Xavier, for they stood by him in the crime but were also among the first to agree to the restoration, committing time and labour and battling to keep others' spirits up to do the same. André once privately admitted to him that he regretted what they did that night and would change things if he could. They clinked beer bottles in commemoration of the thought.

The newlyweds lived in Mrs. McCracken's old house while building a new home by the riverside on property formerly owned by Skootch. He got himself arrested, and Tara, now Raine, defended him. Payment turned out to be a willingness to sell a chunk of land he originally inherited, which he bragged was worth a million and it might have been, except that he sold it for a song to the man who arrested him and the woman who got him off. She kept busy, with her practise and her portion of Willis Howard's store, and also represented local artisans who now sold their wares across the continent thanks to her budding distribution network. So busy, yet everyone's labours these past years were slowed by the communal effort to rebuild.

All those whose hands were placed upon this structure—they will grip his hammer, too. Loggers, both good friends and strangers, who performed the initial and arduous task of clearing the river of old timber, their hands clasped his. And Denny thanked those who gave countless hours of time and effort, tree huggers, and crazy Skootch himself, in and out of jail, who coughed up cash and supplied additional labour and agreed to truncate the baseball schedule so that men were free to donate more hours on the bridge. Chances are, whoever broke into Mrs. McCracken's house, adolescents probably, grew up a bit and worked on the bridge, too, even to demonstrate that they were sorry. Perhaps not, but Denny hoped so, and thanked them anyway. Quietly, privately, he thanked other workingmen and -women and businesspeople and just plain folks who claimed no particular affiliation to one industry or another, whose desire was nothing more than to participate in forming an object of grace, of singular perpetual beauty, to seize a chance to create something in the company of their neighbours with their hands and their hearts and through an affection for one another and through a sense of abiding love.

"I doubt that I can even lift that hammer," Denny whispers, although his son and his father, who hear him, do not know the reference, and he does not explain himself, so deeply is he immersed in his reverie, "without their help."

His whole torso an ache, he returns back to the silence on the rooftop of the bridge and that strange, unfathomable majesty. Denny will never know, few do, who starts up, but one lone hammer does break their code to commence its labour, a gradual, rhythmic, decisive crack and *twiing! twiing!* and a crack and *th'wonk!* and then it begins on the next nail *twiing!* and each man and woman, proud to be upon the rooftop on this night, galvanized by the light of the moon and by the river and by the company they keep, by their work and by the hammer's defiant song, crawl back into position, and take up a nail, and grip a hammer, and in the old-fashioned way begin to pound.

Twiing! Twiing! Th'wonk!

Across the bridge, then, under the soft moonlight and shimmer of constellations reflected upon the turbulent waters below, every darkened form, in bright, holy rhythm, starts to pound, and pound, pledged to undo what had been done, to begin, inexorably, again.

ACKNOWLEDGMENTS

Out of the blue one day I received a commission, for which I am now particularly grateful, from the magazine *L'Actualité*, to be among ten writers who would each visit and describe with some intimacy a different region of Quebec. I chose the town of Wakefield, and the communal piece went on to earn a National Magazine Gold Award. In my investigation of the town, I was given a personal tour of the Wakefield Mill Inn by its owner, Robert Milling, from whom much history was gleaned, useful for the article initially and subsequently the novel. Weekend stays at a local cottage in the company of Dr. Robert Dorion helped deepen my knowledge of the area and added local stories, as did returning to regional provincial parks in my tent. The second iteration of this material came as a short story, which was never submitted anywhere except to students to whom I was teaching creative writing at Concordia University. I learned from their comments but kept the story squirreled away. Next, the tale travelled on to become the genesis for a film script, and the author is thankful to SODEC and Telefilm Canada for their funding and to the director

Leo Bélanger and editor Shea Lowry for their insight. That effort had to be abandoned, as the story was growing out of its earlier forms more rapidly than it could be contained, demanding to be born as a novel. So here it is.

I extend my deepest thanks to Bruce Westwood and Carolyn Forde of Westwood Creative Artists, to Kevin Hanson, Alison Clarke, and the full crew at Simon & Schuster, Toronto, to production editor Linda Sawicki and her team in New York, and to Barbara Berson for her vigorous and thoughtful edit.

ABOUT THE AUTHOR

Trevor Ferguson is the author of seven novels under his own name and another three under his pseudonym, John Farrow. One of his novels became a feature film, *The Timekeeper*. Four of his plays have been produced, including an off-Broadway engagement; one seen by more than 22,000 patrons in a single run. He teaches creative writing at Concordia University and lives with his wife in Hudson, Quebec.